The Adventures of D'Artello

Book One:
Love and War

Rebecca Tilley

Donald Previe

More action than twilight!!

Love,
Donald Previe

iUniverse, Inc.
Bloomington

The Adventures of D'artello
Book One: Love and War

Copyright © 2011 Donald Previe

All rights reserved. No part of this book may be used or reproduced by any means, graphic, electronic, or mechanical, including photocopying, recording, taping or by any information storage retrieval system without the written permission of the publisher except in the case of brief quotations embodied in critical articles and reviews.

This is a work of fiction. All of the characters, names, incidents, organizations, and dialogue in this novel are either the products of the author's imagination or are used fictitiously.

iUniverse books may be ordered through booksellers or by contacting:

iUniverse
1663 Liberty Drive
Bloomington, IN 47403
www.iuniverse.com
1-800-Authors (1-800-288-4677)

Because of the dynamic nature of the Internet, any Web addresses or links contained in this book may have changed since publication and may no longer be valid. The views expressed in this work are solely those of the author and do not necessarily reflect the views of the publisher, and the publisher hereby disclaims any responsibility for them.

Any people depicted in stock imagery provided by Thinkstock are models, and such images are being used for illustrative purposes only.

Certain stock imagery © Thinkstock.

ISBN: 978-1-4620-4216-6 (sc)
ISBN: 978-1-4620-4217-3 (hc)
ISBN: 978-1-4620-4218-0 (e)

Library of Congress Control Number: 2011913948

Printed in the United States of America

iUniverse rev. date: 9/22/2011

For all of my supporters, *if all we ever needed was a dream …*

Preface

Are humans inherently good or evil? Are good and evil all perception, thus making humans inherently neutral? Does having no bias make one soulless? If someone told you right now, you had to be more than a man (or woman), that you had to be a hero, what would you say? If you had the opportunity staring you in the face, would you take it? Would you rise? Or would you pass the buck and not envy the individual whose fate is such?

    What if you were appointed? What if you didn't have a choice? What now? Would you end your life, or would you fight your heart out? Make your choices, because tomorrow will not wait, and neither will its challenges. What are you doing then? Don't sit and pray for a miracle; get out there and make your own.

Acknowledgments

Much of my imagery and ideas are born from a
music genre about fighting the good fight.
A special thanks to:

Nightwish
Hammerfall
Shinedown
Within Temptation
Edguy
Manowar

Rock on!

Chapter 1

*I*T was dark ... like shadows at midnight under a moonless sky. Cold, D'artello rose to his feet and began to examine his surroundings. Short but heavy breaths evacuated his lungs, as if he were waking from a nightmare. He walked steadily with his hands in front of him, staggering to find a wall. Eventually, the tips of his fingers met rough stone. It became quickly apparent he was wading through knee-high water, as his feet scraped against the rock below the surface. Treading carefully, he ran his hands along the stone—hitting each distinct abrasion along the way, trying not to lose track of the wall, his only guide. He cautiously shuffled down the corridor, narrowly bypassing invisible objects and holes in the floor. *A cave?* he wondered.

D'artello's long, wet, white hair drooped stuck heavily and flatly to the sides of his face. He moved his hand to sweep away a sopping clump from his sky blue eyes and youthful face, swiftly so that he could replace the hand on the wall. Perilous blackness all around, his eyes struggled to adjust.

Looking ahead, he noticed a greenish light at the end of the aquatic cavern. It was not enough to illuminate his surroundings, and from this distance it was no bigger than a pinprick, much less the diameter of a pea. Anything was better than what he was doing. Biting his lip, considering the best course of action for the span of a fractional second, he shuffled onward rather than retreat toward nothingness.

It was then the questions turned over in his mind. "Where am I? How did I get here?" he coached quietly, trying to remember what he was doing before awakening in this place. He remembered his family, his friends, and his life before he'd awoken, but nothing within a day of this event. *How long have I been here?* he wondered.

As he continued to move, his wet shirt clung to his chest, while his baggy, blue, guard-slacks waved gently in the water around his legs. With each step, he feared the worst: a hole, sudden trench, or some sort of lurking creature. Hearing a small splash echo from behind, he spun around as if his life depended on it, expecting to see something. Nothing. A moment was allowed for his throbbing heart to return to a calm pulse. D'artello continued toward the greenish light.

He began to feel the water give a slight push forward as a current gradually stirred with each inch he took. Of this he was certain, as the stream's pull caused his pants to cling to him from behind. The front of his pants were dancing in the current, assuring him of forward motion.

Close enough to the light now, shadows began to recede, and his surroundings were beginning to materialize. The walls were not the cavern-gray he had picked out in his mind. Instead they were of a beautiful, golden, glistening gradient. The color, normally representative of wealth or power, for some reason gave him a feeling of lust or tyranny; thus he never let his guard down. The water was clear if not invisible entirely; there was nothing to cloud it, no drifting debris, and not even bubbles to ruin its mica finish on the golden floor. His fingertips left the wall, and he began to walk more confidently, boldly into the unknown.

The sound of crashing water from over yonder came into earshot, yet still no end to the cavern. Despite the increasing speeds of the current, he wandered mentally with only the possibilities of how he ended up there. The sound did not frighten him. It was a peaceful white noise, a supporting melody for his entrance, becoming a distraction of itself. Glancing down, he gave a salutation to the hands he was glad were still there. This reunion was interrupted by another splash. He turned and saw only the blackness, the steps left behind.

As he progressed, the current began to move faster, rocking his tall, fit physique, while the sound of crashing water became gradually louder. Then he heard a much larger splash. He spun around again, certain of some aquatic beast thrashing toward his heels. A rock had dunked in from the ceiling and now bathed under the water. Wishes of having his sword began to flee along with the pounding of his heart.

After a few more steps, D'artello began to feel a vibration in the floor. He slapped a hand back to the wall to brace himself. A second tremor bellowed from within the walls. Rocks began to writhe themselves out of the hemorrhaging walls. To his horror, the cavern was collapsing.

The water gave a harsh jerk, as if telling him to trust it. Hesitating, he looked back at the cart-size boulders that were rapidly getting bigger and more plentiful. He dove into the water carefully, so as not to scrape the floor. The current swept him up, carrying him faster and faster, while the collapse gave chase. Fear alone made his legs paddle to out-swim his tomb to be.

He drew closer to the light, and the sound of the crashing water, although muffled by falling rocks, grew louder. Logically, there had to be waterfall, a drainage point for this stream. Illogically, he was racing toward a wall. Whether or not there was a waterfall just before it was no question of survival. Desperately he tried to grip the rock below with his boots; he'd be dead in just mere moments if he couldn't slow down.

Just before impact, he took a sudden drop. He suspected it was there, but still it surprised him. The formidable free-fall punched his stomach, forcing a cry to escape his lungs as he fell into the soft light. He spun around to turn his back on the landing so he did not have to stare death in the face. The mother of all boulders followed his descent to catch and crush him when he did reach the bottom. He let out a louder scream at his likely doom while the light blinded him. For what it was worth, he put his arms up to shield himself.

Finally his vision returned, revealing a mysteriously lit cavern. The source-less light was an overlooked fact. He first noticed his whole body up to his neck was submerged, and he swam instinctively to keep his breath free while gasping for air. Its walls were the same color as the narrow corridor in which he began. Looking up at a small hole in the ceiling, *that must be where the waterfall empties,* he deduced. The waterfall had trickled its last drop, thanks to the boulder now plugging the hole from which he entered.

Am I trapped? Did that stone seal me in? he wondered. He sloshed about in the water, glancing quickly, looking for a way out. To his right there was a tunnel, just big enough for him to crouch through, and more light coming from the other side.

Conveniently, a few yards to the left was a rocky ledge that allowed him to climb up onto dry land, which was a thin ring of footing around the shaft-like room. He swam ashore. Looking only ahead at the golden hallway, he entered the tunnel. Just a short walk to the other side, he found only another nearly identical cavern, with deep water at the bottom of a large cylindrical shaft.

Screening his surroundings one last time, he saw nowhere else to go but down. Taking a deep breath, he dove feet-first toward the water, remembering his father's words: "Hit with a sprawl, and it'll feel like a wall."

The speed surprised him, but because he did not fall as quickly as he thought he would. He seemed to slow and drift down, like a leaf, as if an invisible force was carrying him gently downward. His arms hung loosely at his sides while his eyes scanned the cavern for the source of this phenomenon.

D'artello expected to feel the cool, heavy texture of wetness engulf him at any moment as the pool got closer, but it never came. His toe touched something hard, something he could not see. He was now standing on some sort of stone-solid membrane on the water. It was like ice, but an aqueous solid. To ensure sturdiness, he stomped a couple of times, and the water in turn responded with ripples dancing about his feet. No doubts now, he couldn't believe it, he was walking on water.

An exit was not readily apparent, so he looked for someone else occupying the room. Nope, still alone. However, since he had awoken in this place, he'd felt a presence—a nonthreatening presence, but one eager, like a child.

What is this? I don't understand, he thought as he stepped forward, looking down at the ripples, listening to the splashes of his steps. *What an odd sensation.* The feeling could not hold his attention long, for he began to run his fingers along the walls to try to find a way out. The room had about a fifty-foot diameter, he guessed, and other than the echoes of D'artello's walking, was completely silent.

"D'artello," a faint whisper called, bouncing from the walls up toward the endless ceiling.

His examination of the walls stopped abruptly. Any quieter and he wouldn't have heard it. Was someone trying to wake him from this dream?

"It's … it's you, you're the one," the whisper hissed.

D'artello looked around, sure he'd heard it this time. He peered down into the water, trying to find who or what was speaking to him. "Who are you? Why have you brought me here?" he shouted, assuming this entity was the cause of his peril.

An echo slithered each word into his ears and through to his brain, "Your time has come."

Am I dead? His stomach dropped. *No, I'm too young. I've done nothing to bring this on myself.*

"Not dead," the whisper followed his thoughts. The voice began as a whisper, but ended the statement rising in volume to a woman's soft tone. "Your world is ending," the voice went on. "You have been chosen to save not only it, but the entire universe; you will be a hero."

"What if you have chosen wrong?" he argued.

"It is a simple game; the selection is mine to choose a champion. It is prophesized that this champion will save the universe and complete the ritual to seal away the dark mistake that I have made," she chanted.

"Champion? Ritual? Prophecy? I don't think I can do that," he responded. His words were what he felt were the right things to say, but in his heart, he really wanted her to press the issue. The very prospect excited him.

"My dear D'artello, it is foretold, my proposition excites you."

How could he hide from an obvious mind reader? And how did she know his name? For most, it would be a difficult decision, one *most* would probably turn down, but not him.

The water before him began to boil. Something was coming to the surface. A grand, golden suit of armor rose from the depths. Like none of any country he'd ever seen, it was simply breathtaking. The helm had a trident-like emblem on it, the points stretched out past the limits of the headpiece. The shoulder armor, rounded and bowl-like, bore strange symbols decorating them symmetrically. The chest plate, perfectly forged, resembled a bulky chest of a man with prominent muscular features, a warrior's physique. The gauntlets were thick and weighty slabs of molded gold; on the right, the thick fingers grasped a giant sword, firmly using its intricately crafted joints that fit together like jigsaw pieces, as they were a one-of-a-kind connection.

The greaves and gauntlets were voluminous as though only a giant could wear this suit. The ankle joints pressed and twisted, emitting a clacking sound as the armor took an aggressive stance. The most notable part of this armor was the absence of a warrior inside. The self-piloting suit was decorative with pictures engraved in every part of it; they were small and hard to make out from ten feet away, but he *could* make out a winged being sprawled across the chest.

"There are those who will try to hinder you," the voice called to him. Pointing the sword, tip first right at D'artello, the armor called him out. The sword itself was a work of art, with a silver blade that started wide, narrowed toward the center, and then gradually widened again toward the tip, like an hourglass. Decorative glowing symbols covered the blade. They were an ancient language D'artello could not read, but he had seen them in religious books. The hilt was embossed with rare jewels from distant lands all around the world. The metal itself was pure gold like the rest of the armor pieces.

"Warrior, take this to defend yourself," the voice called as water right next to D'artello bubbled in a similar fashion to the entrance of the armor. An identical blade to that which the suit clutched rose to his side, showing the very same glowing symbols.

Quickly, D'artello snatched the sword, which rang out like a wind chime, as if it had been pulled from a glass sheath. He pulled it into a defensive stance, not knowing how exactly to react to fighting a suit of armor. The sword was heavy at first, much more so than the one he'd used to train, but D'artello adjusted to wield it skillfully with one hand, as he preferred. This stance gave the rest of his body superior movement and agility, and the sudden implementation of his other hand could create a surprising power that could throw his opponent off. To him, strictly two-handed weapons were awkward and limiting. With a blade bouncing in his right hand, a skirmish was a second home.

The armor charged him with a heedless ferocity, taking ridged swings one after another. The sheer speed alone made it difficult to evade. The armor was whipping its sword around like a toddler swinging a twig. However, it was rather easy for D'artello to predict the influent moves of his opponent. Inevitably the armor drew closer, step by shambling step until he just couldn't feasibly avoid the next attack. As it came down overhead, just before the sickening sound of steel slicing flesh, a clash of swords sounded like a screeching hawk.

D'artello leapt backward using his free hand to spring himself into a back flip, giving him fair spacing between him and his opponent. The memories of graciously passed-on swordplay coupled with acrobatics training with his father were vivid in his mind now. Compared to his usual sparring partner, the armor had left many openings. It was no more than a warm up for someone of his prowess.

The fighters circled, D'artello focusing straight into the empty helmet, picturing an enemy warrior looking him in the eyes right back. His hands at his sides now, he gave a swagger as they cautiously paced, staring the other down until finally the armor came in swinging, lunging with a second influent, but stone splitting, vertical-overhead strike. D'artello spun to the left avoiding the assault. The armor unwound backhandedly for a horizontal slice at neck level, but D'artello was too fast. He rolled to the right, underneath and against the current of the swing, leaving a wide gap, something he'd become well attuned to after fighting this opponent long enough.

D'artello tightened his grip and then took a rising, two-handed swing that cut the opening where a man's arm would be. To his surprise, the gauntlet lopped away—*splash* ... It had fallen into the water, as it should naturally, sinking to the bottom.

Distracted by this, he soon felt the cold hardness of the other gauntlet slug him in his chest. The potent force drove him off his feet, sending him flying backward. He landed hard on his back; this was awfully firm water. *Guess only winners get to stand here. Losers sink to the bottom then,* he confirmed. Without being given the chance to recuperate, the tip of the enemy's sword was thrusting down on him. Instinctively he had rolled to the side, avoiding his attacker once again. The steel clashed against the floor. He rose to a kneeling stance and waited for another opening. When the armor lifted the sword again, he dove between its greaves and then somersaulted to his feet. Here was his chance. D'artello had his enemy's back now, a favorable position.

The suit followed around tirelessly to continue the fight, but by that time, D'artello was already in the air. He flipped overhead, his blade held out tightly. The force of his maneuver, with a loud sound of grinding metal, caused the blade to split the helmet of the armor right down the middle.

D'artello landed gracefully on his feet, once again behind his opponent. The armor went limp and fell piece by piece into the water, sinking to meet the gauntlet that had before. He twirled his blade in a showy circular fashion. Only after the water had returned to its calm state, and the armor had reached the bottom, presumably, which D'artello could not see, the voice began to sound again, "Well done, my dear D'artello."

He nodded, self-satisfied. "Now, may I go back to where I came from?"

"Soon enough," the voice responded. In front of him, a white cloak seemed to fade into existence, forming out of thin air. At first he had mistaken it for a glare on his eyeball, but it became solid soon enough. Just on the other side of the shaft, the ghostly white cloak hovered a foot or two above the water. Sticking out of its bottom left was a vitreous, gray sword that D'artello's eyes traced carefully. At first it looked to be made of stone with its jagged and toothy blade. Just looking at it gave him the feeling of his flesh being sawed apart by this slaughter tool. It too had strange religious symbols unrecognizable to him.

Near the top of the cloak, a stubby appendage … a head looked up at him. There was no face. Only two bright blue eyes peeked out from beneath the hood. Their inhuman, pupil-less stare made it hard to tell if they were in fact looking at him. Given the situation, it was hard to convince himself otherwise.

There was a cloth over the space where the mouth would be, assuming it would not be shrouded in darkness like the rest of its face. A white gauntlet pulled free of the cloak and pointed at him, parting the cloak just enough to show off the rest of its armor, engraved entirely with designs difficult to make out from this distance. Its eyes were affixed on him; he could feel it. Then the being gave a horrid roar that seemed to vibrate every chasm of D'artello's body, calling him out as his previous opponent had.

"Let us see how this suits you," the voice suggested. Without a moment's hesitation, the figure pounced on him like a ravenous cat turned loose on a freakishly fast mouse. The dark being, or what D'artello perceived to be a dark being, swung its blade wildly, sending noises through the air like small gusts with each loose and agile motion, much more fluent than the armor. D'artello dodged attentively, thinking in his head how each stroke was just too close for comfort.

Picking out the final motion with his speedy eyes, the blade swung so very close to D'artello's face. His hair swung backward uniformly to catch up to the sudden jerking back of his head.

He had avoided the attack by just fractions of an inch, losing but a few ends of hair in the process. Before they hit the ground, D'artello had retaliated, flinging himself back toward the being and stabbing it through the area where he was certain a heart should be. He did not stop there. His muscles tightened as he clasped the sword. He gave a sharp and violent twist of his wrists and then yanked his blade free through the monster's rib area.

There was no blood of any kind where it should have poured forth like a great crimson fountain. Nonetheless, with a shriek, the creature fell to the ground. D'artello turned his back on it and began to walk away, neglecting the fact that his previous opponent sank to the bottom once defeated.

"There. I have beaten this one as well," D'artello said, dropping the sword and looking at the ceiling, as if it were the source of the voice. "I will not fight for your entertainment anymore."

No sooner did the words pass his lips that a rustling came from behind. D'artello turned around to see the legless torso rising. He stared at it in disbelief as each of its limp limbs regained consciousness. The being gave a low moan before flying at him with a flawless ferocity, besting the rage with which it had previously come at him.

The being sliced horizontally, barely missing him as he leapt backward, landing lightly on his toes and then dropping back into a stance. He glanced down at the sword lying where the creature's feet should have been, to acknowledge where his weapon ended up.

Letting out another roar, the creature attacked with wide slices at D'artello. He could feel the sweat on his forehead; he knew this vicious creature couldn't be avoided forever.

Thinking fast, he looked over at the wall and then made a run for it. His heart was pounding out of his chest at the sound of the creature giving chase. Once close enough, D'artello leapt with one foot in front of him that seemed to grab hold of the cave wall.

He scampered a couple of steps vertically up the wall. The creature swung its sword at him, barely cutting a small tear in his shirt. D'artello kicked off and soared over his opponent, landing behind it.

Bolting back in the other direction without a moment's hesitation, he recovered the sword. The creature, quick to catch on, followed, meeting him there. The clash of steel sounded. Highs and lows, verticals and horizontals, the exchange went on for quite some time.

Finally the blades embraced each other. Both fighters pushed hard to overcome the other like two young stags fighting for the season's prized doe.

D'artello could feel his muscles tensing up. The being was strong; its ghost-like visage could never have suggested such power. He hopped up and then kicked off the apparition with both of his legs, keeping its sword in check by his own. The force was enough to send D'artello airborne, twisting away from his enemy and forcing the cloaked being to stumble awkwardly on its aerial footing. D'artello flung the sword like a one-bladed pinwheel.

It guided itself straight toward his foe, seeking home in its forehead.

Landing again gracefully, D'artello watched the figure stagger about on invisible legs and then collapse a second time. He approached the heap and withdrew his sword from the creature's body. Still there was no blood. Backing away slowly, he never took his suspicions off of it.

"No heart, but it apparently has a mind," he announced, waiting for the voice's call. Just as he'd said it, the curiously invincible sword-wielder came to once again, its arms regaining strength first while its eyes peered over at him. When it could balance upright, it let out another vengeful roar. Wearily, D'artello raised his sword, grasping the dauntingly heavy blade in both hands. This was easily the most difficult fight he'd ever had. He wondered, *Am I to fight until I die here?*

The creature came charging at him again with its sword held overhead. With barely any fight left in him, D'artello braced for impact.

The shrieking was cut off midsentence, and silence befell the shaft. There was no clash, no roars, no more fighting! The being had been replaced by a woman with dark, silky hair hanging all the way down to the middle of her half-exposed back.

She had a lean but endowed figure. He waited for her to turn around. Then and there, he swore an oath not to lower his guard until he was certain of this being's intent. She held her hand out to the side as if she were painting with the air. In front of her was a dissipating mist.

Had she gotten rid of the beast? he wondered. She was covered with shimmering garments that were flatteringly revealing. The silk was a divine cream color, complimenting her smooth, tan skin tone. Her right leg was completely exposed, slender and lined with small, fair muscles. Only the left leg was covered completely to the floor with a mere draping of the translucent material, easily conservative enough to imply what the eyes could not see. The cloth covering her upper body was wrapped around her chest, but did not cover her shoulders, arms, or lean waist. He felt she was a very strong and imposing presence. Was it because he was alone in this mysterious monster-filled cavern? *No, there is something different about this person.*

"Do you not think impure thoughts of me, mortal?" she asked, lowering her arm finally. She had posed the question in a way suggestive of her knowledge of the answer. He immediately recognized her voice as that of the whisperer. D'artello lowered his sword when he saw her shoulders relax.

Her voice made his chest tighten as if some airborne pressure was pushing him away, or pulling him close; he could not tell. "I have not even seen your face, and now is not the time for impure thoughts," he said, beginning to ease upright into a casual stance.

At long last, she turned around to face him with her radiant beauty. Her eyes were a hypnotizing blue color. D'artello immediately fell into them, as any man would. Her lips were lush and soft in color, and her nose was small and perfectly symmetrical. She had a very young and narrow face, and her appearance heeded the prime of her years. She was a paragon of a woman.

"Thank you for getting rid of that monster, but where am I and who are you?" he said, suddenly remembering his manners and trying not to gawk at her.

"You do not know who I am?" she asked uniformly even though the question sounded like it would come as a surprise.

D'artello rapidly scanned his memories but had no recollection of this woman. "N-no," he replied, nervous of her power. Something about her was desirable but also had him shaking in his boots. There was a definite unnatural air about her.

"My dear warrior, I am a Peacemaker, Harmony," she announced.

He had heard the name before—the church of Harmony; Harmony's sacrificial grounds; the clergy of Harmony; the town of Harmony; she was a deity. He bent to one knee in front of her as he would a king, but not because he wanted to; he swore the air tugged at him just then.

She gave a smirk. "Rise, my warrior, as you will save all of humankind," she claimed.

Doing as he was told, he said, "You keep saying that, but how could I accomplish such a feat?"

"Oh, my dear D'artello, you will know soon enough. Enjoy the last of your life with the mortals. Soon you will soar with the Peacemakers," she said. "I must bid you farewell for now."

"Wait!" he called, reaching for her hand, but by the time the motion was carried out, a white light enveloped them, swallowing his vision …

Chapter 2

REPLACING Harmony's voice in his head was the calling of a youthful girl, waking him softly from sound sleep. The voice was a cross between the coo of a dove and the cackle of a cock and just as familiar as those two animals. A light blanket lay lazily over his body, made from the higoats that were probably out in the fields feeding on the milky morning grass. The blanket escaped him as he threw his feet up, elastically springing himself into an erect stance. To his left was a bureau made of a dark, luscious wood. His father had given it to him, as his father's father had done for him, and so forth. It was hard to believe that the worn finishes and aged brass handles on the drawers were ever once new.

A pile of clothes sat at the foot of his bed where he threw them each night before he fell to his slumber, a multicolor, textured heap. In the corner of the room lay a sheathed sword attached to a belt that stood on its point leaning against the wall. A real piece, as D'artello would say, but it had much story behind it, having seen the hides of many a man. It was his father's sword, back when he still used them.

A noble man was his father, but D'artello knew it was difficult to match a warrior of such stature. So using a sword was fine for now. The bedposts of his twin-size bed were made of the same material as the bureau. They stood tall with their spherical heads at chest level. A glass pane let a golden glow from the morning sun through, imbuing the bare white walls with a beige tint.

D'artello had lived in this room and had called it his own from a very young age. Like most people these days, he was housed in a flat within a large, shared housing unit. It had communal baths, and each living space was one room. This particular flat was built as an attachment to a stone fort wall. It was small and he did not own it, but these details mattered little to a nineteen-year-old of his careless nature.

He ran his fingers through the morning-dried shock atop his head, ordering it to lay flat and be presentable. Normally, higoats would have to fly for him to answer a shout at his window in the morning, but this voice was special and held many happy memories, for which he was thankful.

Rubbing the sleep from his eyes, D'artello staggered over to the window and peered down upon a young blonde girl shouting for him. In doing so, he exposed his youthful, training-beaten body to the tempered sunlight that was surprisingly soothing. The old wooden window squeaked open, letting in a cool wind that sent chills down his back.

The girl's hair glimmered in the sunlight as she looked up at him with big blue eyes. Her smile was as bright as the sun and twice as innocent. She clasped her hands, blushing cutely, rocking back and forth on her heels as she often did. Tanya and D'artello were not related by blood, but they still shared a sibling's bond. She whistled banteringly when she saw him.

D'artello examined the dirt street on which she stood. Contemplating, he looked toward a balcony that was one room over and one floor down. The balcony was a thick-sided metal slab that jutted out from the building. *I can make that if I...* he thought. It was black with skinny poles and a railing that was about chest height, high enough so that a person could not fall off.

The entire balcony was just big enough for one person to turn around on. *If I jump from here to there, then where next? ... Aha!* He then shifted his gaze to a stone archway that stuck out over the entrance of the building. Its bricks were awkwardly bulbous, protruding out just enough for someone to stand on top of it if they were flat against the wall. *There. It's perfect,* he deduced.

"Come out to play with me, D'artello," she called in her young, high-pitched voice.

"Just a minute," he called down, turning around to sift through the piles of clothes. He prospected out a white shirt with short sleeves, sniffed it to make sure it was clean, and then pulled it over his head. The shirt was wrinkled because it was thrown into the giant heap without being folded or pressed, but it fit tightly anyway, so it was barely noticeable. The sleeves and collar were black. His baggy blue pants were already on from the previous night. The bottoms fell around his feet until he put on his boots. He did not want his commanding officer to catch him without most of his uniform at least.

The boots were rugged, black, and worn; the shiny gloss of a new boot had long since faded away. They had spent as many days out in the fields as he had. D'artello slipped them on without untying the laces for convenience purposes, as tying them was a waste of time for his on-the-edge lifestyle. The bottoms of his pants were to be tucked in, but lazily he left them out today. As a result, they covered most of his footwear, leaving only the toe to peek out from beneath the baggy bottoms.

He glanced over at the sword that lay in the corner of the room. Hesitating, he wondered if it was necessary, but then walked over and began to thread the belt through each loop in his pants. *At least Tanya thinks it's cool.* He clicked the metal buckle shut, fastening the belt that fit loosely around his waist.

He walked back to the window and looked down at Tanya once more. "What'cha still doing up there? C'mon, let's go! We don't have all day," she called impatiently. Always nagging, always in a hurry, a feeling to which he definitely could not relate.

Lethargically confirming his surroundings, he grabbed a firm hold on the left side of the window frame. He kicked his two feet up, next to his hand, crouching sideways now on the window frame. Springing off toward the balcony, he even managed to pull off a front flip, making smooth contact with his target.

Kicking off of that, he flipped again, landing safely on the stones. He finished his stunt with a backflip that landed him firmly on his feet right next to Tanya. She applauded gleefully at this show of athleticism as he gave a self-satisfied bow.

"Thank you, thank you," he gloated, as if to a crowd. On the third bow, he looked up, his face only inches from hers. Her hair was tied back as she usually wore it. Today she clad herself in a small white top with no sleeves to accommodate the very mild temperature. She wore black pants that were made for trekking through the woods, the toughest material that could come from a higoat. They reached a bit past her knees but did not cover her ankles.

"Do I look pretty today, D'artello?" she asked, dancing around.

"Oh yes, very, fair maiden," he responded.

"Then what will you do with me? Such a pretty girl?"

D'artello swept her off the ground, spinning her around in his arms. The pair laughed while he pecked her on the cheek and then returned her to her feet. That sort of salutation had some history. They had always used it to make a mockery of the church folk within the town.

Since the last war, officially ending just ten years ago, the church had become a much more potent force in Vaukry, D'artello's country. Everyone worshipped, and everyone abided by the same set of rules. It was stuffy, it was strict, and it was certainly unacceptable for people, such as D'artello and Tanya, not to worship. With their salutations, they threw their happiness, despite their lack of faith, into the faces of the Harmonic clergy.

"So what are we doing today?" he asked as their laughter quieted. Today was a special occasion, Tanya's birthday. She had just turned twelve and wanted nothing more than to spend the morning with D'artello before his guard shift at midday.

"You promised you would take me to you-know-where," she said with a giggle.

You-know-where was a world-splitting chasm on the outskirts of the village, Battalion Bluff. It was named for the light that would toil across it each morning, quite the sight to see. It was just a short walk in the woods, but not safe for a girl her age to go alone.

D'artello looked up at the pale, fresh, morning sky. "There's still plenty of time," he said. The chasm was outside the west gate, and together they walked through the open grounds, past the higoat stables. Tanya looked away from D'artello each time they passed a stable, trying to catch a glimpse of the husky, ropy-haired animal.

They took a right on another of the main roads, this one leading directly to the west gate. It also led into the wilderness of the commerce area, which was steady this time of day. A few old folks minded their own business, murmuring about something unclear, meandering and mingling in their usual scattered morning affairs. Some of them watched the pair walk by, as if there were nothing more interesting to look at. Some gawked, some whispered, but most acknowledged them in a friendly manner. D'artello gave a wave back. It was easy to come to know most of the people in this fort city.

One thing was certain; there was far more living space than population. The village, to an outsider with fresh eyes, might look scrunched, an intricate pile of granite structures pulled tight by the walls that surrounded it. Because of mercenaries from the most recent war, it was considered foolish to settle oneself beyond the sturdy walls. This fact worked against them, as new flats went up a few years ago. It was projected that the population would spike upon the settlement becoming a living space.

Contrarily, many decided that they didn't like country life. D'artello couldn't blame them. So the layout was left clustered yet uninhabited. The exception to the clustering was a town center that offered a beautiful fountain with plenty of legroom, the lawn for all those who could not have one, as almost all of Fort Carrie's residents lived in flats just like the one he did.

Overlooked by four towers, the settlement sat in the center of a ring of hills, mountains, and forested areas, an additional wall to the outside world. The towers were at each corner of the square. They were lookout posts that hadn't seen real use in quite some time.

All in all, the royal stonemasons were a talented force and had done quite well changing the large fort into a small town. The only real militarization going on in the town these days were the makeshift guards stationed there.

The Adventures of D'artello

D'artello had been part of it since he was old enough to grasp a sword. He took it less seriously than most, wondering why anyone would want to make a life out of it.

Even though it was settled that the Kingdom of Vaukry be granted independence just ten years ago, the fighting had really stopped almost twenty years ago.

Mercenaries, who were unhappy with the results of the treaty, remained in this kingdom roaming the countryside, occasionally finding their way to Fort Carrie. Only the dumb ones, that is; others knew there was a fort there. Fewer still dared to challenge its composite-stone walls. In short, because of the exceptionally stupid mercenaries, the guard remained in place. D'artello recalled a day when just their one town archer fended away fifteen men.

D'artello despised war, despite his world's history being soaked in it and his kingdom being born of it.

One sight, however, did catch the pair's eyes. More toward the west gate was the Cathedral of Harmony. It was easily the tallest building in the settlement, and the royal masons put the most time into its construction. The spires on the square structure reached for the skies as the stained glass of Harmony's endeavors stared outward like signs at a fruit stand, blessing passersby with their serenity. The blue and white exterior gave it a heavenly look. It was almost as majestic as the sun coming up each morning. Out front was its enormous water clock being refilled by one of the white-robed, blue-hooded Harmonic priests, as it was every morning. Water dripped onto a lever, and each tenth second, it would empty into the pot below. D'artello did not need a time-telling device, for his father had taught him not only to read, write and fight, but to tell the hours of the day by watching the sun. Through the years, his perceptions of time had grown naturally acute.

Four more priests, circled the building, consecrating the ground for the sermon due to take place in a few hours, as it did every day. This was truly when Fort Carrie would become a ghost town, which was why D'artello was always the midday guard.

Among the priests, all old, hunched, and fatty beneath their garbs, was a much daintier robed figure, a young woman whom D'artello knew well. For a moment, he stared at her, wondering if his father's words of what she would become were true, or if they were merely bred from his exquisite hatred for the church.

D'artello stopped and recalled the voice in his dream and the woman who claimed to be Peacemaker Harmony. She had looked nothing like her depictions on the church's windows. He breathed a sigh of relief. *It was just a dream,* he thought.

Tanya looked up at D'artello. She had never been in the cathedral, and to her knowledge, neither had he. "Why don't we pray like everyone else, D'artello?" she asked.

There was never a reason why, but he *did* know the answer his father had sternly given him ever so long ago, when he had asked the very same question. "Because when darkness comes, Harmony will not save them." That answer was never good enough for D'artello, let alone a curious little girl like Tanya.

"I don't know," he responded blankly. "Just never really have. I don't think it's for me, but maybe you should try it sometime," he suggested, even though he hoped to whatever higher entities bore down on him that she would never mention a notion like that to his father.

In passing the church, they were coming upon the west gate. Much to the unordinary, there were guards today. His shift was usually the first. They were usually foregone this early in the morning. D'artello met gazes with one he knew well. "Joseph!" he called as he waved.

The heavier set of the two guards turned to face him, clad from chest to toe in fading royal blue armor. He was not much older than D'artello, but he was much bigger. He had a round nose to match his body shape. The muscles on his arms could be seen bulging through his shirt as he hung a large axe over his shoulder. His eyes were small, black dots in the middle of fat white ovals. One of his mahogany eyebrows ascended at the call of his name.

"D'artello, it's about time ya got up," he said with some lecture in his voice.

"Why? I'm not on guard duty until noon. Isn't it early enough?" he said, stopping to stretch just a few feet away.

Joseph took a step back, D'artello's questions slapped him in the face. "You haven't heard?" he asked. "Everyone is talkin' about it after this mornin's alarm. There's a big ol' alpha on the loose in the woods. Henry got mauled last night on the usual route. Man, you *are* oblivious sometimes. You're in fer it when yer dad finds out."

D'artello's stomach sank. He knew that if he did not respond to an alarm, there was hell to pay when his commander got a hold of him.

That must have had something to do with my odd dream, he thought. D'artello looked over at Tanya, who was inattentively kicking at the dirt, and then looked back at Joseph. "It's her birthday, Joe. I wanted to take her to Battalion Bluff," D'artello whispered.

Joseph looked over at Tanya, paused, and then said with a smirk, "She's a little young fer you, ain't she?"

D'artello shot him a look as the other guard gave a chuckle.

"Relax. You know I'm just kiddin'," he laughed. "Here. I'll go with you. I'm sure you and I can take jus' one alpha. I gotta give 'em one for Henry anyway," he said as he picked up a helmet off of the ground and slid it over his brown hair. The helmet was crowned with a small golden bear. The bear represented a sort of weight class in this small guard. D'artello's helm depicted a hawk.

Joseph raised his hand, giving another guard the signal to open the gate. The crank was atop the wall, and the guard up top shook his head. *No, we're not supposed to let anyone out.*

Joseph put his hand up and waved again, this time more forcefully. *Just do it!.*

With a loud clack and bang, the enormous, wooden gate began to slide sluggishly. A sunburst of colors filled their vision as they looked out over the fields beneath the fair weather.

The green fields were vibrant, along with their kindred souls. The hills-upon-hills makeup of the land held many memories of the backbreaking, sweat-inducing, blood-shedding training that D'artello and Joseph had endured. It was under the aging blue twilight of these lands that D'artello got his first kiss, and many more since.

Mountains could be seen just beyond the forest in the distance. They were purple giants that stood in a crowd to watch over this place. The three, led by D'artello, traversed a rocky dirt path that would take them to the woods.

"So it's your birthday?" Joseph asked Tanya. "An' he's makin' you walk?" he said, pointing at D'artello. She nodded, gazing wide-eyed upon the large man. "Here, grab my arm tight, lil' one," he said, reaching out to her. His arm looked like a tree trunk when he held it out to the little girl. She grasped it tightly, allowing herself to be lifted from the ground and placed on Joseph's shoulders. She let her legs hang down over his husky chest.

"There you are. Rest yer legs," he said.

D'artello grabbed Joseph's side arm from his belt. A short sword looked like a long dagger in his hands and a knife in Joseph's gargantuan hands. He spot-checked it for a moment, giving it a quick shine on his shirt, and then handed it to Tanya. "What is this?" she asked.

"It's your very own sword, Tanya," he said.

"Wait! That's my—" Joseph protested.

"Shh …" D'artello interrupted with an elbow to his friend's lower chest. "My father is the head of the guard. I'll get you a new one, I promise."

With a shrug, Joseph let Tanya down. "How's about you play with that on the ground. Don't need to lop my head off, do ya?"

"Thank you very much, D'artello," she said, throwing her arms around his neck, slightly weighing him down for a moment. She gave a playful spin of her sword. "Hah! Now I don't need you to protect me anymore."

He laughed, ruffling her hair. "You would be completely lost without us."

"Hey!" she called out, straightening her hair as the two older boys laughed.

The woods lay now in front of them. An army of trees stood like a border of tower shields, separating the open fields from the dark, multicolored, canopied abyss. Beneath the trees, the texture of the land was moist and earthy. It was uneven with gray boulders lying dormant underneath, occasionally breaching the surface.

D'artello stepped down into a teen-frequented walking path. To stray from the path would be to enter an impassable thicket of shrubberies, thorns, and nests of rodents, reptiles, and insects. Tree branches sheltered overhead, sealing off the brush tunnel that was the walking path. The trees along the path were so thick they seemed to make porous walls, confining the group only to what they could clearly see.

On bright sunny days like this, D'artello's father had always told Tanya, "Sound travels much better." Today was no exception. The birds chirping, bugs buzzing, chucks chattering, and twigs snapping were crystal clear. The group grew silent to open their ears and eyes to nature's boons.

It was breathtaking. The greens, browns, and exaggerated bird colors made D'artello, Joseph, and Tanya each look about as if this were their first trip to the woods. "Sure is nice this time o' year," said Joseph, breaking the silence finally.

"Yes it is, very pretty," said Tanya, bending down to examine a flower just off the path. It was purple with a yellow center.

"Are you sure it was an alpha that mauled Henry?" asked D'artello.

"That's what he said, but you know Henry. It coulda' been a wolf or, y'know, something that lives around here. He is sort of a wimp! It wouldn't surprise me in the least if that wasn't the case," Joseph responded.

"D'artello, what is an alpha?" asked Tanya as she stepped over a hole in the path.

"Well it's …"

"It's a big, furry beastie. It comes from the north, and it's got huge claws that can take down a tree. And it eats —" Joseph started.

"Joseph, cut it out. Don't scare the kid," D'artello said. "Just don't worry, we would never let anything happen to you," he swore, looking into her widened eyes.

"Promise?" she asked.

"Promise. Isn't that right, Joseph?" he asked, looking up at the large man.

"Oh yeah. We promise; no way is any big, mean alpha gettin' his claws on you."

Looking ahead, they could see an end to the trees, and an end of the walking path. The three walked over to the edge uniformly, gazing over into the chasm.

For millennia, the frothy-rushing stream, hundreds of feet below, carved out a world-dividing rift. Toward either direction, it ran endlessly. Its walls were not like the gray stones peppered across the forested land, but instead a rusty red-brown. Their colors were layered as well, defined by ages of terraforming. Tanya's eyes filled with bewilderment, and her breath escaped her when she looked down. Below them were streams of rainbow light that danced like ribbons in the wind. The red, blues, greens, purples—she told D'artello and Joseph it was the most magnificent thing she had ever seen in her twelve years.

"It comes from the crystals that line the walls of the chasm," D'artello said, smiling at her. He pointed over her shoulder toward the seven or so scattered, spear-like prisms that jutted out of the walls, capturing the sunlight permeating through the dancing canopy.

"It's so ... beautiful," she said, mesmerized.

From behind came a stealthy rustling.

D'artello turned to face two beaming eyes peering down from above bushy shoulders about twelve feet tall. The creature raised its two log-sized arms and cartwheel-sized hands to show off its sword-size claws. It gnashed the pointy teeth jumping every which way from its hanging, dripping jaw.

The oaken-furred beast towered over the group—even Joseph—with its arms spread like a bird stretching its wings, as if aiming to take all three of them out at the same time. D'artello turned and dragged Tanya to the ground while quickly shifting his lower leg to trip Joseph. The two hands made a horrible ear-piercing clap where their heads had just been. The beast roared with an intense frustration that shook the bones in their bodies.

Tanya shrieked, challenging the creature's attention. It raised its gigantic foot over her. D'artello's eyes met Tanya's, full of fear. It was too late for him to get up and react.

Before the earth-shaking stomp made its descent, the monster was tackled off balance by Joseph. He grunted, hugging the beast around the waist, pushing with all of his weight. It dwarfed him by about five feet and was twice as wide as he was. It was miraculous that he could stop it at all, if even only for a second.

"Get 'er outta here! I can't hold it for long!" he yelled through his strain.

D'artello looked over at Tanya, who lay on the ground looking up at the creature, utterly stunned with horror. She had probably never seen anything scarier in her whole life. He reached down, scooped her up, and then gave her a shove. "Run!" he said to her as he rose to his feet. She scampered off, looking back once to check on D'artello.

Dashing at Joseph, he leapt into the air, boosting off of Joseph's back with his left foot, jumping and thrusting a dropkick into the beast's face. This knocked the already imbalanced creature back a bit. The blow seemed to cause it minimal damage but aroused maximum anger.

Joseph took this opportunity, as D'artello landed next to him, to grab hold of his battle axe he'd laid behind him. Without looking, he took a low swing for the monster's legs. The blunt pole hit the lower back ankle of the alpha. Losing its balance, between Joseph's notable might and the drive of the axe, the beast plummeted onto its back. Using this momentum, Joseph came back around to drive the axe downward toward the alpha's exposed chest.

In its discontent, the beast slashed at the oncoming attack, deflecting, severing the axe head, and sending it spinning away.

D'artello took his opening by jumping onto its chest, drawing his sword. The alpha squirmed to get a hold of him while effortlessly climbing to its feet. He brought his sword down like a lightning bolt, digging into the thick hide with a sickening tearing, but it did not stop the animal.

I must have missed the heart, D'artello realized. In no time, it had gotten a hold of him and he was in one of its enormous hands.

The beast got back to its feet while holding D'artello, arms pinned, in its clutches. It then hastily hurled him toward the chasm with an overhand pitch. D'artello was sent rolling across the ground and over the edge. Before falling to certain doom, he managed to get a grip with just nine of his fingers. There was a sharp pain in his side from scraping over a stone. He looked down. Just to reaffirm the fall would kill him.

The beast loomed over him from above. If he had a few more seconds, he'd be able to pull himself up, but the alpha didn't look merciful. Just when he thought it was over, a roar of pain echoed out over the open chasm. Joseph had punched its lower back. The beast arched backward just enough to let Joseph reach up and get a hold on its head and lower jaw. With a pushing of his hip, he was able to twist its body, using his sheer weight throw it to the ground. It landed with a heavy crash.

Ignoring the alpha, Joseph extended an arm to D'artello. "I told you to go with Tanya," he said, pulling his friend up.

"You'd be dead," D'artello said, abruptly glancing around Joseph to check on the alpha. It had thundered off as quickly as it had appeared. Panicked, he realized that Tanya must have taken off too. The woods were not a familiar place to her.

D'artello looked around hastily. "Where is Tanya?" he cried out. A high-pitched scream from the left sent a death rattle down his spine. He took off with great agility in that general direction. Zipping through the thicket of trees, evading left and right, jumping over rocks, ditches, and anything that could slow his pace, he could feel his heart sinking lower each time a roar sounded from the beast and with each shrill cry escaping little Tanya.

There was time for him to envision a thousand horrible fates of Tanya before he came upon a small clearing. A broken circle of trees enclosed him and the beast, and the small clearing had a stream that ran just behind the feet of the alpha. There was a burrow in the side of a five-foot step in the landscape with an adolescent oak growing from it. The creature lay as a hunched mass in front of it, dredging with its massive claws, shoveling dirt back, and grunting sadistically. *Tanya must be hiding in there,* he thought, hearing the yells from that direction.

"D'artello! Help! No!"

The hole was barely large enough to accommodate that claw, and judging by the shape of the step and the amount of dirt being shoved away by the alpha probably got narrower as it went deeper in. The Alpha was really scratching away, looking for even a toe to yank the little girl out by.

D'artello rapidly scanned his surroundings to try to find something to take the monster down, as his sword was still embedded helplessly in its chest. A rock or even a large branch, anything he could use to cause enough pain to draw it away from Tanya.

A gleaming ray of hope screamed into his eyes. In the clear water of the stream, he spotted the glint of the birthday present he'd given Tanya. Sprinting, his feet pounded the ground as he plucked it from the water with his right hand. He leaped into the air, and as soon as he had, he thought better of it. For that fraction of a second, he knew the lengths he would go to in protecting not just Tanya, but anyone in desperate need. Latching onto the beast's back caused it to thrust up its shoulders, trying to heave D'artello away. It reached behind its back, clawing at him ravenously, leaving bloody scrapes in D'artello's shoulders. Still, he held on tight until he could get a good grasp on the sword.

He found the strength to hold on to a tuft of ropy hair with one hand, while the other dug the short sword into the neck of his foe. He grabbed it with both hands and gave it a sharp twist. The breaking spine made a sickening snap. With it, down came the monster. It let out one final roar before it fell to its knees and then collapsed forward like a giant tree.

D'artello slid down the back of the monster and onto his knees, splashing into the stream, which cleansed his clothes of blood. The cool water dampened his pants and his waist as he sat facing the cave, breathing heavily. His heart was pounding, and his mind was racing with millions of possible combat outcomes, the natural high that he'd always gotten from a fight. "Tanya," he called out through his panting.

Upon hearing her name, she flew out of the burrow and into D'artello's arms. He caught a quick glimpse of her dirt-covered face just before she began to bawl hysterically into his chest. Miraculously, she was alive. Stroking her hair gently, he tried to quell her. "It's okay, I've got you," he said wearily as she choked on her frightened tears.

Joseph came barreling through the trees seconds too late. He examined the dead alpha and then looked over to see D'artello holding Tanya in the stream. Despite the events that had just taken place, it was relatively calm. Only the talkative stream could be heard rushing against D'artello's waist while sparkling in the morning sun. Tranquil and quiet now, it was as if a great plague had been lifted from the land. "I knew you'd get it," Joseph said quietly to his friend, but almost to reassure himself…

Chapter 3

D'ARTELLO, Joseph, and Tanya had made it back to town in just an hour, fortunately in time for the midday guard shift. D'artello planned to see Tanya again once his patrol was over. He'd calmed her and sent the little girl home to clean up and get some food. Joseph had parted from them as soon as they'd come back in the gate, probably going to hide out from their commander as to avoid confrontation about the alpha.

It was now nearing the end of D'artello's shift and the day. One loose end remained before he could retire to his room. Sali was the daughter of the only noble in Fort Carrie, Harmonic Bishop Adriel. Society across all of Vaukry was compact. Commoners lived in flats or complexes like D'artello did. Only lords had houses or lawns. Adriel was the town's lord, the only one in fact. In the capital or other larger cities, D'artello had seen houses that were boxy but had their own personal courtyards in the back. However, in Fort Carrie, space was scarce, so this house's courtyard was foregone. It was still a much larger and much nicer living space than any other Fort Carrie citizen.

He made his way through the streets under the darkening sky and cooling nightfall. He approached the torch-lit house, peeking through the window of the kitchen to see red-haired Sali and her mother cooking dinner, having a great time. Right now they were in the middle of throwing flour at each other, laughing hysterically. What a moment to walk into.

He swung around to the front door and knocked, listening to the rapid footsteps climbing the stairs just beyond the door. Sali's mom must have run to tidy herself for company, lest Adriel find out about the blasphemy going on in his own kitchen. Sali pulled open the front door leading into the atrium. It was a broad room, bigger than his living quarters, with four supporting columns arranged in a compact square near its center. There were decorative vases, for their fashion, not function, strewn neatly about on miniature pedestals.

"Oh … uh, D'artello," she said, pulling her hair behind her left ear and out of the way of her emerald eyes. "Relax, Mother, it's just D'artello!" she yelled up the stairs.

"Ohhhh," she cooed. "Well bring him in and give him some food. Nice to see you again, hun," she said even though there was no possible way she could see him from upstairs.

"We were just … baking bread," Sali giggled.

"Heh, yeah I see that. Looks like fun," he responded with a wholehearted smile.

"You here on guard duty?" she asked, astute to the sword at his waist.

"Uh … no … it's a little more personal."

"Oh?" she perked. "Is it about Tanya?"

"No, she's fine. Got quite the scare today though."

"Oh really? What happened?"

D'artello shook his head. "You'll worry too much if I tell you." Even as he said that, he knew an answer like that wasn't good enough for Sali. He took a deep breath. "It's a long story."

"Well, c'mon in. It's rude to linger in doorways," she said. He stepped up, dwarfing her by about a foot, letting her close the door behind him. She led him through the atrium and the arch-doorway to the parlor. It was a comfortable room with three plush couches, one for her, her mother, and Adriel. White, red, and purple respectively. He could sleep on them just by pillowing his head on one of the bean-shaped arms. On the far side of the room was a fire he knew Sali would want to sit by to talk.

An hour flew by. He knew how to stretch it, a good storyteller, which was apparently true of his father too. Even though he'd never heard any war tales pass his lips, only the lips of others boasting about sharing a species with such greatness. Sali pushed herself up off the floor and dropped her flour-covered body onto the higoat-wool sofa. White on white so that Adriel would not readily notice before she had time to clean it. D'artello placed himself ever so carefully, crouching next to her, far enough away as not to impose, yet close enough for friendly conversation. "So what's the matter?" she asked.

"Well … whoow." He blew a white cloud from her hair. "I'm here to get back with you, pretty girl," he said.

"Really?" Her jaw tightened, and her eyes widened in surprise.

"No," he said without missing a beat. He was about to go on, but she interrupted him.

"Y'know, you could really be hurting my feelings and not even know it," she said, looking away, lowering her eyes.

He thought for a second that he may actually have taken it too far this time. "Aww, Sal, I'm sorry. Really, I won't say it anymore," he pledged.

"Ha! You're so stupid sometimes. I wouldn't say yes anyway. So what are you really here for?" she asked, patting the couch for him to sit down next to her. Obediently, he pivoted his body to plant himself.

"You may want to get your text for this," he said, giving a solemn look.

Looking away, she took a deep breath. "Okay, D'artello, it's really not funny when you make fun of the church." If he did not stop her now, she would go on a long rant about how it was her life's path, whether he liked it or not, and that he should join the church too, because it was an important element to growing old.

"No, Sali. I'm serious this time," he said.

"Uh … oh, okay, just give me a minute to clean up," she said.

In minutes, they were lying in front of the fire the way they used to, this time with her book, and she even put on her blue and white garb, as if she was giving a practice sermon. "Nice robe," he said, exercising latent sarcasm.

"Cute." She responded. "Now what's your question?" she asked, opening the cover of an old, thick book. It was the testament of Harmony, a text used to build a nation and form an army. It was a book that had been written so long ago that no one remembered its conception. It was brown with black bindings, and the pages were thinner than most books. They were comprised entirely of finer text, more so than any other book he'd seen.

"Well, I had a dream. Peacemaker Harmony visited me," he explained. "I know nothing about her, or even really what a Peacemaker is, so why me, I guess?"

"Okay, well one thing at a time." She began flipping through the premier pages. The text yielded abruptly; there were many pictures in a row. "These are Peacemakers," she said, turning the pages gradually slower. She stopped on a very unfamiliar face. It could have been the drawing, but it looked nothing like the person he'd seen in his dreams. Nor was this person clad like her. The woman in the picture was very modest, with a dress that covered all the way to her ankles. The drawing was in black and white, but the hair wasn't shaded at all, leading D'artello to believe that the artist thought Harmony was blonde. "This is Harmony. She's a very beautiful Peacemaker and loves us all. In fact, she is said to be the Peacemaker of love as well, but don't let that fool you, she's powerful and smart too. That's why we worship her and none of these other ones. Harmony became a Peacemaker when she made a sacrifice greater than her own life. She had to offer up her unwilling loved one as a tribute to stop Ruin."

"All right, so I'll assume Ruin is a bad guy," he responded.

"Uh ... yeah. So is this the person you saw?" she said, pointing, staring as his eyes studied the page.

"Umm, no, it doesn't look a thing like her," he said after a time, never once looking back at Sali.

"Are you sure you saw Harmony then? Because this is her," she argued.

"Listen, I know it sounds crazy, but I know that when I dream, everything thinks and acts generally the way I do, or the way I want it to. This person was way too free-thinking, and she wanted to test me, said I had to save the universe. It sounds farfetched, but I can't stop thinking about it."

At that very moment, a subtle wisp tickled the fine hairs on his ears. *She will not understand.*

At first he brushed it off as his own inner voice, a self-made sense of doubt in his friend. It was an easy mistake to make given the circumstances.

"Shhh ..." This time he knew it was no thought of his own, for it echoed in through the vortex of his ear, passing into the brain and out the other side, perceiving it as he would a voice.

"Did you hear that?" he said suddenly, looking at the fire. For some reason, the yellow light trapped his gaze.

"Hear what, D'artello?" asked Sali.

"There was a ..." He caught himself and froze again in his mental quest for words. Whatever the voice, it had penetrated so deeply into his heart that making something up would be to compare it to something worldly. How could human materialism compare to the power of Peacemakers? He swallowed hard at the prospect of looking crazy.

"There was a what?"

"Ugh ... nothing," he said, coming up with a lie and rubbing his head, mimicking the symptoms of a migraine. "Just ... so much training lately, you know? I think I can hear my old man's voice still," he joked.

"Okay then ... so ... save the universe?" she prodded skeptically. "I think your head is just big. I guess let me know if you keep having these dreams, or if you just want to learn your own religion." She took her shot. "But you should leave. My dad is gonna be home soon, and you know how he feels about you and your dad."

"Wait, there's more. Harmony mentioned a prophecy. Does your book have anything about that?"

"Prophecy? As in the future?"

"Yeah I guess," he said, reaching toward the tome, beginning to thumb across the pages himself. She pulled it away abruptly.

"You know you can't touch this, D'artello," she lectured. "Only high-ranking clergy members like me can touch it," she said, as if that were some sort of achievement. Her father was head of the church in the northern region of the country. Of course she was high up in the clergy. With that, she escorted him to the door, letting him stand halfway between the dark cold outside and the warm inviting inside.

"Well, okay, how about a kiss good-bye then? For old time's sake?" he asked ever so innocently.

When she leaned in to give it to him, he pulled away. "No way!" he shouted and then proceeded to walk out the door, leaving her grinning and shaking her head.

* * *

That night, D'artello held onto Tanya's motionless body. She had fallen asleep in his arms while in his room, still frightened of the alpha. The little girl snoozed silently with tiny breaths. A blanket was hugged in close to keep her warm while she snuggled into D'artello. She slept so comfortably without a care in the world, while he could not sleep a wink. The recollection of the alpha, the pondering about his father chewing him out first thing in the morning, and the nightmare of losing the ever-precious life he held was easily enough to keep his eyes wide open.

Rarely ever did his father have to find the words to say. He was usually an infinite pool of advice, wisdom, and if necessary, discipline. This time, D'artello had stumped the old war vet. The words behind his father's famous stone-cold stare were simply, "I can't believe you right now. I really need time to think about this." Those words hurt more than all of the push-ups and practice swings in the world. D'artello was being forced to stew, slow cook his thoughts about tomorrow's impending punishment.

That day made him realize how frail life was. At any moment, Tanya could be plucked from life, for any reason. It sent a chill down his spine to hear her screams in his head again. She was so small, so defenseless, so in need of his protection. Her parents were long gone. He was all she really had, and they weren't even related. Honestly though, he needed her as well, something to hold onto. He could not envision life without her, a part of his family.

Yet somehow, he did not envy Tanya's worriless sleep; she was entitled to it. Everyone who slept soundly deserved to do so.

"I will protect you," D'artello whispered into her ear.

This statement, in passing, evoked wonders about others in faraway places, others who were defenseless like Tanya. Did they have someone to protect them? He thought about Harmony's words: "You will save the universe," or something like that. It was a full-time job keeping just one person out of harm's way. This kept him awake for another few hours.

"You will protect them all," he heard the familiar whisper course through.

His eyes flung open, and he slowly perused the moonlit room. This was the fifth time he had heard the voice since the initial encounter at Sali's house. He was growing accustomed to it now, reinforcing his thoughts.

* * *

With just a blink in the night to the light of morning, D'artello awoke alone in his bed. Eyelids hanging heavily, he was surprised not to have heard his father's voice coming to yank him from sleep. He sat up. Tanya had apparently covered him at some point. The door opened to his left, and she entered the room.

In her hands, she cradled his sword and scabbard. "Here, D'artello," she said, handing it to him.

The sword clicked out when he pulled the hilt. The blade shone with a new finish. No blood or spots from the hide of the beast he had plunged it into.

"I cleaned it for you," she said.

He held it up right, scoping it out, noticing his reflection. *Stunning!* he thought. Then he lowered it so he could look back at her.

"You got up early just for that?" he asked.

"Of course. I knew you wouldn't," she said, sticking her tongue out at him playfully.

"Scary stuff, huh?"

"I was *so* scared," she said. "No matter how afraid I was though, I always knew you would save me."

He laughed a little and stared into her happy eyes.

"Gramps is looking for you," she said abruptly. "He told me when you woke up, to go down out back and see him. He is very mad. He said a word that I don't often hear him say." She shifted her eyes to the left, probably trying to keep a straight face while recalling the word.

"Gramps" was what she was permitted to call D'artello's dear old dad. This by no means meant a frail, old, friendly elder that comes to visit every once in a while. Well maybe to her. D'artello knew him differently. Just because he was his father didn't mean he wasn't hard on him when it came to guard duties. In fact, quite the contrary was true. Even when D'artello was younger than the other guardsmen, more was expected of him.

In a flash, he threw his covers to the side and dressed in his full uniform. He sheathed his sword while speeding out the door, giving a quick "bye" to Tanya, who had commenced tidying the room.

Down the stairs he went, flight by flight; he lived on the third floor. He had tunnel vision only for what lay ahead. The building had an upper-class look. It had white walls with a red carpet that seemed to stretch endlessly down the complex. The walls were lined with doors and paintings of famous guardsmen and commanders. All were good men who'd fought beside Gerrik in the most recent war. Their elegant frames sometimes made him forget he lived in a flat. Each corridor was militantly lit no matter what time of day it was. Finally he approached a dark wood, double door near the center of the building. Since this building was an extension of the fort's outer walls, it led directly outside to the fields.

Stumbling into the atrium, he cornered a hard left toward the door leading out to the fields. He pushed through, thrust into daylight. The grassy fields were alive with valor, ready to charge into a day of harsh training.

Hustling, he made his way through the dew-flooded field toward a hill with two figures awaiting his arrival. *Oh man,* he thought. *Missed the alarm yesterday, and he's already started punishing Joseph. This is not good.* D'artello took attention with hands at his sides, following Joseph's suit. The two guardsmen stood still like statues. A wind whipped in from the north. The fields about them came alive, dancing fluently, making the pair seem all the stiller.

The man standing before them was Gerrik, D'artello's father and the most powerful warrior in all of Vaukry. This aging man's arms were huge, easily the first thing to catch the eye, especially beneath his current sleeveless attire. Naturally, one's vision would travel upward to see his plate-like pectorals showing through his shirt. By this time, one would notice the cold stare he was giving the two younger men, just a bit above his beard that robustly covered his neck and the lower part of his face—much in contrast to his short, neatly trimmed hair.

Gerrik was a tough commander, because he wanted each and every one of "his boys" to grow smarter, to learn a thing or two about combat. In a world with no communication accept for a messenger's thundering steed, Gerrik had earned a renowned reputation as a manslayer. A past he held secret, seemingly only from his son, who felt a deep disdain for that part of his father's attitude.

Two black vests lay at Gerrik's feet. They were weighted and made of itchy cloth infused with the sweat of many a lesser man. These were senior training vests. They were used primarily for punishment in these days of peace, and they weighed a hundred pounds apiece.

Gerrik set his shattering gazes toward Joseph first, his voice more intimidating than the growl of an alpha. "I want you to do push-ups," he ordered.

"How many, sir?" Joseph asked quickly.

"Until I am done lecturing." He tossed him a vest. Obediently, Joseph slipped it on and began the push-ups at a steady, rhythmic pace.

"D'artello!" he barked.

"Yes, sir," he responded, as his father kicked a line in the dirt with his boot.

"Put this on." He chucked the other vest at his feet. D'artello immediately followed his instructions. Much to his surprise, the vest weighed only fifty pounds. He gave his father a look of misunderstanding, to which Gerrik responded with a nod of his head.

"I want you to do backflips starting at this line. Each time you finish a flip, you will hustle back to this line and start again. And I mean hustle!"

D'artello began his workout. The powerful legs on his lightweight frame let him "become part of the wind," as his father would say. Each flip would lift him off the ground, sending him on a quick journey backward. His form was perfect, as he had done many flips throughout the years. Even with a hundred-pound vest, it wouldn't be a difficult task. After a few flips, his father's voice began to sound again.

"Joseph, I know you heard the alarm in the morning and attended the meeting discussing the alpha. You let a fellow guardsman—my son, nonetheless—and a civilian through the gate. I will not ask you to explain yourself. You failed to follow orders. That is why you are here before me now. You let a citizen fall into danger, and you risked your own life needlessly." He looked back toward D'artello, his turn now. "You were not there in the morning for the alarm. You also went through the gate even though you heard about the alpha, endangering yourself. You also endangered Tanya. What were you thinking?" he said, his biceps never leaving their crossed position.

The concern in Gerrik's voice made him sound like a father, not a commander. That meant he and D'artello were going to have a talk. "That is all, Joseph. You can go, and I took it easy on you both because you did save me some time and probably a few lives. Thankfully, neither of you was hurt. This way at least no one else will end up like Henry, or worse. Good job, boys," he said as Joseph rose to his feet and D'artello stopped flipping. The two removed their vests, quite puzzled.

"Now return to your post, Joseph," he laughed. This was the real him, a kindhearted man. D'artello just never could tell what Gerrik was thinking; his father had a way of flipping between tough and kind without warning. Joseph trotted away, bidding them both a farewell salute, probably figuring it best to leave quickly, as not to push his luck. D'artello never had been mistreated, but his father did have high expectations of the future commander.

Gerrik's eyes narrowed. "Listen to me, son," he said softly. "I hope you know how proud of you I really am; you are strong and nothing less than a strapping young soldier." Before D'artello could accept that compliment, Gerrik added, "But you are so stupid sometimes. How could you be so reckless? Really? Are you really that bored that you have to go looking for trouble?" The mighty warrior looked just like a concerned parent now.

"Dad, I'm sorry. It was Tanya's birthday, and she wanted to see the chasm at Battalion Bluff. Don't blame Joseph either. I talked him into it."

"Ah, son," he said, shaking his head, "always protecting everyone else. What will they do if something happens to you then?"

"Guess I can't let anything happen to me."

"Pig headed as always!" He grinned at his son. "You're just like your old man though, sharp and quick."

"Don't you mean sharper and quicker?"

"Okay then, but you still don't have any of these …" Gerrik raised his arm, giving it a tight flex. The bicep bulged like a bear stirring from hibernation. He then gave his son a friendly shove.

Abruptly changing his demeanor, Gerrik combed the scruff on his neck, weeding out the words to say. "I … I have heard some news," he began. "I'm sorry, son. Please come with me." He wrapped his arm around his boy. D'artello looked up curiously at his father. "You are old enough to understand now. Your king needs you."

D'artello's heart never sank so low in his chest, "Wha-what are you talking about?"

"Our capital has fallen, D'artello."

The boy's head began to spin with that absurd statement. The capital was the most protected city in all of the country, one of the most powerful cities on the continent. How could it have fallen, and under the expert command of King Garo III? "Who would make that kind of move?" he asked. "Especially when our allies are so close?"

His father's eyes wandered, and a look of shame crawled across Gerrik's face. D'artello realized that he'd answered his own question.

Gerrik pressed on, "I've heard they are our former allies, the Genzak Kingdom. Bensel has declared war on our country."

Bensel was the king of Genzaks and had always been like an uncle to D'artello, and a brother to Gerrik. D'artello struggled against this logic. If Bensel attacked the capital, there had to be a good reason for it.

"Dad, you know that Bensel would never declare war on us. How do they even know that it's him? There are plenty of mercenaries out there stirring up trouble," he argued.

"Actually, a group of Genzak scouts was sighted near our border," his father explained.

"It could be a mistake. Dad, please think about this."

"I have. There is no option for us, D'artello. We must follow Our Majesty's orders, which are: the launch of a task force to flank the Genzaks. The king knows of my talents. When he heard that I had a son, he demanded your presence as well in the elite force. That being said, this gives us one month to train together, my boy. Just you and I. Joseph will run the guard for me."

"What about Tanya? She needs me ... and you for that matter."

"What about the child of every man who stands up to fight, every woman waiting for the return of her husband? You are merely another one of these men. What is most important is that *you* survive to come back to her," Gerrik said.

"That *I* come back?" D'artello said angrily.

A long silence divided them. D'artello had pulled away from beneath his father's grasp now. The pause allowed them to recuperate as they walked back toward Fort Carrie. The wind blew again, animating the scenery. Clouds were beginning to appear gradually as the morning went and the day began. The conversation carried on.

"I am not as young as I used to be, D'artello. We've had many years of peace, and I am no longer the young and powerful soldier that I once was."

D'artello stared into his father's eyes, trying not to show his saddening distaste for the thought.

"I *will* be gone someday. For now, I'm more concerned with your safety than my own. I will protect you ..."

* * *

Those words rang on in D'artello's head throughout the next few weeks training with his father. His desire to protect all who needed it overrode his desire to stay with Tanya.

Throughout the month, he visited her sparsely, usually one day a week when his muscles would cry for mercy. At these times, he tried to put everything in perspective, but it didn't make things any easier. His distance was growing noticeable. Sali cried when she heard the news and soon stopped talking to him. He presumed she'd rather distance herself from him instead of worrying about his safe return. With his relationships falling apart, he felt it best to try to detach.

He and his father sparred at least twice a day, and sometimes that was all they did from dawn until dusk. Gerrik would practically ambush him out of bed each morning. It started out with a giant gap of skill between D'artello and Gerrik. His father was miles above his level in the beginning. Eventually they began to even off. One thing was for sure; he now understood why his father deserved the credibility he had as a warrior.

Gerrik was a beast; no other word could describe the man's fighting skill. It was the birth of the evening in the very same field where he had met with his father thirty days prior. The sky was black with swollen clouds that forewarned the fury of a storm. The entire guard stood in a circle around D'artello and Gerrik, who faced each other ready to leap into their most intense sparring round yet. D'artello wore only the undershirt and pants of his guard uniform. It revealed his practice-beaten body, and its telltale scrapes, scars, and bruises. His frame was a bit larger than it had been before he started training. Now he did have the muscles to show off, the two were almost the same size. A crackle of promising thunder sounded over the mountains. Not much time to wrap this up.

D'artello held his sword at his side as a few cool drops of rain fell on his face and bare shoulders. His father had his arms bowed in front of him, with open fists at the ready to grab and contort. Gerrik did not use swords; he had killed too many men in his prime, and many nightmares ago, he had vowed "never again" to grasp another hilt. When he held a sword, all he knew was to kill. He cared nothing for anything or anyone else. Nowadays he used metal bracers on each arm that blocked blades for him. He wore the same thing as D'artello did, although his pants were red instead of blue.

D'artello took this moment to visually embrace his peers. Most were friends with whom he did not interact on a daily basis. They were all uniformly clad in armor, with hawk, bear, and tiger emblems representing their classes. They all had dense blue armor that covered their shoulders and chest. Their gauntlets were metal from the wrist to the elbow, and loose leather covered the wearer's hand, allowing easy manipulation of their respective weapons. Their greaves were relatively light, with thin metal and cloth on the inside for comfort while walking long distances. In this formation, they served as much purpose as gargoyles; they had eyes, but would be unable to fully witness the sparring round between the two combatants.

It was among the crowd that he picked out his three closest friends. Henry, Joseph, and Michael were all epitomic representations of their respective classes. Joseph bore the bear, which represented strength. He proficiently wielded a mighty battle-axe. Bears were few and far between because not many could stand up to the demand of such a weighty weapon.

Michael was labeled as a tiger, a medium sized man, much like D'artello. He had a black head of hair and a goatee. He spoke the least, but meant the most, a hard thinker. This pertained well to his title as a tiger, as the class represented cunning and they were respected as tacticians. Michael was studious to the art of war. Tigers wielded spears, a secret art that was not an easy learn.

Henry was a smaller man with a small dog complex; his attitude easily outweighed his strength. He had slicked back, brown hair and a crooked nose that was once broken in a sparring match with Joseph. How like Henry to pick a fight with someone so much bigger. He was titled a hawk, the most common class. Most often on a battlefield, the hawks were first to charge. Their one-handed blades could carve flesh almost as easily as they sliced the air. The techniques were swift, but if done correctly, the most lethal means of combat.

D'artello shifted his gaze back to his father, who had left his fighting stance in exchange for a less formal stance, dropping his weight to both legs, crossing his arms, and impatiently perusing his son's alertness. "He tests you," called the whispers in his ear that he'd become well acquainted with over the last month. It took him by surprise when his three friends came at him with their respective weapons in full swing.

Henry came in with confidence, but D'artello blocked faster than he could make his attack, as if he could read Henry's mind. Shock spread over his friend's face, but not long enough for D'artello to counterattack. When he made his move, Henry was on it just in time. Joseph and Michael had no synergy whatsoever. They both went for D'artello's legs, allowing him to dive away and create some thinking distance between him and his three opponents. Joseph's weighty axe snapped the head off of Michael's spear much the way a twig snaps underfoot.

D'artello sprang from his roll and landed a powerful back fist to the side of Henry's face, which sent the small man flailing to the ground.

The loss of the pointed tip was little more than an inconvenience to Michael, for he was still a tactful bo-staff wielder. He twirled it skillfully, exchanging it from one hand to the other with sightless speed to show his affinity. A distraction.

Henry thrust back to his light-footed stance and with Michael charged D'artello, who retreated with well-practiced backflips to open some distance.

His flipping motion halted suddenly as he reached the downward incline of the hill. He stopped dead to a handstand for a brief moment before springing forward through the onslaught of the blunt stick, where his feet could tear through Michael's stance, sending him crashing to the ground. D'artello landed on top of him, and even with armor, that must have hurt. Michael's breathlessness delayed a writhe in pain from underfoot, giving D'artello ample time to exchange a few clashes with Henry.

He gave a hard swing, which was followed by an ear-shattering clash that ejected Henry's sword from his hand. The blade stuck into the ground a few feet away from where all four men tussled. Henry took his eyes off D'artello to find his sword. This mistake gave D'artello the time he needed to send a roundhouse kick to Henry's upper chest, slamming him again to his backside.

Joseph's axe head swooped in at him again. Timing it, D'artello was able to leap up, and in just two steps, travel from the axe head to the back of Joseph's neck and land behind him. This force sent the large man stumbling to the ground on top of Michael, pinning him. Turning around after he had landed safely, he threw his sword at the fallen axe that was but three inches from Joseph's face. It sliced into the ground, cutting off the head of the axe. The air from the flying blade tickled the fine hair on Joseph's nose; he was too shocked to make another move.

Henry had retrieved his blade and had come at D'artello one last time, swinging horizontally and then vertically, grunting loudly with each effort. D'artello bobbed and then weaved low and to the side while kicking out both of Henry's legs. He spun all the way around, swinging his foot high toward the side of Henry's face.

Henry found himself lying face up once again, not fully aware of what had just happened, his sword flipping helplessly away. D'artello's foot rested on the man's throat, pressing lightly as not to hurt him anymore.

Relieving the pressure after a short moment, D'artello held out a hand to pull Henry to his feet and then gave him a pat on the back once he could stand up straight.

The other men around them were in an uproar, hollering at the pleasing spectacle. Joseph, Michael, and Henry all vacated the ring. Apparently they had been briefed ahead of time for this test.

A booming voice cut the cheering from the spectators. "Now your final test, my son. I want you to come at me as if your life depended on it," Gerrik said, taking his stance, knees bent with arms out in front of him. Without hesitation, D'artello rushed him, throwing and receiving punches and kicks that both fighters twisted into in order to partially absorb the strikes. Turning allowed the blows to strike more favorable parts of their bodies.

The slapping noise of the men hitting each other was enough to make any less fascinated observer flinch. They were evenly matched for a while, until D'artello noticed a smirk spread across his father's face. A second of distraction was all Gerrik needed to take D'artello's legs from underneath him with a well-placed sweep.

D'artello landed hard on his back. He was not there long, for his father picked him up by the scruff of his collar and hurled him over his shoulder, sending him a good ten feet through the air into a forward roll, from which he unwound upright.

Father and son leapt at each other to meet in the air. The speed of the fall was nothing in comparison to how fast the pair's fists were flying. This created an illusion of gentle downward floating as they exchanged blows. At what seemed like long last to the people watching, they were both on the ground again.

The other guards gawked in awe as if beholding Harmony herself; it was like art—beautiful, wonderful art. The two men's moves were so intricately well timed. It would be easy to forget that this was actually a fight rather than a staged show of acrobatics.

D'artello saw a chance; his father threw a straight punch toward his face. He ducked under, then grabbed his father's wrist and the inside of his father's elbow, creating a devious tension that allowed him to move the large arm to a contorted position behind his back. They didn't maintain this pose because Gerrik dropped backward with an elbow to D'artello's midsection and then reached around his neck to grab his stunned son by his rear collar. With a twist of his waist, he would have sent his son flying over his shoulder, but D'artello was too fast.

Shifting his weight, using his arms around his father's neck as a pivotal point, he jumped and swiveled around his opponent. When he landed, his legs wrapped around Gerrik's. A sideways push was all he needed to send his father sprawling across the ground. Gerrik, instead, dove into a fast forward roll, from which he sprang to his feet. They now stood a good few yards apart from each other.

His father readjusted himself to be in the same stance that he started in. D'artello climbed to his feet and took a similar stance. They stared each other down for a few moments. The other men could only watch. The wind and heartbeat of the coming storm were the only sounds to flood their ears.

It could have been ten minutes, or it could have been an hour. No one really noticed the time passing. The fighters did not budge an inch from their stances. Rain continued to trickle down, moistening their clothes and hair. Violent thunder and a rampart of lightning threatened to defeat their will.

Abruptly, Gerrik stood upright. "You have proven your talent and now your focus. Well done, D'artello," he said in a soft voice. His gaze never left his son. "Listen up!" he called out to the squad. "Tonight we drink and we feast, for tomorrow we will train one last time together and then march onward to the capital." The men gave a gleeful cheer. They continued to cheer all the way to the pub.

This past month had taken D'artello from boy to man, but he wondered if a man would be enough if Harmony was truly speaking to him.

Chapter 4

D'artello focused on the beating rain against the wooden roof of the pub, unwilling to partake of the festive affairs of the night with his fellow guardsmen. For a moment, he thought about the rain and how big the drops must be to make such a ruckus, but then he drifted off into a waking dream. A mental high took him over as his mind came alive like the storm outside.

Glancing around the bar, he looked at each of his friends and began to wonder about the people he wasn't on a personal basis with. What would life be like without them? What would he miss out on if he or they died at such a young age? His senses deafened and he was lost in some old memories from his times spent with each of his close friends.

Overhanging oil lamps gave off an orange glow in the plank-walled building, comfortably lighting the tavern. The tables were plentifully scattered across the floor, and the waitresses were running about and batting their eyes at the young men. A gruff-looking bartender attentively served drinks to many raving guards at the polished oaken bar. D'artello watched as one of the men escorted a pretty blonde waitress out the door.

The man was Billy. He was just a couple of years older and loved nothing more than to chase women. Although chasing was hardly the term to be used because he had a natural charm that made many girls in town look his way, another trait of the men on the guard team. Billy had always said, "I'm a lover not a fighter." Surely such a man would die on the battlefield.

Taking another look around the room, D'artello could almost point out who would live and who would die. For that moment, he fancied himself a grim reaper, watching the animated souls just before the bells tolled for them.

This was a local, shabby guard team for the most part, not a band of war heroes. His father's training was good, but the mentality of these kids would not help them survive. His mind quieted, leaving him thinking only how his father should have spent more time training the whole guard, not just him.

He glanced over at Gerrik and saw him throw a playful punch at Henry. He laughed while spilling sips from his wine. D'artello wondered about losing the person he valued the most. His mother had left this world long prior to this day, during his birth no less, so he had never known another parent. His father had shown him all that he knew, including when to be bold, tough, and kindhearted, and he was willing to give all the knowledge any man could possibly bestow upon a son. Gerrik always knew best, somehow even when he was wrong.

The dream that never slept and the voice stabbing his brain over the last month was enough for his legs to carry him from the bar out into the rain, letting a sky of tears fall down into his hair and clothes. Traversing the swollen, muddy streets, he needed to find an escape. Those days, Tanya was it. She and sparring were the two things that could force the voices out of his head.

The memories held dear propelled him forward toward the large orphan flat where Tanya lived. He needed to see her one last time.

Killing a man or dying was still a mystery. Both he feared at this very moment. Taking a life might be to die inside. It scarred Gerrik for life, making him into an engine of death and forcing him to give up the sword. D'artello wondered if he would go down the same road. Only time could tell if he'd rather end up dying.

Going to see Tanya these days was almost a fix, a time when he could leave his stress behind. Together they could laugh like nothing in the world was wrong.

The stairs of the complex lay just a few feet ahead. He could see the stone pillars standing like guards in front of the door. Depicted on the pillars was the symbol of separation, a heart split in two by a dagger. The official symbol of Harmony's sacrifice, as he'd recently found.

Gazing up at the downpour, he let the rain cleanse his eyes of sorrow and fear. Tanya deserved a happy good-bye, not one filled with crying as he'd selfishly planned on the way over. Tears were not for him.

The solid double doors slid open as he stepped into the atrium, lit comfortably by the ever-common oil lamp. The two floors overhead silenced the rain. He was in the center of the first floor, so respectively, there were two decorative archways he could enter to reach the stairs at the end of either hall. He took the left. Windows being licked by the storm outside were on one side, doors on the other. Tanya lived on the second floor, and her room number was CCIII (203). The town was not large enough to have that many orphaned children; the CC (200) simply meant she was on the middle floor.

Normally there was a guard chaperoning the hallways at night, but tonight they were all at the tavern. D'artello paid no attention to the room numbers on each passing door. Now his head hung as low as his heart. The blood-red hue of the carpet began to make him nauseous, making him think again of all of the people on his guard dying or becoming injured beyond recovery. He envisioned all-consuming fire, a hell on earth, ripping the green fields of his home apart. He saw his father dying in his arms, a horrible thought that made him shudder.

Standing there at the funeral, who would comfort him then? With his father being put into the ground, Gerrik would not be there to say, "It's okay, D'artello."

What bothered him the most about war was the fact two men could start a fight and then make others settle it for them, instead of settling it themselves. He thought too about the other king, Bensel, the one who had been like an uncle to him. His father was a brother to that man. In fact, friendships with that family had existed for many generations.

Even though he had never heard his father's war stories from the man himself, D'artello had heard plenty from people he'd been introduced to. In most of those stories, Bensel was present, accompanying Gerrik. These two men were kindred, yet Gerrik was willing to follow the orders of a man he barely knew, King Garo.

King Bensel was one of the most influential people in D'artello's life. His country embraced innovation because they had such a small population in comparison to the surrounding nations. Still, under his formation, Genzak was a force to be reckoned with. They were truly unpredictable, as their soldiers wielded weapons and arts that no one could expect.

Is war really more important than friendship? he thought. *Is it more important than feelings, than morals, and coexisting with the ones you love?* Right now he lacked faith in his father's judgment. Still Gerrik was right; he was training D'artello to grow colder because the battlefield was no place for his feelings.

The carpet ended, and a granite floor began. With his wet boots scraping against the smooth surface, he ascended a spiral staircase to the second floor. D'artello left his mental daze back on the first floor, and the room numbers became suddenly visible. He really did not want to show Tanya how sad he was. The numbers passed slowly … CC … CCI … CCII … then finally CCIII. He turned to face the door and then took a minute to peel the wet hair from his face and put on a smile. He knocked on the door lightly, twice, leaving exactly two seconds between each knock.

Tanya recognized that knock. She folded the large blanket off of herself, rose from her bed in the dark room, walked over to the gas switch, and then slid it upward to release more gas. Wall-mounted candles lit up softly, flickering to life. Most of the town's lamps were oil, but this building used a gas and pilot system. All of the lights had a pilot flame that was blustered by the release of gas when a switch was flipped to light a candle; it was a cheaper alternative to oil once the installation work was done. She then lowered the switch back to its off position, just before shuffling across the carpet in bare feet to the door.

The door opened with a slight creak. Tanya had her hair tied back, as she did every night, and was dressed in a long white gown. D'artello could see the happy excitement in her tired eyes for a moment before she jumped into his arms. "I didn't think I was gonna see you again," she said, holding on to the back of his neck. His hands found their way around her waist. He held her for a few seconds to regain himself, before she could catch on to the gloominess.

"C'mon now," he began, "I wouldn't leave my little sister like that," he said, pecking her on the forehead.

She pushed off of him and landed on the floor, "You're all wet! I have something for you," she said, going back into her room. "Don't just stand there! Come in!" she insisted, walking back and giving his wrist a tug.

He followed her in and closed the door ever so lightly. Her room had the same layout as his, right down to the lamps on the walls. Fort Carrie was fascinated with repetitive group living quarters. The fundamental difference was the lack of clothes all over the floor. Tanya knew how to keep her room tidy. The dresser was spotless, as was the mirror that she surely used every day when getting dressed. Even though she had already been in it, the bed was still neat, the large blanket barely folded over on one corner to let her in and out at will.

"Sit here," she said, pointing at the end of the bed. "Close your eyes too," she ordered. He did as he was told, feeling suddenly bad about his wetness as he dropped down onto the bed, and awaited the next command. He could hear her rustling about under the bed.

"Don't peek," she commanded. He felt her weight plunge onto the mattress beside him. A small arm brushed gently against his hair. He felt a delicate tension on the sides of his neck that rubbed up and down as Tanya wove her hands in a curious motion, a knot he guessed. Then her voice pulled him from the darkness of his eyelids. "Open your eyes now," she instructed.

He looked down at his chest to see a pendant that was a deep purple amethyst, with five small multicolored gems lining it, forming a star—an emerald, a ruby, a sapphire, an onyx, and a diamond, all cut into triangles. It was attached to a golden chain that hung loosely around his neck. "It's a promise charm," she explained. The pendant fit perfectly in the palm of his hand as he turned his wrist side to side, taking it in, letting the light bounce off it.

The gems were rare. One could only acquire such jewels by going to distant lands. They flowed in a circle, each one from a different continent, and no matter how far away the respective continent was, the circle would always make it back home with the jewel native to this continent: the the bright green crystal in the center.. This was a promise charm, usually more appropriate for couples.

"It was my mom's. She gave it to me when I was real little." From behind, she placed her chin on his shoulder, allowing her to peek at the charm in his hands. "I know that spending time with me gets your mind off of fighting and stuff, so I wanted to give you this so you can think about me from time to time. But you have to promise me that you will bring it back one day," she said. "Those are the rules."

He was taken aback at how wise beyond her years she was just then. Clenching it tightly, he was about ready to take it off, to give it right back, but he paused for a moment and uttered the words, "I promise."

The two sat up for a while chatting idly about memories and how much they would miss each other. With a promise to return home safely, D'artello got ready to depart back to his room for the night. Tanya's face began to moisten with her gentle tears, and then crying took her over suddenly. "You can't go to war," she sobbed, throwing herself onto him. "You would never kill anyone! How could you be a real soldier?" she said, her voice muffled by his shirt.

D'artello let her have a moment. "Getting a little old for this, aren't you?" he asked softly. She looked up at him, giving a slight sniffle, clearly dissatisfied with that last question. "Look, Tanya." He bit his lip, captured in her weeping eyes. "Sometimes we *have* to do things."

"Why?"

"Just ... because. I have to go to war. I need to know that if I don't come back, you'll be okay."

She shook her head and her manner grew nearly hysterical. "You can't die. I don't know what I'd do without you, D'artello. You and Gramps are the only family I have left." Wrapping her arms around him as far as they could reach, she begged, "Please don't go. Just stay here with me forever." He snuck his forearms under her lower back and stood up, cradling her in his arms. Sticking his forehead to hers, they would have to look at each other.

"Hey, look at me," was his way of saying, "Open your eyes". "Everything's gonna be all right." A wild grin spread across his face. "Just smile, see?" he said, showing his teeth. She managed to sputter a giggle, trying her hardest to let the smile curve her lips. D'artello repeated the face, allowing a laugh to choke through, and the smile became candid. He put her down on the bed and tucked her in. Sitting at her side until her uneasy soul could rest for the night was the least he could do.

"Do I look pretty today, D'artello?"

"Oh yes, very, fair maiden," he responded.

"Then what will you do with me? Such a pretty girl?"

He kissed her on the forehead before uttering his response. "Why, come back to her of course."

She smiled warmly, sniffling one last time, and closed her weary eyes. Leaving after she had fallen asleep was the hardest thing he'd ever done.

* * *

He walked the night streets back to his room. Surely the festivities at the pub were over now. This kind of weather was desirable for conscious thought. When it rained, it was the only sound; there was no hustle and bustle of the streets or shouting children. Just firm, consistent, pounding raindrops like a multipendulum metronome.

On a whim, he took the long way home. He walked along the west wall of the town, the only wall that had not become a flat. It was tall, but not as tall as the others. One could consider it a weakness in the structure, but there should be no threat coming from the west as long as King Bensel reigned over the Genzak nation. D'artello continued to ponder why his dear uncle figure would declare war on Vaukry, the ally whom he'd helped gain independence. What would it be like to meet that man on the battlefield?

An out-of-place scraping entered his ears. Too distracted at first, he pushed it aside, letting it pass by. Then he heard a shout from the other side of the wall. *It's probably one of the guys, drunk,* he concluded. A clash from overhead made his heart jump. It sounded almost like a sword—*a fight!* He backed up all the way to a building across the street to get a better view of the top of the wall. There was something, very difficult to make out because it was thin. It was curved and had a firm hold from the other side. D'artello's jaw dropped when he saw a hand come up to retrieve it.

A huddled figure pulled itself up. A man, no a soldier, adjusted the hook-like device and motioned to his apparent comrades below. D'artello scrambled to the wall, hoping he was not seen.

They carried sheathed blades at their waist and began to toss spear-like instruments up into one another's hands. His eyes focused a bit more as he desperately tried not to make himself noticeable. The first man kicked his feet off the side. He was about to descend. D'artello's heart raced. *Could they be Genzaks?* Time to find out. He pressed himself against the wall, waiting for the man to drop beside him. He reached down for his familiar hilt. Where was it? Did he leave it at the pub?

Things may have turned out differently had he heard the man say, "Remember our orders. We are not to attack, only to defend ourselves."

Clack! Heavy metal grieves hit the ground right next to him. Another foot to the left, and the soldier would've landed on top of him. He noticed D'artello almost immediately. The soldier barely had time to let out a startled gasp before being grabbed by the shoulder and forehead and slammed against the wall. The helmet cracked against the hard stone, making the man dizzy, causing him to stagger about for a moment.

D'artello looked down at the small sheath hanging around the soldier's waist. Seizing the steel hilt from his opponent was the last conscious decision he made. He pulled the short sword from the scabbard, drew back quickly, and plunged the sword into its master's heart. It had been done; he killed a man. Despite all of the practice swings, there was nothing quite like a piece of living meat on the other end of the sword.

Ripping the sword from the man's chest, he backed away from the wall. The man clenched his bloody wound, trying to catch the life pouring out of him. He fell first to his knees, then down, dead. Another three jumped down from the wall with their long spears in hand. It was amazing he could see them at all; visibility was terrible despite the torches lining the streets, trying to fend off the rain. The soldiers dipped in and out of total blindness as they drew in. He backed away slowly as the men prowled around in attempts to surround him. "Halt in the name of King Bensel," one of them said. So it *was* this so-called uncle. Then it was settled. He would fight against this man in the name of his country.

D'artello flew quickly at the first soldier. The man took a skillful swing toward his face. Using the edge of the spearhead was a very skillful tactic; this individual obviously knew what he was doing. He could keep D'artello at bay forever with that kind of range.

D'artello raised the sword to block, which worked out better than he'd anticipated. The wood gave into the blade easily. The spearhead fell to the ground behind him. The wooden pole missed his eyes by mere inches as the guard swung around with the other end. He didn't flinch or falter. He quickly closed the gap between him and the enemy to establish an upper hand on the long weapons.

One soldier had surprisingly dropped his spear and retrieved his sidearm from his waist-mounted sheath. *Why would he immediately draw his short sword?* D'artello thought.

"This is your last warning!" the man called out. Seeing that his opponent's aggression ceased none, the soldier took a swing.

D'artello ducked under the sword that hissed quickly toward shoulder level, the maneuver perplexing him. *That attack would've disarmed me,* he thought. He thrust his leg at the soldier's kneecap. It buckled. The man let out a cry and then fell to the ground, predictably dropping his sword that was immediately scooped up by D'artello in a fluent motion. While rising, he sliced through the underarm of the staff-wielding soldier, cutting the tendons and causing the arm to go limp. The stab had never come faster, so practiced, pinpointed, and powerful; the second short sword was driven through the chest of the man as well. The other, whom he had kicked in the knee, tried to crawl away, dragging his bum leg, crying out for help. His hands were acting without command, and it was mortifying to him. Yet there was some sort of addictive rush, knowing that to flesh, steel was the executioner.

As he pulled the sword from the man's chest, he plunged the other into the soldier on the ground, aiming for no spot in particular. Wherever it was, he left it there to allow himself enough time to jump to the side to avoid the third man's spear. D'artello landed gently in a crouching position near the handle of a fallen spear that the dead soldier had fumbled.

He lifted the spear up as he twirled and rose to his feet. The motion caused the spearhead to float gently up, savagely slicing the enemy at eye level with its bladed edges. The soldier dropped his spear. His hands flew to his face, covering the spurting gauges. He began to cry out, running toward the wall. D'artello leapt at him like a hungry wolf, delivering a hard kick to the man's back that forced him to stumble face-first into the wall. He instantly went limp and fell to the ground, his body sputtering its last few moments of life. D'artello began to feel queasy, and his knees quaked at the sight of the bodies. Just then, a whisper pulled him from this squeamish pathology. "Run, warrior."

"Who are you, dammit!" he cried out into the night sky.

"Patience. Now run."

Looking back up at the wall, he saw many more men waiting to join the fray. Twenty or so of them jumped down to meet him. Then another twenty took their place on top of the wall. D'artello caught a glimpse of the third wave as he turned tail from the high tide of soldiers. *There are so many of them,* he thought as his feet pounded the streets and alleyways.

Behind him, he heard an awakening roar of over sixty soldiers. The patriotism in their voices erupted and was enough to make his soul quake. Fear for his life, fear for the people of the town, and fear of killing more men swept over him, making his veins run cold. He glanced down at the blood-soaked sword he carried in his right hand. The streets had exploded into chaos. Some citizens had begun to stir, running about, trying to escape their attackers. The soldiers ignored them, with the exception of a few ornery men wielding clubs, chairs, and other objects to fight off the invaders.

Where are they all coming from? Why are they drawing these people out? he wondered. He ran toward the guard flat across town, but came upon a surrounded Joseph in a four-way intersection of two alleyways.

The Genzak dogs circled his friend, closing in. Joseph swung his mighty axe to back them off. The first three men took a step back to avoid danger, for the axe was a good foot longer than even their spears. The fourth jumped unarmed unto Joseph's back. Bad idea; D'artello had tried that one before. Joseph tore the dwarfed assailant over his shoulder, throwing him to the ground. Noticing that the other three men had begun to close in again, he regripped and swung his axe horizontally once more, in the opposite direction now, trying to back them off again. One of them didn't make the two steps back in time. The axe caught him like a higoat's back kick, sweeping him off his feet, sending him flying. With a loud clack, the soldier landed a few yards away, dead.

Now only two men stood to face him. Joseph held his axe ready for either one of the men to make a move. They circled one another cautiously, knowing one blow could end it all.

D'artello ran to his assist. He'd noticed a man running in from behind to stab Joseph. D'artello thrust his heel into the running soldier's face. The stricken soldier got up almost immediately, only to take another blinding kick to the face.

"I owe you one," Joseph said as they took each other's back as they had done in practice many times before.

"If we get out of this, I'll collect," D'artello responded.

They were trapped in the alley, and soldiers poured in from two of the four possible directions. Parts of the mob that had chased D'artello from the wall were coming in to get their revenge now. The first armor-clad man sprinted toward him with his sword held out at his waist. His piercing gaze showed D'artello that he was ready to taste blood, and as he leapt into the air, raising his sword above his head, all D'artello could think of was that blade cutting into his neck, killing him as he had killed the premier Genzaks climbing the wall.

By the time he broke hesitation, there was no dodging the advance, but he was able to parry the lethal part of the attack. The soldier kept going, however, stumbling into him shoulder first. The heavy armor was enough to bump D'artello backward into Joseph. As quickly as it had happened, two enormous hands caught him and threw him back to his feet. "Try to stay standing!" Joseph called from behind.

The soldier climbed to his feet for only a second. With an adrenaline-fueled tunnel vision now, D'artello only saw a fist blindside the man. A familiar companion then threw the soldier to the side like a ragdoll. Shocked, but relieved to see him, the great Gerrik, war hero of the kingdom, had come to their rescue. He made quick work of the other two Genzaks coming toward him as Joseph finished off a couple more.

Not long after, the remaining, blue-clad members of the guard poured in from the third direction. Using Gerrik as an opening, they were able to overwhelm the enemy in this alley quite easily. D'artello felt lucky that his father had been so close. He knelt and breathed hallowed breaths, the taste of death in his mouth enough to make him gag. He felt a hard pat on his back as he swallowed hard.

His father lifted him up and put his face so close he could feel the warm breath of his words. "Are you all right?" At first his words seemed slowly spoken and underwater. "Are you okay? D'artello. Hey!" Gerrik moved him gruffly, checking him for any stab wounds.

D'artello nodded his head in between breaths. "I'm okay, I'm all right," he said.

He wasn't sure what strings in his mind took over at that point. Something compelled him to charge into the massacre, gallantly letting a war cry escape his lungs.

"Now," his father spoke, when all was more orderly. "How many of us are left?"

"Seventeen, Captain," Michael reported, getting a quick head count.

"We're not done yet, men," Gerrik barked, as the remaining guardsmen took their spots in line at attention. "We are going to split up and find the rest of them. Make sure there are no stragglers running around." D'artello watched his father dish out orders in such a bold fashion. Despite all of their private training, he felt there was so much more for Gerrik to teach him.

The group disbanded after being given their orders. With Michael and Henry at his side, D'artello's orders were to blaze a path to the furthest gate, the south. The three quickly moved through the town, helping injured people as best they could. The ground was littered with bodies of fallen citizens, soldiers, and guardsmen alike. No matter the side, a corpse looked the same to D'artello.

The town glowed with an orange haze, as someone had started a fire that had spread enough to light up the night streets. It created an ominous mist as the rain from above failed to douse it. Despite the shabby shape of the town, there were no signs of any more hostile soldiers. Somehow that did not sit well in D'artello's mind. He knew that at least sixty men came pouring over just that one wall.

It was then, as he passed a dark alley that escaped the illumination of the fires, he spotted a white-cloaked figure. By the time he stopped and backtracked to get a second look, the entity was gone. There was something oddly familiar about what he'd just seen. *That cloak!* he thought, remembering his dream. *That beast in the cavern is here?* In doubt of his own eyes, he approached the alley cautiously, leaving his friends behind.

"D'artello, what is it?" Henry asked.

"C'mon," he said, moving into the shadows. The two men followed obediently with weapons in hand.

"What did you see?" Michael asked as D'artello began to hurry.

D'artello had been swallowed up by shadows. Only his voice guided them now. "Shh," he responded, the whispers echoing up the brick walls of the surrounding buildings "Get against the wall," he ordered. His advance stopped when he could wrap his fingers around the edge of the alley. It had taken him far away from the reaches of the light, and now he was running strictly on his secondary senses. Even though he knew every inch of this town, there was no familiarity in the pitch black.

He could hear noxious grunting and muffled screams as he poked his head around the corner. The horrific sight sent chills down his spine. A group of Genzak soldiers and town guards stood over one helpless guard, Billy. One of the assailants was surely the woman he'd left the bar with. He screamed and shouted for help as they began to beat him with their fists. Hideously marking up his face beyond recognition, they continued to rain down on him, like the droplets coming from the sky, until he stopped moving, dead if he had any luck at all.

One of them whipped their head around to look at D'artello, as if smelling his presence. Responding quickly, he folded himself back around the corner against the wall. *What by Harmony's graces is going on here? Monsters!* he thought. Holding his breath, hoping they would not find him, he clutched the charm around his neck.

"Michael, Henry, you have to see this," he finally whispered. In that moment, he realized that his friends were gone. He glanced around the alley. *Did they not follow me?* he thought. It was best to get help, not to engage these enemies by himself. D'artello began to take steps back to the light, in the direction he came from. He glanced behind him every few seconds to make sure no one was there.

The shrill cries of women and children echoed through the town. Some commotion was going on behind him. It was then that five creatures rounded the corner to block his path. These were not soldiers. Some of them were people he knew. Their faces were pale, ghostly, and angry. They screamed, snarled, and grunted like wild animals, and most horribly of all, blood dripped from their hands, and D'artello was inclined to believe it wasn't theirs. Their posture was that of an insane raven, and they growled and shouted like apes. Almost resembling the dead, they were like the shadows of primordial evil locked away in man's heart.

The other group had found him as well, cutting off his only exit. The sound of the creatures made D'artello shake with fear. He fell to his knees and held his head, trying to block the horrible suffering sounds. His sword fell to the ground with a clanging sound that seemed so quiet among their growls.

The first one leapt at him, latching on with both hands around his neck as the hallowed eyes stared into his. They were black and cold, despite the appearance of an elderly woman. The grip was forceful. He thrust his arms upward, ejecting the grip. Before he could strike back, three more of them grabbed him, hissing and trying to pull him off his feet. Down was the last place he wanted to go; Billy got kicked to death that way. He reached desperately for his sword as they yanked him toward a wall, socking him and stomping him. He was pounded in the stomach, the arms, the neck, anywhere they could get an effective fist in.

Just when they seemed to have him pinned, he roared loudly and broke free one of his shoulders. His hand met the hilt of his trusty weapon, and he thrust it into the first heart he could reach. The little boy stumbled back for a moment, causing D'artello to lose his flesh-buried weapon.

He continued to block what blows he could, but there were far too many. The boy who had fallen, who should have been killed, instantly jumped to his feet. He pulled the side arm from his own chest and came at D'artello with it, who was too frightened to notice the boy was not bleeding. The assailant's concentration was broken when he heard Joseph bellow out.

"D'artello!"

"Joseph! Run!" he yelled back, lest he would watch his friend suffer the same fate. The words barely escaped his lungs before another fist struck him in the mouth, causing blood to spill from his bottom lip.

His efforts were too late. Some of the tainted creatures rushed Joseph and tackled him to the ground as well. There were easily enough of them to take on the bigger man too. The helpless D'artello could do nothing except watch and cry out for his Peacemaker's mercy.

Chapter 5

Just when things were looking bleakest, D'artello closed his eyes, and with his dying breath shouted, "Harmony!"

Expecting more fists to come his way, he cringed. The wall turned to mist as the next fist was just inches away. It sucked him in and onto a curiously moist surface. He opened his eyes suddenly to stare up at the endlessness of the golden shaft. He lay on top of calm water, just as he had stood upon it in his dream. Feeling the pain of his bloodied and broken body his muscles sputtered as he tried to detect movement in any of his appendages.

"Harmony?" he called out.

A long pause set in. It was then that D'artello began to pick up a voice. In his mind, he could hear that familiar daunting whisper. "Yes, my warrior, it is I who have brought you to this haven."

"So it was you, that whole time, it really was …"

"Save your energy, my dear D'artello."

He gave a deep, long sigh, taking in the respite from the savage beating. "You have fallen, my warrior," she pointed out, as if she need tell him. She was laying over him, her head pillowed on his chest, one arm and leg wrapped around him. Her sudden appearance startled him, if only his body was capable of jumping. "Beaten so terribly, battered, my hero. What has conveyed this fate to you?" she said, glancing up at him, as if she didn't know.

Why did she show this closeness to him? Why would a Peacemaker like her embrace a mortal like this? "Because my warrior, I will live for eternity, alone, without love. The prophecy has spoken of a hero who loves a peacemaker, who will save the universe. Hold me now, and gain back your strength," she ordered.

D'artello paused, if not for confusion then for the pain ravaging his nerves. His mind raced with the dream he had more than a month ago. First she sealed his destiny telling him that he would become the savior of the universe, and now she was telling him he was in love with her. An eternity of secrets unknown to him, and he was expected to hold her as only a lover would? His skepticism was met with an unseen force, causing his hands to fly involuntarily around her, caressing her magnificent body as she gave a sigh. It was as if some ghost had appeared to pluck his wrists from the ground and fold him around her. She ran her finger all the way from his chest up to the back of his ear, pressing her lips gently across the fine hairs of his neck.

Just as she had said, his wounds began to heal. He brought his hands to his face to feel they were indeed gone, sponging his lip with the tips of his fingers and then examining them for blood. Harmony then disappeared again.

Regaining strength almost instantly, he stood up on the water and brushed himself off. A voice tickled the inside of his ear as a finger drew sensual circles on his chest. "You have grown stronger since we last met, D'artello," she said, suddenly appearing from behind with her arms hanging over his shoulders. He stepped forward quickly to escape, and then turned to face her. "Worry not, my dear D'artello. You will learn to love me eventually. You have yet to comprehend the opportunity upon you."

"Please, Harmony," he said, kneeling on his right knee and bowing his head. "Please, I have called upon you in hopes you would save us from those monsters."

"And save you I will, my warrior, but I cannot vanquish those creatures," she replied. "I must grant *you* the power to be rid of them."

So it was true, all of it, not a dream. Peacemaker Harmony stood before him, asking him to save the universe once again.

One quick thought of the peril Tanya and Sali must be in was the only convincing argument he needed. What was he supposed to do? "Take your time warrior. Decide carefully," Harmony said, as if actually offering him the choice.

He took a deep breath and accepted his fate, whatever it may mean.

"Harmony, I desire nothing more," he responded.

"Do not be hasty. You must learn first, and learn well, my warrior. First, I want you to rise," she commanded.

He did as he was told and returned to his feet. "You have recollection of our last meeting, I am sure."

"Yes," he answered.

"Do you recall the cloaked figure you faced down in these very caverns?"

"Yes."

"These creatures are not of this world, nor of any other."

"Any other?" D'artello asked.

"Yes, they come from the darkest depths of all that is reality. They are a formidable power that you will come to know as a Phantom. They are man's darkest secret, madness. A cancer that lies dormant in the heart of every human. Once madness takes physical form and man loses order, the world around you will become madness. It will be buried in a eulogy of tears. Neither madness nor Phantom is susceptible to death; the only cure for madness is reason."

"These are people I know. They're crazy, not those ... Phantoms," he protested.

"But indeed they are, my dear D'artello. Phantoms wield a peculiar contagion in their swords. Those monsters, of which you speak, are mortals that are tainted with that contagion. They carry darkness in their soul; that is why they have taken on their ravenous methods. Not long from now, they too will don white cloaks and blades, losing their minds to join the ranks of the Phantoms. Also ... do not be deceived. No hallowed ground exists within a pure soul either. Petrification awaits them in mere hours. Both effects are irreversible."

"How do I stop them?" D'artello's expression grew more hopeless by the second.

"Before we part, I will grant you three things of importance. Power, resistance, and truth."

A sword rose from the water below, like in his dream. It came up slowly, seeming to materialize gradually out of thin air. Although half of it was above water, the other half could not be seen below the surface. It bore a shimmering red hilt, with a blade that looked like it was made of white gold. Two fiery ribbons dances from the chain at the base of the blade. Two oblong holes were built into the composition of the one-bladed sword, and at full length it would be waist high to him. Glowing with radiant hearth, it rid the room of all shadows.

"Behold, humanity's reason, the legendary Molten Steel," she said. "Within it lies the power to banish the Phantoms. One cut will slay them as if they were a mortal man. On those tainted, it will reverse the effects of their curse before either transformation is complete. It will glow if it feels the presence of madness nearby. Grasp it, worthy warrior, and pull it to your side; you are its wielder. With it you must slay every Phantom."

D'artello slowly wrapped his hands around the crimson hilt. Instantly, he felt a wave of warm blood course all the way from his fingertips up to his neck, then pooling into the soft spot beneath his skull. The weapon chose him, the weapon needed him, and the weapon lusted for him. The blade was much lighter than he had anticipated. It felt hollow. Holding it made him forget about everything that now troubled him, for he felt the power to conquer anything that hindered his path or harmed his loved ones. Then he felt that the blade in his hands would not be enough. Every Phantom? "Harmony, how can one man kill that many Phantoms? If I miss one, they will return."

"Yes, my warrior, indeed your argument is of concern. Think of a chain hanging over a pit of magma, my dear D'artello. If you sever one link, what is below that link is lost, yes? Well this chain has three links. The bottom-most link, essentially the least important to the army of madness is a Phantom. Slaying one will do nothing other than simply that. Above the Phantoms are Sources. Sources are people who have died with too much darkness in their heart, your King Garo for example."

"My king? You mean King Garo, leader of the Vaukry nation?" he asked.

Harmony nodded. "One in the same, like a ghost, he is bound to this world. As are all Sources, they each carry heavy scars across their hearts. The sorrow for the loss of Garo's queen taints his soul. You must put him to rest before the dark one catches up with him. Sources are like generals, commanding the Phantom army. Now, if the Source's 'link' is severed, the Phantoms below it or under its command are lost. They will disperse. Envision a steel ring, off of which many chains are connected. Those many chains are each sources with their own armies. That center ring or link is the Dark One, another champion," she explained.

"What if I slay the Dark One? Can his sword make people into Phantoms as well?"

"The Dark One's sword works differently than yours. The Frozen Steel has an aura. When it visits a world, madness is introduced, and Sources will spring up whenever they can. The power to change others into Phantoms is daunting on one's life force. It needs a soul of pure madness to function correctly. Each time the Dark One makes a Phantom, he taxes his own sanity. So he is limited in that sense and must use it wisely. If you slay the Dark One, the Frozen Steel will be completely powerless. The Phantoms and Sources will cease to exist."

It was a lot to take in all at once, but everything made sense now; Bensel declared war on the Vaukry nation because he knew Garo attacked him. Harmony approached D'artello as he lowered the sword to his side. "My warrior, I have given you knowledge, power, and now I must protect you from your human weaknesses."

She pressed her lips lightly against his. He began to feel deep nirvana within his body. He felt her tenderness, embracing it as a young man with ambitions would. It lasted long enough to open his eyes to gaze upon her. Tears flooded his sight, making the golden chasm strobe through the ripples.

As she pulled away, a strange, thick, white mist seemed to leave him, entering into her mouth. His anger, joy, lust, jealousy, tranquility, and pleasure all seemed to fade away. He bawled uncontrollably for a moment and then felt no more sadness. The tears along with the last of his humanity trickled into the pool below. A blank and empty feeling was all that remained. He was now awake in a conscious state with no desire.

"Your soul must stay with me, to protect you from the tainted touch," she said.

D'artello fell to the ground, wiping his eyes. He then began to steadily rise with an erased expression. "With no soul, I will not be affected by their curse," he said, monotone.

"Yes, you understand, my dear D'artello," she nodded. "Now go and do not waste any time; your world is at stake."

Her voice faded from his ears as a bright light spread over the cavern. When it passed, he was still in the alley. Opening his eyes, he began to look upon the world the way an animal might. His thoughts focusing toward his goal of stopping the Phantoms, his instinct to fight and survive, his willingness to risk anything for his goal. The enemies that he set his gaze upon were mere obstacles, obstructing this mission. They must be stopped.

"Help!" he heard Joseph cry out. When D'artello's body came back to reality and he could feel the fists hitting him again, he reacted violently, rolling and jumping to his feet. He looked down in his right hand. The Molten Steel shone bright, seeming to await his order to charge into battle. The tainted looked at the blade the way a rat looks at a cat, hissing with fearful eyes.

In a blinding flash, three men lay at D'artello's feet, huddled like frozen animals. Their faces had gone back to their normal color and complexion. They breathed heavily, with their eyes shut tight, shivering in a fetal position. After turning to the mob that was mounting his friend, another bright flash left two more on the ground in a fashion similar to the first three, without wounding them.

Joseph continued to struggle as if they were still on top of him. It took him a moment to realize he'd been saved. D'artello turned to face the remaining five creatures. They kept their distance, looking accusingly at the sword. He rushed them as if he were going to run straight through them. Just before making contact, he sprang from the ground, running on the wall, up and over the muddle, circling behind them.

He latched onto the first man's wrist, jerking it counterclockwise, ripping the man toward him. In one fluent motion, the beast stumbled forward awkwardly, cut by a flash of D'artello's sword. He too fell to the ground. D'artello now had the undivided attention of the remaining afflicted souls.

Joseph held the image for a moment, processing the unbelievable feat with his mouth agape. Shaking it off, however, he joined the fight with the last of their attackers. He grabbed one and thrust him first against one of the tall stone walls, then kicked him into the other three, causing them to stumble while D'artello rolled to his back, kicking his feet up. In doing so, he caught one of his stumbling foes and flipped him over. The creature's arms flailed as it was launched through the air. Before landing on its back, D'artello left a cut in its leg, leaving it shivering on the ground.

Joseph grabbed another while D'artello cured the last two with his shining blade. The one that Joseph had grabbed however was able to muscle free, not before leaving a deep scratch in his arm though. The red-haired, stumbling wretch scrambled from the alley onto the streets to terrorize lesser victims. "I thought I had him," Joseph tried to say as D'artello simply bypassed him, giving chase. Upon exiting the alley, D'artello was attacked by some citizens acting much the same way. Cutting them down, he continued to seek out the red-haired one.

Joseph got up and followed D'artello as best he could, crushing the blood flow of his arm with his gargantuan hands. His muscles began to strain inexplicably. His left eye had begun to swell from a boot that had been there seconds ago, but the pain in his arm from the little scratch was most prominent. Releasing his grip, inspecting his palm, he found a crimson stripe across it. The bleeding had stopped peculiarly fast. Perhaps they hadn't cut him as badly as he thought.

By the time Joseph was able to catch up with D'artello, many a huddled person lay on the ground. Looking ahead into an alley, Joseph could see the bright, lantern-like light coming from D'artello's sword.

"Michael! Henry!" Joseph called out to his friends standing in the shadows.

Henry swung his sword vertically at D'artello. He in turn, made a slope using the Molten Steel, off of which his opponent's sword slid. Quickly, D'artello tripped him, causing his tainted friend to fall on his face behind him. Before Michael could use his weapon, D'artello's boot slapped his wrist, causing it to release.

Michael tried to dive onto him after, but D'artello stepped to the side, pressing himself flat against the wall, allowing tainted Michael to fall right on top of Henry, who was just beginning to get up. He grabbed Michael by the back of his armor, pulling him to his feet, and then slugged him against the wall. Drawing back once, he stabbed the Molten Steel right through his gut, proceeding to rip it the hard way from the body.

Henry snapped upright, looking at D'artello with accusing eyes. D'artello used his foot to slam him in the chest. Henry's body slapped the ground and rolled toward Joseph.

A grunting came from above. Joseph and D'artello looked up to see the red-haired, tainted man climbing the flat wall. He was a good twenty feet up.

D'artello had no intention of letting the creature get away. He whipped the Molten Steel through the air, pin wheeling it toward its target. The sword bounced off the wall, spinning awkwardly elsewhere. The tainted man launched from the wall and landed like a sack of potatoes just in front of them, cured of his ailment.

The Molten Steel came pin wheeling from the darkness into D'artello's hand. He turned and towered over the maddened Henry who nearly got up before being stabbed back to the ground.

Joseph let out a gasp, "What in Harmony's graces are you—" Before he could finish his sentence, he realized that his two friends had become normal again. He knelt down to check their pulse, just to be sure, placing two fingers under the side of Henry's jaw. "By Harmony's will, he's alive."

Joseph heard D'artello's footsteps carry off behind him. He wanted to follow his friend but was halted by the intensifying stiffness in his body. Trying to get up so quickly, his neck jerked backward. He felt the whiplash wedge its way into his spine. Examining his hand, he was turning a gray color. Curiously he tried to pull his glove off. The plush make-up of his chubby fingers was gone. Instead they were like rocks now, completely immobile solids. Pulling his other glove off eagerly with his teeth, he began to run his naked hand across the gray area. Stone if he'd ever felt it—cold, rough, stone. *What is happening to me?* he thought, looking at his inanimate hand.

Suspicious of his worsening condition, he decided not to lose track of D'artello. His strength was depleting, however, and it became difficult to make even the slightest of motions. Along with his hand, his forearm had begun to turn gray as well. Whatever the phenomenon, he was nervous it might spread over his whole body. D'artello stopped abruptly, like a hound catching a whiff of a hare. He turned to face Joseph with an empty expression.

"D'artello? What's happening?" Joseph asked with a quiver in his voice.

"Your hand," D'artello said, reaching out awkwardly. He caressed the petrified glove, churning it between his fingertips. "Stone," he sighed after retracting his arm and letting it rest at his side.

Joseph stared into D'artello's icy gaze. In a way, he seemed lost. He may not have been a tainted, but there was something very deviant about his friend.

D'artello raised his blade, poking Joseph in the chest with its sharp tip. "Wow!" Joseph exclaimed. "What are you doing?"

Too late, D'artello had already pushed it clean through his midsection. Joseph let out a scream as if he were dying. Not knowing what it felt like to cross into the world of death, he opened his eyes, realizing he felt no pain. Looking down and not seeing the ruby-red, life's liquid was evidence enough. D'artello yanked the sword in one clean motion. Joseph stared at his friend, and his stone hand flew to the would-be wound, clenching his shirt. It was then he realized that he could move his fingers again. The familiar, faded brown leather entered his vision. All of his afflicted muscles were reviving. Whatever had plagued him was now gone. Apparently this glowing sword of D'artello's could cure.

"Understand?" D'artello asked with stillness in his voice.

There were so many questions Joseph would have liked to ask just then, but he gave a quick nod instead, signifying his readiness to continue purging the town of the tainted.

D'artello turned due north, back toward the barracks. "Where are we going?" Joseph said. "Our orders are to go south!"

D'artello was busy dancing circles around six more sickly townspeople. They were at the epicenter of an attack, and the streets were crowded with people running for their lives from their friends, neighbors, parents, children, whoever was gripped by this strange blood thirst.

An orange heat warmed their right sides. The lengthy flat, the primary living quarters of half the fort, was burning to the ground, shedding a hellish light over the violence below it. The fire was stoking itself like young love against the all-wooden interior. D'artello had just subdued most of the town bucket squad, and with most of the guard fending off the Genzaks and tainted souls, this building would surely burn to the ground.

Bloodcurdling screeches averted their attention. A Genzak soldier and a town guard were working together to pull a woman away from the blaze. Joseph felt the heat exhaust from the nearby building, trying not to think of whatever or whoever was still inside. There was no way to enter the building now.

It had now become clear to him that the Genzaks were not the enemy here. There was a third party intervening in this fight, something conniving, overbearing, and evil. As soon as he could concentrate on his mission at hand, D'artello was well ahead. "Hey! Wait up!" Joseph called, following D'artello's left turn into the commerce area.

The fire was to their backs now and a couple of blocks away, and as a result, shade took over. D'artello's glowing sword gave away his position but

The Adventures of D'artello

also allowed him to look around the dormant shops. Like tombstones in a graveyard, each shop seemed isolated, standing alone in the mist.

"Oh by Harmony no!" One of the Genzak soldiers stumbled backward from between two of the shops, falling to his backside in horror. He scrambled to his feet and took off with a cowardly sprint, toward the light, where his eyes could grant him sanctity. Joseph started to give chase. D'artello put an arm out that stopped him dead in his tracks. He pointed the Molten Steel toward the dark alley from which the man had stumbled. Neither seeing nor hearing anything, he made his advance as if he knew exactly where he was going. Joseph knew where they were headed, toward the town circle and the fountain. This running was becoming tiresome on the heavy-set man, but D'artello was unrelenting.

Coming upon the large encirclement, Joseph bent down trying to catch his breath as D'artello examined the surroundings with the sword, as if he'd never been in this place. Now there were living complexes between them and the fire. Joseph's eyes took a moment to adjust. He too traced the outlines of his surroundings. Once he'd gotten his bearings, he knew exactly where they were. His eyes jutted to the middle of the circle, the pride and joy of the town, the beautiful statue of Harmony atop the fountain. It had been sliced into perfect stone chunks. His eyes followed a path to the ground where the pile of stone body parts rested. They began to stir to life, as did a figure held captive beneath them.

"D'artello! Over here!" Joseph called.

Immediately the estranged boy turned the light of his sword onto an armor-clad old man trying to pull himself from the heavy stone of the statue. "H-hello?" he called, shielding his eyes from the bright light with his free hand. "Help me, please," he said.

"King Bensel!" Joseph exclaimed. He lumbered over and began to shovel pieces of rubble off of the king.

D'artello though, paid him little to no mind. He raised the blade above his head to illuminate the vacant flats surrounding them. The light beat back the darkness of the stadium of short buildings and windows.

"Up there!" Bensel called, pointing up at a window. There, staring down at them was a white-cloaked figure. The creature gave a shriek as if fearing the light and fled quickly into the cover of darkness behind it.

D'artello gave chase like a dog. Pushing past Joseph, he ran alongside the building toward its entrance. Coming upon it quickly, he thrust his shoulder through the double door, causing it to fling open and shudder against the inside wall. The atrium would have been pitch black and a perfect trap if not for the Molten Steel guiding the way. D'artello knew to head down the left hallway to head his opponent off. This building had the same layout as the one he lived in, windows toward the outer walls and doors on the inner ones.

The light from the sword contrasted his vision; he could not see much ahead of it, and the darkness was like thick fog in spite of a lantern, and just as inviting. Because of it, there was a definitive divide between enlightening illumination and ignorant blackness. Deciding that this was a disadvantage, he placed the sword in the sheath that hung around his waist. The light field was transcended by blindness.

His valorous vision returned, allowing him to outline the objects around him. It was easy, as this building was relatively unfurnished because it had no regular occupants. The windows let in just enough moonlight to see, perforating the hallway. He took to the wall after hearing another whisper, sprawling himself against it, outstretching his hand to feel the doors shut tight. A Phantom had not yet shown him the intelligence to cover its tracks and shut doors behind it. Soon, a slight creak was followed by someone whispering, "John?" accompanied with a quick footstep. "John, is that you?" It was a girl's voice. Shortly after, a baleful roar came from down the hall, echoing through the empty building. The voice inside the room gave a startled gasp and then seemed to coach itself.

"C'mon, dammit, you're a soldier," she tried to encourage herself. D'artello opened the door slowly, so as not to scare her. This gentle action was interrupted as she gave a shout, swinging a sword overhead at him. He pulled the shining sword from the sheath to block. The light startled the black-haired, blue-eyed woman. She fell to her backside, keeping her sword in front of her. The Genzak armor was a marvel among its war-time competitors. The plate was thick but lightweight. It couldn't take the direct hit a Vaukry suit could, but the soldier inside had the ability to get out of the way easier. At each joint, thick gears ground smoothly so as not to hinder movement while protecting the areas where the armor was weakest. They were an industrious and innovative nation, which was possibly why a woman soldier sat before him now. In Vaukry, women were not allowed to become soldiers.

"Oh, Harmony, you're one of them aren't you?" her voice quivered. "Where is John!" she shouted.

D'artello lowered his sword to his side to show her that he meant no harm and then raised his finger to his lips to silence her. She looked at him befuddled. His lips passed no words, yet his eyes told her to follow.

The two left the room under his silent instruction, and she took shelter behind him. They followed a faint snarling forward, and her free hand wrapped around his wrist, crushing it with her emotion-driven grip. "Maybe that's John," she said. "They got him, you know. I saw it. I swear." D'artello pulled away, paying her no mind. Moving swiftly now, easily against the will of his fellow traveler, he approached the room that was the source of the sound. Readying his weapon, he thrust the door open. Gina, the girl with D'artello, jumped back as a horrible shriek pierced the silence. The white-cloaked Phantom burst from the depths of the room, taking D'artello off his feet, smashing through a window. Even though this monster had a good grip on him and hit him hard, in his soulless state, he had an unbreakable wit. He remained calm, catching a glimpse of a second figure emerging from the shadows of the room.

He could only make out a black cloak before crashing to the ground outside, rolling atop the sharp pieces of glass, leaving rips in his shirt and cutting up his forearms.

Joseph was startled by the sudden entrance of the violent hissing, emanating from the legless ghost. Frantically, he lifted a heavy stone from the pile pinning Bensel and then thundered over to help his friend.

"D'artello, hold him still," Joseph called, aiming to drive the stone through its skull. The fraying limbs of the Phantom found reason for just long enough to turn and swing at Joseph. When he stepped back, the displacement of the stone caused him to stumble away and almost fall. He dropped the rock, and it shattered against the ground.

D'artello managed to pull one of his feet between him and the cloaked lunatic. Using his venerable leg muscles, he drove his opponent back, hard against the wall of the building. The ghostly cloak was quick to start back at him. D'artello sprang to his feet just in time to feel a quick laceration split all the way diagonally from his waist to his shoulder.

The monster's anger quelled for a moment as it awaited D'artello's transformation into a tainted. By the time it realized that this was not happening, its rancor climaxed. Joseph watched as it raised its sword to attack the kneeling D'artello. Looking on, Joseph's life flashed before his eyes—the day he joined the guard, the day he met D'artello, all of the things they'd shared in their youth—and he decided that this was worth casting his final lot.

Crying out for the last time, Joseph charged with all his courage, reaching his left hand out to grab the creature and halt its hastening advance. He made contact with the unarmed gauntlet of the Phantom, stopping it for only a moment. With nothing to defend himself, he was victim to multiple stabs to the heart. In and out, in and out, the nasty blade gnashed, spitting up blood with each exit. Despite his valor and strength, five stabs later, Joseph's body was being cast aside. If D'artello had a soul, he probably would have been too distraught by his friend's violent death to fight back.

The Phantom did not give Joseph any more attention. It was as if it were drawn to D'artello.

D'artello rose from his knees, snapping his blade through his foe with a full circle of his wrist. The slash was followed by a crackling sound, the motion being too quick for the noise of it tearing through the ghostly armor. Away went its presence, and its rage, in a thin, black mist, dissolved into the night sky.

Remembering the girl inside, D'artello jumped back through the broken window and set his sights upon the black-cloaked figure holding the soldier up by her neck.

Waiting patiently, his hesitation was obvious. "So, it is you," a deep voice came from the cloak. "A soulless warrior, eh?" he mocked. "I must say, you have exceeded expectation, managing to clear out all of the tainted, and even your first Phantom. Bravo," his voice boomed as he threw the girl helplessly to the ground.

D'artello rushed him, but to no avail. The man leapt over him, his cloak seeming to come alive. D'artello spun to face his foe and placed his other hand on the hilt of the Molten Steel.

"That won't be necessary," the monster said, holding out a leather-bound hand. "I cannot stay here to play with you." He laughed, looking up at the sky. "Like a virus, I have been here long enough to instill the symptoms of this world's end."

A sound like igniting flames rippled through the air, and the man was lifted off of his feet, floating gently on two black, raven wings. "I beckon you, D'artello, pursuit me down the road of madness." Then, staring down at the female soldier, he added, "There are so many things I wish to show you."

"Go to hell!" cursed the girl on the floor, getting her breath back finally.

He returned the comment with a hearty chuckle. "I'm already there. Why don't you visit sometime?" The wings flapped heavily then as he took off into the night.

D'artello gave chase, but his black cloak and wings were ethereal against the night sky.

The Molten Steel was now radiant. D'artello stared into it with a certain hunger in his eyes. This winged man was not a Phantom, and clearly too well spoken to be a tainted, so why did the Molten Steel resonate this way?

Leaving the girl and Joseph behind, D'artello walked back to the guard complex to meet with his father. The location of Joseph's dying body would never leave his uncaring lips.

Chapter 6

A new day began as the sun poked through the cloudy sky, looming over the storm-beaten town. What had been utter chaos had passed into a confused recuperation. "I swear it was here," the female Genzak soldier said to Gerrik, gesturing to the space Joseph's body once occupied. She, Gerrik, and Bensel stood before the carved statue.

Bensel, stocky and stubby under his elaborate armor, scratched his aging beard. Each time he did this, he played a game with fate, for his right wrist had a built-in bow. Just a simple depression in the posture of his wrist could trigger it, sending the arrow through his skull for certain. "Gina is right, Gerrik," Bensel said, equally shocked. "He tried to help me out from under those rocks."

"It was a ghost, a ghost I tell you, if I've ever seen one. It killed him, and now it took him," Gina kept on.

"A ghost?" Gerrik responded, raising an eyebrow. "This just gets more farfetched by the second," he said, shaking his head.

"No, Gerrik, really, it was here. I saw it with my own eyes," Bensel protested.

The two tried to convince the war hero who'd "seen everything" of the events that had transpired the night before. "Now listen," he interrupted. "Joseph was a good man. Whether or not his body is here, he is still missing, and given the horrors of last night," he said, lowering his tone, "I think it best we assume the worst. We will continue with the ceremonies and the group funeral for all who died. I have a town to relocate and parents to attend to."

Realizing Gerrik did not believe a word she or her very own king spoke, Gina neglected mention of the winged man. Bensel must have felt the same way, because he made no mention of him either. She rubbed her hand across her bruised neck, remembering the things that he'd said to her as he held her by the throat.

*   *   *

Hours later, D'artello and his father stood in the proving grounds, among the higoats in front of the guard flat. Together they looked over the main road at the recovering townsfolk clambering about. For a long time, the two just basked in the sun with no words. The town's four higoats traced circles around them. To these five-foot tall, stocky animals, it was just another day.

If what Bensel had just explained to Gerrik was true, there was something amuck at the capital and with King Garo's rule. For a little while longer, Gerrik stood with eyes closed, powerful arms crossed, meditating on the information, and trying to find words to speak to his sullen son.

"This is so … unreal," his father began in a soft voice. "What could this all mean? Our king has gone mad? And what of those soldiers? They kept getting up, like the living dead, the horrid living breathing dead."

D'artello didn't seem to pay his father's words any mind, nor did he seem the least bit shaken up by the events prior.

"And what of you, my son? Why aren't you upset by the death of your dear friend Joseph, or even puzzled in light of recent events?" he asked, trying to look into his boy's eyes.

D'artello looked back at his father with an ice-cold stare. Gerrik tried to read his body language, but it said little more than his lips. The silence grew awkward. "Joseph's death will not be in vain. He's done his part," he uttered finally.

"Is that all this is to you?" his father shot back.

"This is war. You taught me that."

"D'artello, this wasn't what I meant to teach you. Joseph was your friend, just as Bensel is mine." Gerrik paused, mortifying himself with the memories of his boy doing the bloody work of a soldier. "You don't express any passion or mourning for his death. Surely one night couldn't have hardened you this much. What's the matter?" A shameful frown crept across his face.

D'artello turned his head away from his father and looked back at the white, wooly higoats. "Bensel didn't want things to happen the way they did last night. So it turns out he's not our enemy. Instead, our own king has turned on us." Letting that simple statement sink in, he spoke no further.

"If this is a way of saying, 'I told you so,' then you should know that this is hardly the time," his father responded sternly.

"You made your best guess, I suppose," D'artello said, beginning to walk back toward the barracks.

"Hey!" his father exclaimed, grabbing hold of his boy's wrist. "What do you want from me? I'm trying my ... soldiers have to follow orders ..." He lost his words, realizing none of his answers were good enough before, and certainly not now.

"Let's fix it," D'artello interrupted, pulling away.

"What do you mean fix?" He asked, giving chase.

"Our good king must be put out of his misery."

"Oh really? You and what army?" his father said.

"I will go alone if you choose not to help me. It is my destiny," he said, pulling the Molten Steel from the sheath on his belt.

His father's eyes widened when they fell on it. "Where did you get that sword?" he gasped. D'artello looked back at him for a moment, ignoring the question, and then turned and kept pace with the sword at his side.

"Harmony," Gerrik said. Letting D'artello go, he walked further into the proving grounds. When his son was fully out of sight and earshot, he cried out, "Harmony!" All was quiet after his voice echoed across the sky. He waited for a response. The birds stopped chirping, and the wind stopped blowing. On the main road, an old woman stopped to watch him. Admittedly, Gerrik had never realized how fast clouds actually moved until they stopped.

A light slowly enveloped his vision, until the lush greenery and higoats were gone. Soon it dimmed to reveal the warm, inviting golden glow of the shaft-like cavern, as he now stood on top of the dormant pool. There he waited until the fine hair on his ears was brushed gently by the familiar whore's voice. "What business does a mortal have beckoning a Peacemaker?"

He turned around quickly to face the half-naked deity. "You know why I called upon you," he said, before even laying eyes on her, letting his deep-seated rage bleed from his tone.

"However angry you are, you mustn't forget to whom you are speaking, Gerrik," she said.

"You take my first son from me, then my wife during the birth of my second son, and now you want him as well?"

"He is the hero I have chosen, and he has no choice, just like the rest of us."

Gerrik turned and threw a hard fist at the cave wall, letting out a powerful roar. Blood dripped down the wall slowly in its imperfections, trickling through a vertical stone maze as he drove harder. His anger not sufficed, he turned his head so that he could barely see her out of the corner of his eye. "Mark my words, Harmony. Even a Peacemaker can pay someday. When my life ends, I will make you regret this," he swore.

Harmony let a smug laugh leave her lips. "Even when you do join me on this immortal plane, your power will hardly compare to that of my own," she scoffed.

"We shall see," he responded.

"Face me," she said, pointing a finger at him. An unseen force jerked him into an upright position that was so involuntary it could have snapped his spine if he wasn't half expecting it. "I have answered your call for a reason," she began.

"Harmony, you always did put your personal affairs over governing the universe," he shot back.

The water below them began to boil fiercely. "Mortal, you try my patience," the calm-looking goddess spoke. Her smug expression was wiped clean off of her face, and she was left with a deep frustration clenching her fist. "I have answered because I am commanding you and Bensel to aid D'artello in saving your planet. You two will be his vassals in his quest to clear away the Phantoms. I know you will not protest. You must protect your son—am I not correct, Gerrik?" Silence befell the moment. He wore a look of pure resentment and hatred.

"I bid you good-bye for now, Gerrik. Your son will leave for the capitol, due south in the morning." She gave a wave of her hand.

"Wait! Don't you blink away from me, you harlot!" he yelled. Whether or not she heard him, her laughter came along with the holy light that once again carried him off, back to the proving grounds. "Wait!" He continued his curses onto deaf ears, "You can't have him! I won't let you! Do you *hear* me?" He yelled, shaking his fist at the sky.

The very same old woman he'd seen earlier stared at him as she would pity a crazy person.

* * *

D'artello, Gerrik, and Bensel sat in a closet of a room that was dark like a cave. The wall mounts flickered desperately to beat back the shadows of the windowless room, but it was as if the walls were painted black. There was not much for décor either; nothing stood in it but they and the wooden table with a continental map sprawled in front of them. Not even chairs dared stand beneath them. This was a room of absolute focus for Gerrik. Sometimes when something bothered him, he would lock himself up tight. It was a keep where he could have a long, uninterrupted think. Today was one of those days. Just twenty minutes ago, he'd been alone since his encounter with Harmony. It was now well into the dark hours.

"Are we clear on what we are up against?" D'artello asked. "They are Phantoms, and I am the only one who can kill them. I am also the only one who can be cut by one. Be sure to inform the soldiers to stay as clear away as possible if they see them."

Bensel nodded. Despite his mountain man appearance, something gave him the air of a noble man. Just by looking into his aged brown-eyes, one could be aware of his unconventional wisdom.

Like D'artello's father, Bensel was also a revered warrior, but he made full use of a sword and shield. His exploits were nearly as renowned as a commander, truly an asset to D'artello on this difficult journey to the capital.

Bensel began to speak and assess the situation. "I am sure King Garo knows that we will be at his gates soon. We made quite a ruckus here last night, and your son has slain one of his monsters ... a Phantom. He will be missing it when it does not return."

"My lookouts haven't seen any peculiar activities from the watchtowers; we are only just north of the capital. If Garo perceived an attack from this direction, his troops would probably mobilize on top of those hills. Anywhere beyond that, we will have the high ground, thus an advantage with your army and my guard. Speaking of which, how many soldiers can you account for?" Gerrik asked.

"Once my reinforcements arrive from the capitol at midday tomorrow, on the front lines, I will have exactly 2,322 men," he responded.

"Well I've only got fourteen good men left to spare. The rest will be staying here to guard the home front," Gerrik said. "We are a little short, Bensel. The capital has nearly eight men to our one," he pointed out. Five Fort Carrie guards had died in the night's struggle, and Gerrik knew all of them personally.

"Indeed, it will definitely be all about blocking the right pathways," Bensel said, laying his palms out on the map. "The north gate would normally be the weakest, but since Garo is probably expecting us from that direction, it is doubtful. That leaves the west gate across the great bridge," he said, referring to a mighty structure built by the capital. It was a bridge that was two miles long, stretching over a wide river mouth that divided the east and west continent. "He is allied with Vashti. They have a treaty, as you know, and they wouldn't dare raise a sword against each other. Also, he could never expect a full-out attack coming from that bottlenecked position." Vashti was a neighboring nation whose explorers colonized the country of Vaukry; they had not had a war since Vaukry earned its independence just a meager ten years before.

"We will have to move quickly after we cross the bridge though. Unless we can hit every fleeing messenger, the capital will hear of our treason long before we arrive. It's a grueling walk from that bridge to the capital, at least fifty miles of sloped terrain. Our men will be exhausted," Gerrik said.

"Why would we even need to enter Vashti? Can't we just go straight to the capital?" Bensel proposed.

"What's the matter with you? Are you really getting that old? Crosspan, Chapville, and Steepleburg all line up on our route. They are some of the largest cities in this country, not to mention the clergy is already on us about this plan. Those towns are hotspots for those zealots. It would be much quicker to go through Vashti. We also wouldn't have to cross the river until we reach that bridge."

"We will have to hit every messenger then. We will have to make sure that all of our archers aim only for the fleeing mounts," D'artello said abruptly.

"It will be an uphill struggle with the enemy archers pelting us down as well," Bensel grunted. "Once we reach the bridge, that is."

"We cannot afford to let a messenger go," D'artello stressed in his monotone voice.

Bensel let out a heavy sigh. "He is right. It's just … all those men for so little gain."

"We will have to stop in this city, Belren, to rest up for the night. Perhaps your reinforcements could seize the bridge. Again, we cannot let any messengers through. We will have to seize the town under military control and have our archers sleep in shifts, guarding the borders. They will have to shoot anyone trying to leave. We can't afford to take any prisoners. We also can't afford a riot. We will have to do this in such a way that no one knows if a messenger makes it or not." His father spoke with a grim expression.

"Assassination of townsfolk? Truly a dark march," Bensel said. "Got to be honest here, I am not comfortable with spilling innocent blood." he stated, laying his hands flat on the table barring further conversation until his concerns were tended to.

"We have no other choice, it is worth so few lives," D'artello stated.

Gerrik couldn't believe the heartless words that came from his own son's mouth. Harmony had already taken him. D'artello was a walking shell now.

"Well, with such short notice, this is really the best we can do," Gerrik said. "The walk is so long, but I suppose we can't afford to be spotted on our march past any still-loyal towns. It's settled then."

D'artello was closest to the door, and Bensel had to walk by him to leave. He placed a palm on D'artello's shoulder. "I never thought I would have to fight alongside the little tyke I used to teach to swordfight. I always hoped peace would outlive me. A boy has become a man too quickly," he said. D'artello paid little mind to his commentary. This was Bensel's way of criticizing Gerrik's parenting. "Tis important to relax a little, my boy. We all make mistakes," he said, referring to the previous night.

"So how's your daughter?" Gerrik finally said, breaking the awkward moment and ignoring Bensel's hidden remarks. He walked over and put an arm around Bensel, leading him away. "We've had a rough day. Let's go have a few drinks and catch up."

Just as the two were headed down the hall to leave, a clergyman entered. Not just any clergyman though—Adriel himself, and he was furious. Adriel was not a big man. He was pale and skinny, as his practices had left him. However, he had arrogance about him. His silky white garb danced daintily around his stride, sweeping the floor with each step.

"Where do you think you are going, Gerrik?" he said. His thick black eyebrows twitched into an agitated perch, and his dirty-bearded lips pursed. He pointed a long thin finger into Gerrik's chest, lecturing as if to a child, "Declaring war on our capital? I will not have it. Powerful warrior or not, you don't run this town." He adjusted the coin-sized specs cradled on his nose.

"Adriel, don't you get in my face," Gerrik said, his friendly tone instantly turning harsh. Indeed this was Adriel, Sali's blunder of a father. To Gerrik, he was hardly a man, and to Adriel, Gerrik was a demon. It had always been that way, getting worse when D'artello "unpurified" his daughter.

"Spare me, Gerrik. The Peacemakers have granted us a reprieve from war," he said, gesturing to the ceiling and then narrowing his already squinty eyes. "It's people like you and this mountain troll of a king that work against them."

"Now listen here," Bensel began, but he was interrupted by Adriel.

"You are godless, Gerrik, no better than those mercenaries that rampage our lands. People like you are the reason our citizens cannot live outside of these walls. Just look at the catastrophe of last night, and … oh my Harmony!" he exclaimed, catching a glance of D'artello's hollow eyes. "The boy as well?" he poked. "You have subjected him to your godlessness as well? For Harmony's sake, Gerrik, if you wish banishment, don't drag the poor youth down with you. Impermissible! As town clergyman and governing official of Fort Carrie, I will not permit you to take your troops to the capital."

Gerrik exploded back with equal force, "You listen to me, you little rodent. A mouse like you has no place telling a man like me what is right and wrong! With the path you have chosen for your daughter and the defiling you will let the clergy commit to her, you have no right telling me how I will raise my boy. I will take the troops, because each and every one of them will follow me with or without your permission."

"You will be exiled then!" he shouted. "Exiled I say! You will truly become one of those homeless, godless mercenaries."

Gerrik snatched him up by the scruff of his collar, and Adriel's flailing arms knocked over a vase that had been standing on a pillar beside them.

This was not an ideal place for a scuffle. Even Bensel was shocked at Gerrik's readiness to grab a clergyman as if he were some street hoodlum.

"What are you doing? How dare you?" Adriel protested.

"You and I are going to have this talk outside."

D'artello barely listened to the conversation carrying on toward the door. However, a couple of Genzak soldiers were coming down the hall, just crossing into the atrium, headed to the pub as well.

"I just don't know, man. I don't want this war. I'm going to tell king Bensel that I'm staying here," one of them said.

"Where's your loyalty, man?" a deeper tone sounded.

D'artello took notice of the men. One had short brown hair and was of medium build. With a clean-shaven face, he had a youthful complexion. The other, the pro-war debater, was a tall and lanky man with short blond hair, thinning in his middle age.

"This isn't going to fix anything," said the shorter, younger man. D'artello was unaware this was John, the man whom Gina spoke of. "It's cyclical. Didn't you pay attention in school? This area is war after war; they never get enough."

"Then I suppose being a soldier isn't for you then," said the taller man.

"I'd guess you're right. Listen, Art," John said, retrieving a small piece of paper, folded into quarters, form his pocket. "Let's go have a drink. Then I want you to give this to Gina for me. I'm leaving town tonight."

Art took the letter and scanned it briefly. "Looks like you've thought this all out then," he said.

Finally their trot brought them past D'artello. "Hey there, brother, come have a drink with us," said John. "It's my last night in town, so the more the merrier."

D'artello just looked at the pair with an unnerving stare.

After an awkward silence, Art tapped John on the shoulder and whispered, "C'mon, let's just go." With that, the two walked on, much more silent than they had come.

* * *

D'artello lay face up in his bed, staring at the ceiling wearily. His new, soulless body was callous and ignorant of sociality, but it was efficient at getting what he needed, when he needed it. There would be little rest in the days to come, so sleep was a priority. The feeling of drowsiness was absent on this night; like a candle, his consciousness blew out.

Soulless during the day, he did not feel anything since the previous night when he was beaten within an inch of his life by the tainted. During the night, his dreams still tormented his nerves by playing back everything that would normally be of importance to him from then until now. The voices of his friends came in eardrum-splitting whispers.

First there was fire. He stood on a lone, stone pillar, surrounded by flames, shaping into long fingers, beckoning him to come near. The heat felt like it would melt his flesh.

They were swept away suddenly, and D'artello's hair wrapped around his eyes. When he pulled it away, he was among the clouds and blue sky, losing all air in his lungs. He was higher than he'd ever been. There was a slight draft that was relieving after standing in the middle of the inferno, but it grew colder and colder still until he could feel the fluids in his spine crystallizing.

The discord of whispers was not enough to rattle him awake, but this dream seemed to trail on forever. Even this did not faze him. Nothing meant anything to him now—not the concern of his father, the conversation with Tanya about leaving her, not even the death of Joseph.

As long as he slept, he would tumble around beneath the sheets in unrest. His eyes split open to the rousing sunlight, and he was plagued by his nightmares no longer. There was a curious, viscous, moisture in his ducts that he inspected by swirling it between his fingertips. It was of little concern without a soul.

Normally he suffered from fatigue in the morning, struggling to get out of bed. Today though, his consciousness snapped to life. He had no remembrance of the turmoil that ensued the previous night. He peered out the window at the sun just coming over the horizon, casting an orange glow over the reflective clouds. He rose, dressed himself, and then fastened a second sheath on his belt. On his left side to draw with his right hand was the Molten Steel, slayer of the Phantoms. On his right side to draw with his left was his father's steel sword, which would happily kill anything or anyone the Molten Steel would not.

To the left of his bed were various armor pieces, irresponsibly strewn about, awaiting their warrior's return. It was a new set, for he had gone up a size since the beginning of his training. His father had proudly presented to him a new midnight blue armor.

The torso plate was perfectly forged, shaped to look like a warrior's chest. The gauntlets and grieves were light, comprised mostly of higoat leather. There were bolts in the metal that reinforced the leather, allowing superior movement of the joints in the hands, wrists, ankles, toes, and even one near the arch of the foot for maximum comfort in doing almost anything. The inside was lined with silk-like wool that also came from the useful higoat. The pauldrons, shoulder armor, were shaped perfectly, hammered out so that not even a boulder's weight could crush such resistance and architecture. And last but not least, a helmet, with a golden hawk perched on top in a frightening position like a crouching gargoyle. Its wings were bowed over its body like a shield of feathers. He scooped it all up into the chest plate and slung the mass over his shoulder and then proceeded to the east gate to meet Gerrik and Bensel.

Never looking back, he shut the door to his room, his normal life, and his home since birth.

He walked passed Gerrik's room, noticing the door was cracked, meaning he was already up. D'artello pushed open the double wooden doors, taking his first soulless step into a new day. He traveled down the main road under a whimsical dawning sky. Not even the higoats were running the proving grounds in front of the flat yet. He took a left at the first crossing, past the cinders of the burnt flat. It was the living space for half the town, and some patrons were digging through the ash for anything that might have survived the fire.

"D'artello, you are up early!" Henry yelled as he approached east gate, leaving his post to talk to his friend. "I actually was hoping to see you. I wanted to thank you for saving us the other night. I'm not too sure what happened, but …" Henry seemed to lose his place in his words, as he often did when he got excited.

"I bear sorrow to hear of Joseph's demise," Michael said. "He died a hero. He'd always told me, if that be his fate, to perish protecting something or someone dear to him, he could rest in peace."

"Yeah, I still can't believe he is gone," Henry said with a sigh, his eyes were welling up a little. "I just, I guess I never really thought things would get this rough when I joined the guard. If I had known that I would lose a friend, I probably would have stopped him from joining in the first place," he said.

"Ease your sorrows, friend, and regret nothing," Michael said. "You have to remember that this is where Joseph was happiest. And again, he died doing what he believed was right. D'artello is able to stand in front of us now because of him, and there is a reason for that."

"I wish we were going with you. We are stuck taking the safe bet while you are out risking your neck. I guess what we want to say is: come back alive." Henry stepped forward to give D'artello a friendly hug. His efforts retreated, however, when he saw the emotionless expression on D'artello's face.

"I know how you must feel, D'artello. You were closer to him than I was," Michael said, seeing the awkward situation. "Joseph wanted you to live on, and you should honor that request." Another awkward silence broke out. They expected D'artello to speak on this matter. No words came. "Open the gate, Henry," Michael ordered finally.

Henry nodded and began to ascend the ladder to the top of the wall. The loud clicking of the chain busted the morning silence as he cranked open the only barrier left between D'artello's home and the world outside. Without hesitation, he made his way past his emotionally conflicted friends.

The sun had not yet risen high enough to enlighten the fields to their full color. It lacked its usual radiance, or it could have been D'artello's uncaring perception of his surroundings. It had been much time since he'd taken a good look at a daytime sky. The clear summer days were gone. By this time of year, clouds had matured throughout the sky. Whatever the weather, he spotted Gerrik and Bensel sitting atop a hill. Just a few steps out before the gate closed, the loud bang directed Gerrik's attention. Spotting his son, he waved for him to join them.

D'artello approached but did not sit down. For a time, they all looked outward at the forest ahead that stretched on for miles. Much like every other town, Fort Carrie and its fields was an eye in a hurricane of wilderness. Often, there was a path from town to town, much like their path to Belren. It hadn't been used in quite some time. It was probably overgrown, barely distinguishable from the rest of the foliage.

"Come, boy, you should heed what I have to say," Bensel said finally. He cleared his throat.

D'artello moved closer, standing near his father and staring at Bensel as if he were ready to listen.

"Just start from the beginning, Ben. He should hear this since he knows more about our enemy." Gerrik leaned back onto his elbows and stared at the porous overcast.

Bensel took a deep breath. "It was two fortnights ago today, I was in a meeting with my ambassador when the scout burst through the doors to my throne room. Coincidentally, we were about to make trade with Vaukry. That aside, the guards held the youth back as he clawed and bit his way through their arms. It was not until they held their wounds in pain did the young man kneel before me. For a moment, he was like a cornered animal; he would have done anything to make it to my feet. After apologizing for his intrusion and outburst, he stood telling me an army had mobilized on the horizon, from the Vaukry border. It was my perception the man had gone crazy. It was as if Ruin himself chased him into my chamber. I drew my sword, lest he attack me, yet I let him continue. He told me that the army howled like wild animals, that they were not human, that they dressed in white cloaks only to muse at the bloodstains on their garments.

"He told me there were thousands on the way. The man was hysterical, and I ordered my guards to lock him up, as his ravings were farfetched to say the least. Surely his crazed yells would incite panic throughout my city, but not on this premise alone. Given his blood-stained face, I assumed he'd killed his two comrades, as they did not return with him. I could not stay this mind-set, however; I sent my ambassador and a few good men to the Vaukry capital just in case. Only a couple of days later, my nightmares were brought to life. Thousands, hah! Tens of thousands of white cloaks poured onto my streets. No warning, just the shrieking of women, children, and the cries of innocent men.

"What remained of my city guards made it back to the palace in small droves with survivors. Despite the surprise attack, we were able to hold ourselves up for a few days. Their maddened screams did not heed, it was as if they sensed our flesh, needed it. They wanted no one to survive our attack. From the castle, we saw horrible things, men crawling across the ground like wolves, and women being dragged mercilessly into city streets only to be mauled by the white cloaks. No matter how hard we fought, and no matter how hard we hit them, or which way we sliced them … they were beyond death. Every time, a seemingly limitless amount of times, they would rise again.

"Because of this, they became reckless, sloppy, and had no sense of self-preservation. Snarling like dogs, there seemed not a scrap of humanity left in them. My men could not fight them. Furthermore, many of my own men turned against me. I watched people I knew become monsters right before my eyes. The most disturbing part was how the dead began to walk.

"Each time I would strike one down, they would get back up. After just a few days, when the lookout announced the rest of the city deserted, our world began to fall apart. The wind became a hurtful moan, and my soldiers' tears fell as roses. Our home had been lost. Then the fires came, springing forward from banishment itself. With no ignition, our capital burnt to a pile of cinders. I left with my remaining troops, wandering until we followed a white cloak to this fort, and that is why we took the precautious invasion we did."

Not a word was said, silence befell the group for a moment, and the king had a look on his face as a beggar might. "That is not the only oddity. Our journey here was difficult. Though the first wave most certainly came from Vaukry's borders, we encountered them from other directions. Other countries have either been seized or have adopted use of the Phantoms as well. What's worse, I sent my daughter and Sir Elan, my head vassal, with my main force to camp the capital. I do not know what has become of them."

"If your country was sacked as heavily as you say, then what of our reinforcements?" D'artello asked coldly.

"Roughly two thousand of my elite task force remained when we parted. My capital defenses, my elite guard if they made it to the capital, are a rather rough bunch."

"What are you talking about, Ben?" Gerrik asked. "Elite what? How come I don't know about this guard?"

Bensel gave a momentary sigh. "You know, sometimes in your old age you start to get a little paranoid. I know this isn't what you wish to hear, nor will you approve once you've heard it."

"C'mon, man, out with it," Gerrik prodded.

"They are mercenaries, Gerrik."

"Mercenaries? Bensel, you can't trust these people. Their mentality is far too frail to follow orders," Gerrik argued.

"That, my friend, is debatable. Some of them only know how to follow orders. At any rate, I told them to camp outside the Vaukry capital. I also told them to attack if they had not gotten my signal in a week's time. But we still have three days left, and it will only take us two days to travel."

"What makes you think they'll wait until then?" Gerrik said.

"Now listen here, Gerrik, I've lost everything."

"Even if they do wait a week, and we don't make it in time, they will kill everyone—women, children, priests, everyone."

"It makes little difference who reinforces us," D'artello spoke coldly.

Normally Gerrik would have told his son that he had no idea what he was talking about, but he realized his words thus far had fallen on deaf ears.

"You have much blood on your hands, my old friend. Do you really want this as well?" Gerrik asked. He stood up and turned toward Fort Carrie, as if to bid good-bye to the life he'd fought so hard for.

Just then, the chain was heard, rattling off in the distance. The gate slid open, letting through the parade of red armor, speckled with the blue guards. In tow were two wooden, covered wagons, each pulled by two of the fort's higoats. Bensel stood up, aligning himself between D'artello and his father, awaiting the troop's approach. These were all fine soldiers, chomping at the bit to avenge their fallen kingdom.

"Soldiers! You stand here today against tyranny and to …" So the speech ensued. Gerrik was a charismatic speaker. His voice would rattle the frames of the naïve grunts, awakening a special drive within them.

D'artello looked on, meeting gazes with the girl he'd seen during the raid, two nights ago. Her gaze left him to look at Gerrik, but his stare was a distraction to her; she kept glancing back every now and then.

In minutes it was over, and the men gave a hearty "Hoorah!" Filing out of the field and into the woods, it would not be long before they did not recognize their surroundings. In the last month of training, late summer had turned to early autumn. Although the forests to the southeast were much like those near the chasm, most of the luminescent emerald flora had transformed into burnt, earthy oranges. Just in front of the walking path were two boulders, each the size of fully-grown higoat females. Fortunately, they were spread enough to fit the cart through.

The quarter-mile line of soldiers marched single file through the woods, brushing against the arms of the shrubs that seemed to want to pull them back. Sunlight peeked through the canopy of trees, showering them with warmth. Twigs snapped underfoot, especially under the hooves of the two higoats pulling the carts strenuously through the foliage. Soldiers in front of them used their swords to cut down plants that stood in resistance. All the while, the squeaky cartwheels sounded above nature's melody.

Gerrik and Bensel, as well as most of the soldiers in line, chatted idly, watching as D'artello walked a good twenty feet ahead of them with no company other than his armor slung over his shoulder. Just behind the war vets walked Gina.

"Jonathan," she sighed, thumbing a letter she'd pulled from her pocket. "Why did you go? Why did you leave me all alone?" She stared down at the folded piece of paper. She knew what the note said, but she hadn't read it. Jonathan never cared for war. He was strictly against it, in fact. "I thought we'd grown so emotionally apart, I thought it was implied, and then you gave me this," she said, clenching it between her thumb and index finger. "I really, really thought I was over you, yet I ask why?" She held back the tears. "Heh, I'm making myself sad again." Her inner focus was startled when Gerrik called for her. Gerrik and Bensel were whispering to each other like two little boys keeping a secret. Gerrik had his arm around his shorter friend and they both leaned in to the conversation.

They stopped as she hustled to catch up to him and her king.

"Yes, sir," she said, meeting their pace.

Gerrik leaned in close to her. "You see D'artello up ahead," he said, motioning toward the lonely soul.

"Yes—your son, sir?" she replied, remembering her encounter with him two nights ago.

"You see, he hasn't been himself lately, a little down if you would," Gerrik began. "I think a pretty girl like you could break him out of it."

"With respect, sir, I am not sure I know what you mean," she said.

"I was hoping that maybe you could go at least introduce yourself to him. Perhaps you can take his mind off of whatever is bothering him. Just talk, that's all."

Gina took a deep breath readying her speech about being a woman soldier, but when she looked her childhood hero in the eye and caught a glimpse of something broken inside, the speech burst into a deep sigh. "Yes, sir," she said.

"No need for the formalities, Gina. That was a favor, not an order," Gerrik said as she began to walk ahead.

The dark-haired, crimson-clad girl walked toward the silver-haired

D'artello ahead of the line. At first she cursed the thought. *I'm not here to entertain these men, I am a soldier, dammit,* but as she drew closer she realized that this could be good for her. *Well, I suppose he is kind of cute, if he ever smiled, that is; he's always so serious.*

"You think that'll really work?" Bensel asked.

"I don't know, Ben. I hope it does, but I have noticed since we left that she has a problem as well. Maybe it will be good for the both of them."

"Hmm, bet you think you are pretty clever," Bensel said, giving his gray whiskers a stroke and smiling. "You sound like you have given up hope on your own son though."

They watched as Gina put on her best act to speak with D'artello, turning and walking backward to face him with her arms placed cutely behind her back.

"I was a boy once. I know what he is going through," Gerrik said.

Chapter 7

COUNTLESS hours slid by. Ever since they had stopped for lunch, the time sped up. The forest changed as they entered Vashti. Vaukry's forests were thick with brush up to knee-height, but the trees were big and sparse. In the Vaukry forests, trees had domain all their own. Here in Vashti, trees were smaller, huddling together to bed larger animals. It seemed less of the season's molt had made it to this area as well. The gray boulders had also left them behind some few hours ago, judging by the sun's late afternoon position.

Pacing backward along the path, Gina was now on her fifth attempt at courting D'artello's attention. She gazed up into his callous eyes, trying to look her best. He was impervious to her femininity and kept his eyes only on the path ahead. "My name is Gina," she had already given her name to him once before, but his lack of response suggested perhaps he hadn't heard her. "I am a soldier of the Genzak army, sworn vassal to King Bensel himself. I am a *high-ranking, female soldier,*" she emphasized.

Still nothing, not even a blink. *Okay, let's talk about you then,* she schemed. "How about you? What is your name? What is your rank in the Fort Carrie Royal Guard?" she asked. No response, just one heavy footstep after another. Gina had never felt so invisible. This was nerve wracking to say the least. She peeked around him at Gerrik, hoping she was done with this favor. He gave a sweeping motion with the back of his hands, urging her to continue.

"Umm," she cleared her throat. "You are sir Gerrik's son, are you not? Tell me, what's it like to be heir to such a commendable legacy?" No sooner had she uttered the words did her heel catch a root curling out of the ground to trip unwary travelers such as she. Despite her resisting flails, her armor pulled at her. Too late to regain balance, she clenched her teeth and accepted the impending fall.

She stopped though, as did everything else around her. Something cradled her just below her back, supporting her weight, protecting her from the hard ground. When she opened her eyes, D'artello was looking right at her. His armor was slung over his shoulder, gripped by one hand, and she hung out in the other. He'd stopped her fall.

Hugging her shield to her chest out of reflex, she stared into his eyes for a while. "Th-thank you," she said finally. Regaining his posture, D'artello pulled them both back up. Just like that, he dropped his arm and continued to walk past her.

"I am D'artello," he said to no one in particular.

Gerrik was tickled to see her run back to D'artello's side and recommence the conversation. Begrudgingly, Bensel slapped a coin into his palm.

"Told you," Gerrik said. "Nothing like the attention of a beautiful woman."

The day was mild, but the brisk wind would weave through the thicket of trees occasionally to cool the travelers. Soon it would be night. The day's travel had gone off without a hitch, and they were nearly halfway to the bridge, ahead of schedule.

"Genzak was the third nation I tried to be a soldier in. I was rejected twice before because I am a wom—" Not that she felt D'artello was listening anyway, but he perked up suddenly; he was definitely paying attention to something.

Just like the wind, a cry pierced the woods. At first Gina had no idea what it was, but it echoed out into a bloodcurdling scream. Following it was another louder sound, causing many of the smaller creatures in the woods to flee in terror. D'artello, Gina, Bensel, and Gerrik all stopped to look at the woods behind them. The few soldiers preceding them did the same. Before anyone got any sort of visual confirmation, there came a loud crunch, and then something big and limp was thrown from the brush behind, landing in front of D'artello and Gina.

It was a Genzak soldier. He hit the ground and then rolled over, dead. There was a monstrous, four pronged claw-mark in his chest plate. Luckily for this poor man, whatever hit him killed him instantly. Gina was about to panic, but another four men came bursting from the woods, pushing many of the soldiers and King Bensel over in their attempts to escape.

"Alphas!" they screamed, stampeding ahead.

Before Gina could even look back, D'artello had already jolted to life, charging back toward the end of the line. In passing, he scooped a stone into his right palm. The thirteen-foot tall behemoth loomed over one of the Carrie guard members. It slashed, tearing away the brave man's shield, knocking him over, leaving him vulnerable to the shredding claws about to dive into him.

A fist-sized stone snapped into the back of the alpha's head. It turned immediately, frustrated only a little by the pebble's impact. D'artello leapt from the ground to a nearby tree, springing off of it to reach head-level with the beast. In one motion, he drew his father's sword, slicing its throat, and planted his feet on the dead-instantly alpha's collarbone. It hit the ground with an impressive ruckus, cushioning his fall, as he now stood on its bulging pectorals. Gerrik, Bensel, and Gina followed him through the bushes. They were too late to take on the first alpha, but there were many more to deal with.

An orchestra of low bellows and screams rose over the tranquil forest. It was apparent through the convergence of noise from all directions that the formation of the line had been broken.

Another alpha pushed in from the left. It rose from all fours to its hind legs, peering down at the adolescent under D'artello's feet. It was broader and at least three feet taller than the one under D'artello. Gerrik and Bensel stepped forward to take it on.

"D'artello! Go help the cart at the back of the line!" Gerrik barked, but his son was already on the way to try to save their only provisions.

The beast took a telegraphed swing at Bensel, who was ready with his shield. Despite its predictability, the driving force behind that claw was enough to knock the warrior king sideways through the air. A tree stopped his flight short, but his armor protected him. The very same claw swipe gauged the trunk of another nearby tree. Skinny and tall, it was getting ready to topple. Gerrik helped it out with a powerful dropkick, sending the timber the alpha's way. By the time the beast was aware of its impending doom, it was too late. The tree had probably crushed its lungs. It would certainly suffocate in minutes.

Reaching out his hand, Gerrik pulled Bensel to his feet. Without words, the two headed back to join D'artello. Gina followed. D'artello almost ran them down when he burst from the bushes, headed away from the cart. "Go the other way!" he shouted. Three more alphas headed them off; they were bent on making this the small human army's grave. One of them reached out preemptively, arresting Gina in its claw.

"No!" Gerrik yelled, running and then leaping to catch on and save her. One of the other alphas swatted him out of the air. Gerrik hit the ground with a forward roll; he had already deduced the correct response. He unfolded his body and sprang feet-first toward a tree with his powerful arms. The alpha scuttled after him, just in time for Gerrik to pounce back toward it. The two collided somewhere halfway, with his elbow in its furry throat. The force of it snapped the animal's neck. It stumbled wearily before taking its last breath.

The remaining alpha hunched on all fours. It barreled toward D'artello with its mouth agape. Bensel hurled his shield at it, which found its way into the beast's jowls. It reared back in pain, trying to pry the embedded shield out of its mouth. D'artello wasted no time. He jumped at the alpha's face and kicked the shield. This caused it to dig further into the creature's ebon, leathery lips. The bloody shield then fell out, but not before the beast had already decided enough was enough and turned tail.

Gina, grabbed around the waist, as luck would have it, was able to reach her sword. With both hands, she plunged it into the side of the alpha's leather skin. Then she dragged it across its hand, slicing a painful gash deep enough for the creature to drop her to the ground. She landed hard, lying face up, giving herself a second to gaze through the canopy as her blurry vision returned. Kicking her legs, she sprang to her feet. Gina charged between its hairy legs, taking powerful two-handed swings at its ankles, chopping up the tendons. The alpha fell to its front arms. She back-flipped onto its shoulders and stabbed the alpha's spine, snapping it with a twist of her wrist. As the beast went down, she slid off of it and onto her feet.

Gerrik darted by. "Let's go!" he called out to her.

"Gerrik! What about the cart?" Bensel yelled.

"It's gone, Ben! Just run!" he responded.

With D'artello in the lead, they tore through the woods, ripping the leaves and branches from their path with their bare hands. The alpha pack roared again, as if telling them never to return. Bensel and Gerrik had their only maps. If the soldiers left behind could not find them, provided they made it out of the woods with their lives, they would be unable to find their way to the capital.

Running for a bit longer, the group hit Belren's clearing. They were sure of it. Just as they'd left the woods, another scream from a recognizable Fort Carrie Royal Guard member sounded. Gerrik turned around, fully intent on charging back in, but Bensel and Art, the only other soldier to make it out, grabbed him, stopping his advance before he risked his life for someone who was probably already dead.

"Dammit!" Gerrik screamed, putting some strain on Bensel and Art. "Alphas! They aren't even native to this kingdom!" He fell to his knees, weeping for his lost men.

D'artello stared back into the woods without so much as a heightened pulse. The sight of Gerrik so upset was rare. Something welled up inside him just then. A solid ball of anger worked its way up his chest into his mouth.

It emerged as a roar that caused the small animals to flee, just as the alphas' did.

"My men, the carts, what will we do now?" Bensel asked.

"My king," Art said, reading the despair on Bensel's face. He approached him but was waved off, as the old king needed time to recollect himself. That left Art to the confines of his own thoughts, which were enough to bring him to knees and stare at the blades of grass before him as if they were each a lost comrade. Gina followed suit.

"Do we go in after them?" she asked.

"No, we have to wait here. Just in case any of them come out, I want to be here," Gerrik said.

The group stood about for a few more minutes before Art took the initiative to find firewood. It would be dark in little over an hour.

Using the friction of two sticks, Bensel got the fire going. He knelt over it, blowing into the infant flame. With the dried grass they had used for tinder, it caught quickly. Bensel, having completed his job, fell to his backside and then rolled onto his side to talk to Gina, who was curled up with her arms wrapped around her knees. She could feel his stare on her.

She sniffled, then swallowed. "You do not weep, sire. Am I weak because I mourn them?"

Bensel thought for a moment. "It takes a long time to get used to this kind of loss. This is war now; it will change you." His tired eyes glanced at the fire and then back at her before he spoke again. "My lack of tears ... it is no strength, just merely an acquired taste to the feeling of death. You must learn to endure. Do not let them die in vain. Do you understand? I want you to know, it is your passion for their deaths that will make you stronger. So cry now, let it comfort you, for someday ... the tears may never come."

Although she had no rebuttal to her king's advice she still defiantly fought back the tension in her neck that was begging her to keep crying.

D'artello and Gerrik sat on the other side of the fire, not paying any mind to the two on the other side, or Art, who was isolated enough to begin a conversation with himself.

D'artello sat with his legs folded in, watching the fire hypnotically. Gerrik reclined with one leg out, his elbow resting on his other knee. He stared at his son, pondering his recent attitude change. It was all he could do not to cry out loud, cursing Harmony's name. In front of Bensel, Gina, and Art, this type of sacrilegious behavior would probably not sit well.

However, his mind and body were at certain unrest. They would not let him keep his mouth closed. They would not let him sit still. He took to his feet rather abruptly, causing everyone around the fire, except D'artello, to look at him.

The rest of the group sluggishly followed suit. Gina wiped her eyes clean with her arm, and Bensel gave a loud yawn accompanied by a hardy stretch, but D'artello's eyes had not yet left the flame. Gerrik cleared his throat, placing a hand on his chest. In a low tone, he began to speak over the subtle noises of the night. "We cannot stay here any longer; we have not only lost our provisions, but many good men as well. I am sure that none of us will forget them and their courage, for it was key, certainly, to our escape. We should bow to give thanks to their souls for giving up their bodies to allow our safe passage. Glory to you, brave men," he finished, falling to one knee, giving a second ovation to those lost in the woods.

When they finally rose, D'artello had already slung his armor over his shoulder and had begun to walk away. This did not sit well with Gina. "You didn't even kneel? Do you even care, bastard?" she screamed. Throwing her shield to the ground in frustration, she sprinted after him. Gina stood face to face with him now, seething with anger. "You are not going anywhere until you pay your respects. They are the reason you were able to escape and survive!" she ordered.

"Maybe they should have been smart enough to get out when we did," he responded.

His words were met with Gina's open hand across his face, leaving a five-starred red welt. This was barely enough to move him. He reset his vision on her, his bangs hanging over his face, which remained unchanged.

"Your answer is not good enough," she said through clenched teeth. She pulled her sword from its waist-mounted scabbard. "You will kneel for their respects now," she said, another tear rolling down her cheek.

"Gina!" Gerrik called to her, but she was as stubborn as D'artello.

She separated her stance, clasping the hilt of her weapon and tensing both arms until she felt her veins about to pop. D'artello straightened himself out so he could stand square to her. "Kneel!" she called out, taking a horizontal swing with her sword. In her anger, she'd forgotten that Bensel had taught her never to lock her arms up. Her knuckles were white with tension.

Bensel gasped in shock. As quick as she had given a motion with her wrists, D'artello had drawn the glimmering Molten Steel from its sheath, pulling it safely in front of her weapon. Gina's sword struck the Molten Steel like a wall. He stared straight into her eyes, looking at some fool misguided into thinking she could win a fight he'd seen a thousand times.

Gina wasn't about to stop there; she fell to one knee and then swept her right foot to take him off balance. D'artello avoided it by leaping clear overhead, landing softly behind her. His bored posture made this feat look far less impressive than it actually was. She scrambled to her feet, turning around to face him in a ready stance. He seemed barely challenged by her, just standing there emotionless, a spectator at his own fight.

She cried out in frustration, letting forth repeated swings, each one colliding with the Molten Steel clashing in the night. Bensel shouted to his vassal, "Gina, stop this at once, before you—" He was interrupted by Gerrik's hand on his chest.

Gerrik also grabbed Art by the wrist to prevent him from stopping the fight. "This is just practice for him," Gerrik said, letting his solemn eyes fall over the conflict.

D'artello blocked about ten swings or so before he grew weary of the sport, sidestepping the last one. His form was never better. He thrust his sword right through her chest. She looked up at him accusingly. He pulled the sword away and sheathed it with a single graceful motion as she dropped.

Gina placed a hand on her chest and then pulled it away to examine it. There was no blood, no pain.

Gerrik's words followed. "Do you recognize that weapon, Bensel?"

In fact, he did; he remembered it from his war days, and the anger that came along with it, when a very young Gerrik used to boast of false encounters with Harmony.

Hearing the commentary, Gina looked down at D'artello's waist acknowledging that the other sword could have taken her life.

"Gina," Gerrik called out, shaking his head. "He is not himself. Stand aside, and we will follow him," he ordered.

She hesitated, absorbing a second piercing from D'artello's gaze. In them she noticed her own reflection, something she had not noticed before. His mouth remained closed, but his eyes cried out for help, for someone, anyone to be there. She pushed her sword back into its case, rising defeated. Her eyes were affixed on his as she felt her pounding pulse begin to wind down. She then slouched to the side so that her eyes still would not leave his as he passed.

She walked on and tried to put together the puzzle that was D'artello.

"You are still young," Gerrik said to her. "It is easy to hate him right now, for you feel wronged by him. Well the truth is, he's only wronging himself. The least you can do is give your pity to a person. Think of it this way; if you were lost, as he is, wouldn't you want someone to be there beside you?"

Gina gave a slow nod, closing her eyes in shame for her folly. She then turned her sight back to D'artello, who walked up ahead by himself again. Unable to get her mind off of his eyes and Gerrik's words, she found no point in staying angry with him. There had to be something wrong with him. She vowed that she would not rest until she found the remedy, until she could know the real person behind those beautiful eyes. Jogging to catch up to him, she slowly began to wrap her hand around the inside of his. Their fingers stitched together now, he looked back at her. She made sure to lace her lips with a slight creak of a smile.

Together they walked miles onward into the early hours of the morning. Gina knew the route well. Beyond it was a life known by only herself and a few others, the life of her past. Even Bensel believed her to be Genzak born. They did not know she had been born in Vashti and was of noble blood. What she expected to see coming over the horizon was her great city, basking in the midnight moonlight. Instead, an orange glow could be seen polluting the starlit sky just ahead. A hazy bubble seemed to peak further as they climbed the hill in front of them. "What is that?" Gina called, releasing D'artello's hand. She looked back at Gerrik and Bensel, "What is that? What's going on?"

Gerrik, Bensel, and Art walked on, a grim look across their faces. D'artello continued his melancholy stroll, paying little mind to this phenomenon. It was as if the sun were rising again, touching the planet on the horizon.

As they came upon it, the light became a thick bearing on their faces. A virulent dance of smoky light wriggled upward into the sky. "What is that?" Gina said louder this time, jogging away from D'artello back to Gerrik. "What is it?"

Gerrik looked off into the distance, squinting slightly.

"By Harmony, it is a blaze!" Bensel yelled as he picked up his pace, starting to run slowly in his heavy armor. Gerrik's footsteps followed, surpassing Bensel's easily. Gina followed the two quickly past D'artello, who continued to walk slowly as if he were unaware of the sight. Art rushed past as well to assist his commanding officers.

D'artello reached his right hand into his sheath on the left side of his belt to pull the Molten Steel from its case, examining it as if looking into his own reflection. The sword illuminated the early morning darkness around him. He then lowered his arm to his side and looked off into the distance toward the flames. The group was already yards ahead of him.

He was able to keep up with Gerrik despite the heavy armor on his back. In front of them, the hill seemed to sink as the flames rose upward, belching forth a vicious cloud of smoke blacker than the sky. D'artello and his father stopped to behold the sight, while Gina then Bensel caught up to do very much the same. D'artello dropped his armor to the ground and began to pick the pieces up one by one, placing them onto his body. He pulled the leather lined with silken hairs over his body where appropriate, and it drew an immediate sweat when faced with the fire. Looking back at the Molten Steel, in such a short time it had leapt in brightness from a glow to a shine. He slipped the helmet over his matted hair and rushed straight toward the city.

Gina pushed past Bensel in her haste toward the inferno. The city of Belren, the stop on their march to the capital, was now burning to the ground in front of them. "Go in, check for survivors, be careful, and do not go into any buildings!" Gerrik shouted beginning to run again.

"This ..." Bensel began quietly, "this is the same as my capital, burning completely to the ground."

D'artello burst into the inferno. Wherever he looked there was hot smoke blocking his vision. The static of red, orange, and black was mindboggling at first, especially with the heat tanning his face. The once proud buildings burned like fallen black giants, their crumble hard evidence that this was not a fresh blaze or an exhausting one.

D'artello took a swing at the flames to part them just long enough to reveal the Phantom hiding behind them. It wasted no time either; upon seeing him, it burst through the fire, attacking with a horizontal slash.

D'artello crouched below the swing, bending at the knees gracefully, at which time he heard another noise, like a lion's deep purr. A second Phantom flew out, flanking him from the left by giving a mighty vertical swing of its sword. D'artello struck up the Molten Steel with an ear-piercing clash that even caused the fire to arch and heed its cry. He thwarted the Phantom's attack. He thrust his piston-like leg into the other Phantom that was raising its blade, just about to strike. This would only give him a second before it would recuperate to come after him again.

In one fluid step, he pulled the other sword from his belt and jammed it into the ribs of the Phantom to his left. It backed off in pain, stunned from the impact. D'artello hopped forward, giving an outward flick of the Molten Steel, slicing through the Phantom and turning it to mist. His father's sword dropped suddenly into his hand, just in time for his other opponent to come back for more. A block from his regular sword and then a swing from the Molten Steel made quick work of his careless adversary.

He wasted no time in darting further into the burning city, following the glow of his sword. Meanwhile, Gerrik and Bensel were able to make it into the middle of the town, listening closely for shouts of survivors. Spotting something among the flames, Gerrik called out, "You there! Come here before you burn."

The figure hovered slowly toward him. Like a ghost, no legs and no heed to the hot flames. No human could have restraint enough to pass straight through the fire so ominously. Gerrik took a readied step back, digging his stance into the warm dirt. At the same time, Bensel drew back his sword in his right hand and held his shield out in front of him.

The figure drew closer and closer, and suddenly a slight raspy breath entered their ears from behind. Bensel turned around to face a pair of glowing eyes shaded beneath a thick white cloak. The Phantom lunged into a powerful stab. Without heeding an inch, Bensel blocked the sword with his shield, butting it to the left, leaving his opponent open. He stabbed the sword through its gut and then bashed the Phantom with his shield, sending it hard to its back, cooking over a pile of flames.

Bensel could hear Gerrik struggling. He turned and depressed his wrist, launching the arrow from his gauntlet bow into the head of the other Phantom.

Gerrik had managed to get hold on the arm of the Phantom in front of them. It screamed wildly, trying to free its hand so that it could use its weapon. Gerrik pivoted his body, thrusting his elbow into the monster's gut, causing it to fold around his mighty arm. He stepped backward with his left, letting his weight fall freely, dropping hard onto the Phantom's hunched body. Never letting go of the secured arm, he jumped to his feet and then flipped the limp body over his shoulder, contorting the arm in horrifying ways that would probably tear a man's arm completely off. It smacked against the ground lying motionless.

The pair stood back to back as the Phantoms pincer attacked inward. Gerrik was on guard. His kick sent the Phantom in front of him flying. "They're going to keep coming," Gerrik said.

"We have to look for a way out," Bensel said, blocking the other foe, both persistent beyond death. Gerrik looked around, but it was hard to see through the raging fire. An incoming swing sparked off of Gerrik's bracers as he thwarted another attack from his foe. He threw a stiff arm toward its midsection, hunching it over like a drunk at a bar. He withdrew his attack only to smash against the back of his foe with another hard elbow.

Meanwhile, Gina was just beyond the fire. She could see little of the commotion but knew that Gerrik and Bensel were in trouble. The flames separated the group in a hazardous labyrinth. She looked to her right, spotting a wooden pillar, possibly a support beam for a house that had crumbled around it. Once mighty and unheeding, now it struggled even to support itself. She stood up on her toes to try to peer over the fire to see exactly where her targets were. Having just a rough idea, she bounded over a few piles of flaming debris to reach the pillar.

With both hands, she gave a stone-splitting horizontal chop with her sword. The wood was frail enough to allow the sword to penetrate deep into its body, coughing out embers with each hit. She pulled her sword out, ready for another swing. It was no axe, but in this soft wood, it was easy for her to make progress. One last chop and then she positioned herself behind the wood. "Get out of the way!" she grunted to Bensel and Gerrik as she raised her foot, giving the pillar a mighty kick.

On the other side of the hot colored mosaic, Gerrik and Bensel heeded the sharp cracking noise by leaping to avoid getting trapped by its trajectory. Gerrik grabbed hold of one of the Phantom's arms and flipped it onto the ground right as the giant pillar toppled down on top of it, leaving it pinned under heavy weight.

The pillar had made a convenient bridge, parting the sea of flames, which they both crossed without hesitation just before the heat engulfed it to finish it off. Gina was not on the other side to greet them, however.

Gerrik looked around frantically for her. He did not have much time to consider it, for the pinned Phantom had reawakened. It shrieked angrily, pushing the flaming pillar up with one of its gauntlets. Once on its balance, it grabbed hold of the fallen debris and began to swing it in a circular motion that left the two warriors crouching for their lives.

Gina had come upon a triangular castle in the middle of town. It looked like a flaming centerpiece of the city. The triad of bastions stood to both sides, reaching high up into the air like colossal candles. The castle's stonewalls were spewing fire from each window. It threatened at any moment to melt from the face of the structure.

In front of her was the large wooden gate. Like the blazing mouth of hell, it promised nothing within except more fire. She took a deep breath while deciding she would take that risk for her family that might be trapped inside. Gina took one final breath of outside air and then flew boldly at the door. A forceful splintering noise gave way. Diving into a forward roll, she landed safely in the garden. What would normally be a place of tranquil green colors with perfectly sculpted shrubs looked very much the same as the rest of the town. She ran on a stone path that cut through the forest of flame. To her left, what should have been a statue of Harmony was now a pile of well-carved rubble. Someone or something did not favor the Peacemaker.

To her right was a statue of Peacemaker Unity, still standing tall. He was a powerful-looking man, clad like a gladiator. With a vest and armored leggings, he stood with his great arms crossed in front of him, peering down as if over an entire world from a heavenly height. His long hair hunched over his head, flowing down to his mid back, tracing his cape that boldly streamed from that point to the ground. This pose was often how he was portrayed. He was gallant, righteous, and unforgiving to those with evil souls, but where was he now while his sister crumbled?

She had no time to admire the artwork, but it was a clue as to who conducted this miserable, burning orchestra. She dashed ahead, trying to find the door that would grant her entrance to the castle. The inner cloister of the castle was a triangle pointed in the opposite direction to separate the gardens. She did not know what to expect. Instead of charging through, she managed to dismantle the door almost entirely with her greaves. It seemed that the castle had just begun to catch fire on this side. The hallway was dark but warm, lit subtly by the fires that burned on rugs, tapestries, and décor strewn about. The halls were filled with thick black smoke. She pulled the scruff of her collar up to her nose, breathing through the sweat-ridden fabric.

Realizing the moisture on her brow, she wiped her forehead with the leather part of her gauntlet. She was beginning to feel a little lightheaded, so she decided to walk rather than continue her hustle.

"Gina!" she heard Art call from behind. The skinny man pranced over the fires and crouched beneath the burning beams that Gina could just pass under. He ran toward her shouting, "Don't move! I'm coming to get you! Where are you going?" She turned away from him, and a falling beam stopped him in his tracks. Now, not only did she need to brave the inferno, she also had to do it quickly and tactfully as to avoid being dragged out by Art.

"Mom! Dad!" The heat was staggering and stealing each breath she tried to take. She began to feel weak. Even though the cloth in her armor protected her skin from burning, it was a formidable insulator in an already warm environment. Her sweat drenched almost every inch of the inner fabric, causing further discomfort. She pulled the cloth away from her mouth once more to give another holler at the top of her lungs. "Marie! David!"

She then heard a strong movement somewhere ahead. Something definite, other than flames, it had to be; she was certain of it. Proceeding with caution, coughing the smoke from her lungs, she honed in on that one specific sound. Had she heard it? Had it been there? Was there someone up ahead? "Hello!" she yelled, trying to make her voice distinguishable from the white noise.

An ear-piercing sound startled her, causing her to jump back. Good thing too, because if she hadn't, the sword now sticking from the wall would be in her head. It sawed in and out of the wall, breaking pieces from it with each thrust. Accompanying this noise was the all too familiar acoustic of the Phantom's shrieking voice. It had mauled an opening large enough for its head to snake around the corner at her.

When Gina decided it was a good time to retreat, she was cut off by another Phantom. She ducked under its horizontal swing, and as it went for a swift second strike, Art grabbed it from behind. His arms locked under the Phantom's. He was able to hold it back long enough to shout "Gina! Run!" and allow her escape. In a panic, she did as she was told, running past the other Phantom that was ripping the wall in front of it down. Once it had broken free, it immediately went after its agitated companion. As she darted away, Gina watched the Phantom stab through its comrade mercilessly and frantically to get to Art. She heard him cry out, trying to press on.

Breathing hard in the ash-thick air had put a strain on her running speed.

She was coming upon another large door. This door was finished and coated in steel for extra enforcement. In it she could see herself and the dozen or so Phantoms that had joined the race to catch her. She threw herself at the door, grabbing the handle. It slid easily on its handcrafted hinges, slamming against the inner wall, leaving a mark shaped like the handle. She turned around, thrusting the door shut. A second later, a vicious pounding came from the other side. Slamming louder, pounding like her heart, the Phantoms shrieked like demons. She barred the door and then took a short respite to examine her surroundings.

The tower was airtight to the rest of the castle, having yet to catch fire. At this point, she felt privileged to breathe such comparatively clean air through her fearful sobs. She looked up four stories worth of spiral staircase at a crystalline, pyramidal chandelier. It was jagged with hundreds of tiny mirrors, hanging in the cross section of four windows. Normally the ornament would reflect the sun from the outside to light the dark tower, but at night, if not for the light of the fires outside, it would be pitch black in there. It had always frightened her when she was a child.

With just a brief hesitation, she ran quickly toward the staircase. Due to her haste, her boot did not quite catch the first stair, and with a sharp slip, she slammed her shin hard on its unforgiving stone edge. She rolled onto her back for a minute, holding it tight and trying to suppress the pain, clenching her teeth. The impact hit in just the right place to leave a sizeable dent in the leg piece. Lifting her chin to look back, she could see the door hinges beginning to give way to the relentless rapping.

She rolled to her feet, putting both her hands on the next step and beginning to limp upward toward the next floor. Once there, she flung the door open, only to unveil a hallway filled to capacity with flames. The heat nearly bowled her over the side of the railing, plummeting to her death, before she shut the door. Upon doing so, she heard the heavy door below slap to the ground. The Phantoms began to pour through. Sick with rage, they flew straight up at her in their ghostly fashion. She continued to climb as fast as her injury would let her.

She felt a cold fright as one approached, sounding out with an unholy cry. Her sword came screaming from its sheath, guided only by reflex. The Phantom went immediately on the attack.

Running would prove futile. She paused and hunted her opening. Sure enough, an overhead swing came her way. She leaned her body to dodge it, causing her assailant's sharp blade to get its steel teeth stuck in the wall. She pulled the Phantom in by the muffler scarf that covered its face. Her sword thrust in and out of its would-be neck. The stunned, limp body fell onto one of its flailing kin, ensnaring two more in the frantic descent, catching them off guard pulling them all toward the floor. Without looking down to see the effects, she limped up to her next exit.

She ripped it open, stepped inside, and then quickly socked it shut and slammed the bar down. This hallway burned subtly as her first impression of the castle did. She began to shout again, "Mom! Dad! Marie! David!" She began to hack.

The walls were lined with elongated arches, almost like a church. The enormous windows were yet unbroken. She used to spend much of her time here, gawking at and dreaming of the training grounds. This was where she would watch the soldiers practice and show off their masculine talents, forbidden disciplines she'd wished to acquire.

During her abrupt reminiscence, between her injured leg and the strangling smoke, she was growing very weak. Her body encouraged her to lie down, to sleep as the heat pressed on her. Her run sputtered to a walk, and her short breaths strained her muscles. Her armor felt so very heavy. Falling to her good knee, she sheathed her sword as if conceding defeat, soon after falling to her stomach.

Phantoms began to come down the far end of the hall. The Phantoms behind her would make quick work of that wooden door. Soon there would be no escape. Just before her fading breath, her eyes stayed open long enough to see D'artello burst through a window to her left with the shining sword in his hand.

The Phantoms were immediately drawn to the Molten Steel like moths to a flame. D'artello, facing the direction of the tower, glanced behind him to see the crowd of Phantoms lunging in, and an exhausted, unconscious Gina before him. The hallway had turned out to be an excellent place for him to make his stand as only two Phantoms at a time could come at him from either direction proficiently. The Phantoms were cautious at first, examining the sword as if it were some strange form of life. Their hollowed eyes were fixed on it, giving him enough time to pull his second sword from his sheath.

It did not take them long to rush at him recklessly, snapping from their hypnotized fascination into fierce anger. He blocked one while stepping to the left. His leg unwound from the cross-stance and slammed into the next one, sending it smashing through the window opposite the one he'd entered. In one motion, the Molten Steel went through the blocked Phantom, and was thrown at the Phantom he had just kicked out the window, turning them both to black mist.

The remaining Phantoms surrounded him. D'artello evaded a slice from his left by pushing forward, his shoulder abreast the Phantom. He had to move again as another attack came from his right. He tossed his arm behind his head to block a rear attack with his father's sword. One of them had snuck in beside him, in front of the window from which he hurled his precious Molten Steel. Calling the sword back, he reached his hand in that direction. Faithfully, the weapon came flying back through the window and the Phantom adversary.

Two swords back in hand now, he leaned forward and stabbed the Phantom directly in front of him with his father's sword, and then he turned around quickly to slice the one behind him that was readying itself for another swing. He followed the motion through, cutting the one with the sword stuck in it and causing the other sword to fall past the ethereal mist and into his palm, placed aptly behind his back. The rest crawled on him like a swarm of ants, but their efforts were futile; they were unable to overcome him in his soullessness. The lack of hesitation and untiring motion made him into an autonomous slayer. His actions were so certain, like instinct resonating from every fiber of a wild animal.

Each Phantom dropped after its predecessor. Truly a testament to the victims they had claimed before, a testament to humanity's strength. The commotion caused more Phantoms dwelling in the castle to stir and meet him on this narrow pass. It was risky, but the fact that there was only room for two at a time to come at him made little difference to his adversaries.

They were so adamant about trying to shred their foe that they pushed and shoved to get their chance. More came in from the windows, and the clustering made them easier for D'artello to manage.

Even though his soulless motivation told him to take the fight to a more open-ended battlefield, such as the training grounds, somewhere he would have the space to move around or escape if need be, he would not leave until Gina was safe. He'd slain dozens thus far, but as the endless supply continued to pour in from all sides, the castle would tolerate such a rumble less and less.

As for the hallway itself, it began to shake while the whole structure gave its death rattle. Flames began to breathe through the floor, igniting the carpet in certain spots while the smoke grew thicker. D'artello found himself getting a little short of breath. He slew another Phantom in the hallway and turned around, sheathing both of his weapons. He slid his arms under the motionless Gina, one supporting her back and the other under her knees. He knew that more were coming, but he could ignore the impending danger of staying in the burning castle no longer.

He flew as fast as his feet could carry him toward the next tower where he would make his escape from the flames that were reaching for him like greedy hands.

Meanwhile, Gerrik and Bensel had taken their fight out of the town. They had made it all the way to the other side onto the fields that lay to the south of the giant bonfire. On their way, they had attracted the attention of several more Phantoms. The old soldiers took them on well, holding their ground and avoiding the attacks at all costs. "I guess this is it!" Bensel shouted over blocking then cutting one down only to take on the next.

"Just hold on, Bensel!" Gerrik said. "D'artello will come!"

"Right. Remember to stay optimistic," he shot back.

The Phantoms backed off suddenly, encircling the two men, standing still like a forest with eyes. Bensel and Gerrik did not let their guards down. They looked back toward the blaze to see D'artello, and in his wake were the flames that promised to reduce the rest of the city to ashes. His arms cradled Gina. Black soot war paint was blotched across their faces. His brow was low, as if he were beginning to experience disdain for his foes, the first facial expression any of them had seen in days.

The crowd of Phantoms moved in unison, stampeding toward him as they all howled. "Bensel! He can't defend himself!" Gerrik yelled, beginning to run behind the white cloaks. Bensel picked up speed as well, but the two could never hope to be fast enough.

A sound pierced the sky, a loud thundering cry. Then like lightning appeared a magnificent beast standing as a stone guardian between D'artello and the crowd of ravenous Phantoms. On its back was a giant of an armor-clad man, wielding a great claymore in his right hand to show his youthful power. The beast resembled a mighty stallion with crow's wings. They outstretched more than twenty-five feet while it perched up on its hind legs, kicking its two front sets.

"A slepne!" Gerrik called out.

Seated atop it, skillfully pulling the reins, was a man clad in the signature red Genzak armor. His helm covered his face with slanted, intimidating eyeholes and an open mouth area. A spike thrust to the heavens from its top. Near the rear of the animal, gripping the rider tightly, was a young woman with long blonde hair, dressed in an accentuating sleeveless white blouse and brown leggings, with a lavish pink drape that covered her right leg all the way to the ground.

"Sir Elan! Sandra!" Bensel called out.

"Hold on," D'artello heard the rider say.

The animal gave a hard flap that pounded the air around it enough to give lift straight into the thirty or so Phantoms. The rider held out his claymore as the animal went into a daring corkscrew dive, cleaving away and stunning each Phantom that the blade passed through.

This maneuver bought Gerrik enough time to retrieve Gina from D'artello. No sooner did he begin to run away did D'artello have to pull his father's sword from its sheath and halt one of the savage beasts. His teeth clenched now while he kicked it back. He pulled the shining sword and began to use them both in unison. Blocking with one, slicing with the other, he had to be careful as these foes were always on the attack.

He jumped backward, trying not to get surrounded as he herded them back toward the blaze. With only about a third of them occupied by Sir Elan's effort, that left the rest to take any tactical advantage over the young warrior. D'artello would not let up though. As they began to surround him, his blades whirled around faster. He killed three more in a uniform fashion as the others began to learn his pattern and fight more defensively.

Gerrik put Gina down next to Bensel and then ran back to help his son. Taking a short hop to get his momentum going, he leapt through the air, landing on one of the Phantoms, planting his right foot square in its back. Without words, the father-son duo worked as one. While D'artello defended himself, Gerrik pounded and threw the Phantoms into him so that he could get a cheap shot with the Molten Steel.

Five Phantoms later, some of them began to turn on Gerrik. With little surface area, his bracers did not block so many attacks gracefully. He was unsure how long he could keep this up, much less strike back. Fed up finally, the Phantoms began to use their fists as well as their swords. The two weren't ready for it. Gerrik and D'artello were taken off their feet by the super strong foes. Just as a Phantom was about to bring its sword down on Gerrik, a whizzing sound was heard coming from Elan's side. An arrow pierced the air and the head of the Phantom.

Another arrow came to aid D'artello. This momentary distraction was enough to let them get to their feet to keep fighting. When they had gotten a chance to look, they saw the blonde girl, Sandra, with a longbow standing next to Bensel. Her accuracy was as gorgeous as she was. She pulled each arrow with such serene grace, letting it fly freely into the bodies of their ghostly foes. Bensel too fired his small arrows from his wrist-mounted bow, pulling them from a deposit in his leg armor.

D'artello immediately laid waste to the arrow-stunned Phantoms and then continued to fight his remaining four. As more arrows came, more Phantoms fell. Soon Gerrik and D'artello had cleaned up the fight. This left only the Phantoms that Elan had stunned.

Elan had landed among them, proudly examining his own work, his own killing art. "Elan! Get out of there!" Bensel yelled. It was too late. The Phantoms were already beginning to get back up for revenge. Off guard, his Slepne took a hit, causing it to panic. Thrown from its back, he had no time at all before they dove all over him. He managed to fight most of them off but did not get away unscathed.

Left with his cuts, the Phantoms backed off for a moment as D'artello had seen them do when he was cut across the chest. Elan had wounds on each of his arms, right through the metal plates of his gauntlets, one across his face, and one across his chest. The saw-toothed blades had ripped the armor open like tissue paper.

"Elan!" Sandra screamed as he stood in shock, not lifting his sword. Dropping his claymore like it was on fire, he immediately flung his hands to his face and began screaming. His cuts felt like they were being cauterized. It was as if his flesh was burning. He fell to his knees, screaming louder and louder.

"D'artello!" Gerrik began. He was already on top of it though. He cut his way through the remaining Phantoms that were fascinated with their work. By the time the group had turned from this spectacle, they were too easily dismissed.

"Elan!" Sandra yelled, taking life and limb to run toward the group. The young and spry blonde was too fast for Bensel to stop. Upon hearing her voice, Elan became enraged and rose from his fetal position. His shoulders were hunched over his maddened grin. Elan let out an inhuman roar. Preoccupied, D'artello could not prevent the tainted lover from pursuing his former mate. Elan took off with sword in hand to meet his beloved in the middle of the battlefield.

Quickly realizing that her dear Sir Elan was no more, Sandra began to run in the other direction. He chased her ravenously back toward Bensel, who stood with his sword at the ready to protect his daughter. Sandra hid behind her father as the brute stepped in with tree-chopping force in a hard swing. Bensel blocked it with his sword and shield, using both hands to cushion the impact of the much heavier weapon.

Pushing the sword to the side, Bensel readied for a stab, but Elan had already redrawn his attack, much quicker than Bensel could have anticipated. Just before the blade was about to fall, the Molten Steel came thrusting through Elan's chest. Sandra screamed at the sight of her impaled companion.

D'artello grabbed him by the shoulder and ripped him backward. As Elan stumbled in shock, D'artello delivered a back kick that thrust him violently to the ground. Sandra ran out from behind Bensel to Elan's aid. D'artello grabbed her wrist, halting her suddenly.

She stopped and stared at his eyes for a moment, long enough to realize that something about him was very strange. He said nothing and simply pointed to Elan's chest, where the wound should have been. Upon further examination, she realized that he was still breathing, that Elan seemed to be perfectly fine. He let her go so that she could kneel by his side and see his breaths. She looked back at D'artello once more and said, "Thank you."

"Sandra, my daughter," Bensel said, opening his arms and dropping his sword.

Once she was sure that Elan was okay, she looked into the eyes of her old dad. Rising, she entered his arms and threw hers around him as well. "Daddy, I'm so glad you're safe," she said.

Chapter 8

A couple hours later, the sun had risen to its morning roost; it was the dawn of a new day, choking away the darkness. Elan rubbed his eyes, gave a loud yawn, and stretched his arms. "My king, it eases my sorrow to see that you are alive," he said.

"I am glad to see you as well, my loyal vassal. Thank you for bringing my beloved Sandra safely back to me."

"Please, Daddy, I saved Sir Elan enough times as well," she said, crossing her arms.

Elan's hand flew to his head, "Oww," he began. "My head ... what the hell happened? I remember fighting those ghostly figures and ... Oh my Harmony! Thunder!" he called out, clenching his teeth as his headache drilled in. Making clicking sounds with his tongue, he looked around for his faithful steed. After seeing it and breathing a sigh of relief, he walked off toward D'artello, who was trying to pet the jet-black animal on the nose.

The slepne did not panic, but it seemed to back out of his reach and purposely avoid eye contact. "Thunder," Elan said, then making the clicking sound. The animal immediately turned its attention to him and trotted over, allowing itself to be groomed by its master's touch.

D'artello just stood watching, his eyes fixed on nothing in particular. "Thank you, warrior," Elan said finally. "If not for you, those creatures would have killed us."

"Not killed," D'artello said simply, looking up at the sky dreamily. As odd as this was, his sense of awe at the sky was the most human thing he'd done in quite some time.

Elan timidly directed his attention back toward the other survivors.

Among them, he recognized Gerrik instantly. "Oh my Harmony!" he said with the excitement of a little girl.

Gina's bare leg lay in Gerrik's hands. Once the dented leg piece was off and the pants were pulled up, the hideous bruise reared its ugly black, blue, and red centered head. Gerrik thumbed in circles to feel the bone. Gina cringed at his strong pressure. "Hold still now," he said, closing his eyes to concentrate. "Good news: it's not broken, but you're going to walk funny for a while. Your armor wasn't so lucky." He motioned to the piece with the stair-shaped dent in it. Gina's face showed little interest in the dent or the joke.

"You are Sir Gerrik?" Elan asked finally.

"Yes," Gerrik responded, not even turning to look at him, but instead continuing to check the bone.

Elan paused for politeness, but he could not control his excitement. "I have looked forward to this day almost all my life. Your exploits are legendary," he said.

He put Gina's leg down and stood up abruptly. "Look …," he began.

"Why, it was you and my very own king who held back an entire army alone. You felled almost half of them by the time reinforcements arrived. Wonderful!" Elan interrupted.

"Now listen," he tried to say kindly, as his son was in earshot for these stories.

"The epic battle of Vaukry's independence, it was your tactical genius that led your regimen to victory," he said. "During the darkest hour, it was you, your strength, your sword that—"

"That's enough," Gerrik stopped him, taking a quick glance to see if D'artello was looking. "What I did, had to be done; otherwise I wouldn't have done it," he said, as if Elan's words of praise were a persecution. With that, Elan stood puzzled as his childhood hero walked over to D'artello.

Much a mystery to everyone around him, Gerrik never talked about his past or his war days with anyone except Bensel. Not even D'artello knew the vivid details of what happened during those years.

"I apologize for the disrespect, sir," Elan said, turning and giving a salute to his back. He watched him put a hand on D'artello's shoulder. Eager now to change the subject he looked down at Gina who lay flat on the ground with her hands folded over her chest, as if she were to be buried.

"Such is the glory of being a knight," Elan began with a sigh. He turned to look over the smoldering city. It had burned all night long as the group collected themselves. Now the ashes smoldered quietly, extinguishing the last evidence of human inhabitance.

"That was my town," Gina said, her eyes welling up.

"Aye," Elan said, "there is no looking back." His armor clacked as he sat down next to her.

"No bodies though," she said. "So maybe everyone is still alive somewhere. Maybe they just burned the village down and took everyone hostage to the capital or something. Sir, I ask you to leave me," she said rolling over onto her side so she could sob in peace.

Even though she could not see it, he gave a slow nod and got up, beginning to walk away. He overheard the conversation between D'artello and his father. "The source must die," he heard the boy say.

"D'artello I don't know if we can keep going like this. We've lost all of our men, and we have no provisions. Son, please come out of it."

"The … Source?" Elan asked. After a brief pause, he said, "Ah, King Garo, the scoundrel of a war monger he is, burning this town to the ground. Death will be fulfilled; no forgiveness." He raised a fist into the air, expecting to rally D'artello. Of course nothing came of it. D'artello merely kept his vision in the same direction as if watching a ghost drift across the field.

Gerrik walked away shaking his head, moving to talk to Bensel, who was entertained with the quiver and bow strapped to his daughter's back. "Sandra, where did you get that?"

"Oh this? Sir Elan gave it to me. He said it belonged to his grandfather," she said. "Daddy, I know how to shoot the bow," Sandra protested with her father's arms positioning hers. She was a childhood friend of D'artello's and any friend of his shared an enthusiasm for adventure. Sandra was a princess, but certainly Bensel's daughter when it came to her raw audacity and independence.

"Now, now, just trust your old man," he assured her. "Your aim is good, but your technique needs a little work."

"Ben!" Gerrik called.

"Hmm?" he responded without looking up. "Hold on a second, Gerrik," he said as he saw Elan approaching. "Elan," he called.

"Yes, sire," he said kneeling.

"Elan, I'm going to tell you what I told Gina; I do not want your formalities," Bensel grunted.

"Sire, I do not understand."

"There really isn't a Genzak kingdom anymore. I have no loyal subjects. I have to come to terms with this and don't need a constant reminder," he explained.

"I am your loyal subject forever, my lord," Elan said.

"Get a brain of your own," Bensel said out of frustration.

Taking no offense, Elan continued to argue, "With respect, Your Highness, that is why I am a great commander in the Genzak army, sir."

Bensel could see that he was getting nowhere fast; one could not become a renowned tactician as he was without having a great wit. "Well, if you are so loyal, then I hereby order you to be at ease and forget your formalities," he ordered, folding his arms behind his back.

Elan was dumbfounded at the nature of his orders. "O-okay, sir?" he said as if it were a question. "No, wait, that's not right ... a thousand pardons, Your Higness."

"Enough, Elan. I have a question to ask you. Did the other soldiers ever make it to the capital? When did you separate from them?"

"Separate, sir?"

That response caught the attention of Gerrik and D'artello as well. Sandra strutted over beside Elan, before her father. "We were attacked. The scoundrels came in droves of thousands, too many for myself and those lawless mercenaries," he said looking down.

"Elan, you had two thousand men under your command, the last of my elite guard," Bensel stated, lowering his tone and leaning forward, smelling a lie.

"My king, that was irrelevant at the time," Elan answered, staring straight ahead and sticking his chest out.

Bensel's eyes widened, and his lips tightened. "Wh-What did you just say?"

"The soldiers were irrelevant," he repeated.

Bensel turned his back for a second and scratched his beard. "Why is that?" he asked, turning back around to face his elite commander.

"Sir Elan and I were off in the woods, Daddy," Sandra butted in.

Elan placed a hand across her chest. "I will tell him," he said.

"Tell me what, boy?" he asked harshly.

"I wish to have the princess's hand in marriage," he finally said, his resolve unchanging.

"So let me get this straight," Bensel said, walking toward him. Elan backed up as Sandra watched on. "Even if I didn't care, *and* I do, you left your post and the entire army to make off with my daughter?"

Sandra could see where this was going all too quickly. "Daddy, no, I ..." she swallowed hard as her father's gaze met hers. "I love Sir Elan. He and I have known one another since childhood and we have grown fond after all we have been through," she explained. "He is the man I want to marry, and he will gladly take on your legacy better than any other man in the kingdom. I love him Daddy," she pleaded with her hands out in front of her.

"You left those men for the slaughter," Bensel said. "It doesn't matter how much you *love* each other, I can't believe this."

"Sire, please," Elan began. "Those men were crude and hardly loyal—"

"Elan, you defied my orders," Bensel said. "Do you have any idea what you've cost what's left of the Genzak nation? Perhaps the world?"

"Father, please, you have to forgive Sir Elan because your first order was to protect me," Sandra reminded him.

"What are you talking about?" Bensel asked.

"You really have no quarrels about sending me off with those mindless scoundrels? They looked at me like I was a piece of meat. You are lucky that Elan was the strongest of them. If not for his bravery, I would have been violated. He was so very close, Daddy, and it didn't matter to him how many times I said no."

"What?" he said, looking at his commander.

"Just as it looked bleakest," she said, "Sir Elan burst through the entrance to my tent and pulled the knave off of me."

"Is this true?" Bensel said, lightening his tone.

Elan nodded carefully. "Although that went well, it did not sit with the rest of the camp. After I pulled him from the tent, he kept coming, and soon the entire camp was on his side. He was a widely respected warrior in their minds. Humiliating him in front of the crowd only made matters worse. I did the only thing I thought I should have done; I scooped her up in my arms and called Thunder to my side, and we fled the camp. I assume they were attacked soon after, as we approached the deserted camp just hours later."

"Ben, we need to talk for a moment ... privately," Gerrik said, as Sandra eyed her uncle figure.

Bensel bid leave to the conversation, though not without vowing his return to it. "D'artello wants to go on. There is no convincing him otherwise," Gerrik said.

"Gerrik, we have no supplies and no men."

"I know, that's what I told him, but he will still go."

"You expect me to drag my very own daughter into battle?" Bensel said. "Since when did you become so soft? Since when do you let your son make your decisions for you?"

"You don't understand what is going on here, Ben."

"Like hell I don't!" he whispered loudly. "I followed you into every stupid, daring, life-risking fray that you just couldn't avoid. He's like you; he is not thinking of risk, only the fight. You haven't done your job as the boy's father to keep him out of business like this."

"That hurts, Ben," Gerrik said, pausing a moment to reflect on that remark. "I feel the loss for my guard boys, and I know I am asking too much of you again, old friend, but I am trapped here. Surely you can see that."

Bensel stood listening, his arms crossed, waiting to hear a good reason.

"D'artello is a man now," Gerrik said. "I can't stop him, but I can still go with him."

"This isn't your fight!" Bensel said. "Haven't those Phantoms, or whatever they are, made that clear to you? You can't kill them; only he can. Otherwise you'd have that sword."

"Is that how you feel about all of this? It's not our fight? Then why did you seek me out in the first place?" Gerrik asked.

Bensel opened his mouth to respond, but his words fled when he realized there was nothing he could say to that except: "If I were you, Gerrik, I would take your child and run for your life. This is the battle to end all battles."

"Look at your daughter," Gerrik said, motioning to Sandra practicing her shot according to her father's instruction. "She made her choice when she picked up that weapon, her choice to fight. I can see it in her eyes, in Elan's eyes as well. Their kingdom, their young hearts broken over the only home they've ever known. Backed into a corner, even the youth know that they must fight. To see their king give up would crush them. Don't think I can't see what you've been doing here. 'Stop the formalities, you say, as if you were some helpless peasant. In all reality, you are hiding, denying responsibility for a problem too large for you to take on. Like it or not, you are Bensel, lord and king of the Genzak nation, and these youths all look at you that way. You are still my companion, even in our aged state, you are still the warrior—no, brother—that I need by my side."

Meanwhile Gina had gained enough strength to stand and limp over to D'artello. The pain was harsh, it still being a fresh bruise. He ignored her hand on his shoulder she used to brace herself on his strong frame so she could stand without stumbling. "What is going on here, D'artello?" she asked. When he couldn't even be bothered to look her way, she began to get irritated.

"C'mon, I know that *you* know something. That was my town back there," she said as her eyes burst into tears. "My parents, my family … D'artello, please tell me they are going to be okay. Tell me that you can help them." She clutched his shirt and plunged her face into it. With her flat palms she gave a couple of hard pounds to his chest, but they didn't seem to faze him. A feeling inside made her long for her hero, for someone to be there for her, for D'artello to caress her then and there. As her hopes that her parents lived on died, her hopes of D'artello's empathy did as well.

She hugged his body around the waist and sniffled a bit, trying to calm her nerves. His hands clenched her shoulders suddenly and pushed her away. He stared into her eyes. To everyone else, he was being his new usual self, but she saw his eyes meant to say indeed, "Everything is going to be all right." Though very little emanation came from his soulless body, she drew as much as she could from those tiny messages in his stare.

"I-I'm sorry, D'artello," she said after a moment. She limped from his grasp and let herself tumble gently to her back, lying on the cool grass. She looked up at him now. In her mind, she acknowledged that he'd saved her life by pulling her from the burning castle, and for that she was grateful. Asking him to save her parents was asking too much; it wasn't his fault they were gone.

He sat down beside her and whether it happened by accident or not, his hand fell on hers, not gripping it, just simply lying atop it. Almost instantly, she arrested it and clasped it against her chest, embracing it, wishing more of it, and looking at his neutral expression with her tired eyes. It was hardly a substitute for comfort, but it would have to do for now.

Gerrik called out to them, interrupting her moment. "We're gonna get going. We have to make it to the bridge by sundown. I will carry Gina because I don't have armor weighing me down. Pick up your things. Elan, get that slepne ready to leave." He was in his commander mode, barking out orders to avoid more conversation. He trotted over and hoisted Gina up with one arm under her knees and the other supporting her upper back.

Beyond Gerrik's shoulder, Gina got the last look at her beloved Belren she would ever have. She hoped for her parents' survival, but after seeing Art's helpless struggle and Elan's sudden transformation, she began to doubt their safety with a degree of certainty. Between the hours of early morning and high noon they had made it a few long miles into the woods south of Belren. The group now headed southwest toward the bridge back to Vaukry.

In the distance, they could hear the rapids of the river. At Fort Carrie, it was responsible for Battalion Bluff, but it dove due south whereas the group had traveled southeast. Eventually it would catch up with them by banking southeast, forming the mouth, over which the bridge to the capital stood. They were close. For Sandra and Gina, there was no time, only night and day. The other warriors were far more experienced and could tell the sun's daily lifespan. Sundown was about eight hours off.

Gerrik carried Gina through the woods. She was comfortable enough despite the rustling from the foliage underfoot and the wind flapping through the trees. Here was her hero, a man so powerful and revered that an entire world knew of his exploits. *With so many casualties under his belt, I would think it would have driven him insane,* she thought. *I thought through my training that I wanted to be just like Sir Gerrik, but he is human too. There are things about his past that bother him. Harmony teaches us not to hold personal conviction and progress spiritually, but Gerrik. Is this the fate of a warrior who does not lose their mind? A regretful man?*

Gina took a moment to reflect on her earlier days in the Genzak army. She remembered what it was like to take a life, every detail of it. *He was a thief who had never really stolen much, just a little every time. At first he was nothing more than a nuisance, a street vermin. The man was stealing to survive, just some bread and the occasional dwelling. These habits evolved, however. Probably sick of being chased away from the bread stands, he turned to mugging travelers. He found it easier to steal money to buy things.*

When I finally caught up with him, the young fool decided that he had nothing else to live for if he were to go to prison. He resisted, and I killed him. That ruby red liquid dripping down my sword and his limp body lying over me, still I wake in the night, she retold the story to herself. *I have taken other lives since, but none of them easy, and this one sticking out in particular. Maybe Elan is right, "such is the glory of a knight,"* she pondered. *Gerrik has had to do this multiple times. I wonder how he feels about it. Was I even cut out to be a knight? Should I have just stayed to become a baby-making housewife to a wealthy lord the way my parents had wanted it?*

"Sir Gerrik?" she said.

"Hm?" he said, taking his eyes off the path and then looking down at her. He was tired too. She could see the weakening resolve in his gaze, though he cradled her still in stiff biceps.

"Why …" She swallowed hard, afraid to ask the question after Elan had gotten his head bitten off about the topic. "Why did you become a soldier?"

"That … is a good question," he said, contemplating it. "For a number of reasons. To protect my country and my family, to find myself, and for a woman," he answered. "But you have to understand that back then it was a different time. When I came of age, this whole continent was at war, and the enemy was right over the wall. You really didn't have to go anywhere to see a massacre or marauders coming through the town taking money and women as they pleased. I wanted to oppose them. I really wanted to be the savior. And there were many of us who felt this way. I was just one of the lucky ones," he explained.

"Wow," she said. "Your reason is way better than mine," she admitted, thinking of her parents.

"I have seen worse men enlist for lesser reasons, I am sure, or women I suppose," he corrected himself, giving her a teasing wink. "Think you can keep up?" he asked. She nodded her head. He let her down, and she began to limp quickly toward the front to meet with D'artello.

She turned and said, "Thank you," before hobbling away.

As she walked by, Bensel gave a heavy yawn. The lack of sleep was beginning to wear down the whole group. It had been almost an entire day and night's passing since they'd had food, and even longer had they gone without sleep. Astoundingly, it was harder on the younger soldiers. Gerrik and Bensel pressed on hard like true seasoned veterans. They had straight marching posture while Elan slouched under his armor and Sandra leaned forward on the neck of the slepne, resting her eyes. Whether or not D'artello was feeling the effects was as most things were, uncertain.

There came a rustling from above in the branches. The only ones who noticed the sound were Gerrik and Bensel. Gina walked silently beside D'artello for a little while, about ten minutes or so before she got the strange feeling of stage fright. As if many eyes were on her. She glanced up at the trees and around the canopy. She looked back at the rest of the group to see that Elan continued his trot and Sandra had now fallen asleep on top of Thunder. Bensel and Gerrik remained poised but vigilant. Not once did they turn their heads, yet they scrutinized the canopy.

A loud snap cut the silence, and without warning, a rope tightened around Thunder's ankle. With a whizzing, the unsuspecting animal was hoisted high up into the air. The slepne gave a frightened neigh, struggling frantically to gnaw at the rope. It flapped its wings heavily, trying to pull itself loose. "Thunder!" Elan cried out for his mount. He knew that the thrashing about would only hurt it. The rope trap was slung over a thick tree branch like a pulley and trailed off behind the brush. Sandra jumped to her feet, startled by the suddenness of being thrown off of the animal. She looked and stumbled about for a moment, collecting her thoughts.

"Oh no, Thunder," she said. "Get him down, Elan, before he hurts himself."

Distracted by the spectacle, Gerrik let a sword sneak around in front of his neck, but not before he secured the arm holding it in his powerful grip. With a sharp twist of his waist, the man came tumbling over his shoulder, flat onto his back. His attacker was clad in a black hood that made the face unrecognizable. Bearing the signature red Genzak plate gave away his identity. They were being attacked by the remnants of the Genzak royal guard.

Gina yelped as a sword came swinging toward her face. Luckily, D'artello was far quicker than the hooded assailant in front of him. Managing to draw his sword, he thwarted the attack. D'artello kicked the man's exposed upper body ferociously, sending him off of his feet and into a tree just behind him. The man's head violently jerked back and whipped against the bark. This sent a shockwave to his limbs, causing his body to come to rest in a heap on the ground.

With little time to avoid it, they were surrounded by hooded men clad in the familiar red armor. "Wait!" Bensel cried out. "These are my men!" he desperately shouted. The encirclement of hooded mercenaries stood still with their weapons in hand, ready to kill at any moment. Everyone on the offside except Bensel stood ready, waiting for a struggle even though the troops were familiar.

"I don't think that matters anymore, Ben," Gerrik said, never once taking his eyes off them.

"Release me! Animal!" they heard Sandra call from behind. They turned to see a wiry, shirtless, man holding a knife firmly to her throat.

"Sandra!" Elan yelled. "If you hurt her, soldier, you are all dead men," he swore, holding his sword at the ready.

"What is the meaning of this?" Bensel asked.

Only maddening chuckles answered his question. Breaking the inhuman laughter was a deep masculine voice. "We need that Molten Steel, old king."

"Seraph!" Gerrik and Bensel exclaimed. The crowd parted abruptly and stood at broken attention, letting an aged man through. He had jet-black hair that reached his mid-back, and he bore the very same red armor of the Genzaks.

"I'm flattered you remember me, Gerrik, but I'm not looking for a fight today," he said, staring D'artello's father down.

"That's enough," D'artello sounded. "You are in the way. This is your last warning to back down."

"Quiet, boy, the adults are talking," Seraph rebutted. "My demands are simple—the princess's neck for the Molten Steel."

"What?" Bensel asked.

"That boy over there carries it," he said, pointing to D'artello.

"Seraph! Release the princess right now, or you will kneel before the king with your last breath," Elan threatened.

"You are in no position to make threats, whelp," he responded.

"That's commander to you!" he shot back.

"You've been overthrown, you pompous idiot. While you were out gallivanting with the princess, horrible creatures attacked us. We lost so many men, and for what? Time to find out … you will hand over the Molten Steel or we will take it," he commanded.

"How is it that you know of the Molten Steel?" Gerrik asked curiously.

"An axe-wielding man from Fort Carrie. He also told us that it is the only weapon capable of defeating those creatures. To leave it with you, such a small group, would only allow humanity to fall into the wrong hands, so just hand it over."

D'artello dug his foot into the ground, determined to have them try to take it from his cold dead hands.

Gerrik looked over at his son. He knew that D'artello would never let it go, not without dying first. He would have to talk his way out of this one.

"Still playing war hero?" Gerrik asked sarcastically.

"Many men died at the end of my blade, surely as many as the *great* King Bensel. I taught *you* how to kill for Harmony's sake, and look at what became of that," Seraph pointed out. "Can you deny that kind of credibility, the title of war hero?"

"Hmph, that's not what I was talking about. You always had a thing for women that said no," he remarked.

"I deserved it after the conditions I had to live through. You should have tried it sometime, Gerrik. It's the thrill that makes it more fun."

"That's all it ever was to you, huh?" Gerrik asked. "Just some thrill? You don't know what it's like to fight without a choice. That's why you are no hero. Now let us pass."

Seraph's face evolved from smirk to toothy grin. "We can sit here debating my role as a hero, letting more towns and more of the countryside be ravaged by those white-cloaked barbarians, or we can get down to business and you can hand that Molten Steel to the only worthy man left to wield it. Think about it, Gerrik. You laid down the sword long ago. At least that's what the rumors say. And this broken king is no more fit to touch it than the boy who holds it now." He took a few steps forward.

Without warning, Gerrik dropped his stance and swept Seraph's leg from underneath him, causing him to fall clumsily to the ground. It all happened too fast; the seasoned vet was unable to react in time. "D'artello! Take Gina and run!" Gerrik shouted.

Seraph didn't even hesitate. "Stop him!" he called out. By the time he'd blurted the order, there were already three men barring the escape path. Trained killers as they were, they were still no match for D'artello's unhesitant nature or his fighting skill. Making quick work of them, he tugged Gina by the wrist and darted into the cover of the trees.

"Get up! Go after him!" Seraph commanded, standing up and then slugging Gerrik hard across the face. "You old fool, don't you see that I will readily kill the princess?"

Gerrik spat the blood from his lip and stood right in Seraph's face. He could tell that even this hardened man was slightly intimidated when staring *him* in the eyes. "You know as well as I do that you wouldn't dare. You know that if you kill her, you will have to kill me too. Should you be so lucky. D'artello certainly isn't going to trade that sword for our corpses. Killing us is not a move you can afford to make."

Seraph stood clenching his teeth and fists for a moment. "Let me tell you something. When your son comes back for you, I will kill him too. All you've managed to do here is buy some time and anger me into killing the boy. I will make you look him in the eye before I take his head off." He spat at Gerrik's feet.

"We will take them to the prison," Seraph grunted to the men around him. "Take their weapons!" he commanded. "Hand them over willingly or the princess dies, even if we have to face you, Gerrik."

Galtaria Prison? Gerrik thought as he looked at Bensel, whom he was sure was thinking the same. *How will D'artello find us now?* It was time to devise his own plan and quick, but how?

"Do not let go of the princess," Seraph barked. He stared Gerrik down a moment as if to curse him. Then he took one step away, and then he turned and delivered a sucker punch with his shield to Gerrik's stomach, causing him to fold over a little and grunt. "So help me, old man, if I get that weapon, I will kill you and everyone else here," he threatened.

"Just kill them, Daddy! Don't worry about me!" Sandra yelled. The men had begun to collect the weapons and cut the still hanging Thunder down. Somehow even the animal knew that this was not the time to resist.

That punch hurt, but Gerrik knew that he had to take it. He had to do anything just to know that no one would die. *I hope I'm right, D'artello is strong enough, there's no doubt, but he is not himself. Hopefully Gina can convince him to return for us.* The fact that his own son would need any sort of convincing to consider a rescue hurt much more than the hit from the shield. For now, he had done his part.

* * *

D'artello darted through the trees, holding Gina by the hand. The men were catching up fast due to Gina's lingering inability to run. He took a sharp turn that whipped Gina behind him as he secured a thick tree branch. He bent it backward and waited for his prey to run by.

Not seconds later came the thick rustling as the first chaser jumped over and sliced through foliage. D'artello waited in silence and then put a finger up to his lip for Gina to quiet her breaths as well. Just as he was thundering through, D'artello let go of the tree branch and it snapped back, taking the man clear off his feet and breaking his nose.

D'artello leapt on him, picking the mercenary up by the scruff of his collar. "Wait!" Gina yelled. Too late. With a brutal heave, he sent him headfirst, stumbling into a big and unforgiving oak trunk, twice the thickness of his own shoulder length. The impact knocked him out cold.

"Let's go," said D'artello. He let her lead the way as they blazed through the forest. He dove on her abruptly. At first she thought he'd tripped, until he wrapped his arms around her and pulled her to the ground on top of him to break the fall. An arrow whizzed by, tearing leaves off in its wake. She stared straight into his face for a moment before being pushed to the side as he jumped to his feet and delivered a snapping jab to the eye of another man coming their way.

Before the man could regain his posture, D'artello closed the gap with an uppercut to the diaphragm, followed by a driving back fist that sent the hood to his left knee, where he then took a powerful roundhouse kick to the side of the face.

The brutality both excited and horrified Gina. *What strength*, she thought. For that instant, she looked upon an animal, a beast mauling these poor men until a chill snapped her out of it. She began to feel a rush and a sharp shudder surge through her body as the adrenaline kick started her muscles.

She jumped to her feet to intercept the next attacker. Her fist led the way toward the hooded head, but the soldier was smart enough to dodge it. She avoided a retaliatory decapitation easily. She rose, pulling her sword from its sheath, and with the momentum drove the handle into the knuckles of her attacker's hand. The stunned and broken fingers released the sword to the ground. The pain must have been excruciating because she was able to pull him into another hilt strike to the face.

Just as the man fell, another arrow came ripping through, this one a little less accurate. The couple left the injured soldiers on the ground and ran for their lives. They stayed low and swift as to avoid the arrows coming their way; it would only take one to end it all. They shot by every now and then. Whenever the trees did not cover them well enough, the archer would take his chances. Zigzagging as much as possible, they had little trouble avoiding them. The bolts were sent through the air with formidable speed and accuracy, and whenever one would collide with a tree, it would drive itself halfway into the wood.

A damn longbow? Gina clued in. *Only a longbow could deliver that kind of power, but I don't remember seeing one back there, and there's no way he could chase us through the woods like this and still be accurate.* Her pondering was brought to a halt as a large mercenary came in from the left and grabbed D'artello, throwing him to the ground in a grizzly fashion.

D'artello thrust his hip and leg to move the man off of him. Then he jumped to his feet and gave the warrior a boot to the side of his face. Another one came in from behind him and grabbed hold of his shoulders for his comrade to begin wailing on him, but D'artello dropped his weight while thrusting hard elbows into the man's chest and gut. Eventually the pounding caused him to let go, despite his armor's protection. D'artello's armor proved much harder and much better quality than the former Genzak soldier's.

The other man had gotten up and gave a feral roar as he took a wide swing with his hammer-like fist. D'artello bobbed under it and smashed the edge of his hand into his attacker's neck while clasping his windpipe in his arm. He dragged the stunned man into a punch coming from the other hood behind him, and then launched his captive into his comrade. The man stumbled forward, catching himself at the last moment so as not to topple into his friend.

Ruthless as D'artello was, he was not about to let the man regain balance. He wound up and delivered a sharp hook to the backside of the man's head, knocking him to the ground, leaving only his friend standing, who closed the gap in hopes of grappling with the more wiry D'artello.

All Gina could do was close her eyes and hope that the arrow on its way did not hit him. She heard the bolt come slapping through the leaves behind and cringed, ducking her head.

The bolt stuck in, heeded by a bloody blemish seen through the cloth. A loud scream came after as the pain shot through the shoulder of the hooded man. His attacker now concentrated on his own wound, and D'artello was able to pull away, grabbing hold of the arrowhead that poked all the way through. Using it as a handle, he smashed his forehead into the nose of the warrior, dropping him to the ground instantly.

He turned to Gina and motioned for her to follow. The two hurried their pace and stayed low to escape the woods.

Chapter 9

FINALLY, they had made it to an open clearing. As soon as they hit the fields, they stood upright and darted into a full sprint. Ahead lay Tombstone Bridge, the crossover between Vashti and Vaukry. Its name came from the seven men who died during its construction. Katakeun was a royal stone mason, dedicated wholly in body and mind to his work. Katakeun was obsessed with crossing the river that divided southern Vaukry and Vashti. His disciples were loyal. Four of them worked to death simply carving the bridge's pieces. The other two died installing the oversized stone leviathan that dove in and out of the turbulent water. The bridge was wide enough to walk an entire army to the other side. The gargoyles sitting atop each merlon, raised brick, were erected from each bank inward, so the middlemost were unfinished and had been that way since its opening the morning after Katakeun's body was found, chisel and hammer still in hand. What had become of his remaining two students and cobuilders was still a mystery.

D'artello and Gina raced to Tombstone Bridge's gateway. There were usually Vaukry guards surrounding it all day long, but not today. Only upon approaching it would they know if the hooded mercenaries chasing them now sacked the squad, or if the Phantoms had gotten there first. Only tell tale bloodstains or not held the answers. Their feet went from romping on the soft ground to pounding into the heedless stone.

The cold sea breeze, traveling down river from the north, whispered through their hair. Even though they were at least seventy feet above the water, they could still hear it trickling against the thick legs of Tombstone Bridge.

The couple made it about halfway before sharp pains crackled through Gina's shin. She collapsed and then rolled over onto her back clutching her leg. "I think I pushed it too hard," she said, clenching her teeth. D'artello stood watching and waiting for her to recover. "I think we've gone far enough anyway," she said, opening her eyes to the sun and sighing.

"That was close," she declared, staring up at him. She noticed his hand placed firmly against his right shoulder as blood trickled down his pauldron. "Oh," she said, recalling the image of the arrow sticking through the mercenary's shoulder. It was then she heard a snap come from the woods, and then a sharp whizzing sound. D'artello dodged to the side as another arrow shot by his head.

She sat up and turned to face the bowman yards away, coming through the arched entrance of the bridge. In his arms was a steel crossbow. Remembering that this weapon was only in its early stages, she also recalled its uncanny power to puncture even stone, let alone through two men. It was lightweight and very wieldable. Now it all made sense; this was how he could stay accurate with so much power, even in the woods. D'artello began to walk slowly toward the archer despite the wound in his shoulder.

"No, D'artello, you can't. You'll die!" she yelled after him as the wind picked up. Envisioning him with an arrow through his chest or in his head was a grotesque thought. Yet she watched on. Her eyes widened as the bowstring gave another sharp twang. The arrow took off at blinding speed, and in what looked like a flash, its pieces fell pathetically to the ground behind its target. His right arm now extended, D'artello held the Molten Steel out to his side, maintaining its follow through. At first Gina was unsure of what she had just seen. When her mind caught up to her eyes a second later, her jaw dropped. He had cut the arrow from the sky.

The man strung and shot another. To the naked eye, D'artello's arm never moved from its awkward extended poise, but each time one of those arrows came screaming through the air, it failed and fell the same as its predecessor. One after another, as he backtracked the bridge to his foe, he cut them down. Even though, in the archer's panic, some of the shots were completely off aim, D'artello still cut them out of the air. His wounded shoulder proved no hindrance to his soulless resolve.

Too close now, the man frantically tried to string yet another arrow from his waist quiver and fire, but before he could raise the weapon to even suitable height, D'artello released his clutch on his wound and arrested it under his arm, letting the arrow twang off toward the ground, splintering and skipping off the stone, over the edge, into the water below. In the blink of an eye, he swung the Molten Steel, sliced the metal, and tossed the head of the bow over the side as well.

The hood immediately turned to run, but he was grabbed by his hood and pulled to his backside. Gina breathed a sigh of relief that there would be no more arrows. When the mercenary tried to get up, D'artello kicked him back down to his rear and put a foot on his chest to prevent him from doing so again. He sheathed the Molten Steel, looking down as a predator upon his foe.

"Where?" D'artello shouted as the man flailed his arms to protect his face.

The man whimpered, too scared to utter any words.

"I said where are they?" he said. "Where will your men take my father?"

"The prison ... Galtaria Prison," he said.

D'artello had never heard of this place before. He picked the man up by the scruff of his collar to peer in at him through the hood's eyeholes. "Where is that?" he asked. His eyes told it all, that he would do what was necessary to get the information he wanted.

"It is ... to the south. Just a few miles," he answered.

D'artello released his grip, letting the man fall to the ground and scramble away, back toward the woods. Putting his hand against his bleeding shoulder, D'artello started to walk back toward Gina, who was already on her way to meeting him.

"We have to go back and go south to Galtaria prison," he said.

"Wait, stop," she said, softly trying to sway him with her arms. "Your shoulder."

He paid her no mind and began walking south, pushing his way past her.

"I said stop! We are not going anywhere until you wait a minute and hear me out!" she said, hobbling and stepping in front of him to block his way.

He beamed down on her with his cold eyes. She gave a shudder. Though she hadn't feared him before, after seeing his latest display, reason was beginning to creep in.

"You are not invincible, D'artello. Look at your arm."

"A wound like this will take time to heal, and we don't *have* time," he said blankly.

"Just come here," she said, putting her hands around his waist, guiding him like a blind man to kneel down with her. "Now let me see it." She grabbed his hand to pull it away from his pauldron. Around the arrowhead's gouge, the metal had buckled inward, but the wound was still difficult to make out. "I can't see it," she said, beginning to tug at his armor.

Obediently, he shed the metal pieces and placed them on the ground. "Hold still," she said as she cut his black shirt down the middle with her sword, revealing his powerful upper body. He watched her curiously as she peeled back the cloth from the wound, not cringing at all. Soon his shirt lay on the ground with his armor. "Oh thank Harmony, it's clean. They didn't use poison," she said, remembering her training days with the bow. "Not that they would need it, huh?" She laughed a little. "Went right through both of you."

Chest plate, shoulder pieces, and gauntlets, she removed her own upper body armor, revealing a lean and powerful yet surprisingly feminine figure. What she was moderately endowed with revealed itself when she unbuttoned and removed her red overcoat, leaving only the first layer of undergarments and the second layer of fine, white, long-sleeved shirt, draped lightly over them.

"The jacket is heavy and your shirt is no good," she said trying to sound displeased, but her face turned red as she pulled the shirt out and began to unbutton it. Removing it revealed her smooth, fare skin and most of her shapely breasts.

Her body was definitely not what he'd expected. She had obviously taken good care of herself and seemed somewhat mindful of her appearance. This was not typical of a soldier. "Here, this'll make a fine bandage," she said, grabbing the shirt by the shoulder and tearing a sleeve off using her teeth. She scooted up beside him and began to work.

She took his left hand in hers, placing it on her lap, and then wrapped the cloth around the wound, swooping underneath his arm and around the top of his shoulder. She pulled it firm after two rounds and then knotted it to make a tourniquet. She tore off the rest using her teeth once again as a reliable tool.

"There," she said with a shiver as she reached for her jacket. There was a period of uncouth silence, not that this was anything unusual for D'artello.

"I think we should stop at the town nearby. I know that sounds crazy, but I *cannot* go on without any rest. Just a little sleep is all I'm ask—"

D'artello stood up. "If we must go charging into a trap, then at least at night we will have better cover," he reasoned, beginning to walk toward Vaukry. "We need a plan, because we cannot fail."

* * *

"My Harmony, we've walked all day and now we're at the coast," Bensel whispered in Gerrik's ear. "Even if D'artello does decide to come back, there's no way he'll make it in time. Hope you've got a plan."

"Don't worry, Ben. Just take this time to get whatever rest you think you can," he said quietly.

"Rest?"

"What's the matter? Not exactly the royal chambers?" Gerrik poked fun.

"Hey, you two, cut the chatter," a large man barked from behind, giving Bensel a hardy shove.

"How can you joke at a time like this?" uttered Bensel, catching his balance. He examined Gerrik's silent face.

They could smell the coals burning that eased the death chill hollowing out the tower. Warm winds wafted by as they climbed the windy slope via a path nestled between two jagged rock walls. They had been marching for most of the day. At the top of the gritty walk, they approached two great wooden doors. Attention was diverted to a window near the top of the tower jutting from the earth. Peering down at them from his perch was another hooded soldier.

A soft creaking averted Gerrik's eyes to the catwalk above the door, the strings of so many bows being pulled back, aimed probably right between their eyes. There had to be at least a hundred black hoods with sharp arrows ready to storm down on them.

Gerrik scratched the hair on his chin, assessing the situation. The thoughts of snapping the neck of the soldier in front of him, grabbing Seraph, and taking him hostage had now fled from his mind. Too many eyes watched them now.

Seraph gave a wave and then a salute with his right arm against his chest, followed by a gallant thrust of his purple over red cape. A momentary silence. The men then lowered their bows, nodding to one another. The man in the window gave a confirmation nod and disappeared back into the building. They heard a loud bang and then a heavy rattling. The door cracked slightly at first and then with a heavy scratching noise, it began to slide across the ground.

Galtaria Prison. Never had man or nature devised more a diabolical structure. Its orange steam belched out from its daring posture out over a boiling sea. This prison was as renowned as Harmony's blessed wrath. Within that hellish smokestack, not even dreams could healthily sustain themselves. Starvation and torture were constant plagues for its guests, and thriving insomnia overtook its guards, driving them into a mad, abusive furor.

Inside, the air was dry and burned the nostrils as it was inhaled. Burning wood was an almost overpowering odor if not for the smell of so many sweating bodies. "By Harmony, it's hot in here," Sandra complained. Never having been to a prison, she did not know this was a common tactic to wear a man down. The room had an orange glow that showed off the windowless stonewalls. It was a tall, hollow, shaft-like tower with loft floors circling above the fire pit below. The pit itself was a bowl of shriveled remnants of men, poorly clad, poorly fed, and poorly bathed. In the center breathed a stack of smoldering coal.

The sounding of a whip directed their attention to the barebacked bodies of the prisoners shoveling black charcoal into the pit. One of them fell to their knees using his shovel as a cane. "Get up," they heard the guard say before giving a crack of the whip, leaving a bright red gash in the back of the scrawny, bearded man. The poor man stumbled into the fiery coal. Sandra hid her face and shielded her ears from the agonizing screams.

"What right do you have to keep these prisoners? Just let them go! You don't need them," Bensel protested.

"Have you forgotten?" Seraph asked. "These are the dogs of the motherland from which we clawed our independence. They have life sentences to fulfill, and far be it from me to under mind the very justice I fought so very hard for."

"They are not involved in this, Seraph, and you know it," Gerrik said.

"Someone's got to keep the furnace running," he said, leading the group in and onto a stage that loomed over the fire. The door clacked and cranked, shutting tightly behind them as Seraph turned to face his tour group.

"Take the princess away and give her the special treatment. That's what she gets for having dogs that bark too loudly by her side."

"No! Sandra, my daughter!" Bensel cried out. "Seraph, if you hurt her, I'll—"

"You'll what? I'm in control now, you old fool, as a true warrior should be."

Sandra began to writhe in the man's arms and then stomped hard on the top of her captor's foot.

"Agh, dammit!" the man screamed, throwing her to the ground. Instantly, another man scooped her up and raised a knife to her throat in one motion.

"You are a feisty one, princess," he grunted, then tapped her on the behind.

"You'll lose your head for this," she sneered, jerking up straight as the man put tension on the blade.

"Seraph, you'd better not do anything stupid!" Bensel threatened. "I'll wrap these old hands around your neck until your last breath if she is harmed." His roar was so intense and so promising that Gerrik half expected the tower to level around them. Quickly he noticed that everyone, prisoners and guards alike, stared at the intense scene. They'd indeed made a spectacle of themselves.

"Don't worry, my king," Seraph sang.

"I am not your king!" he yelled. "A dog like you has no right to even serve me. Your place is on the other end of my sword," he declared.

Elan could watch no longer. A sharp twist of his waist jutted an elbow into the fleshy diaphragm of the man escorting him. He did not stop there. The rope that bound him slipped right off, and that was when Gerrik realized why Elan had been quiet for so long, purposely not drawing any attention to himself. Ensnaring the hood by the shoulders, Elan thrust his knee into his gut. He then put his gauntlet up to block the sword coming in from his left, setting off little sparks that danced to the ground. With that momentum, he threw a powerful counterpunch toward his attacker's face with his other heavy gauntlet, dropping him and knocking him out or killing him, it was hard to say for certain.

Seraph signaled at the guard with the knife, and Sandra let out a scream that sent chills down everyone's spine. Elan looked at his lover, relieved to see that she was still alive, but the man holding her had dug a red line in her shoulder with his knife.

"Elan, stop!" Gerrik barked finally.

"That's all the excuse I need, Seraph," Elan said. "When we get out of here, I'm coming back for you."

"Do you fancy this some sort of game? Some sort of fairy tale? Take the princess to her room and these dogs to their kennels," Seraph said, shrugging off Elan's threats. He took a minute to look at the hood Elan had just punched out. "Take this one and strip him of his armor. Then bring him to work the pit. It seems he needs to be broken," he ordered, pointing at Elan.

As the men filed out with their respective prisoners, Seraph managed to catch the look in Gerrik's eyes. "Hold," he simply ordered. The two men on Gerrik halted suddenly. "I know that look in your eyes, Gerrik. Are you angry? What's the matter? You can't be the hero this time?"

"Just a little disappointed in an old ally," he said.

"Oh come off it. You're pissed, aren't you?" he shot back, licking his lips.

"Anger ... is not something to be directed at someone."

"I figured you'd say something like that. Get him out of my face," Seraph ordered. "Now!" He faced the rest of his hoods in the immediate vicinity and said, "Go and prepare for our visitors. No doubt they will be here within the day."

* * *

In the meantime, D'artello and Gina had walked miles in the grassy plains. As they passed deeper into Vaukry, the grasses began to dry, turn golden, and grow up to their knees. Still they hadn't seen a town. Gina's legs grew weary, and D'artello was in desperate need of new clothes, as he was still sporting his shirt cut down the middle. Over his shoulder, he carried both of their body armors.

"I don't remember there being a town here. It's not on any map I've ever seen," Gina said out of frustration. She really had no memory for such things.

D'artello stared down at her for a moment. "If we were near a town, you'd think we would've seen it by now," she complained.

As they came over the hill, something came into view. "Is that a fence?" she said. A fence there was indeed—a big one with a herd of husky, fluffy animals grazing about. "Higoats!" Gina shouted, beginning to walk faster. "Female ones." From their height, they could see a small cottage with four large, circular fenced-in areas around it. They quickened pace, walking toward the small wooden structure, taking the path that led between the first two fences.

The pair watched the animals munch idly as they passed through the two encirclements. An odious stench filled the air from the fresh animal droppings. There was very little difference between the male and female higoat. One had horns, and the other had a maroon utter mounted beneath it. Mouth full of grass, one of the higoats raised her head and gave a low honking noise, as they were known to do when acknowledging a stranger's presence.

Gina gave a short giggle. She had always found them to be funny animals, especially when they made their sound. She recalled that her father used to make the noise on purpose just to hear her laugh when she was little. Unable to contain herself, she strayed further from D'artello's side to try to provoke one of the nearby woolies to honk again.

A loud bark, however, directed their attention to the fence on the other side. This fence held a group of ters, large lizards with wings. They had arrow-like faces and lightning-fast jaws that could snap logs. They were lean with elongated, bony limbs, standing at a height equal to a grown man's waist. If one was to perch on its hind legs, it would certainly be taller than any man, and easily a few heads over, due to their serpentine necks. They had small curved claws that stuck out at the end of their three independent toes. They looked like big flying lizards.

These were males identified by their bright, grassy green skin, mauve underbellies, and their long whip-like tails. Two of them were hissing and barking at each other, obviously settling some sort of mischievous rivalry. D'artello and Gina watched as one pounced on the other and they began to roll around in the warm field. They bumped into a larger stud that gave a snort to warn the younglings.

Ters, along with slepnes, were mounting animals, but due to their pale beauty and fractured domestication, in comparison to the winged horses, they were often sold at a cheaper price to riders. This was balanced out by their abundant litters, however. So a couple of ters with good genes could yield many younglings and provide a fruitful profit. They had much longer lifespans than slepnes as well. All studs though, whoever owned these fields was seeking profit; a stud with good genes was worth a fortune despite the fact they couldn't be ridden.

Too distracted to see it at first, they noticed a bitterfruit tree. Its arborous stature stood sullenly slouched over the shack. The succulent, orange, fist-sized fruits hung freely and deliciously, allowing their scent to swath gently through the air toward Gina's nose. Normally their scent was light, but Gina was so hungry that her sense of smell had become hound-like. Not even the manure in the air could quell her prolonged hunger. Feeling the saliva well up in her jowls, she jogged over to the tree, looking up at it with begging eyes. "D'artello, look!" she said. "Food! Harmony, am I starving," she said, placing her hands on her stomach.

D'artello glanced at the green giant that blocked the sun and graciously cast its shadow. It was far too high to pick the fruits. He drew his Molten Steel and wound his arm back. "Catch," he uttered as he hurled the blade through the air. The blade cut one down and let it fall into Gina's eager hands, then returned to him after cutting down another. Off guard for only a moment, Gina extended her hand at the last second to catch that one as well.

Approaching her, he sheathed his sword and accepted the fruit she held out to him. D'artello stared at it for a moment while Gina peeled back the firm skin and began to dig in. Soon he followed suit. Even he could feel that his body was starving, but their feast was soon interrupted.

Catching wind of the little girl hiding around the other side of the tree, he put the fruit down. Busy eating, Gina did not see her, but she paid close attention to D'artello carefully circling the tree. Coming around, the little green-eyed, red headed, impish child stared up at him timidly. D'artello straightened his posture in an unthreatening manner and knelt down to her level, giving a half-cocked smile. She wore a blue sundress that reached to her knees with a blue ribbon tying back her hair. She could not have been more than ten years old, almost Tanya's age, and her eyes reminded him of Sali's.

Gina took notice of the gesture. This was the first time she had seen an ounce of humanity in D'artello anywhere but his eyes.

Hiding behind a wooden ladder and a basket full of bitterfruit, the little girl stared at him cautiously, never blinking. This only lasted seconds before D'artello began to slowly advance. She let out an ear-piercing scream and began to run toward the cottage, abandoning her work entirely.

"Wait!" Gina gargled with her mouth full of fruit. Placing a hand on her chest, she swallowed the generous bite. "C'mon, we should follow her," she said, taking off. D'artello noticed a straw hat she must have dropped when he startled her. He picked it up and observed it for a moment.

They chased her as far as the stairs of the small wooden home, which upon second glance was rather homely. It was not large but two stories tall and at least three good-sized rooms wide, comprised of superior craftsmanship. The wood was tied together with rope made from high-quality Higoat fur, very strong indeed. It was more a cabin than a cottage. The little girl ran through the brinebark door and slammed it shut. Brinebark was a tree famous for its light blue tint.

"Dammit," Gina said, climbing the stairs to the wooden porch so that she could get a better look through the windows. D'artello tried to stop her but did not climb onto the porch. Not a moment later, the door swung open again.

A tall man ducked out of the low doorway, his dark red hair just barely missing the frame. He had a round face with a burly mustache that covered his mouth, the same fiery color as his hair. He had huge, vein-laced forearms that stuck out like logs from his gray shirt, which hugged his muscular chest and draped over his small belly, and his brown work-slacks reached the ground around his big black boots. He pointed and fixed his gaze on Gina. "You best leave here," he said in a deep voice.

"But, sir," she protested.

"Listen here, missy, no one wearin' those red metal slacks is allowed 'round here," he said, referring to her leg armor. "What'se matter? Y'all don't hide yer faces n'more?" he asked.

"Wait … wait, I honestly don't know what you are talking about," she said, raising her hands defensively.

"Them hoods!" he yelled. He now seemed suspicious of her instead of angry with her. "Don't play dumb. Y'all come 'round here an' steal some o' our crop an' goats too."

"Wait," Gina said, pulling her sword out and laying it on the ground. "We're not with them."

"Why you dress like 'em?" he asked.

Gina took a second to find the words to say. "They are traitors. We were all members of the former Genzak army. Please, you've got to believe me."

He took a second to assess the situation and then pulled his spectacles from his nose and polished them with his shirt. Her sword was on the ground, but D'artello still wore two of them around his waist. Taking a minute, he scratched his beard and looked into D'artello's serious eyes. "He ain't dressed like you, an' he don't look like a liar."

Gina was surprised at the notion of simply guessing if someone was lying or not, but whatever this man's reasoning, she was not going to argue.

"I am Gina of the former Genzak army, and this is D'artello. He is the son of Sir Gerrik. Surely you have heard of his exploits?"

He snorted and spat toward the grass off the edge of the raised wooden porch. "Yeah I've heard o' him," he said. The man scratched his beard.

"M'apologies, miss ... why don't y'all leave them swords out here and we'll go inside an' sort this out," he said, turning to invite them in.

D'artello approached the stairs and laid his father's sword down on the first step but kept the Molten Steel by his side.

"Hey, boy, you hard o' hearin'?" asked the man.

"Oh ... no, sir, he's just strange about this particular sword, it ... it um means a lot to him," Gina tried to explain.

"Don't worry, son. Just put it out here against the door. Nobody's comin' 'round here, I promise," he said. D'artello hesitated for a moment and looked at Gina.

He leaned the sword down, and the pair filed in, walking across the creaking floorboards and into the cabin.

The interior was surprisingly inviting and lit by slow breathing candles. They entered what looked like a kitchen, with a black cast iron woodstove right next to the door, a wooden table and four chairs on the far side near the entrance to another room. Apparently this man was quite the craftsman. Everything from the table and chairs to the shelves were handcrafted then sanded to silky perfection. Gina took a second to peek through a window strategically placed toward the sun for optimal lighting in the morning. They did not have wall-mounted oil lamps like most of the royal structures she was used to.

The man walked over to the table and pulled out a chair. "Ma'am," he said. Gina smiled at the gentlemanly gesture and sat with her arms below the table. "Jus' sit anywhere," he said to D'artello, who then sat to the right of Gina. The man sat down directly across from her and sprawled his forearms across the table, clasping his hands together. "I'd offer y'all some juice, but you interrupted my li'l sis from picking them bitterfruits. There anything else I can get ya?"

Gina and D'artello declined the offer. "The name is Jarod," he said just as two children came from the other room. One was the girl they had seen in the field, and the other was a rough looking little boy. Red hair and green eyes seemed to be the family trait.

"This is my brother an' sister, Joyce an' Jayce," he said. They huddled together, gawking closely at their visitors. "C'mon now, come shake hands with yer guests, show some manners."

"Sorry fer how I was," Jarod said as the two children came in to shake hands with Gina and D'artello.

D'artello handed back Joyce's hat, and she perused it carefully, as if to see if there was anything strange or wrong about it.

"We been havin' some trouble with those black hooded folk," he explained. "They been stealin' some of our higoats and ters."

"Really," Gina said. "Where are they taking the animals?"

"To that prison 'bout twenny miles south. They been tellin' some stories o' monsters an' a magic sword that'll save the world, but I don't believe none o' that. Soz long as I keep my bro and sis safe. Nuf 'bout me though. Start talkin' why you walkin' 'round in these fields? Yer far away fer sight seein'."

"We are lost," Gina began. "Our friends were taken by the men in black hoods, and we are planning to attack the prison tonight. We came here to treat my friend's wound, and rest until then, um if that is okay?"

Jarod looked at D'artello's shoulder where a splotch of blood was beginning to soak the makeshift bandage.

"Tonight's not far off, an' how can I say no to such a pretty young thing," he said, pushing away from the table as he spoke. "I'll fetch some bandages and some alcohol. Kids, show 'em some hospitality; give 'em what they want," he said before walking out the door.

"What happened to your arm, mister?" inquired Joyce, with a concerned pout on her face.

"An arrow hit him," Gina responded, getting up and walking over to the two kids. She knelt beside them.

"An arrow? Really?" said Jace with excitement.

"That's terrible," Joyce responded, shooting Jace a sisterly look. "Was it one of those mean hooded men?"

"Mmhmm, but D'artello sent them running." Gina boasted.

"You did? Really?" Jace asked. "Even with your arm like that? You're strong, mister."

"Yup, he is," Gina said, placing her hand on D'artello's arm and giving the kids a smile.

"How come he doesn't talk?" Jace asked.

"Yeah why doesn't he talk?" Joyce repeated.

"Umm ..." She looked back up at D'artello, "that's a good question."

"I like your name," the girl said to D'artello.

D'artello smiled.

Jarod came back, and once the wound was tended to, D'artello and Gina were offered some fruit and bread, much to their satisfaction.

* * *

Soon after, they found themselves out on the porch. The sun was close to setting, and they would be in perfect view as it came down over the horizon. It was almost time to leave. Gina rested her eyes, opening them periodically to glance over him. When he smiled, she leaned her head on his shoulder and pressed her face against his neck.

Although the two had never spoken heart-to-heart, she felt a deep and growing bond with him. Even though she knew it would never happen, she really wanted him to wrap his arms around her and hold her tight. She wondered where their journeys together would take them.

This time, she felt *him* move. He looked down at her and even gave that smirk she adored so much. Stomach aflutter, looking back at him expecting a kiss at any moment, she closed her eyes and slightly puckered her lips. It did not come though.

"Are you rested?" he asked. Only a sigh followed his question. "We must rescue our comrades. I fear that our time is far more limited than we would like to believe." He climbed to his feet and walked back toward the door. "There is no time for this right now," he said.

Right now? she thought. *Did he really mean that? Did he mean that this will not happen or it will not happen now but later?* Just about ready to write the notion out of her head, she followed him in. "Wait," she said. "We could trade our last armor pieces for a couple of ters. They're cheap mounts, right? I mean, how much different could they be from slepnes?"

Moments later, they were in one of the rear enclosures. "Here. Pick the ones you like," Jarod said, waving his hand among the females. Females were the mounts; they were a tad larger than males and had few but fundamental differences. The girls were brown and had paddle-like tails for increased maneuverability. Since they usually carried the heavy young, they needed all of these extra features to do so.

Joyce came sprinting out of the house to wish the two good-bye. She stood next to D'artello and tugged on his arm for a moment. "I wanted to say thanks for bringing my hat back," she chirped. "Can you guys stay a couple more days?"

"I'm sorry, Joyce," Gina said. "We can't stay. There are many things that we have to do."

"Like what? Get married?" she asked.

Gina gasped. Was she so easily read that a little girl could point out her feelings for D'artello? *No of course not,* she thought. *Little girls always dream about love and marriage; surely that was where she drew her question.*

"No, it's nothing like that," Gina answered. "We have to save our friends, remember?"

"Yeah, I remembered that, but what about after? You couldn't come back?"

How little she understood. It was far too harsh for her to comprehend that the two of them may not survive the night. That Gina herself was bound to her duty before being bound to anything as trivial as love. "Why did you ask us if we were getting married?" Gina asked. She had to know.

"Well you gave him that thingy around his neck right?" she asked, pointing to a twine around his neck. She had noticed it but whatever was attached to it was always in his shirt.

"Can I just see this for a min ..." she asked, getting lost in mid-sentence, pulling the pendant from the grip of the collar. The promise charm that Tanya had given him hung in her hand and swiveled freely as her hopes fell. She felt a slight tremor of confusion and embarrassment in her chest at this discovery.

Her jaw began to tighten with the bitter, tinny taste of jealousy. She recalled minutes ago wanting to kiss him, that she leaned in and puckered to meet nothing. Now she realized why. Her eyes lowered only slightly at her feelings of foolishness. Letting the promise charm fall, she crossed her arms, embracing herself slightly, but making it look like she was warming her skin.

D'artello forced the charm back into his shirt as if protecting it with his life, with his heart. "We need to go," he said.

Maybe I just need to back off a bit, yeah ... that's it, we have a duty, she thought. Her thoughts stayed on the pendant, a symbol that now defined D'artello.

Looking on, her eyes met Jarod's round face. Reluctant to take the incomplete sets of armor, even he was roused upon examination that this armor was far more valuable than a cloth shirt and two *female* ters. He pulled a rag from his shirt and waxed the sweat from his brow, as he'd just pulled two of the lizards from the fields. One of them seemed to have given him some trouble, but an arresting tug of the reigns around its head was enough to tame it. "Here, these are good ones, best two I've got," Jarod said proudly.

"I'm no tactician, but you should fly southwest o'er the ocean, get the jump on 'em," Jarod said to Gina, who had begun to mount the brown lizard. Joyce ran back toward the house. She climbed up onto the porch and faced the fields, blanketed by the orange sky.

"I've never ridden one of these before," Gina said as the animal underneath her gave a low growl that vibrated her seat.

"Now don't you worry none. Ridin' one o' these is jus' like ridin' a slepne, except they're a lil' more sensitive ... you'll get the hang of it. The animal's not gonna crash itself into the ground. So like I said, don't you worry none, jus' feel it out. One more thing," he said, tossing a brown leather pouch to D'artello. "That should square us off."

"Thank you," Gina said as D'artello fastened the pouch to his belt.

"Good luck. Don't go gettin' yourself killed," Jarod called as the pair gave a kick to the sides of their mounts. They could feel the muscles and bones loosen up as the animal prepared to run. Their flat feet pounded the ground as they darted off at surprising speed. The riders flattened themselves out to avoid the pressure of the wind against their faces.

Gina's stomach pulled tight as the lizard leapt toward the sky, hugging the wind with its deceptive wingspan. On the ground, their wings looked like crumpled sheets. When they jumped and spread them out, they were a sight to see. The fully outstretched wings were no less than thirteen feet long each, large enough to lift the heavy reptile, along with their riders, off into the post-mature sunset.

They were fast, and the sudden burst of speed made Gina swallow her breaths. "Oh my Harmony, oh my Harmony," she repeated as a quick mantra. Ahead, the forest's tree line was coming up fast. Gentle as she tried to be at first, the beast could barely feel her tugs. She looked up at D'artello, who had already flown high enough to avoid the trees. He was looking back down at her, his eyes shouting: *Come on! Up!*

She pulled hard, reeling in her hands, clenching her eyelids, and biting her lip. By nothing short of a miracle, just mere feet from the tree line, the ter gave a low hum and shot straight up into the air. Excitedly, she screamed as they soared upward, rocketing above D'artello's elevation. Out of reflex to hold on for dear life, Gina pulled the reins tighter and tighter. The ter responded by doing a big somersault. Only shortly did she catch a glimpse of the ground that was far below.

In a panic, she gave a frantic tug to the left, and the lizard responded with a fast corkscrew and a leveling dive. "Woohoo!" She exhaled with joy now as the beast stabilized. Jarod had been right; it was kind of like riding a slepne. She remembered only having to pull lightly for a slepne to go up, but the ter responded much quicker and much faster to a sudden motion.

"Show off!" she shouted playfully to D'artello, who seemed to have tamed his beast easily enough. Maybe he rode this animal before, but his skills were overly impressive nonetheless. Accompanied by his lack of emotion was a lack of fear, and foolish or brilliant, it gave him a confident air.

Affixed on their destination, they flew side by side into the cooling dusk. Jarod watched from below and wiped the sweat from his brow again. Joyce walked up beside him and hugged her brother around the waist. Breathing a heavy sigh, he said, "Gerrik's boy? The las' time I saw Gerrik, I was just a youngin'." He looked down at Joyce. "Wonder if they'll be okay."

"I reckon they will. D'artello is very strong," she pointed out.

Chapter 10

THE wings flapped heavily and stealthily in the blackness of the night as the ters slithered through the air. The pair pulled back on the reigns, and the creatures opened their veiny wings wide like fleshy parachutes to slow to a crawling glide. Descending upon the lit prison, Gina held her breath, spotting the crossbow-armed archers on the roof. The twenty-story obelisk leaned out over the ocean like a sadistic lighthouse of torture and death. Like an active volcano, it spewed thick black smoke that burned Gina's nostrils as they passed through it. *Archers at night?* she thought. *They must be expecting us. Too bad they are looking in the wrong direction,* she mused as they put their backs to the waves and icy ocean breeze.

For the ocean, it was a rather eventful night. The tides crashed continuously against the craggy coast below. This was a perfect muffle for their landing. The two circled like vultures, spiraling down toward their bounty. It was as if the ters understood perfectly their role in this plan. They stayed very quiet as they touched down on the dark side of the catwalk. The lizards' feet still made a slapping sound upon landing, but not loud enough to draw attention.

D'artello and Gina dismounted, then pulled the ters into the shadows where they lay down, calmly wrapping their lengthy necks around each other's. D'artello set his gaze to the first hood clockwise around the tower. The man was bent over the side, peering down at the path just ahead of the front gate.

D'artello noticed the instrument around his waist, a horn for sounding the alarm no doubt. "Wait!" Gina whispered as D'artello began to creep toward him, but it was too late. He had already left the safety of the deep shadows. Without a sound, he made it an arm's length from the man and tapped him on the shoulder. Gina could imagine the hood only getting a short glimpse of D'artello's knee before being knocked unconscious by it. Going limp instantly, D'artello caught his body before it could hit the ground and make a noise. He dragged the heavy hood back into the shadows.

"Are you trying to get us killed?" Gina whispered. "Oh!" she gasped hearing a voice coming from around the corner.

"Did you hear something?" one of the other archers called.

"Nah … don't worry about it. It's probably just Gary messin' with us," another voice responded.

D'artello looked down at the body and began to unfasten the armor pieces. He pulled off the hood, revealing a middle-aged, battle-beaten face. A scar ran across the man's cheek and reached all the way up to his dirty-blond eyebrows and thinning hair-line. His fuzz-lined lips hung open loosely as the rest of his body hung in D'artello's arms. A good sized, egg-shaped shiner had already erected the black eye that D'artello's knee gave him.

"Put this on," D'artello ordered, handing Gina the hood.

"What?"

"And the armor, all of it. Put his clothes on," he repeated.

She began to tie her hair back so that it wouldn't show through the bottom of the hood. She reached out for the man's crossbow, but D'artello's hand met her wrist. He shook his head. "They don't belong in this fight," he said.

Pretending to understand what the statement meant she continued to play along, letting the crossbow rest. Just as she pulled the black hood over her head, one of the ters looked up inquisitively. It gave a low growl that crackled through its leathery lips.

"What in Harmony's name is that noise? I know I heard it this time."

"Whatever it is, I'm gonna beat it out of you, Gary! Cover my spot for a minute." The other hood sounded angry now, and his footsteps were beginning to close in on them.

"Go!" D'artello pushed her from the shadows.

"Wait!" she said, wanting to ask what she should say, but before the thought could finish crossing her mind, the other hood was in front of her with crossbow aimed right between her eyes.

"Bam!" he yelled. "That's all it's gonna take, buddy. Now stop screwin' with us. This is war," he said, muttering off. "Freakin' kid."

Gina heard a scream come from the other direction, just as the hood was beginning to walk away. "What was that? Gary, d'you hear that?"

Gina was too afraid to speak and reveal her identity.

"Behind you, man!" he shouted, pushing gruffly past her. Seeing him reach for the horn, she realized a decision had to be made now. If he was able to press his lips to that horn, they were as good as dead.

Taking a deep breath, she swung her armored leg hard at the back of his head, knocking him down and smashing him face-first into the stone. He stirred for a moment but didn't get back up to attack her; he must've been out. Upon hearing the scream, the other guard must have had his lips pressed against his horn by now. She cringed and waited for the sound.

Little was she aware that around the corner, D'artello had already yanked the horn from the other man's hands and was ready to duke it out with him. "Hey! Guys! Sound the alarm! They're here, they're here!" he pleaded, but D'artello just closed in cautiously. Once it set in that the cavalry was not coming, the man brought his crossbow to killing level. But when his hands felt the sting of D'artello's roundhouse kick, they immediately flung it to the ground.

"Heh … If that's how you wanna play, let's dance," said the hood, putting his hands up. D'artello barely avoided the lightning-fast lead jab. He then had to block the savvy fighter's quick follow-up kick coming toward his midsection. Once he had a firm hold on the leg, he drew inward with a quick elbow to the throat, then wrapped his arm around the neck and rearranged him over his shoulder, slamming him hard against the ground. Just as the hood was trying to get up, D'artello knelt down and devastated him with a powerful punch to the face.

The snipers taken care of, they began to drag the bodies off into the shadows and pile them up near the ters. "Okay, so you're going to put one on too, right? No trouble at all, just disguises? In and out right?" she asked.

He stood up, answering her with a meager headshake.

"What do you mean no? This is our free ticket," she argued.

"To do what? Just walk out the front door with Seraph's bargaining tool. Did you really think that would work?" he asked. "That disguise will only get you in while I create a distraction."

"A distraction?" She pulled the hood off of her head. "D'artello, these men are ruthless. They'll kill you if they catch you."

"I know, so I'll have to make sure I don't get caught then," he responded.

"I won't let you do it. I won't let you kill yourself," Gina said. D'artello just put a silent finger across his lips. *Damn him and that promise charm. I should just let him do what he wants,* she thought bitterly.

"You know there is no other way. This place is huge, and you need time to find everyone," he pointed out.

Crossing her arms, she turned to face the opposite direction so that he would not see the tears in her eyes. *He doesn't care what I think. Why should he? He just has his girl at home.* "You don't care about what I think!" she stated, letting her inner voice out.

"Gina, you're acting childish," he said heartlessly.

"Childish? Are you even capable of feeling, or do you have no soul in that body?"

"I will go with or without your help," he said. "True, the choice is yours. But tell me, what do you suppose my chances are without your help?"

Gina immediately turned and slapped him, as she had before when he didn't pay his respects to the fallen soldiers. This time was different though. There was something else behind that slap. Something that made D'artello's hand fly to his cheek as he stared at her with the same blank look.

"You sit here and stop me from killing these men like we should be doing, as if you care, as if there's some care that still runs through your veins. Then you step all over my feelings again. Do you step on your girl's feelings too?" she said, pointing to his chest.

Tracing his palm along his shirt, he felt the promise charm Tanya had given him. "Is this why you are acting so strangely?" he asked. "This charm and its promise are important to me … but they serve an entirely different purpose than that which you aim to serve," he said, stroking her hair behind her ear. "I cannot promise that you will never again watch me run headlong into life-threatening danger, but I live on. This I can promise," he said, untying the necklace.

"What? Wait … D'artello, no," she said trying to fight him, but he was much stronger than she was.

"Time for you to make me a promise," he said when she finally gave in, placing her hands around his wrists. While fastening it around her neck, he spoke their contract, "When I survive, and when we meet again, you must return this to me. Promise? Meaning you can't die, or else you will break that promise."

"You bastard," she said quietly, clasping him tightly. "Do you have any idea what I've been through?"

"Say it," he said softly, leaning into her ear.

"I … promise," she agreed with a squeezing of her grip on his wrists.

Patting her on the back was the signal for them to ignore their feelings once again and continue with their mission. Pulling away, she couldn't take her eyes off of him now.

"Now put the hood back on. We've got work to do," he said as they made their way around the smoke stack to a door leading inside. Upon pulling the door open, the awful stench of burning wood mixed with sweaty bodies invaded their nostrils. Gina leaned to the side of the waft and gagged, then stopped herself. They made their way down a narrow, torch lit, windowless, spiraling stairwell comprised of stone steps and walls that circled the central smokestack. When they came to the end of the well, they peeked through the door-sized opening into the main hall.

If they were to leave now, they would escape onto a loft that circled the smoky cloud coming up through the center of the room. It was hard to determine how high up they actually were, but they were on the top floor. There were guards, more black hoods of course. Poor planning on Seraph's part. His guard would have been impregnable from the outside had they taken the normal route, but inside these walls, his influence was loose. Though few, these must have been rugged men to stand in the heat with their heavy armor.

"This place is huge," Gina whispered. There must have been quite a few floors, because just two guards patrolled this top floor. That Phantom attack must have drained Seraph's resources. Two more guards were climbing a ladder just to their left, coming to the top to join the watch.

"I wonder where they are keeping Sir Gerrik," Gina said.

The two bunched themselves up a couple of stairs so they could peer into the pit below. Just below them was an enormous, oaken, tri-bladed fan. Cranking from below, the prisoners were probably breaking their backs rotating it the hard way. This fan forced the smoke and more tangible side effects of the fire pit below out the top of the smokestack. Just level with that was another loft, connected to the top floor by a lowly wooden ladder. D'artello could see two more lofts below that, also connected to their predecessors and successors with the very same crafted ladders. He was inclined to believe that these lofts went all the way down to the ground floor. It would be a hopeless climb down, without much distraction.

The third loft down, he noticed a door that must have led to holding cells. So it was reasonable to say either every third floor had cells, or every floor below the third from the top had cells. Since the building was cylindrical, the prison halls must have been circular around each floor. It would be like finding a needle in a higoat's coat. Gina would need more than time; she would need the disabling of several guards.

"When I run out, chase me to the edge so you look convincing, and then in the confusion, start looking for them," he ordered. With no further warning, he sprinted from the hallway, the sudden motion immediately alerting the guards on that balcony as he made a mad dash toward the railing. Giving chase, she followed him until he pulled himself up to balance on top of the railing, as if taunting the guards and stirring their attention. Gina gasped out loud and tried to grab hold of him as he plummeted forward down the long shaft. Her drive to save his life just then looked that much more convincing.

She had to hold her breath as he threw himself over the side. What looked like her relentless pursuit as she peered over the railing was actually watching him miss the gigantic fan blades and catch on to the rail just below to climb up to the next loft down. She could breathe again. Now it was her turn. *I have to hold up my end of the plan*, she thought, running to the nearest ladder to slide down. It was an odd feeling, knowing who she was, but completely fooling the frenzied guards with her disguise. Each time one of them passed by, she expected to be attacked.

Meanwhile, one of the hoods wasted no time in attacking D'artello, who had just pulled himself up. The man drew his lightweight saber and swung hard. D'artello pivoted his whole body into a block with the Molten Steel. A loud clash alerted everyone else who already was not astute to D'artello's presence, and sent the saber careening over the edge of the pit. In pivoting his body so harshly, D'artello's knee buckled that of his opponent, keeping him stationary for a second.

With two steps outward and a leg thrust into the guard's diaphragm, D'artello sent the man reeling, who did not lose balance, but stumbled about trying to find his breath.

Two more guards circled in, one with a club and the other with a chain. Crude weapons, but these were Genzak soldiers, masters of improvising. D'artello could see in his peripherals that more and more guards were starting to pile onto this floor, and that these two only wanted to stall him long enough for reinforcements. The club-wielder came in at D'artello's head.

At that very moment, the chain found its way around D'artello's Molten Steel, making it useless in defending against his other attacker. However, he took soulless flight with a sideways roll, smashing both of his feet against the club-wielding hood, the first into the weapon, knocking it away, and the second to the side of the head, wrenching the neck in an unnatural way.

D'artello landed on his feet and then fell to his backside, yanking the chain-wielder, helplessly attached to the Molten Steel, inward. The unsuspecting hood stumbled into his extended leg that acted like a lever, throwing him over D'artello, forehead first into the stone floor. Spinning back to stance, D'artello freed the Molten Steel of its entanglement.

Three more men lined up to get their piece of him. The fall of their allies meant nothing. Fearlessly, they charged. D'artello tripped the first one, wielding a sword. He stumbled into the path of another knife throwing hood, whose blade wound up in his friend. D'artello grappled the imbedded handle. Using it as leverage, he flipped the stumbling, wounded hood over his shoulder, flat onto his back.

The knife thrower drew another blade from a pouch on his waist. Giving it first a quick flip, he waited this time more carefully, so as not to hit his spear-wielding ally advancing on D'artello.

D'artello drew his father's sword, and in a flash, it tossed the knife vertically into the air. Mounting his Molten Steel on his forearm, he deflected the spear, sending it off to the side. This man was good though. He was already retracting at impressive speed for a second stab.

Jumping and landing flat on his chest, D'artello avoided the second stab. He arrested the pole of the spear in his right hand and then rose, twisting his grip on the weapon in a way that created tension on his attacker's wrist. He swung a foot toward the falling knife. It batted the blade right back at its owner, lodging itself in his shoulder, causing the hood to cry out in pain.

All the while, D'artello had risen completely to his feet and slugged the spear-wielding hood in his unguarded head. He then wrenched the spear free and swung the blunt end. Just after the knife had buried itself in the knife-thrower's shoulder, the spear handle smashed him out cold.

By this time, men had poured in from top and bottom. With nearly thirty men surrounding him, D'artello was beginning to consider other options.

Clenching both swords out in front of him in a threatening manner, he gave a roar, which was just enough to buy some minimal but much needed time. They were all shocked when he replaced both of his weapons and straightened his posture. Without warning, he back-flipped up and over the railing behind him.

They all watched the suicidal maneuver in awe, as he was way too far out to catch onto the next railing down. D'artello flew gracefully like a dove, his hair picking up the gentle swath of movement. Staring down at the fools, he began to plummet, when suddenly he was swept to the side, landing on a blade of the massive oaken fan.

Seraph, watching from below in the riotous shoveling pit, threw his goblet of wine at the fire. No fool to the simple tricks, he noticed a hood running in and out of the prison hallways, the only one not joining the brawl upstairs. He cocked his head to the side. "Curious," he spoke to himself. All around him, the prisoners who once shoveled coal were in a frenzy. They fancied their lack of supervision an opportunity at freedom, but not the few that stumbled or were thrown into Seraph on his way through to catch up with this mysterious, renegade mercenary. He used his long two-handed sword to butcher men's flesh as if it were foliage or shrubbery in his way.

D'artello knew he could not stay on the fan. With no prisoners providing power, it would surely wind down fast. On his first pass around, he noticed the soldiers had formed two lines, equal in length and facing one another. They were making a strange motion, pounding their fists in the air. On the second pass, he found out they were cheering on the one brave man who jumped and caught the blade D'artello was on.

He couldn't kick the man to his death. He had to fight him carefully. This was clearly not the intent of his attacker, however; for once he grasped firm footing, he immediately charged D'artello with a hand axe held high. The wood bucked under his running weight, as the fan was not made to support any bystanders, even less so when D'artello avoided the attack and tripped him, driving the axe deep into the thin plank.

The man got up and tried to yank the axe from the wood, but the hooked edges were embedded. A loud splintering noise echoed through the prison. Most of the prisoners below, and even Seraph, found themselves staring up at their impending doom. They began to panic, pushing, shoving, and trampling. The mass of bodies moshed around Seraph, taking him off balance. Driving his sword toward the ground like a cane, through the shin of a prisoner, was the only thing keeping him from being buried under greasy flesh.

D'artello shifted his eyes toward the side of the balcony opposite that of the mob of hoods. When he took off running, so did the man behind him. Bounding through the air with a front flip, he was able to clear the railing and make it safely on the other side. The soldier behind him was not so lucky, as his jump was only high and long enough to allow him to catch the railing with one arm. He let out a scream as his shoulder popped out of place. Immediately D'artello ran back toward the edge and pulled the man over the rail, flat onto his back. He didn't stop there. With a hard punch he knocked the man completely out.

The guards began to stampede to the other side of the loft, but by the time they made it, D'artello would be long gone. He got up and ran to the first ladder he could reach, sliding down without touching any of the rungs and taking off to not the first but second door he could find.

Running down the dark hallway, he stopped abruptly when he realized that the Molten Steel was shining far brighter than it ever had. Upon unsheathing it, the whole hallway was illuminated in its pale, benevolent light. In addition to this indication, even his body began to quake. Feeling something, he turned to look down the hallway at a golden door he hadn't seen before. It must have been the doing of the sword. One thing he knew, there was something of importance behind that door, something dark and familiar.

Killing his moment was another spear-wielding hood. In this hallway, there was nowhere to run; it was block or die. Pulling his second sword from the sheath, he deflected the attack and then cut the head of the weapon with his Molten Steel, leaving the guard unprotected. Then in a swift and fluent motion, he swung the bloodthirsty blade at the man's neck.

Just as it would have spilled his contents all over D'artello, the sword made a miraculous halt, so close but not quite there. In that moment, something within cried out, "No!" He realized that Tanya someday would ask him how many people he killed, and it would be plenty painful to even tell her about the Genzak soldiers, let alone any additional casualties.

He began to feel sadness and regret. He longed for his father and Bensel and feared the man in front of him. During this moment of emotional contemplation, the soldier pounded his gauntlet into D'artello's chest, knocking him to the ground. The man picked him up and slammed him against the wall, socking him again in the stomach. By the third time, D'artello dropped his long sword. The blade seesawed to the ground, while its owner took another punch to the stomach.

The soldier picked up the sword. "Get up, you worm!" he shouted. D'artello held his hand against the bruise on his midsection. "Where is the fight in you now?" hollered the man. The black hood was never more fitting as he raised the sword to behead D'artello.

It was then he saw his life flash before his eyes. What he felt more than fear was the twine that had until minutes ago hung around his neck. He had promised Gina he would stay alive. In the darkness of his mind, he found the solar light of the promise charm. The green gem in the center was staring straight at him, and it felt like Tanya's very own eyes. "Get up, D'artello! You have to bring that back to me someday," he heard her saying.

"What a disappointment," he heard as the sword came down. His muscles tightened instantly, and he leapt to his feet defending with the Molten Steel. With a mighty elbow, he regained control of the situation. After the hood fell hard to the ground, D'artello leapt and landed on his chest, knocking the wind out of him. D'artello stared down at him with fire in his eyes; he grabbed the man's head and jerked it down at the floor, knocking him out.

He yanked his sword from the loosened grip. His heart pounded in such a way he swore he could hear it. For a second, he even became convinced its drumming would give away his position to the other hoods. Strangely enough, there were no lamps down this hallway, just the shiny golden door and the pale light from the Molten Steel. All of this provided adequate vision of the barren walls and floor, and the body that lay next to him. This hall was not dedicated to prisoners however. There were no cells as he envisioned it. Where did his soulless body take him?

From what he gathered, he was conscious the entire time and could remember every detail he'd been soulless for. Since he was not in control of his thought process or his body, it was difficult to piece together the former intent of his soulless self.

The door ahead was as voluminous as the stone corridor. It looked wooden and shabby, with presumably rusted bolts fixing it together. However, it shone with an untold, wealthy golden finish. *Is this the doing of the Molten Steel?* D'artello wondered.

He drew near and began to finger the handle. Giving it a flick, he concluded it was sturdy, that it wasn't just his imagination. "He's down this way," he heard an angry voice say. The hoods were catching up with him. *Now or never,* he thought, taking a deep breath and grasping the handle. Pulling the door quickly, he jumped inside, slammed it behind him, and waited for the soldiers to try to break it down.

They never came. He heard not even so much as footsteps coming from the other side. He almost wanted to pull the door open and have a look for himself to see what became of their exploits.

Releasing it and his thoughts of being pursued, he felt dankness. The air in this room was burdensome, as if there were hands, claws of the restless dead pulling at his ankles, keeping him rooted. It was cool, like a basement or a cave, a place that never saw fire or sunlight, slightly chilly. He shuddered as his eyes began to adjust. Even the light from the sword could not illuminate this room.

He meandered a moment just before he bumped into something hard. It repelled him like the reverse polarity of a magnet and slammed him against the hard floor, which repelled him much the same way back to his feet. It hurt, but he ignored it to reach out and touch what he could not see. When it cooled his hand, it felt almost like water, flowing downward, frigid and full of motion, but when he pulled his hand back, it was not wet. Now the pain coursed through his body. The impact agitated his shoulder wound and sent a shocking shiver down his spine.

Finally, his vision returned, adjusting to the room that was ... nothingness. This room appeared to be made of aqueous shadows. The walls seemed to run down with the solution, just as four pillars in the center seemed to push this substance up toward the ceiling, like a continuous fountain of darkness.

The room jolted to life, causing him to stumble to his knees, and the continuous flow of shadows halted to stare at the newcomer. The whole room was still, slightly more uncomfortable than its previous fluid movement. Even the air stood still. They began to recede, as if the room were growing, as if it were alive.

D'artello held the Molten Steel close, carefully watching this phenomenon. The shadows slithered away toward the door. He was glad they were leaving, but he began to feel eerily alone. They made an ear-piercing hiss, like powerful winds in all of the grass whistles of an entire field.

They fled through every pore of the door, the cracks in the wood, the space above and below it, and the lock hole until they were all gone. Left behind was a great white hall. At first it was blinding, from pitch-blackness to bright marble light.

His eyes came to and allowed him to see what he assumed to be the real room. The pillars now stood like glossy, white giants, holding up the roof, and beyond them was an obtuse set of stairs draped over with a velvet red carpet that was widest at the bottom and narrowed toward the top. Shields that depicted a white raven were polished and bore his reflection from their wall-mounted placement. The picture was familiar somehow. *That's the picture on the chest plate of the Phantoms.* He concluded that he should not be welcomed by this room's deceptively bright nature.

Scrutinizing the stairs, his gaze climbed them and came to rest at the top, upon which sat a throne facing the far wall. Was someone sitting there? Without thinking, he gave a shout, "Hello!"

No answer came. He crept toward the steps, holding his breath, trying not to make a sound, gently placing one foot in front of the other. His toe stopped against the first step, and he gave another call as he could now see, indeed, a heavy someone sitting in the throne. "Hello!"

Still no answer. He swallowed hard and took a deep breath of the thin air that idled in that chamber. The hall still felt empty somehow. He had never felt so alone. "Heh heh heh," a familiar laugh came as the throne began to rotate, revealing its occupant. D'artello gasped but experienced a sudden relief.

"Joseph!" he called out. "You're alive!" He ran toward his friend. He stopped about halfway up the stairs when his friend did not rise to greet him. Standing at his side in his left hand was a sinister, gray battle axe that looked similar to the swords the Phantoms carried. Notably, he was clad in full body armor, even his helm, and it was not like Joseph to wear his helm unless he absolutely needed it. An uncharacteristically angry stare gazed down upon D'artello, red like blood and hatred where the whites of his eyes should have been. Accompanying the stare, like a maddening fungus, a crazed smile had grown across his face.

D'artello stepped back, unsure whether or not to raise his sword to a friend. "You … are not Joseph!" he barked angrily.

"That's right," it spoke. The voice was an entangling of many, but the central one, or at least the one that spoke to D'artello the clearest, was indeed the voice of his dear friend. "You threw me to the wolves!" he said.

"What is this?" D'artello yelled as a tear began to roll down his cheek.

"This is revenge, D'artello," he said, jumping down the stairs swinging that axe overhead. It would have chopped D'artello down the middle if he had not found the strength to step aside at the last possible second. It smashed the tiles, digging in and splintering the stone. With ease, he pulled the axe up onto his shoulder, readying for his next cleave. "Fight me, D'artello! Do it! Finish what you started!" he yelled, taking a neck-level swing over D'artello's crouching body.

"No, Joseph, I won't," he said, placing the Molten Steel back into its sheath. As hard as he pushed, however, the sword would not enter all the way into the sheath. The would-be Joseph peered down on him as he tried with both hands to force it back into the worn, brown leather. He slipped, and the sword was vaulted toward the wall behind him, and his eyes followed it back before returning his vision to Joseph.

"See?" he said, holding up his empty hands.

Joseph chuckled. "Then dodge me, D'artello!" he responded, winding back and taking a full swing.

Meanwhile Gina had attracted the attention of many as she ran through another torch-lit prison hall. She knew Seraph had caught on to her disguise. "Gerrik! Sir Gerrik!" she yelled. "Bensel! My king!" Her steps pounded the stone floor as she tried to out speed her pursuers. A sight down the hallway stopped her in her tracks. She felt her heart drop as she stared at the white cloak hovering just above the ground. In less than seconds, its beaming eyes detected her.

It shrieked to acknowledge her, snapping her out of a frightened trance. Raising its blade overhead, it flew diagonally at her. Gina stood her ground; there was no point in running in the other direction toward the approaching hoods. Lowering her stance, she got ready. Diving downward into a forward roll, she narrowly avoided the vertical swing of her opponent. The Phantom's momentum carried it far enough down the hall to catch wind of the much tastier mob of prey headed its way.

Gina could sense them standing off with the beast for a moment until she heard one man ask the obvious question: "What the hell is that thing!?" Gina continued to run, but could hear it give another howling battle cry and charge into the clashing weapons.

It was not long before the chorus of horrible screams began to fill the corridor. "Gerrik!" she yelled. Her heart pounded as loud as her feet, drowned only by her occasional voice booming every now and then, echoing down the hallway. "Elan! Sandra!" She gave a winded cough and stumbled for a moment, but pressed on.

"Look out, Gina!"

"Gerrik?" she answered, looking to the left and spotting him behind iron bars. In her momentary distraction she was savagely blindsided, leaving her sprawled on the floor, looking face up at the ceiling. Her face throbbed as she squinted up through her disorientation to see the red-caped Seraph. Blood dripped from his sword, and his armor was spattered with the remains of the men he'd cut down in the pit. He ran a hand satisfactorily through his black hair and watched her squirm.

She struggled to push herself off the floor, but Seraph's boot came down in the center of her back, making her fall again. "A valiant effort, but it's only a matter of time before we track down your little friend as well." He knelt toward her face and began to blow his distasteful, warm words into her nostrils, yanking the black hood from her face. "Sorry, you couldn't rescue your nation, truly."

"Just wait until D'artello gets here. He'll kill you for doing this to me," Gina rasped as he bore down. She spit in his face, and he took a moment to straighten his posture and calmly wipe the saliva. This angered him enough to put more of his weight on, forcing from her a painful grunt.

"You won't live to see it because you won't ever be leaving this spot," he barked, raising his great blade.

"Seraph! Don't touch her!" Gerrik yelled from down the hall.

Gerrik's words were meaningless, but the shriek from down the hallway certainly got Seraph's attention. Halting the tip of the sword before its bloody, steel mass entered her spine, he listened acutely, while peering down the dark depths of the other direction.

Gina had never been happier to see the white cloak emerge from the shadows and tackle someone. As luck would have it, the creature barreled through the air and took Seraph off-balance, casting his sword sliding across the ground. Now being the one pinned, he fought for his life instead.

"Gina, break the lock!" Gerrik yelled. She ran to his rescue but reversed her direction to grab Seraph's heavy weapon. She dragged the sword until in range, and like a hammer, gave a hearty heave of her shoulder, striking the chain.

It exploded into pieces that fell bouncing to the ground. Gerrik kicked open the door and immediately seized Gina's wrist. The two ran back the way she had come. "Help! Have mercy please!" Seraph screamed. The Phantom slugged him in the face. "I can show you to the rest of your comrades."

A roar of mixed tones came from down the hall. The mercenaries who had previously encountered the Phantom had apparently begun to turn wild. Gerrik realized that they did not have much time, and he had no idea the layout of this structure, except the way he had come in. Although Seraph had proven himself a menace, they needed him, especially if they wanted to leave with Bensel, Elan, and Sandra.

Gerrik leapt over and gave a sharp kick, sending the Phantom a few hollow steps backward. Seraph scrambled to his feet a few paces behind him. The Phantom rushed back with much irritation.

* * *

D'artello flipped over the huge, careening axe, barely missing the leg-severing blade. The momentum drove it into the marble wall, blasting ugly scars into it, and halting the advance for the moment. "Joseph! Stop this! I'm sorry," he yelled. "This is crazy!"

"This is power," Joseph hissed, his muscles visibly straining. D'artello had expected him to simply retract the axe from the wall, but instead the wall began to crack more. Chips began to pinch away from the wall, violently expelling themselves. Joseph's red, blood-filled eyes fixed on D'artello's as the axe forced through and escaped the rest of the wall, barreling toward D'artello's neck.

Unable to react in time, he threw his hands up to block. The Molten Steel that once lay on the ground now sailed to his aid, blocking the axe with its broadside, while being thrust back into its wielder's hands.

The block was not without repercussion. D'artello was sent flying backward, spanning the forty-foot width of the room, slamming against the far wall. He could feel anger flare up inside of him, a power he could not control. Joseph leapt at him, his weapon leading him in a vertical swing.

D'artello rolled to the side as the blade struck and drove into the floor, smashing the stone tiles as if they were dried clay. D'artello arched his back and sprang off his arms gracefully to his feet, ready for more.

"You are going to have to kill me, D'artello. Kill me if you want to live, if you even *want* to live this life!" Joseph said.

Life. His had been taken; he had been an emotionless slave to his Peacemaker. Never to love, never to hate, never to feel again, and to only love her and feel for her—to hell with that. *If I cannot live my own life, is it worth living at all?* "Joseph," he addressed his friend.

Joseph charged, but D'artello did not budge an inch. He wanted to end the loneliness, meet his mother, and soar in the heavens. Let the axe pierce the shell of a man he was, releasing his spirit, letting it fly free, no longer a slave to a Peacemaker.

Joseph drew closer, and D'artello's mind salivated with those desires. But for now, he *could* feel. He loved his father, and he longed for Tanya and his newfound friend, Gina. He felt sorry for Joseph and all those who would fall without the mystic sword. Unsure of the path he would take, he felt a deep anger for the being that held his friend captive. It was for these feelings that he would fight henceforth, battling for his soul. Unexpectedly, he blocked the axe and used the counter momentum to serve up a powerful kick, driving the behemoth of a man down.

Clenching his teeth, Joseph climbed to his feet. "So! You do have some fight left in you, but do you have it in you to beat us?"

D'artello could hear the voices of the dark soul speaking through his friend now. It was then he realized, even though he could hear his friend's voice in the muddle, there was no man behind the monster. Joseph had died that night in Fort Carrie and was buried the next morning. The only way to save him was to free his soul. He planted his boot to the tiles and waved his sword into proper stance. The two gave a war cry and charged.

* * *

Gerrik and Gina had charged past the Phantom, blocking their path. Gerrik tossed Seraph against the wall and slugged him in the stomach. He picked him back up off the ground and held him up by his neck. "If I don't see Bensel or Elan in the next few moments I'm going to break your legs and leave you for that Phantom. So if you are thinking of leading us into a trap, know that my patience grows thin," he threatened.

"He's just up this way," Seraph said, taking a moment to catch his breath then leading the group with his cape streaming behind. The entire prison had erupted into an orchestra of cries and screaming swords. Seraph pulled the keys from his belt midstride, approaching a sturdy wooden ladder. "He's up top!" Seraph pointed, but not without another threatening look from Gerrik. Gina grabbed the keys in her teeth and drew her sword, climbing the ladder erratically. Poking her head up and tasting the tin in her mouth, she glanced around to make certain the coast was clear.

"Gina!" she heard. Pulling herself up quickly, she unlocked Bensel's cell. "Where are the others?" Bensel asked, pushing the heavy set of bars open. She pointed down the ladder hole, and then without hesitation or further words, they rejoined the group at the bottom.

"Where is my daughter?" Bensel grabbed Seraph by the collar and began to shake the life out of him. He stretched the man's cotton undershirt across his windpipe with a predator's looks in his eyes.

"My king, please," he gagged on his words.

"I am not your king!" Bensel said, tightening his grasp. Gerrik's hand came to rest on his shoulder.

"Bensel, the Phantoms are here. We don't have time for this. He will show us where Elan and Sandra are being held."

Bensel shoved Seraph back onto his elbows.

Seraph caressed his neck, which now bore red fingerprints. "I put Elan to work in the coal pit, and the princess in my private quarters on the other side. Elan is on our way in that wide-open center of this prison. But we've got to hurry," The group ran down the hall back in the direction they had come.

The Adventures of D'artello

Along the way, they encountered some hoods that acknowledged Seraph and tagged along. By the time they reached the large wooden doors leading out to the central area, there was commotion sounding from the other side.

Gina's heart sank as they heard the howling and screeching of grown men. Then they could faintly make out Elan's familiar voice. "Fight on, men! For King Bensel!"

Gina cracked the door and looked into a terrarium of hell. Some of the hoods fought with their weapons to suppress the prisoners, and some of the prisoners fought back against them with shovels and chains, whatever was accessible. Some used their shovels like catapults to throw the hot embers at the hoods. This was not the only thing awry in this room, however. A third party interjected the norm. This third party was made up of men crawling around like animals, jumping on, dragging away, and mercilessly beating other men.

She opened the door a little wider only to be startled by the swing of an escaping prisoner. She ducked and thrust her sword through the heart of the escapee, not on purpose, but a reaction from years of conditioning, a testament to how easy it was to take a life. Scruffy, dirty, and beaten as he was, his still human eyes stared at her accusingly in his last moments of life, before his body slid down to the floor.

Gerrik and Bensel gave war cries and pushed past her with the ever-ready band of hoods. Watching them through her peripheral vision, she began to shake.

How did they do it? How did they take so many lives? How was it that easy? She watched Gerrik battle against three others. Powerful as he was, she now did not question his ways of giving up the sword. This sight troubled her more than her first kill. She watched the ever-amazing Gerrik fight, taking on three other armed men with just his bare hands. *Only the strong have a choice,* she realized. *Only the strong have the choice of taking a life in this world. D'artello and Gerrik, they are truly amazing men, but Elan and I, even King Bensel, we are all slaves to our weapons. What can I do except charge?* she speculated sadly.

* * *

"Joseph, if you're in there, I don't want to hurt you," D'artello yelled to the kneeling hulk a few feet away.

"Even if I fail, I have done my part. Just remember it was my Phantom that crippled your spirit!" the creature spoke. "Die!" Joseph screamed, reaching a hand out. A black tendril darted from his palm and caught D'artello by surprise. With his hands pinned under the mysterious black mass, he was unable to writhe free. It felt like thousands of beestings piercing and burning his flesh. It lifted him off his feet. He struggled helplessly.

"Joseph!" he grunted. "I'm sorry, Joseph."

"Huh?" it seemed that somewhere inside the monster, Joseph's consciousness still peeked through. The tension around D'artello grew tighter still.

"I was not myself. Harmony took my soul. Even I did not know what I was doing. That's the honest truth!"

"D'artello ..." Joseph's voice could now be heard much clearer.

"Yes, it's me."

"I don't believe ya. Soulless? How could ya lie to me?"

"Joseph," he said, gasping for air. "I'm telling you the truth. Harmony took my soul to protect me. I know what it looked like. Trust me, your death already kills me. Not a day goes by that I don't wonder what I deserve, but I am not the source of your pain. Let go, Joseph," he said. "I promise I will avenge you against whatever has done this to you."

"His story is flawed!" said the now deep voice that overlapped Joseph's. An odd process ensued before him. The voices that had spoken as one were beginning to separate and interact with one another. "Do you really believe he was soulless?"

"Joseph!" D'artello called out, continuing to defend himself. "Look at what's happening! Is it *that* hard to believe? I didn't seem different to you at all?"

"Yes, you were different ... it ... was as if you weren't there, as if you *weren't* my friend."

"I would never have let you die, Joseph. I'm ... sorry!" he grunted as the tendril forced the air from his lungs. He was no longer able to inhale. Whatever Joseph's decision, he'd better make it quick. There were barely a few seconds of life left in him.

The tendril released him abruptly, and Joseph with his hands pressing hard against his head began to cry out. "I believe you, D'artello!" he shouted.

"No, he's lying. He will kill you."

"No, it's not true! I am already dead!"

"Stop, you fool!"

"D'artello ... now! Do it now while I got a hold of it."

D'artello held his Molten Steel in one hand and supported himself with the other like a cane. Breathing heavily, as his blue lips returned to their normal color, he thought about the decision before him. It was much more comfortable when he felt Joseph was indeed dead, and not this monster. Now it had shown him otherwise. He had seen that at least a part of his dear friend was still alive. D'artello stared in horror.

* * *

Gina looked over the morbid scene surrounding the fire pit. Innocent men shed blood, and the tainted remained unscathed. Despite the skill of the warriors, the furious persistence of the tainted was unmatched. Bensel butted one off with his shield and then stabbed it through the midsection.

Bensel was not left alone for long. Another tainted man leapt at him from behind, pounding on his back. The best efforts of Bensel's armor were not enough. The force of the pounding was indeed substantial. He fell forward into a hood, holding his own against two tainted. Unfortunately, he stumbled to his knees, giving the tainted their moment to dive on him and drag the poor man away.

"They are getting back up!" Elan yelled.

Bensel had turned to face his thrashing opponent. He would have been able to handle just the one, but the tainted slain just moments ago rose back up to fend off the old king. Bensel skulked away, behind more human combatants, to avoid being dragged off as the other man had.

The pale faces and famished legs of the tainted showed their transformation beginning to take hold. Soon they would all be full-fledged Phantoms. Then they would have real problems. In backing away, Bensel's back met the ever-familiar Gerrik's. "This is going to hell quickly!" Bensel shouted.

"Agreed," Gerrik responded in a mid-roundhouse kick, bowling over another tainted. The veteran soldiers could see and hear the room being taken over. Hoods and prisoners that did not have excessive skill like Gerrik and Bensel were dying off rapidly. The sheer number of tainted would have been enough, but the fact they wouldn't die made it even more overwhelming.

"Elan! Gina! We've got to push through!" Bensel yelled.

Gina was scared stiff. She had not the stomach for the way the tainted crawled about, as men never should. A heavy iron ball careened to her feet, smashing into the stone floor, taking the guesswork out of what such a weapon would do to the human body. Her eyes followed the links of a chain attached to the ball, to the hands of its hooded wielder.

"Blast," she heard a grunt from beneath the hood. The weapon was unwieldy, and the man behind it obviously had a hard time using it, thank Harmony. Gina was grabbed suddenly by her hair and pulled gruffly backward.

Realizing at last that her hesitation would get her killed, she sprang to life. Drawing her sword, she circled back around her neck and severed the strands at shoulder length, freeing herself from her captor in time to dodge the metal ball soaring through the air at her again. Instead, it fed its violent appetite on the hood that was holding a handful of Gina's hair.

She was sickened by how suddenly the man went limp. That impact to the chest sent him to the ground, leaving him with broken bones in his chest.

Although that could've been *her* lying on the ground, fighting for bloody breaths, she felt sympathy for the poor soul. *What a way to go,* she thought.

Thank Harmony, Elan had come to her aid. Ensnaring her wrist, he attempted to lead the way. He was stripped of all of his armor, except for his cloth slacks and chainmail suit. There was a bloody claymore held at his waist, one that he must have seized from an enemy guard. The hood with the ball and chain was tackled off balance by a tainted while trying to retract his weapon.

Elan led with his shoulder, then unwound with the claymore, blazing a macabre path to the exit. There they could see Gerrik and the others holding the door. Probably an exit to Seraph's private quarters, she figured, remembering the earlier conversation.

They made a mad dash to the door and ran straight past Seraph, who was already inside, guarding the hallway from any flanks to the rear. Gerrik threw one last angry fist, snapping one of the tainted out of the air and back into the crowd fighting for the same door. Upon slamming it shut, Bensel was already smashing down the iron bar to lock it. A horrible pounding and screaming came from the other side of the door, rattling it with intense fury. Gina had a sudden flashback to the burning tower she had been trapped in.

Elan didn't hesitate a second in shoving Seraph against the closest wall and holding his claymore up to his throat. "Show me where she is or I'll kill you right here." His complexion was serious enough to even catch Bensel off guard.

"Right this way," Seraph said, looking him in the eyes. The king he had called fool, and the soldier he had called boy, were now in full control of each move he made. As soon as Seraph was let go, he gave a flip of his cape to capture what little dignity he may have had left.

As they tread in, the sound of the commotion behind the door grew fainter, as did their scared heart rates. They took a sharp turn down a much better lit hall. The floor was littered with sizeable broken wooden splinters. Surprise spread over Seraph's face, and he ran ahead and began to search every room, looking for the princess. Elan ran to search the other side of the hall. "Sandra!" he called.

"Elan," she answered. Her voice came faintly at first, but his ears pointed him in the right direction. Following the voice, he entered a room expecting to see his love, arms agape just waiting for her valiant knight to save her.

When his eyes fell on her, there were no arms agape. There was a bed on the far side of the room, next to a nightstand providing candlelight. Sandra was atop the bed, looking over at him.

Her hands had lost all of their color, and so had most of her clothes. They were now an ashen gray and folded over her chest as if she were to be buried. She had turned her still colorful face to gaze upon her love.

"Elan … no … shhh … everything's going to be all right," she said, seeing his face grow hysterical. Naturally she'd always hated to see him cry, even when they were little. Kneeling down at her bedside, he dropped his sword and his head, letting the worrisome tears flow. Moving her arm gave off a grinding noise as she touched his cheek, his hand clasped hers. She too began to cry.

Seconds later, the rest of the group rounded the corner. "My daughter," Bensel gasped, running to her bedside.

"Daddy," she moaned weakly.

* * *

"Kill me now!" Joseph said, throwing a fist at the wall, trying to restrain himself. "It's gonna control me again," he strained.

D'artello watched his friend suffer as *he* suffered in his decision. He wanted to cure him so badly, to have Joseph back as an ally and a friend. He could really use his lightheartedness now more than ever.

The only way to do that would be to cut him with the sword, and he was uncertain what the outcome. He would have to treat it like a weapon, like it would actually kill him, and therein lay the decision.

"D'artello, pleeeeeaaaase," he roared. The man was in pain, experiencing a pain worse than death. "I-I forgive you, D'artello. I-I'm sorry it's gotta come to this, but please, my fogivin' ya, is what's lettin' you get your chance," he sputtered.

Making his final answer, D'artello approached his kneeling, wounded friend. "I'm sorry, Joseph," he said under his breath, holding his sword up. He used his free arm to pound across his chest once, a response to his friend's last salute.

D'artello couldn't bear the sight. He acknowledged this as the coldest thing he'd ever done. A childhood memory flooded back just then. He and Joseph were six years younger, just thirteen years old. That day, they had decided to spar with real weapons, and when D'artello came back with a deep cut in his arm, Gerrik had to cauterize it using a hot piece of iron.

Gerrik had told him to look away. He said it wouldn't hurt as much that way, that by the time he opened his eyes it would be over. Imploring a similar technique, D'artello closed his eyes now and awaited the painful sting of knowing he killed his friend. He retracted his arm and then took another deep breath. A chill crept its way over his shoulders and under his hair, wrapping around his neck. He thrust his arm, driving the sword into Joseph's chest.

He had to open his eyes as soon as he'd done it. Joseph collapsed around the Molten Steel and then fell to his back. A black geyser shot up from his body, like an ink-formed soul. It passed through the roof. Having vanished, it left the two young friends in silence. Joseph's eyes began to crystallize, turning white like mist on a rainy morning.

Just as D'artello knelt and wiped the tears from his face, he heard a voice. "D'artello, that you?"

"Joseph?" he asked, looking upon him.

"Aye, it's me," he replied, staring up at the ceiling. He began to cough and sputter as D'artello swiftly approached him. Joseph had not even the strength the cover the wound on his chest. Sliding his hands under the weighty man, D'artello tried to lift Joseph so that he could lean on his shoulder, but with what little strength he could muster, Joseph resisted.

"No-no, please, I've got somethin' important to tell ya," he gasped, giving another gurgling cough.

"Joseph … don't talk, keep your strength. I can save you. Just come with me," he said, trying to raise him again.

"Don't waste yer time. You've already saved me. I have to tell ya … King Garo is a monster, like I was. He's takin' an entire army of those Phantoms to the north. While those monsters got me, like in my mind, I kept hearin' 'find the Dark One, winged man, the Dark One.'" With that, he let out one final gasp and then fell limp and silent.

"Who's that? Wait, Joseph, stay with me! Who's the winged man?" He shook his friend, trying to wake him up. It was no use; Joseph had succumbed to the final sleep. D'artello laid the body down slowly and glanced for a moment at the wound in his chest, a wound that had seen both the Frozen Steel and Molten Steel. *Was that there before?* he thought. *Did my sword do that? Dammit, did I slay him?* For sanity's sake, he would have to assume not. His sword was not capable of piercing the flesh of a man; it was only for killing Phantoms. *Clearly I freed his soul—or did I?*

"We share this, my friend," he said, placing his hand across the cut on his chest the Phantom at Fort Carrie had given him. It was wrapped up in cloth now, but soon he would remove it and there would be a scar to remind him of his friendship. Darkness befell the room, and from the darkness sparked a torch. As the room lit up, he realized he was now kneeling back in the hallway before the golden door, and said door was gone. Emotions as if memories came flooding back for all that he should have felt in his soulless state. He hung his head and gave a respectful moment of silence; a moment for the soldiers, some of them his friends, killed by the Alphas; for the untimely demise of Joseph; for the affections that Gina had shown him; and last but most importantly, the good-bye that he owed to Tanya. "Aaagh!" he let out, throwing his fists against the walls.

Why me? he thought. *Why did Harmony choose me? I'm just a kid from a town out in the middle of nowhere. If there is a universe full of people like she says, couldn't she have asked someone else? This,* he looked at his sword, *this thing attracts them. If I didn't have it, they would leave me alone.*

He wanted to leave the Molten Steel in this hallway, turn his back on it, and never look back. But then Joseph would have died in vain, and his promise to protect Tanya would mean nothing.

* * *

Gerrik and company had holed themselves up in Seraph's private quarters. Gerrik and Bensel stood at the door listening, trying to make something out of the dead silence in the empty hallway. They couldn't help but keep one eye on the progressing affliction that had befallen Sandra. As more of her body turned to stone, her arms became frozen around Elan's face. He kissed her tenderly as if to absorb the last bit of love that was left in her still red lips. "Forget me, Elan. You deserve to be happy and remain pure."

"Never," he said, brushing away tears.

"Sandra, I am sorry I couldn't protect you," Bensel said.

"It's okay, Daddy," she gasped, her neck turning to stone. "I know you did your best. I just outgrew your protection, like all daughters do."

The old man began to cry beside the young lover. "Listen to me," she said. "Please don't seek vengeance, so if you die, you will die pure as I am. I promise it doesn't hurt ... I love you both," she said with her last breath. Footsteps began to sound from outside the door.

"Gina!" Gerrik barked, pulling her from her affixed trance on the dying princess.

She pulled her sword from her sheath and stood next to him, ready to bottleneck an oncoming attack. "Wait!" she said suddenly.

"What?" Gerrik said.

"Phantoms don't have footsteps." They listened closer to the tapping of boots hitting stone floor. They were making an odd footwork, pausing at predictably every doorway on the way to this one. This person was looking for something, or someone. "A survivor?" Gina guessed.

Despite the possibility, Gerrik readied the attack. The only person who could have possibly dodged Gerrik's strike rounded the corner. His fist barely missed D'artello's silver haired head. The gruff greeting didn't upset him; he had expected it from his father. Upon seeing who it was, Gerrik scooped D'artello up in a bear hug. Gerrik could feel his boy's warm feelings again. Finally he had come to. "D'artello, my son, I'm so glad you are alive."

"Glad to see you too, Dad," he rasped through the mighty pressure. When Gerrik finally put him down, it was all Gina could do to stop herself from jumping into his arms to take her turn. She held the solemn look on her face and turned to face her statue princess.

"Oh dammit," D'artello said, pulling the sword. But by the time he could touch it to her flesh, it was too late. The sword refused to dig into the stone to cure her; it had been too long to restore her health. "When did the Phantoms attack? How are all of you still okay?" he asked.

"You didn't see them?" Seraph asked.

D'artello shot him a nasty look; he was as shocked to see him as he was disgusted by him.

"D'artello, almost everyone in this prison became a Phantom—guards, prisoners, everyone," Gerrik responded.

"What are you talking about? There were some bodies in the main hall, but none other to be found. I thought they all escaped."

"No," Gina said. "In fact, they were all on their way down this hall before you showed up. Their screaming stopped about a half an hour ago."

It was then D'artello had an epiphany. *The darkness in the room where I fought Joseph, could that have been a Phantom? Was that what Harmony meant by the source? Was Joseph a source? Then is King Garo a source too? If so, we have to stop him from getting to the north.*

His train of thought crashed with Seraph's body against the wall. "You worm," Elan said, taking Bensel's sword and holding up to the aging mercenary's throat. "I'll carve your eyes out for this," he said. Seraph by reflex had Elan by the throat and kept a steady line of vision, although it would do him no good against the knight's youthful physique or the blade in his hand.

"Stop that," D'artello called. "Quit it, Elan. Don't hurt him."

Elan ignored him and even began to push the sword before D'artello finally grabbed him and threw him to the ground.

"Calm down!" D'artello yelled.

Elan stood up with fire in his eyes. "You would deny me the revenge I deserve?" he asked, swinging Bensel's sword. With a peace-breaking clash, D'artello blocked.

Bensel did something completely unexpected, shoving D'artello against the wall.

"My king!" Gina shouted.

"Hey!" Gerrik yelled simultaneously.

"Gerrik, I suggest you back off and let us do what we please with this traitor," Bensel growled, referring to Seraph. Gerrik tried to put a hand on his comrade's shoulder to calm him, and he was surprised at how blindingly fast the jolly king lashed out, swinging his fists furiously.

"Stop it!" Gina yelled. But the two older men began to tussle, using some skillful blocks and reversals. Bensel could fistfight, but the only reason he was able to keep up, was because Gerrik did not want to hurt him. This was the first time D'artello had ever seen them disagree, let alone throw fists. Elan suddenly came at Gerrik, who was distracted.

Catching his attacker in his peripheral, Gerrik threaded a strong palm through Bensel's hands and shoved him to his backside. Elan came in over the top, but Gerrik pivoted and then slid away from the attack. Due to his emotional distress, Gerrik lost control for just a moment; he snapped powerful blows at Elan's arms, causing him to drop the sword. Just as quickly, he flipped Elan over his shoulder, onto his back, and then locked his neck in his powerful arms. Elan stopped struggling as Gerrik applied pressure.

It didn't take long for Elan to respect that the aging warrior could snap his spine like a twig. "You ever try something like that again, soldier!" he threatened.

The room was quiet now. D'artello put his sword away and brushed himself off. Seraph stood in the corner with a frown across his wrinkly lips. "This is over the boy's head for Harmony's sake," he began to defend himself. "I am fighting for the same reason."

Gerrik shot him a quick look, as if to say, *it's blatantly obvious what you've managed to accomplish here.*

D'artello stood up tall and began to speak. "Do you know how many people in the world are like Seraph? Tons, more than we can count. He's done horrible things, and horrible things have come from his actions ..." he said, pausing a moment to gaze upon Sandra, "but we are fighting to save this world, and like it or not, we don't get to pick who lives in it. Either way, we will be saving countless murderers, scoundrels, and knaves. What would she want?" he asked, motioning to the stone corpse. Taking another moment, he glanced again at his childhood friend with whom he used to play in the training grounds.

A look of shame spread across Bensel's face that was as prominent as the look of utter fear on Elan's, still locked in Gerrik's arms. Even with the mighty warrior bearing down on him, Elan quickly remembered her words, telling him that he was not supposed to seek vengeance, so he could die pure like she did.

Gerrik rose from his knees and then helped him up. "I'm sorry," he whispered. "I'm sorry, old friend," he said, holding a hand out to Bensel as well. Bensel hesitantly accepted his hand and pulled himself up.

"Listen, Elan," Gerrik said, "I know what you're going through."

"I thank you, Sir Gerrik, and I apologize for losing my head, but I will mourn in my own way," he said, walking back to the statue and placing his face back into her stone grasp. The formalities left a sting on his conscience.

"Sir Gerrik," no longer rolled off of his tongue as if he were addressing his hero.

Seraph began to clap loudly, raising his hands up to neck level. "Ah ... the boy sounds with reason," he said.

"And you ..." D'artello turned to him, drawing his Molten Steel and pointing it at his face. "You cannot have this. You don't deserve its power because you try to *choose* who lives. If you still think you can take it from me, then we have unfinished quarrels."

D'artello put his weapon back in the sheath.

"No? Then I leave you with this ... I will not kill you, nor will I let anyone *here* kill you, but when I leave you all alone, here in this prison, your life is in your own hands, and you'll know the mercilessness at the hand of the Phantoms, because they want you. A soul filled with hatred, their favorite feast."

Gina was taken aback at his speech. Goose bumps broke out, and she gave a slight shiver. It put things in perspective for her. When D'artello said, "This is not their fight," that's what he meant. *Even though they may be doing the wrong thing, they are not the ones on trial here, and they are not our enemy. They are just mixed up in a war that they could not possibly win, or even understand, and why would we take the very lives we are fighting to protect?*

"Get running," Gerrik told Seraph as he grabbed him and threw him from the room. "By the time we're done in here, I don't want to see you. If I do, it'll take more than my boy to stop me," he warned.

Seraph continued his dignified posture, though as prideful as he was, he could not deny the luck associated with escaping that situation alive. Not pressing it, his footsteps echoed down the hallway.

Gerrik turned to his son, trying to ignore Elan and Bensel's sorrows for a moment. "Good to have you back, son."

D'artello knew the reason for his recent cold attitude, but Gerrik didn't. It would be too difficult for him to explain himself at this moment, especially in front of everyone. "I'm sorry I acted the way I did, Dad," D'artello said.

"It's fine, son. I'm glad I didn't lose you ..."

D'artello felt as if he'd heard the sentence carry on under his father's breath. Some sort of emotion crossed Gerrik's face then. To the rest of the room, it had never happened because of how good he was at hiding such things, but to D'artello, he may as well have been spilling his guts. His father was keeping something from him.

What could it be? Glancing back in his mind, he filled in his father's life from what he was told, from what he held to be true. Born a peasant's son, grew up a farm boy, best friends with a prince by the name of Bensel, having young loves ... and then he went to war ... after that, D'artello's own eyes had seen the rest.

"So is that it? Did we win, son? Are there no more Phantoms? What did you do?" Gerrik asked hurriedly.

D'artello scratched his head, shaking off his thoughts. "No," he said. The natural magnetism of the response drew sudden silence, pulling the attention of the room right to him. "I know this is going to be hard to believe, but I saw Joseph," he said.

"That's not funny, D'artello," Gerrik responded coldly.

"No really, or ... at least I thought it was Joseph ..."

"You thought?" Gerrik asked.

"Dad, let me finish. I thought it was Joseph. It looked like him, but it didn't sound like him, and it most certainly wasn't. His eyes were red like blood, and he fought me, but I never saw any Phantoms. When were they here?"

"We stopped hearing the screams a little more than half an hour ago," Gina said again.

"That's about the time I defeated the doppelganger," D'artello said.

Gerrik scratched his scruffy chin, pondering the thought for a moment. Considering recent events, it was not hard to believe what his son was saying.

"In his last few moments, Dad," he began again. Gerrik looked up as did everyone else at that moment. "It makes sense to me that Joseph was some sort of leader to these Phantoms. If what you say is true, they vanished just as I defeated Joseph's doppelganger. He told me that King Garo had gone far north to meet the Dark One. I do not know what it means, but ..."

Gerrik moved in on his chance to overtake this venture while his son still had some sense of compliancy. "We have to continue to the capital, and if Garo's not there, we have to go to the north. If he's toting an army of those things, we can't afford to let him march through the country," Gerrik said boldly. "We have a long walk in front of us."

"We won't have to walk," Gina said. "D'artello and I got here on ters. It took us less than an hour to get here from the farm near the bridge."

"A farm?" Bensel asked.

"Yeah, the owners name was Jarod, a big redheaded guy," D'artello answered.

"Jarod you say?" Gerrik said, searching his memory. "I think I know him, or at least his father. Did you happen to mention my name when you met him?"

"Of course," Gina replied. "But everyone knows of you, and I don't know if he really believed our whole story."

"He owes me one. I'll just say that." Yet another curt, vague war story. "I can get us at least a couple more ters, and we can cut our time down, even have time to stop, rest up, and eat. Yes … this is favorable …" Everyone watched as the gears turned in his mind.

Chapter 11

In just a couple of hours, Gerrik, D'artello, and Bensel had flown to and from Jarod's farm, while Gina and Elan located the group's belongings. On their way now, three ters flapped on into the morning. Yet another sleepless night was grinding them down; tonight they would have to stop, one way or another. "I'm not very good at flying them. I'll just ride with D'artello," Gina had said. So then Jarod's debt, whatever it may have been, was repaid with just one additional ter. They had found Thunder tied up in the basement of the prison. So the slepne traveled aloft, adjacent to the pack of ugly flying mounts. From the farm, they continued their southwestward momentum toward the glorious capital of Valor. Named after the very force from which it was erected, this wondrous civilization was a world of its own.

If Fort Carrie was sturdy, then this place was a mountain. Its elevated positioning and layers of stone walls made it an impossible battle. The city was a mass of organized, square, stone buildings, much like Fort Carrie. The wall around the capital was an afterthought though, so instead of being four-walled, the white giants around the capital roped around the city itself. The palace was a titan presiding over and tending to the safety of the denizens living just below its elevated position. Around it was an additional wall, should any force make it through the outermost one. Three large streams that branched off from the main river some miles ago ran through the city's waterways and under its decorative walking bridges. In fear of being taken out of the sky by a hail of arrows, the group thought it best to land outside the castle walls and work their way in.

Garo was the fiercest and most cunning of all the generals to do battle for Vaukry's independence. He became king by popularity. With such a small group, a direct attack would be suicide, but infiltration was easy. D'artello was suddenly glad they were making their move by air.

Leveling off over the city, D'artello had remembered being there on occasion as a young boy. After passing the two walls, there was the market place in the outer cloister, and one was susceptible to the smells of the various foods being cooked up. The food was marketed from the endless trade streets leading to the towering palace that sat in the middle of the town. Not today though, and where once they could hear the roar of daily hustle and bustle, people shouting and bantering to sell their goods to make an honest day's work, only silence echoed across the sky. The idol of a palace with knights practicing formation and combat remained idle.

Gina had her arms wrapped around D'artello's waist firmly, and she had all but drifted off into a snooze. The light stasis was interrupted as her co-rider's shoulder jerked to get her attention. She combed the hair from her eyes and inhaled a mesmerizing yawn.

"Look!" he said sharply.

Peering down, at first glance she noticed the capital through the clouds. Rubbing the teary wash from her eyes, she took a clearer look. The place looked like it had been abandoned weeks, possibly even months ago.

What have we missed here? D'artello thought. It was true that he had not been out of Fort Carrie or its outskirts in a while, but if this trouble were as old as the city let off, one would think a messenger would have come eventually.

The group pulled the reins, and the ters began to circle downward. No cacophony of the crowds came into earshot with their descent. A balancing flap blew some scraps about, clearing the landing for the dry, scaly feet to touch down on the white-stone walk. They had landed on a main street that ran parallel to the outer wall. D'artello dismounted first, and as Gina was swinging her leg over, the lizard gave a shudder and a stretch; she stumbled into D'artello's anticipating arm.

"My Harmony," Bensel said, looking around as if he'd heard his name among the hallowed whispers of the wind whipping through the ghost town. "What happened to this place?" The streets were still white, but the buildings were caked in ash. Some of them had been reduced entirely to gray rubble. The capital had obviously burned to the ground, the way Genzak's capital had, and the way Belren was when they arrived.

"I think we know what happened here," D'artello said.

"The whole army?" Elan questioned.

"It would only take one," D'artello said. "They don't stop."

"That quick though? You don't think they could have caged it or something? And don't you think at least one survivor would have spread the word?" Gerrik asked.

"There are your survivors," Bensel said, pointing down the road. The group squinted down the orderly-graveled street. There was a tarp blowing against something—no, a crowd of something. If the wind turned the right way, it would flap open and reveal statues of people. Some of them stood or lay accepting their fate, and others seemed to be in the process of clawing away from their stone limbs, fighting until the very end.

Then they were like ants popping out on a rock. D'artello looked harder and began to see more and more of these stone citizens. "Evidently they have been quite thorough."

"Make no mistake, this was a clean sweep. No one made it out of here alive, not even women or children," Gerrik said, examining a statue of a mother holding her child's head into her bosoms to shield the youth's eyes. "The question is ... are there any of those monsters still here?"

D'artello withdrew the Molten Steel, sharing its wisdom with the rest of the group. "No," he said. "It glows when they are near, and right now there is nothing. Garo must have set his sights on the capital citizens first. He could make so many Phantoms out of just the population here. I don't understand though, it looks like this took place months ago." D'artello examined some new ivy beginning to nip at the heels of a nearby building.

"If they are not here, then where are they?" Gina asked.

"Joseph said north," D'artello reiterated.

"Fort Carrie," Gerrik said. "He's got to pass our home before he can go north."

"Tanya!" D'artello said. "C'mon, let's go! We don't have time to look around!" He hopped back on the ter, motioning for Gina to hurry. Obediently, the group jumped on their mounts to be on their way again.

Gina was surprised by the speed of the lizard below her, but even more surprised at D'artello's body language. *Tanya, so that's her name,* she thought. Even though she was jealous, she still felt the adrenaline rush when he said her name. Still she hoped for her well-being.

It was hard to be optimistic, as it would be another two hours before they were even close to the town. Each earthen husk of a settlement they passed on the way made it feel less likely that Fort Carrie remained untouched, as they had left it.

A fluttering came in Gina's stomach. She was nervous, as was he, "Oh no," he would whisper as he looked down at each desolate leveling that formerly was a city. D'artello pushed the ter hard, reaching top speed.

No matter the two hours of prelude, Gina was not ready to lay eyes on the fort. It did not look optimistic from above, and the sudden and swift dive of the animal took her breath away. Clenching her teeth just before lethal impact, the animal gave a braking flap and touched down much gentler than expected. D'artello left her in full sprint, shouting off the name, "Tanya!"

She watched him flee for a moment until Gerrik and crew touched down, and then she impulsively took off after him. He had a good five-hundred-foot lead. At times when he rounded corners, she was unsure of where he had gone. They chased past statues of more women and children, but no bodies, just like the capital. His yelling had ceased, and she wondered if he yet grasped the reality of the situation. She thought if he found his love, he would go crazy. His young heart might not be able to handle it.

With cat-like agility, she followed him up to a flat, in front of which was a petrified old couple.

D'artello recognized them, but they were in the way of the door. After practically kicking them over onto their side, he grabbed the handle and gave a violent jerking of his shoulder to open the door enough to slip through.

"Wait up!" Gina called, running and then sliding through the door space as well. She was petite compared to him and able to make quicker work of the obstacle. The windows on the outside wall and the windows from inside the rooms where the doors had been forced open let in the shadowy visibility of the hallway. It was obvious, given the decor, glass, and leaves sprawled across the floor, the Phantoms had come charging through in their white hurricane of death. She passed a bloodstain on the floor, spilled apparently from a statue laying down, holding his side. She could hear boots thumping up the steps as D'artello had already plowed his way through obstacles to the end of the hallway.

He rounded the corner and four doors down to room CCIII. Hesitating to look inside, he took in a deep breath. The door was intact strangely enough, as if he were meant to find this place. He drove his shoulder, as his emotions drove him, through the wood, sending a splintering crack echoing throughout the lifeless building.

The door swung open suddenly, bounced off the wall, and shuddered back to a crack. Gina's feet patted the floor with stealthy prowess as she darted up to the door.

The sight was as gripping as his halted breath. He began to cough and embrace himself on the bed. Gray and cold, like the rest of the people in this town, the twelve-year-old Tanya stood before him. He placed his fingertips on her sandpaper skin, touching the stone that his lifelong sister figure had become. During his tangible scrutiny, he found a tear that had begun to run down her cheek, just before she'd petrified completely.

D'artello went wild now. He pulled his Molten Steel and began to bash it against the statue, not out of anger but out of desperation.

Gina looked on in horror. It clashed loudly on the defensive rock. The first ruckus was so sudden that her heart skipped a beat. Even the second sounding caught her off guard. It was not until the third and fourth swing that she could watch it with just flinching eyes.

"Dammit! Work! C'mon! You said I could cure them!" he shouted toward the sky.

D'artello felt his stomach roll completely over like a raw steak being shaved from its vertical carcass. "Tanya, I'm so sorry," he cried. He could not help the tears that flowed. He stayed for a moment, bowing his head. Shakes ran down his body as sadness and anger were stirred into a new form of mental poison. He gave a hard sniffle and a choking swallow before shouting out the familiar name, "Harmony!"

Gina paid no mind to the phrase. It was not uncommon to take their Peacemaker's name in vain. She raised her hand to the door to open it all the way and console him, but abruptly stopped as a bright light filled the room. Once the light of purity was gone, there stood a woman, the most beautiful woman she had ever seen. The half-naked immortal stood perpendicular to D'artello, staring down on him as if he were nothing, as if he were pitiful. Gina felt angry at the raw audacity of her body language. *Can't she see he is in pain?* she asked herself. *Am I really seeing Harmony? The Peacemaker of Love?* This was an infinitely difficult concept to process. Even in her unconventional lifestyle, her beliefs were steeped in the church. This person bore no resemblance to the depictions she was accustomed to seeing. Could she really be seeing the Great Peacemaker of Love?

A plethora of thoughts raced through her mind as she struggled to discern fact from fantasy. Her beauty was surreal, so unachievable by any mortal. It had to be her; a tightening in her chest told her so. Hearing D'artello speak her name quelled her thoughts.

He remained on his knees, not looking at her even for a moment. His gaze was fixed on his dear friend. "Harmony, please, she didn't deserve this. Please cure her," he pleaded.

"I am sorry, my warrior, I cannot. The Frozen Steel's ailments are steeped in arts beyond my understanding. My power is insufficient."

"I couldn't even say good-bye," he sobbed.

"What are these emotions, D'artello? Your soul is here with me," she said, thumbing a vial around her neck that was next to another vial on the same chain. The fragile containers were crystal shaped and glowed with a hypnotizing, baby blue radiance. "Perhaps some of it remains within you," she reassured, almost to herself.

Emotions? His soul? That must be why he seemed so heartless before. She has the power to take his soul, so whatever is left is what is making him feel again, Gina deduced.

"I must take the rest of your soul. I cannot allow this ailment to befall you as well," Harmony said, referring to Tanya.

I can't let that happen, Gina thought.

"Harmony, this is who I am. I am not truly alive without my soul, and I can cure myself with the Molten Steel, can't I?"

"My dear D'artello, pain is only for normal men. This is for your own good," she declared as he stood up to face her.

"You're right," he said, taking a quick glance back at Tanya before melting into the Peacemaker's eyes.

Harmony placed a hand on his cheek and leaned in to embrace him, but something inside Gina rose up and shouted after her. Welling up her courage, she burst in on their moment and stood with her wrist locked around her sheathed sword. Harmony looked at her with extreme distaste, a stare of intimidating hatred as she lowered her hand gracefully.

"How dare you interrupt us, mortal?" she asked.

Taking a deep, bracing breath, she was about to find out if this really was the immortal Peacemaker. Gina stepped into the ring of fire, serving as a divide between Harmony and D'artello, as she pushed him from harm's way. "Gina?" D'artello asked, as if coming out of a trance. He saw that she had taken a defensive stance, to protect him like a proud knight willing to die for her kingdom.

"Mortal, you dare to deny me what is mine?" Harmony hissed. Gina's stance was good—it was revered as one of the sturdiest in her squad—but it was no match for the will of a Peacemaker. Harmony never once gave her the respect of locking gazes. She looked on at D'artello even though her words addressed Gina

"Quaint, but foolish," Harmony uttered, giving an innocuous wave. Despite the nature of the gesture, an unseen force threw the poor girl from her feet across the room. Tanya's bookshelf broke her fall, smashing into large portions and cushioning her back with jagged, upright spines of the fairytale tomes Tanya had liked to read. "I wield great power, mortal. I can end your life with the blink of an eye."

Her ego took an immediate downturn when she realized the pitiful look on D'artello's face.

Harmony wondered how many times she could do that to Gina without D'artello turning her away. The boy had yet to realize his bargaining chip. Also, his sudden outburst of emotion was rather discerning to the goddess. *For how long will he question his feelings? I know I took all of it. Even if I hadn't, his emotions still would not be this strong. I have to reason with him before he realizes his negotiating stance,* Harmony thought.

"I understand your desire to feel. It is what you mortals live for," she aired. "When you leave for the north tomorrow, your soul stays with me. It is for your protection." She disappeared again into the light, but this time it came and went faster.

"Why did you do that, Gina?" D'artello asked, helping her to her feet and then wrapping one of his arms around her back. "Are you okay?"

"I-I don't know D'artello, I just want you … uh … I mean you deserve to feel," she replied, wiping tears from his face. "Who was she?" she asked, looking over at Tanya.

"Just an orphan," he started. "One of the many left behind during Vaukry's liberation. Her parents were taken by Vashti marauders and dragged through city streets," he said.

Gina swallowed hard thinking of the struggling, screaming couple being battered and bloodied up by the stony walkways.

"Just some sick people, trying to make their point at the end of the war. I remember being just eight when I saw them get theirs. They would have killed Tanya too if not for my father. He caught them, because he knew the couple." He went on, remembering the roar of the crowd as they brutalized the bandits before hanging their comatose bodies publicly. "She never really knew them, her parents I mean, and she was only one year old when my father took her in. She's always been like a sister to me. Closer than most, she is the one who gave me this," he said, pulling the charm wrapped around Gina's neck. "The promise was that I would bring it back to her someday. It belonged to her mother." He began to sob, pillowing his face against Gina's shoulder. She palmed the back of his head and ran her fingers through his hair, letting him get it all out.

"Shh, she's not just an orphan. We'll find a way to fix her. Just don't give up."

"I vowed to protect her. I've always done that, Gina," he cried. "Maybe Harmony is right. My emotions do make me weak," he said, wiping his eyes.

She pulled him away. "Look at me," she commanded, placing her hands on his cheeks, forcing him to look into her eyes. "You're not weak," she said, slowly shaking her head. "You're not weak, and they don't make you weak. Do you hear me? You didn't have your soul, and that's why Tanya is in this state, because you couldn't care about her. You couldn't care about anyone. It made you forget what's really important. I don't want you to think this is all about me, but I need you right now. I need your strength. I need to be protected."

Without her, he lacks purpose, Gina thought. She hugged him tightly around the neck. "Maybe we can meet back up with your dad, and we can give her a real funeral," Gina suggested.

"No," D'artello said. "My dad won't understand."

"I see. I'm sorry you feel that way," she replied, looking down. "Then just us, we'll give her a proper burial."

"No, no funeral; this isn't over," he said. "I know this sounds crazy, but trust me when I say I can still feel her inside of that statue somewhere. I'm going to find a way to cure her when this is over. I made a promise," he said with the charm in hand. He turned and placed her lying down on the bed. "It's okay, you can lay down now. You were so brave, and I'm so proud of you," he said before kissing the stone forehead.

Gina approached and placed her hands to warm his. He looked down at her, taking his eyes off of Tanya as if to let it pass him for now. The pair left the newly established tomb to join Gerrik and Bensel.

* * *

"What a fine blend, Gerrik!" Bensel said, back at the guard flat, taking a few puffs from a wooden pipe. The pipe had a lofty, round, brown belly with a long thin neck stemming from it to his wrinkly lips. They were smoking puffis, a substance that defined a "sophisticated soldier." Pigs dealt with their troubles drowning in alcohol, but men smoked puffis. They sat in the dark tactical room where they had sat before their journey to the capital. Shreds of the reddish leaves were spread out on a large piece of paper. Gerrik hung loosely over a chair he had moved into the room, on which he sat backward, with a pipe in his hand as well.

"See, I told you, *this* is puffis," he declared, his voice rolling. The two laughed hypnotically, without cause, as their minds slipped into a blissful, negligent stupor.

"Head north, yeah right!" Bensel laughed. The plant, like alcohol, had a truth serum to it. The user was usually plagued by blunt honesty.

"What?" Gerrik chuckled.

Bensel took another puff before beginning to speak again. "You must be crazy. We couldn't possible go all the way up there."

"You serious?" Gerrik asked, his laugh soberly silencing. His words were as if the very world had stopped spinning.

Bensel sat up, his eyes slightly bloodshot, partially from the drug and partially from his few days behind on sleep. "You drag me through hell an' high water, I lose my daughter, an' now you want me to go to the opposite extreme of hell?" he asked. "That is a funny joke."

Gerrik decided somewhere in his consciousness to delve with him. "Well you know what is funnier?" Gerrik began to snicker.

"Oh?" he responded looking at him with one eye.

"You don't really have anywhere else to go!" he yelled before giving a hearty chuckle while slapping his thigh at the poor king.

"That's not funny." Bensel straightened up.

"Yes it is, the truth is hilarious," he mocked.

Bensel thought for a moment and took yet another puff. He began to laugh himself. "It is true," he shrugged.

"I don't have anywhere else to go either!" Gerrik exclaimed, continuing to guffaw. Then suddenly he began to droop in his chair, a little saddened by this feeling of homelessness. "Wait, this is actually not so good."

"Oh no, your puffis is starting to wear off, eh?" Bensel said, picking up some leaves. He stuffed them into Gerrik's pipe and carried on. "Either that or you're just getting old and senile," he shot, cracking up as only the jolly king would.

"Oh, I'm old now. Look at you, gray-bearded dwarf," Gerrik laughed.

"Hmm." Bensel thought for a moment, running his hand through his beard. "It's a sophisticated look," he replied, self-consciously smoking the pipe.

"You scared of going up north, afraid to chill those old bones?" Gerrik said after a time.

"You know what I think?" Bensel asked.

"What's that?" Gerrik asked, taking another puff on the pipe.

"You're a bad father because you follow your boy so eagerly. A part of you can't deal with getting old. You could have sent D'artello on his way with the troops; it is after all *his* battle. Instead, you risked your life again to journey to the capital."

"I didn't see you backing down," Gerrik shot back.

"That's fair," Bensel said, putting his hands up in a submissive fashion. "Perhaps I am afraid of the same. Who wants to die of old age anyway."

"Harmony told me to go," Gerrik explained.

"You really are senile!" Bensel laughed. "You know what is really screwed up? I watched my grandpa live out his old age on a royal farm with servants to cater to his every whim, and my father the same. Where is my farm, Gerrik?" he asked.

Just outside the door, Elan sat and inhaled the fumes coming from the plant. *Ah, puffis,* he thought to himself, but thoughts were all he could have, as someone would have to stay sober. Still rolling the thoughts of Sandra around in his mind, he began to torture himself.

Lost for direction, the fact Sandra's smiling face would only appear in his dreams was troubling to say the least. *Will her name ever pass my lips without highest endearment?* Elan had always been a shallow thinker, and this concept would take him time to toss around in his mind. *If D'artello had not been there, I would have beheaded Seraph most certainly,* he thought. He had thought more about his revenge and killing Seraph than about Sandra. There he sat, tasting this icy fact with the subtle twitches of his brow until Gerrik and Bensel finished their merriment.

* * *

Before that happened, it would be midday. The sun was now in the middle of the sky, a pinhole in the vast overcast. Elan and Bensel had gone to find food and a sac to bring it in. Gina hovered about, as she was given nothing in particular to do. D'artello had wandered off on his own after taking Tanya's promise charm back from her.

The sky soon became a twilight mix of black thunderheads and bright sunshine. Rain began to pour down in just certain areas, something uncommon, but D'artello always loved to stand in the rift between storm and clear skies. He found himself in the moist fields with flowers he had picked, and a large, deformed, pyramidal rock he'd uncovered and moved himself. He created a memorial for his friends, a place where he could let it all out, where no one would notice. He rose, holding the promise charm to drop it among the flowers.

Too big a part of him did not want to give up on Tanya. He regrabbed it, tied it back around his neck and then squatted back down to organize the flowers again. He sat for a long time in the field, staring at the ground, giving a self-made elegy to an audience of one. *Tanya…* he thought so hard that he found his arms hugging himself, missing the beloved younger sister. *Joseph…* he felt a brotherly remorse, accompanied by every memory of his hometown and a life that used to be easy. *Dad…*this thought woke him from his trance. Why did he think of his father just then? He cried about him just as long as he cried about the others, but he was alive. For another hour at least, he cycled through his friends, mourning their loss and bawling. So very sad and so very tired.

Eventually, when he was able to stand, he wiped his tears and looked up at the sky and then at the surrounding environment. There was something very wrong. Having little to do with nature, humans aside, his world was trying to tell him something. It was dying. The sun began to glare into his eyes. Soon the rain would trickle to a stop, gradually as all things do.

He perked up a bit at this fact, this inalienable law of nature, a law of gradient. If all things end gradually, then there is still time to save everyone; they couldn't possibly be gone in an instant. Putting his palms to the sky, he awaited this rare phenomenon. Like a startling shockwave, the rain went from downpour to drought. His body even shook with suddenness in the absence of hard droplets. *Sudden,* he thought. Nature had torn his recent epiphany to ribbons, but before he could realize this fact, down came a hawk from the trees, a beautiful brown bird, gliding over the winds and chasing the storm.

At first he paid no mind to it, but it landed just in front of him, perching itself on the memorial, staring at him through its left eye. About three feet tall with gorgeous mahogany and eggshell feathers, the hawk stood proudly as if to coach him through this moment. It was a perfect lifelike example of the depiction on his helm. It outstretched its wings as if to get his attention for words of wisdom it was about to convey. When still he did not stare it directly in the face, it gave a loud screech, obviously directed toward him. It returned its head to the side-cocked position to get a good look and assure he was paying attention now.

The bird's behavior was strange indeed. D'artello had never seen a hawk of this size, this close. Its actions could only conclude it wanted him to come near. Holding his hand out, he approached the animal, getting so very close. Just inches away now, his hand could already ruffle the feathers. Just before the bird fluttered off into the sky, he swore he felt it press its head within his palm. He watched it flap overhead, in the same direction, chasing the storm, beckoning him to come along.

* * *

Afterward, Gerrik and his son knelt upon the dusty floor of a room no bigger than their living quarters. It was in fact, just down the hall—one of many rooms used for storage, as the population did not meet the builders' expectations. D'artello looked about complacently while his father dug like a hound through the numerous wooden crates and chests, shoveling piles of steel blades aside with his callused hands. "Whoa, take a look at this," he said finally just before tossing something leather to D'artello.

He examined it for a time. The musty smell entered his nostrils and the pores of his hands instantly. It was a sheath, and the sword inside of it was short and nicked beyond repair. The object had definitely seen better days. "It's my first sword," D'artello responded, withdrawing it.

"Was mine too," Gerrik said, giving another rattling shove into the crate.

"Wow," D'artello declared, impressed with its age. "This thing is in decent condition for how old it is."

"Me too!" Gerrik laughed. It was never more obvious that he was just trying to cheer his son up, but D'artello's mind was yet again unreachable to his father. Gerrik could not help but feel partially responsible for his son's sadness. After all, *he* forced him into war. The fact that D'artello reminded Gerrik of himself in his younger, war days was a disturbing thought, as those actions were nothing to be proud of. The last thing he wanted for his son was to live in regret the way he did.

"I promised her, Dad," D'artello said.

Ignoring the comment, he continued to rifle through the chest. Just then, as if by fate, a bulky leather pouch flapped open, revealing its contents. A leather-bound pocket notebook rested inside, one easily recognizable as his war journal. Seizing it quickly, Gerrik dusted it off and heard the old bindings snap as he thumbed through the pages, skimming the memories.

By this time, D'artello had put the sword down and began to examine a shelf. It did not take long to locate an old book. It was a tad bigger than the journal and twice as dusty. He blew the dust away from the cover, revealing *Legendex*.

A legendex was a book that compiled myths or dogma that glorified the Peacemakers. A legendex was often used as the basis for preaching in any kind of clergy. The main religious bias in the country Vaukry, and its neighboring nations, was the United Church of Harmonites. "A bunch of smoke blowers," as his father would say, most of them kept to themselves, but the zealots were the worst kind of people. No matter what wrong they could commit, as long as it was in Harmony's name, it was okay. This particular legendex was not one he had seen, however. No label in particular, just *Legendex*, as if it were whole, complete—the end all, be all of interpretation. Slowly he pursed his thumbs and cracked the binding, *Whoa! This book has never been opened,* he thought. The first few pages were blank and read nothing of the Peacemakers. There was no preface or opening prayer, just a table of contents. A list with dotted lines leading to numbers:

The Dawn
The Dusk
The Peacemakers
The Madness
The Swords
The Dark One
The Hero of Light
The Parcef

Those eight categories were supposed to sum up the universe. The ridiculousness of it all kept him fascinated to the point where he was silently mouthing the words down the list. Just as he was about to turn the page, he heard his father call: "Heads up!"

He turned to react quickly and catch the leather pouch with the journal in it. "It's my journal, D'artello," Gerrik said. "Now you can see that I know what you're going through ... when you're ready of course."

Giving a silent and processed nod, he slid the book and the leather pouch with the journal into the bag resting on his thigh.

Gerrik stood up with a pile of weapons in front of him. "There. I think that's everything—swords, shields, helms, extra body armor. Here, help me carry it."

"You still won't use a sword, huh?" D'artello inquired.

"What an abrupt question," Gerrik shot back, a defensive tone in his voice.

"Yeah, I know, but you never really tell me anything. I feel like everyone knows, and it's like one giant secret ... that just I don't know."

"I didn't think you needed to hear those things. I still don't."

D'artello could tell just by the impatience in his voice that he was starting to get uncomfortable, and when Gerrik got uncomfortable, as sparse as it was, he got angry.

"I'm not a child anymore," D'artello argued. "I can handle it."

"D'artello, I'm not talking about this with you, and you are still a child to me, *my* child."

"Harmony doesn't think so," he said, pulling the Molten Steel as if to show his father one more time. Gerrik made a sudden motion that not even D'artello was quick enough to pick up on. In an instant, the armor in his arms was plummeting toward the ground, and with a sharp draining tap to his son's wrist, the sword came free. It flew up against the wall and landed with a clang. The pair locked eyes.

"Is that where you got the weapon?" Gerrik asked. "Has Harmony been visiting you as well?"

"As well?" D'artello asked.

Gerrik silenced and sized up immediately, realizing that for the first time in D'artello's upbringing, he had said too much.

"What do you mean as well?" D'artello asked while Gerrik turned his back to pick up the armor.

"Nothing, it's nothing," Gerrik said.

D'artello nodded. "Yup, of course it's nothing; it always is," he said, calling back the Molten Steel and then sheathing it. Bending at the knees, he began to pick up the weapons and armor piece by piece.

Gerrik closed his eyes and took a deep breath. "D'artello ... I'm sorry," he sighed.

"No you're not. You're still keeping secrets from me, new secrets in fact, ones I didn't even know existed." Having collected all the armor now, he began to walk away from his father.

"Wait," Gerrik said. "The answers are in the book I gave you just now." D'artello took a second to glance down at the bag hanging off his waist. "Forgive me for not being strong enough to speak those words to your face," he said.

After a brief pause, D'artello began to speak again, still not facing his father. "You cooking tonight?" Changing the subject, it was their way of saying everything's okay now.

"Heh, yeah, my stew if we can find the ingredients," he said, the one and only recipe at the man's disposal. It was everything for the strong warrior in one pot. No one would argue about it. Usually D'artello or Tanya would handle dinner if they ever got sick of stew, which was frequent, but tonight, stew it would be. D'artello's stomach squealed with hunger, and just about anything sounded good right now. After being sufficed by soullessness and sadness, he realized quickly how empty he physically was. Making a right and leaving the room, D'artello headed for the street to build a fire.

Left alone, Gerrik's mind was riddled with thoughts of Harmony and what she could really want with his son.

Chapter 12

THE group spent the remainder of the day gathering ingredients for the stew and items for their campfire feast. That brisk evening, they all sat around a blazing, crackling fire, wrapped in blankets they had taken off of the clean beds to warm their outsides. Warming their insides was the scent of the salty, slow-cooked stew that sweltered in the pot before them. Long wooden poles supported the pot, letting the flames tickle it. Gerrik stood over the flame with the wooden ladle, stirring it like a cauldron with his two mighty arms. It was a big pot, but the last thing any of them could count on, even less than a Phantom attack, was leftover food. "There. I think it's done," he said, puckering and taking a cautious suck from the ladle. "Ah," he sighed, licking the remnants from his lips. "I've outdone myself this time."

Eagerly the rest of the group approached the pile of bowls next to the pot and held them out to be served as if they were beggars. And serve Gerrik did, quickly and efficiently. A little spilled on Gina's finger upon exiting the ladle, but she quickly licked it off with a delighted smile in her eyes. D'artello was the only one who did not immediately inhale his dish; he sloshed it about in the bowl for a moment. He smelled it first—it was something he always did—and then began to chow down. It was heaven, no two ways about it in this hellish reality he'd recently become accustomed to. The tastes blasted back the loneliness and sadness that had accumulated in his heart the last few days. Enveloped in the entrancing thickness of the smell and flavor, he could not and did not want to feel anything else.

After about three or so bowls each, the stew had run out, as had their appetites. Bensel and Elan sat on one end of the fire, spread out and rolling over for bed. Gerrik sat up meditating, his legs crossed and his palms toward the sky, much the way his sensei had taught him long ago. D'artello had seen him do it a few times before bed, only when he was unusually stressed. His jaw moved slowly as he chewed the minty mastic leaves that they had all popped in their mouths before bed. This particular mastic ensured dental health; the sticky-pliable texture would pick the teeth clean while freshening breath and taking it away at the same time. Gina had slouched over onto D'artello, moving her bony jaw in and out of his chest while she too chewed. She stopped periodically as she drifted in and out of sleep. She snuggled in more and more, as if she were trying to force herself even closer to him.

The fire gave a pop that D'artello took as a signal; he braced Gina gently with his arms and lay back slowly, cradling her gently down. He too was becoming very drowsy. "Gina," he said.

"Hmm?"

Even this subtle syllable felt like a pounding on his ears; any noise other than his own collective conscious was an outburst. The sudden amp was startling, yet he took a deep breath and continued.

"Harmony is going to come for me in the morning. You can't stop her. I want you to know that no matter who I become, it's still me inside."

"Are you afraid of being alone?" she responded.

He was unsure he'd even heard her ask the question. Ears and eyelids both began to shut out the outside world, and his mind could now take over as he slipped into a dream.

* * *

What felt like minutes later, he awoke to the cold. His eyelids flew open, and his eyes were instantly flooded with early morning twilight. The fire was giving its last few sputters of life to the light casting on the empty Fort Carrie around him. He stood up, and Gina was nowhere to be found. A quick purveying revealed that everyone was gone. Alone he stood, feeling the hot embers burn out before him.

How long have I been asleep? he thought. His ears picked up a noise. He could hear someone whispering his name. "D'artello …" He turned to face the voice, only to watch a paper blow across the street. With each blowing of the wind, he felt whispers brush past. One phrase seemed to lead immediately into the next like a poem or an endless sentence.

"I will always love you, the best intentions,"

"You are not immortal,"

"Are you afraid of being alone?"

"You won't let me have my revenge?"

"I am a Peacemaker. I have no choice, why should you?"

Their discord sent a puncturing migraine through his head, and his hands shot to his ears, trying to block out the subliminal noise. Then through the murky madness came a prominent and unfamiliar voice. "What are you fighting for?" A question that he'd never been asked in his life, a question in fact that he'd only recently asked himself.

He lowered his hands and turned sharply toward the direction from whence it came. Peering down the gray street, he could faintly see the silhouette of a person. Man or woman, he was uncertain, but someone was definitely watching him. "You question love, strength, acceptance, justice, and freedom, so what is it that you fight for?" So close were the words, but the figure was so far away.

He reached for his Molten Steel, but it was nowhere to be found. Where would it go? Did his father take it? Was this a ploy to *protect* him?

"What will you do without your goddess?" the voice asked. As he drew closer, he could still only make out the black silhouette. The person must have been wearing a cloak. The street was much longer than he had remembered it, going on and on, creating its own endless abyss. Taking a second to look up, the buildings seemed to repeat themselves in a noticeable pattern, and side streets were nonexistent. It was not until he passed the smoldering fire again that he focused back at the cloaked figure. It was gone.

After a double take, he let silence hiss into his ears. He was listening for any sound, any one noise that could give him the position of the cloaked figure. *Is it a new kind of Phantom? They usually wore white cloaks, but maybe this one is another source*, he thought.

Without warning, the lecturing whisper sounded again, "Do you enjoy being a mindless puppet for your goddess, nothing but a dog? She could get a million others like you. Do you like having no mind of your own, not being able to feel the loved ones around you *dying*?" It was said sharply like the striking of a snake at his ear. Targeting the voice, he turned swiftly to his right, looking now at one of the buildings he'd already seen three copies of.

D'artello began to clench his teeth to detain his anger. The words were setting him off slowly. "Do these questions hurt? What's the matter? You don't understand." Approaching the door with ample care, he first noticed that it was cracked, as if someone had been there recently. He peeked through to see if he could catch a glimpse of something. Detecting nothing with his eyes, his ears then picked up a repetitive sound. Breathing. Heavy, almost winded pants. They were abnormally frequent like a rodent's heartbeat.

Welling up his bravery, he first looked around to assure himself no one would flank him from behind, and then he opened the door slowly. As the door glided back on its hinges, a triangular wedge of light forced open the darkness of the abandoned inside. An inverted shadow cast on a figure huddled at the far end of the hallway. On its knees it sat, rocking back and forth and breathing heavily, shaking and quivering. The defining features were familiar even though its back was turned.

"Dad?" he called. It stopped rocking and breathing at the sound of his voice, as if its overworked heart froze instantly.

"Dad!" he exclaimed, running to his father. His hand was about to rest on his father's shoulder when it was painfully slapped away with freakish speed. The creature spun to face D'artello as his father. Not for a second did he believe it was Gerrik. He began to fall back into his fighting stance as the creature shrieked wildly, starting to attack D'artello. A quick snap of its leg sent D'artello flying backward through the doorway and onto the street. He rolled and landed on a rock, skidding over it until it created a large gash in his back.

"Well, why don't you ask him what it is he keeps from you?" the voice suggested.

D'artello thought about the prospect and then scrambled to his feet, getting ready to face the faux Gerrik who burst through the door. It was hardly a time to pose a question, but he trusted the voice; perhaps it would stop the creature. "Dad!" he said, calling down his direct attention. "What is your secret? Why do you keep it from me?" he shouted. He had let it go before, letting the book suffice his need for an honest father, but inside he was seething.

"That's none of your business," said the creature, cocking its head freakishly to the side. It leapt toward D'artello, throwing punches and chops trying to strike him down.

D'artello, still unsure of his father's presence, played the defensive, but with each move—he had seen them all—he became less and less convinced.

"Answer me, dammit!" D'artello yelled back as the rock-hard fixtures that were his father's arms left sharp bruises in their wake. The pair fought on, Gerrik still on the offense, but D'artello did not heed an inch; it was almost playful pain, as if he were training again. Their skin slid off of each other's like swords clashing, leaving burns on their barren forearms. Every now and then, they distanced themselves enough to throw a kick. At one point, their shins smashed while throwing identical roundhouses.

The faux Gerrik slipped up as the original never would, and D'artello got hold of a wrist. That was all he needed. In attaining the advantage, he took a cheap shot to the side of the face. Jumping up like a frog, D'artello pressed both of his feet like pistons into the doppelganger's abdomen. Compromised and counterweighted, the faux Gerrik fell over and was flipped onto his back by a thrusting of D'artello's powerful legs. Faux Gerrik landed like a cat would if it didn't land on its feet, flailing and trying to get himself back up quickly.

D'artello didn't stop there. He rolled and sprang backward with his arms, launching him just high enough so he would come down with both feet on top of the creature. Like a descending javelin, his fist came down with sternum-shattering force. The initial impact caused its limbs to kick up for only a moment, and then return to the earth as the life of this thing had. Rising, he breathed heavily through clenched teeth and sweaty locks. "Damn," he uttered, squeezing his fingers in and out to restrain his anger.

"Wow. I didn't think you could kill your father without so much as a good-bye," the voice spoke.

"You're lying. That's not my father," D'artello answered.

"You believe what you want," the voice shot back.

His heart fell into his stomach. *It couldn't have been him. He was way too sloppy. He couldn't have been a tainted either. He was talking to me, it can't be him*, D'artello thought. "You're lying. This is *not* my father; he would have become a statue."

"Is that so? The things he hasn't told you. Now drop it, onto the next game."

Realizing that the voice would give him no answers and continue to speak in riddle, D'artello retrieved the leather-bound book from the pouch around his waist. Anxiously he opened it up and flipped through the pages to find what this voice was talking about. Blank. Angrily, he tossed the book at the ground. "Harmony! Dammit," he yelled.

"She can't help you here," chimed in the whispers.

"Show yourself, coward," he threatened.

"Not until we are done with my little game. I prefer to taunt the tiger beforehand, makes for a more interesting dare," the voice chanted. "Now come and find me," it said.

Glancing around quickly, he noticed a person standing not but twenty feet away. A heavy black cloak covered the person from head to toe and granted no hints of who was underneath. "What's the matter? Lost your nerve?" D'artello asked, walking toward it, wearing the first grin since this whole experience began.

A growling could be heard from under the cloth, a growling that sounded like a million pebbles rolling downhill. With furor, he grabbed the cloth, clenching it tightly in between each finger. He gave an eager jerk of his shoulder, and off came the cloak, but before he could see who it was, what felt like a foot smashed into the side of his face, making him spin out and fall to the ground. Braking with his hands, he turned to see what had hit him. "Are you afraid of being alone, alone like me?" It looked like Gina. Giving a show of inhuman strength, she picked him up by the scruff of his collar with one hand, choking him.

"Gina," he said, gripping her hands, his feet dangling above the ground. "Gina, stop."

"You're pathetic," she said. "Poor Tanya. What about me, huh? My parents are dead, and all you can think about is yourself."

Showing off again, she hurled him across the street and through the door of the guard flat. First came the impact of the door, then the ground, then the slam into something metal and lumpy. He sat for a second and gave a moan. Taking a quick survey, he found that this interior did not match the exterior at all. He was thrown through the door of a living space and ended up in the town tool shed. *What is going on here?* he thought. There was no time to wonder.

He looked for something to defend himself with. The wall was lined with shovels, pitchforks, axes, and picks, plenty to cause a lot of damage. However, he did not want to kill her; he just couldn't bear to think of killing another ally. Coming from outside, he heard footsteps and the unsheathing of a sword; it was faux Gina coming for him. *What did I land against?* he thought, rubbing his shoulder.

Turning, he gazed at his saving grace, a robust chain coiled around a crank, a device used for tying up higoats bulls. As large and brutish as they were, the crank was leveraged enough to allow just one man to deal with the large animal. On the end was the hook that would go through one of the links to restrain the animal properly.

Gina came cutting through the door with intense ferocity. Spotting her target, she wasted no time and twirled in, swinging the blade down from above. D'artello held up the chain that gave a strong rattle as the sword came crashing down. Without wasting a second, he stepped in, ensnaring her arms in it. This was no easy task, as her strength was inhuman. "What are you doing, D'artello? Do you want to be alone forever?" she asked dryly.

In tying her up from behind, he took a reeling elbow to the gut, but he ate through the pain and began to wrap up her feet. One pull of the chain, and she fell helplessly to the ground.

She started to struggle and hiss wildly. All he wanted to do was get away from it. Raising his palms in a submissive manner, he shuffled toward the door. Upon exiting, he closed it behind him and placed a hand on his right abdomen, just below the ribs, where the elbow had struck hard. "Not as eager to kill that one, were you? What's the matter? Not so sure anymore?"

He breathed hard. "You like it too much."

"I don't think you like it enough," it taunted. "You didn't answer my question."

He had kept his cool up until now, but this voice was working his last thinning nerve. "Return my sword, you bastard! Allow me to cure them and then face me!" he yelled.

"Interesting. I take away the puppeteer's strings, and the puppet calls to have them back." At this remark, D'artello clenched his teeth until his jaw felt tense, and he pounded the door behind him in frustration. "Don't worry, it's almost over. Just one more and I will know all I need to."

"Who are you!" he demanded.

As if there were a hand wrapped around his chin, his body, led by his head, turned in the other direction and up toward the third story window. It was like an instinct; someone was looming over him, practically breathing down his neck, a predator. No. Glancing through the shadowy glass pane of a beige bricked building, he could see a gray, stone, familiar face. "Tanya!" he exclaimed. There was another pair of eyes looking down from the window; he was sure of it. Squinting, he could barely make out someone standing behind the Tanya statue. "Dammit," he cursed, darting toward the door.

He lined himself with the door, smashing through it with his shoulder, backed by his powerful body. A stinging ran its way through his nerves and sounded a temporary ringing in his ear, but he did not care. He had tunnel vision for only the destination ahead, missing all of the empty rooms beside him and the blood-red carpeting running beneath him.

This was not Tanya's building; this was not even a building he could place in his hometown. *That bastard, he has defiled Tanya's resting place, and he will pay,* D'artello thought as he charged up the staircase with loud stomps. He didn't even stop to glance down the hallway of the second floor. Instead he continued his heavy ascent.

Upon reaching the third and final floor, he stopped. It was then he'd decided the element of surprise might be important. As if whoever was in that room with Tanya didn't already know D'artello was on his way up, he crept down the hallway slowly, checking each open door along the way, even though he had some idea of which room it was. Inside of each room stood a three-foot statue of a raven, hunched over like a scary gargoyle. Its wings were bowed, and the first one he caught sight of was startling, even unnerving despite his anger. Gerrik had always told D'artello that ravens were horrible misfortune. He began to get the sense he was walking into a trap.

In the hall there were paintings, predictably the same paintings of former guard commanders, generals, and kings, but not this time. They were paintings of him. The first was of D'artello hunched in a fetal position beneath an overcast sky, his eyes bleeding a black sludge that was pooling at his knees. The second painting was him standing above Tanya's apparently lifeless body. He looked like he did it, like he'd killed his young sisterly figure. This enraged a deep, heated breath from his lungs. The third depicted him pounding the life from faux Gerrik, and the fourth showed him chaining up faux Gina. Both of the latter paintings made him look like the antagonist.

By the time he'd seen all of them, he was across the hall from the door shut tight. It was mahogany with iron hinges, thin enough to let D'artello hear what was going on inside if he pressed his hear to it. Once he was sure this was the room, he grasped firmly the handle and ripped it open. The door splintered, and his seething anger nearly took it completely off its hinges.

D'artello took a step into what looked like Tanya's room. "So we meet, brother," greeted the figure just as he entered the room. The masculine voice affirmed D'artello's conclusions of a cloaked man. Although he had never heard the voice in his life, there was something about how this man held himself up, or how he spoke certain words, or his physical build. It was hard to place D'artello's sudden sense of familiarity. He took no stance in particular. Instead, the cloaked man stood before him, simply, boldly, and lethargically letting his hands drop to his sides.

Brother? Is this a joke? D'artello thought. He raised his fists and was ready to go. "I know who you are," he warned. The momentarily meaningless memories of his first soulless night were vivid in detail. "You are the winged man who attacked Fort Carrie a few nights ago," he deduced.

"You weren't listening, brother. That may be true, but that is not how you will come to know me, and as for this miserable creature." There was that word again, *brother*. It was beginning to eat away at D'artello. The man drew a long, one-handed sword from under his cloak. The blade was an unfinished, stony gray, and the guard, shielding his hand, looked like a pyramid of icicles. "Behold," he commanded, holding it out in his black-gloved grip for D'artello to see.

It was a single-edged sword, much like the Molten Steel. With the exception of the colors and some minor details, the two were identical weapons. "Gaze upon it! The Frozen Steel, and with its power, I have and I will do horrible things," he boasted.

A second hand emerged from beneath the cloak, and it too grabbed the handle. D'artello readied himself for an attack. Slowly and smoothly, the blade wound over the cloaked man's shoulder. *Is he announcing an overhead strike?* D'artello thought, getting ready for this premonition to become reality. If so, he knew exactly what he'd do. As the arms had come up, so had the cloak, revealing part of this man's hairless, muscular chest. This man was young, he could tell that much.

The cloaked man took one step forward, and this gesture backed D'artello off a bit, for the movement was as sudden as the halt. A deep chuckle came from underneath the cloak. "What will you do, D'artello? What is it you fight for?" That question again. "I think I know."

In the blink of an eye, the cloaked man was facing the other direction. The sword had started on his right shoulder, and had somehow made it next to his left thigh, the tip pointing down away from its wielder. It took a second, but D'artello registered the fluent motion of this man taking a spinning, downward, diagonal slice, but why?

Like a grand unveiling to his masterpiece, the man flared up his cape. By the time it had settled back to his body, he was standing erect, next to Tanya's statue. *What did he do?* D'artello thought. D'artello watched Tanya's stone face slide off her neck, fall to the floor, and shatter into minute fragments.

"Tanya!" he yelled, at the top of his lungs. All hope and reason to live was lost with her adorable face breaking on the ground. "No," he gasped. "How could you?"

"That's it," said the man. "I enjoyed taking this one personally. She was so *brave*," he mocked, "*wise beyond her years*, delicious, ironic, she will never see those years for which she was wise beyond. You know, I think she partly enjoyed it. Humans are taught from birth to fear death even though it gets rid of all of your troubles, much like insanity. Not this one though, she … heh heh hah … she already knew that she wanted to die!"

D'artello had heard more than enough. He cared nothing for the words of the winged man, nor for his ironies or his tastes. As quickly as the cloak had turned to slice Tanya, he had turned back toward D'artello and sheathed the Frozen Steel in one fluent motion.

D'artello threw a left, then a right, trying to pound in the face of his attacker. The first punch was avoided with a backward step and the second with a bob to the right. His fist slammed into the wall, leaving him wide open. The cloaked man arrested D'artello's arm before it could be retracted, then slammed his bicep, sending pain all the way into D'artello's upper back.

Reacting immediately, D'artello tried a roundhouse kick to the open ribs, but the cloaked figure with mind-blowing speed, switched hands, grabbing hold of the right leg too. With right arm and foot in hand, the cloaked man walked his way back to the middle of the room. Desperately, D'artello jumped up, using his enemy as a center of balance, and swung his remaining leg up to tag his opponent in the face. The cloaked man was far too quick for this; he'd seen it coming a mile off and simply let D'artello's limbs go. As a result, D'artello's attack missed and he fell flat on his back.

He scrambled back to his feet, at which time, for the first time, the cloaked man put his hands up, ready to fight. It never occurred to him that so obvious a maneuver was a trap. When the black-gloved fist launched from beneath the cloak straight at him, D'artello parried and stepped, then turned to retaliate onto his opponent's back.

Recovering his assault, D'artello threw some more blunt blows to the back of the head. The blind attack was thwarted by blind blocks. The cloaked man never once looked at any of his attacks, yet was able to dismiss them so effortlessly. Did he have eyes in the back of his head too? The fact that D'artello was severely outclassed was beginning to sink in. It stunned him, halting all of his efforts.

The cloaked man wasn't going to wait around. He spun and then grabbed D'artello's throat, again far quicker than could feasibly be reacted to. He thrust him against the wall and then held him above the floor with just one hand around his neck, like a hen for the slaughtering.

With his free hand, the man began to fondle around D'artello's neck, the promise charm between his black-gloved fingers. "How adorable. Is this from your lover? Or … from her?" he said, referring to Tanya with smugness in his voice. D'artello pulled his body up and used both feet to launch him square in the face. The man gave a shout, stumbling backward, releasing his grip. Taking his opening, D'artello jumped toward him with two aerial, spinning kicks. The first was to drive him back, followed by a roundhouse that clipped the cloaked man's head. Using that very same momentum, he landed with a punch to no location in particular that sent the man screaming and crashing out the third-story window.

Some excess glass bounced off the floor as silence befell the room for only a moment. Short lived, his ears picked up a noise that sounded like an old crone beating out her bed sheets. Starting with the head, the cloaked figure rose slowly on long black shadows, fluttering from his back. Under the freakish morning moon, the starry ebon feathers revealed themselves.

D'artello took a step back, startled by the sight of the man's body hanging like that of a spider's on its high riding legs. He put his fists up ready for the man to come flying through the window. "Who are you?" D'artello asked.

"Why do you want to save mankind?" the man asked, ignoring D'artello's inquiry once again.

"Because this is a fight between immortals, and mankind has no need to suffer." Even he surprised himself with his wisdom. This sudden burst of insight seemed to come from thin air, but then he remembered saying it to some effect to Gina. "This is not their fight."

"How very flattering. You believe me to be immortal? Or do you believe yourself to be one?" the cloak shot back, revealing a nasty grin.

What a foolish question. Where did that come from? His own brand of narcissism, or did he read it from my face? "That's not what I said!" D'artello yelled back, letting the thought ricochet about in his mind.

The Adventures of D'artello

"I see no one else here, just you and I. Well then, it seems it is out of their hands, doesn't it? I see where it is that you are sidetracked. You hold the only key to humanity; you get to choose who lives and who dies. Makes you feel powerful, doesn't it?"

"I have no such feelings," D'artello barked back.

"What a shame. I certainly do, with the destruction of an entire race between my palm and fingertips," he said, holding up his sword. "You are so noble, D'artello, far more noble than I, one misplaced shard of humanity. If you believe that they should suffer their own fate, I will have to oppose you. I believe that people must be put out of their misery."

"I won't let you do that," he responded, clenching his fists at his sides. The wings collapsed as the man swooped back into the room, his heavy boots bludgeoning the floor. Like silk in the wind, the cloak collapsed around him, covering the wings once again.

"Not me, hmm … let me explain … you see, I am just a spark, just a small sway that stirs the mixture," he said, pulling his Frozen Steel, drawing a circle in the air with it. "I may lay the first cut with my sword, but people choose their own path, to bathe in their darkness." He paused for a moment, licking his lips. "They seem to lose their mind, and that is because they are too weak to fight for their free will. I beckon you, look down at your home. How many did not choose darkness? Statues are the byproduct of a pure soul and one being that could never choose darkness, straight as an arrow. Collateral damage, for the greater good I suppose," he said, nudging Tanya's pieces with his foot.

D'artello's level of cool had all but run out. He had been glancing back and forth at Tanya's broken body, and his eyes watered more each time. Exhaling a battle cry, D'artello rushed his foe. By the time he was throwing fists, his eyes were so welled up that he couldn't even see straight. Before he knew it, the Frozen Steel slid under his neck and pressed anxiously against his tender skin. The man restrained him effortlessly and leaned his head over D'artello's shoulder. "What side would you choose? Huh?" he asked gruffly as D'artello gave another struggle. "Right now it looks like darkness. Right now you would do anything to get up after I slice your throat. You would do anything to get up and show me why I am wrong, wouldn't you? Here's the irony; if given the chance, I would choose it as well," he said, extending his tongue and licking the edge of the blade daringly.

"But, it is your dream. You believe what you want," he explained, shrugging his shoulders and looking up as if to some heavenly audience. He released D'artello, who fled toward the window and then turned to face his foe. "You are afraid of your own failure, and you damn well should be. For now though …" the cloaked man held, examining the bedpost as if it were some foreign life form. He tilted his head slightly, as if doing some sort of mental measuring. He grabbed hold of the four-foot tall wooden post and ripped it from the bed.

The bed teetered for a moment before the mattress's weight caused it to slope in the direction of its newly absent support. The old mattress exhaled a musty breath as it depressed. The cloaked figure took his sword and began to shave the wood, peeling back first the finish, then the dark outer skin to reveal the lighter, tenderer meat of the piece.

"What the hell are you doing?" D'artello yelled. He watched him sharpen the long stake. A critic of his own work, the winged man paused briefly to look at his carving, just to make sure it was good enough, as if he were examining a jigsaw piece to make sure it would fit into his devious intentions. When he was finished, he sent it spinning and sliding against the floor planks. Its rotation and momentum came to a stop at D'artello's boot.

"Here," the voice cradled eerily. "You have to throw a dog a bone every once in a while. I believe you know what to do with this. You win," he said, dropping his sword to the ground.

What is this? Can he call that sword back to his side like I can?

Knowing that D'artello still had a thought process and it was time to change that, the cloaked man said, "Or you can sit there and tell Tanya that you couldn't avenge her, just like you couldn't protect her."

D'artello picked up the pike and began running his finger down the tip. This man was quite the craftsman, smooth as a woman's skin, but sharp as a ter tooth.

Much to his surprise, the man did not heed. He was taken off his feet by the force of D'artello's charge that made a dead stop only upon staking the winged man to the inside wall. His limp body was nailed to the thin wall, and his ebon wings lay open at his sides. Blood began to gush from his gut. "Excellent," he coughed. A warm red spatter drew a line across D'artello's brow.

D'artello pulled the hood off to see his attacker's face. Gasping, he loosened his grip on the wooden stake as a certain sense of familiarity fell over him. The feeling passed as he clenched his teeth, continuing to attack his tormentor. The man's silver hair and physique were almost built after his and his father's. The face was longer, showing a few years beyond D'artello's age. Subtle similarities, D'artello was able to shake them off. Still the man was young, and an arrogant smirk was spread across his cherry-red soaked lips. "Just wanted to see if you had it in you, if you could lose control."

D'artello began to pummel his face, throwing right and left hooks alternately until his knuckles were raw from the friction. Only laughter came from the man who by all rights should have been dead. "Enjoy this, feeble hero, because round two will be far more entertaining. Come to the north, come to the ice palace, and we will settle this. Let's see if you can do this for real."

D'artello could utter no words in response; instead he roared like a triumphant alpha.

* * *

Waking abruptly with a cold sweat brooding from his face, he breathed heavily, holding his chest for how hard his heart was beating. It felt like at any moment some evil black creature would rip open his chest from the inside. *A dream ... a dream ...* he thought, trying to calm himself between pants. *But it was so real ...* Choking air through angry tears and a thundering heart, he felt around for Gina, but she was absent. Standing up quickly, he made sure to get a head count on his father, Bensel, and Elan. *Everyone else is here ... good,* he eased into rational thought as if it were warm bathwater. The flames had long since petered out, but it was not quite morning yet, not for these tired souls.

Shivering, not because of the cold, he recalled the room, the cloaked man, his face, and then Tanya's body. His brain convulsed between fear and anger. He continued to look around for Gina. In his waking daze and the heightened sense of paranoia that came after waking from a nightmare, he felt that he must find her immediately. Looking down the street, he found an immediate clue.

The door of the church was open. It had not been that way the previous night. *She must be there,* he thought. Taking a few jogging steps forward, one over the pile of ash, one over Bensel, and one more for good measure, he stopped abruptly and then slid his hand down to his waist. He felt the cold, metallic handle of the Molten Steel. *Still there,* he thought.

Focusing back on the door, his quickened pace returned. He was relieved to see the door not pulling away from him as it had in his dream. He approached cautiously, swinging his head to look down each alleyway he passed. If it weren't for the moonlight, the town would not have been navigable. Creeping up on the door, he opened it a little more to sneak through. Despite being older now and the end of all life as far as he could tell, the church still felt like a forbidden place to be. Cracking it just a little more, he allowed himself to slip in sideways. On the inside, except for a moonlit sliver coming from the doorway, the stained glass windows ensured blindness in the pitch-black hall. Even though he couldn't see, this was not what he had expected. His father had always told him to stay away from this place, giving it a forbidden allure, as if it were never dark in this Church of Harmony.

The mere acoustics told what his eyes could not see. If it weren't for a burning sound accompanied by a pouring sound somewhere in the back of the church, he would be totally blind. The echoes bounced off the walls of the hollow funnels that were his ears. This was a big and empty room. Entering at long last, he stumbled over something hard and wooden at shin level. His hands flew to the object, patting it, emitting empty drumming noises.

The wall-mounted torches flickered to life, filling the room with light. D'artello looked about the place, absorbing all he could of what he was never allowed to see. The inside had an off-white tinge, like sour milk, the color neutral to the loud gem-finished windows. Conjoined marble pillars that were no more a body themselves than they actually supported the structure, lined the walls. They had been meticulously carved, horizontal ridges that went all the way from the widening bottom to the widening top. At these edges were mixes of swirled brown and white madness, the natural traits of the marble. Each pillar looked like an oblong hourglass.

Glancing back down at the mystery object, he realized he had bumped into a black bench that ran all the way from the aisle he stood in, to the pillars along the walls. On either side, many black posts of the benches stood like soldiers watching him if he dared walk up to the altar. Above hung three glass chandeliers in succession that led down the aisle and sparkled with the flames of the torches.

It was dream-like, as he traced along the borders of a stained glass window. It was a picture of Harmony's sacrifice, the event leading to her becoming a Peacemaker. Before long, his tour was interrupted by a voice.

"What's wrong, D'artello? Are the Phantoms out there?" asked Gina.

He looked up to get an eyeful of smooth skin. There she stood, up at the podium, in front of the candles, in front of the Harmony statue, but behind the podium to modestly cover herself. She had apparently turned the lights on and now waited with a concerned look.

D'artello tried to do the modest thing and hide his eyes by turning his head sideways, covering his face with an open palm. "I'm sorry, I didn't realize you were bathing," he explained, realizing that the fire sound was the heating of the water and the pouring was putting it from the big warm pot into the clergy bath. "S-sorry about this ... really, I'll leave," he said, turning to head for the door.

In this slight meantime, she had managed to work her way down the aisle without so much as a sound on her bare feet. "No ... really, it's okay," she said, grabbing hold of his hand. He looked back at her, drawing his eyes from the bottom up slowly, noticing that she had not stripped completely. His gaze traversed her clad legs and slipped up her bare stomach then onto the white shirt pressed over her chest using her other hand. "Heh," she laughed awkwardly, "good thing you weren't Gerrik or Bensel, huh?"

"Y-yeah," he answered, shaking his head. Her flat, wet hair made her look so very beautiful, heavenly in fact. There was never a paradise greater than her tender, loving gaze looking back into his, for the first time, with real emotion. She had held as much back as he in his soulless state, suppressing a deep agog to make this connection. It may have been her loneliness that drove her now, the cold embracing her like the arms of a lover, or she may have felt that he was the last man still alive in the world, wishing to live through nature's ideal just one more time.

Perhaps the two felt a deep symmetrical lust for one another; they *were* young, fit and attractive. Whatever drove them, their focus was on the tangible reality of a warm salutation, a locking of the lips, uncertain and curious at first, but by the time they had climbed the steps to go through the door into the bath chamber, their lips had taken a plunge from curious to inseparable.

At some point, they realized words were pointless. They began to kiss again with wild passion. He wrapped his arms tightly around her, trying to hold her closer than possible. She wrapped her hands around his neck, unsure what to do with them at the moment.

Never taking their hands or mouths entirely off of each other, they began to shed the rest of their clothing and lower themselves into the bath. To the left of the hot pool was the large pot that was used to fill the bath, roughly four hundred gallons of steamy water now around them and their deeds. Underneath it, the flames still tickled its bottom. The bath was an in-ground bowl, made of smooth, treated stone that had no pores so water could not escape until drained voluntarily. It was carved to seat its patrons around the outer edges, for it was common for the clergy to bathe together to express a Harmony-preached brotherly comfort.

Their movements were erratic but synchronous, a beautiful display of love and power under the holy roof of Harmony. There were smooth, soft moments that seemed to last forever, and frantic ones as their hearts raced with the hours of the morning. There were times when she whispered his name back to him, and times where she shouted the name of her beloved Peacemaker out of shock and reflex, times when they held on for dear life, and others when they explored one another, caressing gently with their fingertips. Regardless of which times they were experiencing, pleasure was constant.

When it was over, she breathed a heavy sigh, as if she'd just had a close call or a rough day. Her body loosened up immediately and fell over his like a warm fleshy blanket. Cuddling her face just under the side of his chin, she spoke to him gently. "Very good," she said as if she were some experienced mentor, proud of her younger pupil.

Admittedly he felt the same way, but he felt more than just a physical attachment as he held her in the turbulent bathwater. Having never had sex for just meager merriment, he looked away and over her shoulder at the stone ceiling, at the picture of Harmony above, staring back down on them. The picture looked nothing like she did in real life, at least not the Harmony D'artello knew. It was then he tried to take his mind off of what he was supposed to do or say next. How could there be such a large-scale organization that worshipped and dedicated their lives to something that they weren't even certain existed? Even as Gina screamed that name in passion, he wondered.

In this place, under the Peacemaker who believed in love, he would give out his heart to this girl now. "Gina ... I-I think ..." he sputtered, not sure if he should say it.

"Hmm?" she asked, forcing her head to turn against his skin to let one eye glance up at him.

Now was not the right time. This could have been from anything. *We're both lonely and we're placed ever so conveniently,* he thought. Convinced things would be different if there were more people around, he simply let it go and said instead, "It's nothing."

"D'artello?" she asked.

He looked down at her with a gleam in his eyes. Gina knew that this was only temporary, but she would enjoy it while it was here. Soon he would remember Tanya, his mission, and Harmony. Then his gleam would be gone and there would be no affection left for her. "Can I confide in you for a moment?" she said.

"What is it?" he asked, holding her body close, kissing her on the lips again. The touch made him feel like they had known each other all their lives and that she could tell him anything. When they pulled away, she gave a shake of her head to toss back the hair in her mouth.

"That town we passed before the prison, do you remember it? Where you saved me from the fire?" she asked.

D'artello could see her face and mood beginning to sully. He nodded his head. "Even though I was soulless I still remember everything," he responded. "I ... It's kind of like sleeping with your eyes open, I don't really control my actions or understand them, I just kind of suggest what I should do next."

"Well ..." she said, biting her lip. It was hard to tell if there were tears rolling down her cheek, but it was entirely possible. She kissed him again to fill the silence. Her lips felt rubbery and loose this time, with a salty tinge; she was definitely crying. She sniffled a little and breathed heavily, the mastic still on her breath. Unable to say what she felt, she melted back into him, holding on tight. "I want you to know that I am glad to have you and that even if the circumstances were different, I would still want it this way," she declared.

D'artello was puzzled at her sudden change of emotion. Was it because he saved her from the Phantoms? No, there had to be something else. Hopefully it would come out before morning, before Harmony came to take his soul again and make him into that puppet. Puppet! The winged man had used that word to describe him and his situation with the goddess.

"Heh, know what?" She laughed playfully. "You might as well tell me since there is no one else to tell."

I could tell you the same thing, D'artello thought, but she beat him to it, fair enough. Even still, he could not say the words that had originally popped into his head, and he tried to get her drop it. "It's nothing. I forgot, so it couldn't have been that important."

"It had to be *something*," she probed, nuzzling up to him again.

No, it would have to wait until this was all over. What if he lost her? Where would he be then? He could not bring himself to invest that kind of emotion yet. One thing he could tell her would satisfy her appetite for conversation, however. "Well, you're going to laugh at me, but I had a nightmare," he began.

"You okay now?" she asked, looking up at him with concern.

"I don't know."

"What do you mean? You can't remember?"

"Oh no, I remember all right," he answered, raising his hand to his chin for a moment, puzzling the words to follow.

"Do you want to talk about it? I'll listen," she said, sitting up again.

"I think it all means something, but I can't figure it out. I started in the street, where we all fell asleep last night, and all of you were gone. The street was endless, and there were no alleyways, no escape. I only found you and Dad, and when I did, you were not normal and you attacked me. I ... I killed my father, and you would have killed me, but I managed to chain you up."

"That's terrible," she gasped.

"Yeah, that's not even the worst part though. It was all this elaborate plan belonging to a winged man, like the one we saw the first night we met. He was *really* there, Gina. I don't know how, but he was. He was way too free thinking to have been my own dream. And I couldn't fight him, no matter how angry he made me. He was just way too good. The creepiest part was when he revealed his face. He looked like an older me. Then he challenged me to come to the north, to the ice palace to face him for real. I feel like he has everything to do with the Phantoms."

"An ice palace?" she asked. "D'artello what are you talking about? There's nothing up there but frozen wasteland." She realized that the look on his face was not kidding, so she prodded more. "Was it king Garo?" she guessed.

"No," he answered simply. "This man was younger, and like I said, he looked kind of like me, and he had these big black raven wings. Really, I think he was the guy from the night this place was attacked. He said something about being a spark. I think he has power over the Phantoms."

"D'artello," she began. She recalled the night all too well. That man waited for D'artello to be preoccupied with the Phantom, and then had grabbed her by the throat. She still remembered his hot breaths in her ear:

Fly away, my little dove
Away until you find love
Until in the clouds above
Then come flapping back
Come when the sky is black
When you come back to me, the sky will be black forever, little birdie.

The last line was an input; how clever he must have fancied himself. The rest of the poem was something that her mother would recite every night before tucking her into bed. As far as she knew, it was a homegrown nursery rhyme, right out of the confines of her own bedroom. Her mother had invented it. When they came upon her burning town, she knew it was he, the black winged man, who had killed her parents.

"What is it?" he asked, placing his hands on her shoulders.

"Nothing," she said without missing a beat. All this time, since she'd seen her burning city, she wanted to exact her revenge. She wanted to make this man pay. If what D'artello was saying was true, and this winged warmonger did have power over Phantoms, then it would be impossible for her.

Bypassing the quickness of her answer, he began to speak again. "When Harmony comes this morning, I intend to get answers."

If Harmony came, the last thing binding Gina to this world would be gone. She lost her loved one, she lost her city and her parents, she lost her kingdom she devoted her life to, and now she was going to lose D'artello.

Now was not the time for her to take that; she needed his kindness and livelihood, not an empty shell of a hero. Dismounting him suddenly, she sat back and stroked the hair away from her eyes. Staring at the ceiling, she contemplated her only option.

D'artello watched her for a moment, wondering why her complexion had reversed completely. She was keeping something from him, and he was afraid that more prodding would hurt her. He had just begun drawing his own conclusions when she rose from the water, letting it drip off of her naked body. Exiting the bath, she grabbed a white towel that read Adriel. Apparently he too had chosen darkness, as they had yet to see a statue of his likeness. There were no members of the town clergy here, in fact, not even Sali's body.

D'artello felt there was something to be said for that. The light of the church apparently did not shine on their souls. What did that say about Harmony? D'artello felt no better though. The winged man was right; if faced with the choice, he would have given anything to get back up and avenge Tanya, no matter what that meant.

Gina dried herself and began to put her clothes on. Something about her body language was not right all of the sudden. Wherever she was going, he thought it best to follow, so he jumped out of the bath quickly, retrieving that single towel that she had dropped and passing it over his skin a few times.

"I'm going to go to the roof for a few," she said, beginning to ascend the staircase to the rear of the bathing hall.

Chapter 13

As the stars faded away, the sun began to bronze the scenery while the two looked out from the highest point of the church. "I can't believe how quiet it is," Gina said, sitting up high on the parapet wall surrounding the balcony. The church was the highest structure in the town, even over the guard towers. From this height, they had a beautiful view of the each building's roof. This was a perspective that not even D'artello had seen, and he'd lived in the town all his life. The highest he'd ever gotten was perched in a guard tower facing the fields. It had never occurred to him how breathtaking a town would look from this angle.

"It is peaceful in a way," she said, hanging her legs off the side of the building. "Makes you wonder why we fight sometimes, right?" She posed the question to him rhetorically, but in reality, she was looking for a reason to go on. Soon she would see if he would pass the test; her life depended on it.

Peaceful, he thought. Could that mean that the scion of his dreams was right? Could this really be what it meant by putting humanity out of its misery? To have peace? He sat next to Gina and hung his legs over the dangerous drop as well. *Peaceful? Here she is, alone with no kingdom, and I am losing all of my childhood memories, all for just a quiet moment? This is peace?* "Are you forgetting the Phantoms?" he asked. "We've come all this way and have seen those battles just to call *this* peace?"

Gina fell sullen at his outburst.

"I feel that peace is happy, loving, and beautiful. Besides momentary sadness and anger, the world is supposed to be truly happy," D'artello said, staring down at a crowd of statues. "This peace feels like death."

She looked down off of the side of the building, and that was when he saw it in her eyes. *Dammit! She is going to jump and end her life right here in front of me. Did I hurt her that badly? Did I misunderstand what she said? Was the peace she was talking about indeed death? No.* He would not let that happen. Quickly he fell back from his perch and put his arms around her, holding on so very tight.

She kicked and sobbed wildly, trying to pull away from him as he lowered her back and away from the edge. "Let me go, dammit! You don't understand what I've been through! There's nothing left for me!" she shouted, crying her eyes out.

"Gina, stop it!" he said, grabbing her and holding her head to his chest. She gave a couple of rough pounds that made a drumming noise on his chest. Some last-ditch efforts to get him to release her. "I won't let you do it!" he said repeatedly, at first shouting over her, then getting quieter until he whispered it in her ear.

"It's the end of the world, isn't it?" she cried.

"Look at me ... *look at me,*" he said, forcing her chin up so that she would have to look him in the eye. He pressed his forehead to hers so that there was no escape now. "I'm not going to let that happen, do you hear me? I won't let it happen. Don't make my efforts go in vain. You deserve better," he said, kissing her again.

"D'artello, that burning city was my home. My parents lived in that castle," she said.

So stupid, so much had happened in his soulless state, he'd forgotten almost completely about that. Gina was not originally from the Genzak nation. When she cried, why could he not place these facts together? This girl was in much more pain than he had originally thought. He said the only thing he could think to say, "I'm sure, wherever they are, they wouldn't want you to die like this, and they are very proud of you finally doing what you've always wanted."

Gina grabbed him tight again, this time her chin like a hook around the back of his neck, "Promise me," he heard her whisper. "Promise that you'll never let me go. Just hold me like this until the end."

That, unfortunately, was a promise that he could not make, let alone keep.

Luckily for him, she began to drift off into an exhausted sleep. Her body and mind could go no longer without rest. Needing it as much as she did, he held her tight for a little while, at least until the sun was in his eyes, then he loosened his grip carefully as not to wake her. Even as Gina slept so comfortably in his arms, the dream still lingered in his mind. Between that and Joseph, it was clear what he had to do to end this once and for all. He would beat the winged man at any cost.

Giving up his soul made him the ultimate fighter, one that did not care about his own life, one that did not hesitate or consider arbitrary details, like *feelings*. If his soul was the sacrifice he had to make, then he would do it for Gina, his father, and the rest of the people left in the world.

Putting her down gently, replacing his warm body and beating heart with the cold and silent stone floor, he slipped away.

As he began to descend the stone steps, he turned his head to look once again at her lean and powerful body lying huddled from the cold, her head flat on the ground, her eyes pressed tightly shut as she slept soundly. Somehow a look of sincerity and a grateful gaze of love still escaped her radiance. "I love you," he said, half expecting a response, but it did not matter, as long as she heard it.

He burst through the doors of the church. Having seen the unknown and the forbidden, he decided that it was not all that great, and clearly religion had it wrong. Harmony was not the amazing Peacemaker that everyone thought she was. She too was hiding information from him, and he would find out now, as he held the ultimate bargaining chip. He began to walk toward the ters when she appeared suddenly, her gleaming light trick feeling like nothing new now. "This is it, my warrior. I have come for the rest of your soul. Has this respite been joyous?" she asked as if she were unaware of his and Gina's activities in her church.

"There was a man in my dreams," D'artello began. "He looked like me and had black raven wings. He was also there the first night that Fort Carrie was attacked, and he was probably responsible for the downfall of the capital and the affliction of King Garo. Who is he?"

Harmony looked at him for a moment as if he had said nothing and then began to speak. "You do not need to know the forces at work here. All you need to know, my warrior, is the clarity of your mission," she replied.

"Fine," he said. "I didn't want to do this, but you leave me no choice. He unsheathed the Molten Steel and threw it at her feet. "If you do not want to answer my questions, then I do not want to save your universe. You'll have to kill me before I pick up that weapon," he threatened, hoping she wouldn't.

Harmony was not shaken by this defiance. The boy had never learned the respectful ways of the church, and she could also feel his unwillingness to die. "Are you sure you wish to travel down this path?" she asked.

He nodded. "Who is he?" he repeated.

"Let us begin with the beginning," Harmony said, casting out her hand. With this motion, all fell silent. It was not as if there were many noises to begin with, but once the wind, birds, and insects quieted, his ears missed their cries dearly. The sun began to dim until D'artello could no longer see. He had only Harmony's voice to guide him in the pitch blackness.

"I sent you that *Legendex* in your pouch to enlighten you beyond my explanation," she noted. "In the beginning, before life, there was only a chord, a voice if you will, but neither you nor I can hear it. The voice, we Peacemakers came to know as the chorus. It is a being above us, and its reason is mysterious and indefinable. It sang of darkness, of endless abyss, the stage for life itself.

"Writhing in the darkness were life forms we have dubbed dark half-minds. They represent merely one half of the human spectrum but are not to be confused with humans. Humans came much later. The chorus sang again, planting small rocks across the endless abyss. These 'worlds,' as you would call them, were alive with separate beings called light half-minds."

"So … these dark half-minds, they're evil, they are the Phantoms?" D'artello asked, looking at the silhouettes that had appeared out of the abyss and on the planets. The black shadow silhouettes were creature-like, many different shapes, and the light ones were shaped like men.

"Typical notion of a human, this is all perspective. They are dubbed dark merely because they are indeed dark, for no other reason. Without the dark half-mind in you, you would be a worm and could never stand up for what you believe in. There was no good or evil yet, just perspective; good and evil were invented by the humans who are later to come. Now … these two life forms met and began to exchange perspective, learning from one another and changing physically thusly."

From the distance, a planet came barreling in at them. D'artello shielded himself just before it stopped abruptly. He and the Peacemaker hovered above the surface of the world, just close enough to see a dark half-mind and a light half-mind touch hands. This made him think, reevaluate his beliefs about good and evil and question its existence. What if everything was all perspective? Could it be possible?

"Eventually, the first human was born." D'artello watched a dark half-mind hug a naked man. "He was the first to gain a perfect understanding of both the dark and light half-minds. By the chorus, this was not unnoticed. It sang for the third time, the first time in many millennia, appointing this human as the first Peacemaker. Wisdom is his name, and he is the eldest of us all. It was under Wisdom's teachings that more humans came to be."

D'artello watched more light and dark half-minds combine to form adult males and females. It was a remarkable process. The information bombarding him was astounding. This kind of knowledge wasn't meant for any man. "By Harmony, this is amazing!" he said. Harmony stared at him a moment as if contemplating the expression. "Uh … oh sorry," he said.

"Not all half-minds could learn from Wisdom's teachings though. Those half-minds became the other species that inhabit the planets today. The creatures are considered less intelligent than humans and generally inferior to them. Wisdom was great, and the other humans felt that being this close to him and understanding his ways made them great as well. They developed a sense of superiority and felt the animals that did not understand it did not want to, and therefore they should be extinguished.

"The humans began to crush the other life forms with their intellect and vast armies. This is not how Wisdom wanted it. As a warning, he set many planets ablaze in eternal fire, so that the remaining planets could look up at the night sky and be reminded of their mistake. Unfortunately, it was not taken that way." They flew away from the planet and back into the pitch-black abyss. D'artello was startled by an igniting of several worlds in the distance. Harmony's face came into view under the soft light. It was almost like a candle.

"The humans responded with an epiphany. Their enemies were not the harmless woodland creatures; their enemies were one another. Immediately they began to blame each other for this occurrence, then take sides, and eventually break into all-out war."

Again they hovered in on a planet, this time just below the clouds to peer over a vast field. Both sides were flooded with weapon-wielding men and women. They clashed in the middle, fighting and slaying one another. Then Harmony averted her attention upward, and D'artello followed suit, to a young man with short black hair, clad in a white robe.

"Wisdom was at a loss. Take heed to this next passage, as no text on your planet or any other will ever speak of this event. The chorus began to sing again, and from its voice came the Phantom army. An infection of the soul that man carries, and because there was no birth yet, this was especially devastating."

D'artello heard the all-too-familiar screeches of the white cloaked monsters. They poured down from the sky, passing him as if he weren't there. It did not take long for them to wedge an opening in the scuffle below.

"These creatures existed outside the bounds of harm, but Wisdom fought hard to rid the universe of their presence. He succeeded about the time Ruin was tricked and sealed away. He managed to seal them in an alternate reality, much like the one I have created for you now, and in the physical world, the disease had to be forged within a blade. The Frozen Steel was placed in the hands of one of the guardian statues. Further, Wisdom sacrificed his eternal youth and much of his power to forge the Molten Steel, the saving grace of humanity should the Phantoms ever rise again.

"So you see, the Frozen Steel has the power to spread the disease again, but once it is out, it is out. Sources will spring up on their own, whenever someone dies a wrongful death with too much hatred in their heart. All that Frozen Steel does is complete the transformation of sources. If the real Frozen

Steel cuts a source, the Phantoms under its rule break free of their master to become their own masters. Meaning you would have to slay each and every one of them, individually, to suppress the infection.

"Conversely, if you cut down a source with your Molten Steel, the Phantoms under its rule will dissipate along with their leader. Much like what happened to Joseph, and what is happening to King Garo now."

"The Phantoms were created when humanity's integrity was in question."

"So it would seem, but the chorus works in mysterious ways. It is hard to tell if it even thinks; it simply knows," Harmony tried to explain.

"So why is this winged man doing this? Why would he be helping the Phantoms along?" D'artello inquired.

"He has much hatred in his soul, more than any man could possibly have, but instead of ending his own life, he chooses to live with it and take revenge on humans," she answered as they flew away from the planet again.

"Revenge for what?" he asked.

"I am not certain," she said curtly. "Much like I have chosen you to be my champion, my brother Unity has chosen him as a champion," she said.

This angered D'artello. Of all the nerve and the infinite wisdom bestowed upon these creatures they called Peacemakers, how could they do something so dark? "Why don't you and Unity hammer out your disagreement yourselves?" he asked angrily.

"We are siblings. It is forbidden for us to engage in combat, and although we differ, we still do share unconditional love for each other. That aside, we cannot wield the two blades ourselves. So it says in the prophecy."

"Then *you* kill the winged man," D'artello said as if it were the obvious answer.

"I cannot," she began. "If I kill him, Unity will kill you, and we will have to select new champions. We have agreed to aid you both, but not to harm the other," she explained.

Clearly there was no reasoning with her. He just let it go and accepted the fact he would have to fight for humanity. What else could he do? He still wanted to know the obvious question, however. "Who is he? Why does he look like me?" he shouted.

"The answer is rather simple, don't you think?" she asked. "The answer is in your father's book. When you believe you want to know, you have the answers in your hands. I would not want to tell you anything your father does not want you to hear."

If he could determine whether she cared about his father's feelings, he might say she had a point. This was just another way for her to dodge the answer. D'artello supposed that it did not matter who this man was; he had to defeat him, and he had to do it alone.

"I can't take them all with me," he said abruptly, referring to Gerrik and the others. The starry surroundings faded away, and he was back on the road of Fort Carrie, headed toward the ters.

"Do you really expect to survive without them?" she asked.

"Yes … I know I can do it without my soul," he proclaimed.

"I don't think you understand the severity of this situation. You would sacrifice all of humanity for your pride?" Harmony protested.

"You want me to bring them to their deaths? They can't fight Phantoms, and I'm not exactly prone to protect them when I don't have a soul."

"Their sacrifice will not be in vain, my warrior," she said, looking up at the sky.

"Don't talk about them like that!" he shouted. Her neck snapped back to a forward locked position. Her eyes targeted his now, and he felt a sudden jolt in his spine from the abrupt glare. "They're not sacrifices," he continued, quickly regaining his composure. "I don't care if you kill me for speaking out," he said, acknowledging her power.

To Harmony, his insolence was familiar. Other people in this world would take her words without question, as they were all tamed to do, through her churches, but not D'artello. He was a wild one and had yet to be tamed. After all, it wasn't his fault. He was brought up without the guidance of the clergy. It was a worthy sacrifice for a warrior of his caliber.

"If you don't honor my request, then you know where we stand," he said, gesturing at the Molten Steel.

"You would throw away the entire universe?"

"If I am the hero you believe me to be, then let me go alone. Now take my soul," he ordered.

Harmony stared blankly at him, pondering modestly about her decision, chewing on the latent disrespect and the raw gall he had to call her bluff. She glanced at the sword once more and then circled her hand, causing it to lift into the air. D'artello never took his eyes off of her flawless face until the sword was shoved back toward him. He caught it by the hilt, closing his eyes as the force pushed him back a few feet. When he opened them, her lips were already on his. This time, he could feel a slight ferocity in her biting embrace, as if to punish him with her lips, and yet somehow she was enjoying herself. As she pulled away, the ghostly stream flowed from his mouth to hers, sucking away the moral poison. The familiar tears began to run and dampen his face as he fell to his knees.

"You may go alone, warrior. Fight on and let me be your guiding light," she said, making her exit.

Truly alone now, D'artello rose to his feet, hollow and unrelenting. He was a child just born into the world, curious and confused. He staggered for a moment, losing his grace long enough to fall to one knee. First he regained his stature, and then he looked at the sword in his hand, as if it were interesting reading material, forgetting about the books in his leather pouch for now. He snapped it into his sheath and lowered his arms gradually to his sides. After a moment, he took off, his steps pounding the ground toward the ters.

They were no more than a block away from Gerrik, Bensel, and Elan. Upon spotting him, the ters scrambled to an upright position. They refused to make eye contact and pressed their backs to the outside wall of a building. They looked like they were willing to push through the bricks to get away from him. Cornered as they were, they dared not try to bite. Fear of his empty being gripped them. Pulling his father's sword, he raised it high above their skittish heads and then brought it down swiftly. The ropes gave way as the blade sliced through with relative ease, and two ters eagerly flew away from the scene. The last one had stopped forcing itself into the wall, probably recognizing the prospect of freedom, but D'artello advanced and held out his hand. The animal gave a few coy sniffs and then lowered its springy body back to all fours. He mounted it.

"D'artello! What are you doing?" he heard his father call. Gerrik had always been a light sleeper; he probably even knew that he and Gina had gotten up earlier. Without so much as a second look, D'artello cut the last rope with his sword, not once looking back at his father, and the ter began to gallop away, flapping its wings. By the time Gerrik had caught up to his son, he was already in the air, on his way to the frigid north. Gerrik slowed his pace, realizing the futility of catching his son now, "D'artello! Dammit!" he called.

Chapter 14

D'ARTELLO soared away, leaving his father's waking curses behind. The animal rocketed into the clouds, embracing the cool, dawning morning. It got rocky for a moment when the animal gave a wavering shiver to shake the dew from its scales.

It was only an hour before his blade began to glow and the air beneath him felt warm. In the silence of his mind and the air around him, he could hear the battle cries of soldiers and the clash of swords far below. The screeches of inhuman tainted souls filled the air, creating a demonic symphonic apocalypse. Under normal circumstances, certainly he would have stopped to help them, save a few more lives, but the mission set in his mind was clear as crystal. If he did not make it to the north in time, there would be no stopping the Phantoms, and his world would end, with or without his interjection. So the shreds of humanity in the back of his mind pleaded, "Fight on, and let me be your guiding light."

He flew all day without stop or rest, during which time these roughshod hotspots came and went as he passed many a battle, while the sun cycled all the way overhead. They were forces struggling to protect their families and homes. D'artello's sword shone like a beacon dwelling in the night sky to those overwhelmed by the tainted populace. As he approached the north, the air grew cold like death.

All was clear to him now. The winged man had claimed many lives, bringing to an end at least two countries. There were others off in faraway lands who needed his protection. In fact, all of humanity was as weak and frail as Tanya lying in his lap just over a month ago. The battles below were fierce but impossible to win. Phantoms were simply too powerful to be suppressed by human troops. On top of that, each battle rolled over by the Phantom army increased its size, the number of Phantoms, and the amount of souls condemned to darkness. It did not take long for the ground below to turn to snow.

He spotted a line of statues, all of the same creature. It was a line of petrified alphas, headed due south. It looked as if Joseph had been right; whatever was up here was nasty enough even to make alphas migrate away. That explained their sudden outbreak in Vaukry and Northern Vashti.

The ter beneath him, being used to a mild or hot climate, was beginning to pant and hack at the dry, frozen conditions. It sounded like a slap across the face every time the lizard opened its mouth. D'artello waited until he could see light from a large settlement and figured it was time for the animal to rest if he intended to get further use of it. The settlement was comprised of tents, walled in by a sturdy fence. Surely there would be food and a place to rest.

About halfway down, he could hear orders being barked out, "Steady your arrows! It's a ter, a survivor!" Drawing in closer, the ter gave one last wing-beat to stagger its fall, then landed on its gelatinous feet within the wooden fence that was much taller than he could perceive from the air. The three-foot thick fence was reinforced with planks from the inside and was no less than fifteen feet tall. These people were obviously anticipating an attack.

D'artello dismounted, and before he had a chance to secure the animal, it turned tail and took off back toward warmer weather, almost dragging his arm and shoulder off with it. Clearly it would have no part of this. D'artello turned to go after it when a booming voice welcomed him with "Sorry 'bout that, kiddo. Ters don't work too well 'round he-a."

D'artello turned to face a monster of a man, massive in every sense of the word. He gave a short smirk under his thick black beard and bushy eyebrows in an effort to seem a little less scary, and not threatening to his new guest. "What place of the world you from, buddy?" he asked.

The man would have to forgive D'artello's rudeness. Without a soul, he was not much for conversation or even giving a friendly smile back. Instead he stared on, standing erect to the walking bicep. A few smaller men scrambled up behind the big man, but they were all built as hell. They began to whisper to the bigger man. "Is he alone?" he heard one of them ask.

"I don't see anyone else …" He could hear just a few words. Clearly they were trying to avoid the impossible, upsetting D'artello.

"The poor lad is too shocked to speak. Wonder what happened," the red-haired man on the left spoke.

Finally the big man grew weary of their exclusive conversation and made a shout to D'artello: "The name's Zack," he said. At a loss for what to say next to this awkward young lad, he led out with, "It's not lookin' like you're going anywhere. Why don't you bunk up and join our ranks."

"Ranks?" D'artello asked, almost too quietly for the men to hear.

"Uh, yes," he answered. He swallowed hard, and the other two bowed their heads in a remorseful manner. "We are the last organized army in the world," he said with no pride. "At least that's what it's lookin' like, but chin up, right? You're here, so maybe there are more survivors. So what do you say?"

With no ter, D'artello was stuck in this encampment. He had no choice but to agree until he could get a mount that would take him to the ice palace. The two muscle men returned to their posts, and Zack led D'artello around a very nomadic town. Tents upon tents sat steeped in the thick snow that even now came down sparingly from the sky. They called themselves an army but they were running from something. He couldn't help himself. He began to feel a tent between his thumb and index finger.

"Pure alpha hide. Good quality stuff he-a. There ain't too many of them anymore though. They been running down south ever since that ice palace sprung up about a month back," Zack said. This explained the sudden influx of alphas near his home. They were running from whatever was in that ice palace. "We'll stop he-a first, the supply tent. Ya must be cold ova the-a," Zack suggested, pulling open a flap for them to step through.

Upon entering, his skin felt a sleeping numbness due to the contrast in temperature. It almost felt warmer to be outside once his skin realized what it was missing, but that feeling passed. "Good job, Joey," Zack said, giving the guard a salute and a little morale boost as he entered the tent. The man gave a smile and a friendly nod. "Need a coat, one about his size ova the-a," Zack requested, giving a nod toward D'artello standing in the entrance.

Joey looked up from his sitting position, pulling back the fuzzy hood from his very short hair. "It's rude to sit in doorways y'know. Eh?" he said. "Come in so I can fit ya." He stood up and turned around. The layout of the tent was simple. The fur floor was barren, barring the pile of clothing behind Joey, which he now rifled through. Joey came up successful and pulled the sleeves of a coat over D'artello's arms. Even he could feel the tension; there was no room for a strapping young lad like him to even flex. He pulled it off, a much more daunting task than putting it on. A few tugs on each arm, and it was back to the pile with it. "Bigger than he looks, eh?" Joey murmured to himself, but Zack nodded anyway. Two or three coats later—it did not matter to D'artello—they found one that was snug but loose enough for him to get the full movement out of his arms.

"Ooh, that one the-a, that's a mammock hide, is it?" Zack asked with an excited perk in his voice.

"Yeh, this stuff is so warm you could go take a bath under the ice, eh, and still break a sweat," Joey said as he brushed the jacket off. It was brown and weighed down on D'artello's shoulders, but when they exited the tent, he felt no difference from the inside temperature to the outside. The jacket was cold proof.

They passed more brown tents. There weren't many people loitering about in the snow, so it seemed a rather lonely place. Eventually they passed a big tent. It looked like it was comprised of three of the normal little brown domes, two small ones in the front and a bigger one in back. The two small ones had entrances to get into the big one, and atop the structure was Harmony's three-pronged symbol. Zack took notice of D'artello's interest.

"Ah, a religious man. Well, stranger, if you wanna pray he-a, the priestess can show you to the men's quartas later," Zack offered. "I have to get back to my post ova the-a," he explained, beginning to walk away.

In truth, this town did not have a real priestess. She was the daughter of a priest off in another town, a small settlement somewhere down south, built from a fort named after a mad king's wife. D'artello entered the big tent. It was nothing like the church he'd spent the morning in. There were no beautiful windows, no benches, no altar, not even a picture of the Peacemaker, just a knee-high, wooden statuette of Harmony's depiction and a fire behind it to warm the tent. In front of the statuette knelt a girl with a familiar figure, also clad in a warm jacket and a warm pair of pants that made her look deceptively thicker than she really was. She was flipping through the pages of a religious text. "Harmony be with you, friend, but I am giving no preaching tonight," she replied to his entrance, not even turning around to face him. He noticed the reddish hair that sat neatly and modestly tied back as it always had been.

She could still feel his presence, and when she realized he wasn't leaving, she slammed the book shut, stood up, and turned around. "Listen, buddy, I—" She dropped the book, and her eyes grew wide. Her hands flew to her mouth, and she began to cry.

"D'artello? Oh my Harmony, D'artello, it *is* you," she acknowledged, running and hugging his stiff figure. Sali pulled away, realizing that he did not hug her back. "Hey, D'artello, it's me—Sali!" She stood awkwardly in front of him. "Um, I'm sorry, it's just, I thought everyone from Fort Carrie had become one of those things." Trying to regain her modest posture she covered her mouth with her hands again, letting the skin soak up some of her tears. "I thought I was the only one who escaped. Michael and Henry and I got away, but they were taken too, and then I was all alone. I was so scared and …" she stopped, realizing she was rambling. "You went off to war, and I thought … that you were …" She sobbed. Sali hugged him again. Everything she had been holding onto and was unable to talk to others about was being poured all over D'artello's jacket in the form of tears. He lacked the will to comfort her.

Within him, a plan was formulating. Sali probably knew where he could get a mount *and* knew the way to the ice palace. She would certainly be a useful tool in helping him achieve his divine goal. He truly meant no harm, but nothing else mattered in his soulless state; only saving the world was ahead. "I need a mount," he declared abruptly.

Sali drew back in confusion. "A mount? Are you leaving?" she asked, the hope dying in her voice.

"I have to go to the ice palace. Do you know of it?"

"The ice palace? Yes, I can find it, but why would you want to? Even alphas run from that place."

"If we want to end this and get rid of the monsters, I have to go there," he explained.

"D'artello, you don't understand, we can't kill them," she argued.

"I can."

"Trust me, D'artello, you can't. We're safer here than anywhere else in the world right now. Let's just stay here and let Zack and the soldiers handle this."

If only she could understand how mistaken she was and realize that slaughter was on the horizon, and as soon as those creatures found the encampment, they would rip through it like tissue paper and leave no one behind.

That answer would have to suffice for now because she was his best bet of getting to the ice palace. He knew that the Phantoms were on their way and that Sali was not going to believe his words unless she saw it for herself.

Sali gave it one last shot. She grabbed hold of his arm as if to chain him. "Please, just stay here with me. I need you right now. It's been so very cold."

Nodding, he figured it best to bide his time.

* * *

Gina could not believe the amount of curses Gerrik now murmured. He had gotten himself a hare and shook his fist up at the circling ters, then proceeded to tie the bloodied ball of fur to a long stick buried halfway in the ground. The plan was simple; he'd gotten himself a net and some bait and would jump on the bitch when she flew in to grab a bite. The meat now in place, he ran like a mischievous child around the corner of a nearby building, positioning himself not even ten feet away.

Gina had already hidden herself and waited around the alley for him, "I'm sorry, Gerrik. If I had known, I—"

"You couldn't have stopped him. None of us could have," he said.

But that did not help her feel any better. Perhaps she could have stopped him if she weren't so damn helpless. Inside, she had beaten herself up since she had awoken, but that was the very problem that led to her suicide attempt. She should have been strong. There and then, she vowed to stay strong, no matter the situation, because people relied on her as much as she relied on them.

Despite her revenge, the one thing running through her mind right now was D'artello, and across her lips slipped the words, "I love you too." In his soulless state, he was weaker than he knew. He had been strong for her, and now it was time she returned the favor. The ter eventually landed, and with the kicking off of her feet came the kicking off of her revelation.

In just a half an hour, the group had wrangled the ters and mobilized the slepne with supplies they would need. They were ready as could be for takeoff. She held Elan's back tightly as the beautiful black steed began to kick, and the wings sent it soaring angelically into the south wind, leaving her comfort zone and her world of pity behind. The only sight was that of D'artello ahead.

Chapter 15

D'artello sat around a feast with many of the members of the encampment, mostly the ones who did not escape with family members. They had all piled into the large meal tent, in which a big fire was lit, warming the inside. The roof was vented to let the smoke out so that it did not strangle its patrons. The hunters and cooks had done well today. There was more than enough food for everyone.

D'artello watched some of the cooks serve up the meal. Then he glanced over at a hunter who was telling the tale of today's game. Most people in this tent were beyond misery now, acceptant of their current lifestyle. There was so much diversity in one room—countries, ethnicities, religions—and none of that mattered now. The Phantoms were monsters true, but Unity's plan had created something beautiful in humanity. These people were working together like an ant colony, not for themselves, but for everyone else so that everyone else would work for them. Here they all looked the same, covered in their big, brown, bushy coats.

There were people like him, pale like the clouds speaking the same way he did, and then there were others. There were the darker men from the other continent, men with strange accents and mispronunciations.

Much of the immediate population consisted of burly, tan men that looked like natives to this region. They were all very strong and knew how to keep warm, as anyone would have to in a place like this. Even the women, the housewives and mothers, generally had much girth and muscle to them. Sali, the poor, cold girl, sat cuddled up next to him.

There were many meats, everything from various large birds and mammock meat to fish. Clearly they must have been by a coast. Not a lot of vegetables to be had though. Farming couldn't have been very good around these parts, but everyone seemed to enjoy the spread just the same.

Sali noticed that D'artello was not eating. She took a second to swallow her mouthful and wipe her fingers with a cloth. "You okay?" she asked. "You know, you really should eat. You have to keep your strength up," she said, running her hand through his hair.

About five minutes passed before she decided there was nothing she could say to fix whatever was wrong with him. Maybe she could get him talking. Taking his hand, she led him out of the tent toward hers, much to the dismay of many a lonely man sitting around the feast. All eyes were on them as they left. They made it about halfway to her tent before he stopped her. The pair stood still in the evening precipitation. Some torches in front of tents remained lit to attract survivors and provide some illumination. The snowflakes reflected the flames as they came down to pile up at the pair's feet.

"D'artello, what's the matter?" she said giving him another tug. He was way too big for someone of Sali's size and stature to move. "What gives? It's cold. We really shouldn't be out here." She pulled her jacket up toward her ears, hugging herself. She looked into his eyes and saw the hard, lifeless expression.

After seeing so many loved ones turn tainted she felt her stomach drop and her heart begin to race. Her fears were put to rest quickly, however, when his hands shot up to her shoulders, startling her. "Listen to me," he said over wind that was now picking up. "We need a mount, and we need to leave. It's not safe to stay here."

"D'artello, what are you talking about? Where else are we supposed to go?"

"The ice palace!"

"I already told you, I'm not taking you there to throw away both of our lives," she said.

He reached into his coat and drew the Molten Steel, causing Sali to take a few steps back with her hands raised submissively. The blade had an odd shimmer about it.

Only D'artello knew that it was glowing because of nearby Phantoms. Reaching out, he grabbed Sali's arm firmly.

"Help!" she yelled. "Help!" she screamed again, kicking her feet and falling to the ground. He raised his blade high above her, like he was going to harvest her spine. "Oh my harmony!" she said with wide eyes as he brought it down onto her. She had closed her eyes to greet death in the darkness, but when she felt no pain, she opened them again. The sword was in her, but she didn't feel it. It was lodged right in her heart, yet she still breathed and felt it still beating. He pulled it out to reveal nothing, no wound.

"Do you see now? This sword cannot hurt you. It was made only to kill Phantoms. They are the monsters of which you speak," he explained.

By this time, he had let her hand go, and she sat huddled in the cold snow. Some men came out of the tent to observe the situation.

"Hey, take it easy, eh," one of them said, approaching him cautiously.

"You'll leave the lil' lady alone if you know what's good for you," another man holding a shovel threatened.

More men came out, their wives watching from the entrances of the surrounding tents, and Sali could not take her eyes off of him. She noticed his hand tighten around the hilt of his glowing sword. "Wait!" she shouted, climbing to her feet. "He didn't hurt me … he can't." In response, the crowd halted its angry advance. "He was showing me his sword—this merciful blade, it can't cut people."

"What? What's this all about?"

"Can't cut people? What's this girl talking about?"

"Don't protect him! How dumb do you think we are, missy?"

The crowd murmured on. She believed his words about the safety of their location too and began to voice his warning. "That sword can only kill monsters, and they're on their way. It's not safe here."

Some soldiers of the last organized army in the world overheard and came out to quell the ruckus. When they caught wind of Sali's words, they did not look happy. Sali and D'artello were escorted and brought before Zack, who looked very displeased. "What are you kids doin' out the-a? What's going on he-a?" he asked. "You can't just go spoutin' off like that, honey," he said to Sali, who lowered her eyes to the floor in shame.

"An' you, stranga, why do you have to come 'round he-a and cause trouble?" Zack said, his eyes narrowing on D'artello. A brief pause, and his voice sounded again. "Well, anybody gonna speak up? What's goin' on he-a?"

Sali looked up. "Zack, D'artello says the monsters are headed this way. I believe him. I really do."

Zack rubbed his eyes. "You kids can't just go spouting off like that. People got high nerves 'round he-a," he explained. "Speak. What makes you think that?"

"His sword," she said. "It can't cut me. He held it right here, right in my heart, then pulled it out. I'm not wounded or even hurt, and he told me it's only made to kill Phantoms, those monsters."

"It glows like this whenever Phantoms are near," D'artello explained, holding up the blade for him to look at.

Zack got up and walked over, scrutinizing it. "What kind of trick do you have he-a? What makes it glow?"

"That's not important," D'artello responded.

Zack stood upright, towering over him as if he could pluck that blade away like a tree branch on a sapling. "Aw, I don't know why, but I believe ya," he said abruptly. "We have to get everyone out of he-a. How long do we have before they come?"

"They're not coming," D'artello said. "They're already here."

A masculine scream pierced the silent falling snow. After the scream came the all too familiar shrieking from a frozen Phantom. The men in front of Zack's tent let out terrified cries as their silhouettes were dragged away into the invisible abyss of the animal hide.

"What the hell?" Zack yelled.

D'artello seized Sali's hand, leading her out of the tent. He stopped, confronted with his first Phantom of the night. It lunged forward in its usual angry fashion, but a block, kick, and slice was enough for this one. Sali was bewildered, as it was the first one of these demons she had seen fall. She felt a great relief well up in her soul when she saw the truth in D'artello's words.

"C'mon," he ordered quietly. "We have to find the mounts before they do," he said.

Among the white noise of the encampment erupting into a battlefield, they heard a loud crash and hideous laughter. Splinters were thrown through the air and poured down over the tents like rain. The outer fence had crumbled like a pile of hay. D'artello stopped to let her lead the way, and the two weaved their way toward the mammock keep.

"Through the mess tent!" she yelled, peeling back the entrance and running in. To her terror, it was filled with Phantoms. One of them turned and charged her, but D'artello's arm raced around her, pulling her aside so he could engage the enemy, giving a quick cut. The Phantoms were drawn instantly to the threatening sword. If through the tent was their path, then black mist would be left in their wake. D'artello held his ground defeating several more Phantoms. One had come in behind them, and Sali screamed, but he pulled her away just in time and cut down the flank.

Taking her in a hostage position, with one arm around her so that she would have to move with him, he took another slice. This one was avoided as the Phantom hovered backward. He pivoted around her so that she stayed standing in the same spot, but he could get closer to unwind and catch a big enough piece to send the enemy to the heavens. One of the former patrons of the mess hall, a tall dark man, had gotten back up as a tainted and came running. He attempted to dive onto the pair and ensue with whatever devious plot filled his bloodthirsty mind, but D'artello tripped Sali and then dropped to a squat, cradling her in his free arm so that she did not hit the floor. The man went vaulting over them, and D'artello stood back up, pulling her to her feet again.

After slaying three more, they began to feel a palpable presence in the air. There were only roughly seven left in the tent, as far as D'artello could count while keeping him and Sali out of harm's way. Finally they could mount an offense and get away from the doorway. Just as they were gaining some headway, two more of the formerly preoccupied Phantoms left their current victims to engage him. Cutting one down came simple as usual, but when he took a swift swing toward the other, a loud clash rang out. Blocked. Not one Phantom had ever attempted to block him.

There was no time for this. Sali knew, just glancing around at all of the wounded bodies, any second they would be overwhelmed with tainted. Looking to D'artello to get them out of the tent, she watched him struggle with his ghostly opponent. In the span of a blinding flash, he managed to pull free his second sword, stab it into the Phantom, and then slice it with the Molten Steel. By the time Sali's eyes could catch up with the motions, the Phantom was already drifting off into the air. Five more Phantoms left their victims to attack. D'artello ran ahead of Sali to give some distance and attract them to the sword they so desired.

They were getting smarter. The crowd was forcing him back, strategically, gradually surrounding them.

Ten soldiers burst in through the entrance of the mess tent. Sali was startled by their intrusion. The last organized army in the world had about all it was going to take of the Phantoms. Although the humans were no match for them, the ten soldiers proved more than an adequate distraction. All of the warriors in all of their different weaponries and styles were too diverse for the expanding Phantoms' techniques and thus they were overrun momentarily. D'artello and Sali took this chance to flee the tent. She looked back at the helpless men, knowing in her heart none of them would make it, so she looked to D'artello for assistance, but his cold stare suggested he had no intention of going back to help. Leaving the mess tent was leaving all hope of saving the camp.

They exited into the middle of a scuffle. The Phantoms were trying to pick off a spearman. One of the two on him pushed him back, almost into D'artello, but he dodged to the side, allowing the Phantoms to get in on their stumbling prey. The pair continued to run from the replaying nightmare.

"This way!" Sali said, waving her hand. "It's just a little further."

At long last, they reached a fenced clearing in the center of the encampment, and within it towered tame mammocks. They were gargantuan creatures, even bigger than alphas. It was no wonder they were worthy choices for making tents out of; even just one could satisfy the amount of material needed.

Their enormous bodies walked on four short, fur covered, support-beam-like legs that hammered through the snow below. They had massive tusks that branched out just above their top lips and a long snout that pushed the snow aside in search of frozen vegetation.

After a quick somersault over the fence, D'artello turned and helped Sali over. They took one last look at the encampment. People were beginning to flee like ants, and two black tendrils could be seen waving in the air. It was a source, King Garo probably, but there was no time to deal with him. Fleeing to the ice palace was the only goal. Killing the source would end this slaughter, but perhaps slaying the winged man would stop it all.

They approached one of the twenty-foot tall mammocks. Its raw size and power was rivaled only by its docility. The creature was more than willing, almost happy to have them as passengers. D'artello sat atop its soft fur and rounded shoulder blades, and Sali climbed on back and held on tight by securing her arms around his collarbone. D'artello gave a kick, but the creature did not need a lot of convincing. It took off so quickly that it almost threw them off of its back.

Even with its bulk, it was deceptively quick on its feet. Apparently the wooden fence had been nothing more than a mental blockade, because the beast tore through it like paper.

They weren't out of the woods yet; the mammock pen was untouched, but they still had to charge through the tents to escape the other side. Instinctively, Sali's hands flew to the reins. She was an expert slepne rider when she was younger, before she became a full-time member of the clergy. Something told her that D'artello would not even try to avoid people if they got in the way.

The bulky beast seemed to avoid the tents on its own, but the Phantoms were all over it. They left cuts in it every which way as it passed, but one of them got caught underneath its titan footsteps. For that instant, being immortal and not able to die must have been a curse, and if Phantoms had feelings or nerves at all, it wouldn't want to get up afterward. D'artello drew his sword to protect the mammock, slicing it once to cure the effects of the Frozen Steel. He then slammed it through the next Phantom coming in from the side.

All in all, Sali was doing a good job for the limited experience she'd had riding mammocks, but suddenly they heard a ripping sound. They had run right into a tent.

Blinded by its former kin's hide, the animal was thrown into a panicked frenzy. D'artello and Sali were vaulted from its back. They landed in the snow, a gentle impact until Sali fell on top of him. The mammock rose up on its hind legs. Its height was nothing short of a small building, and it was certainly twice as heavy. D'artello grabbed Sali and rolled to the left, narrowly avoiding the giant foot crashing down like a meteor. She yelped as a wave of snow buried them and found its way down the back of her coat, stinging and numbing her back.

A loud horn-like noise pulsed from the trunk of the beast. Phantoms were closing in on them and their confused mount. D'artello folded Sali off to his side and climbed to his feet, which was no easy task in more than a foot of frozen powder. Their mammock and their only escape was romping away, smashing into tents and tripping over panicking people. The Phantoms ignored D'artello and went straight toward the stumbling creature, as if they knew, as if their maddened consciousness could think far enough ahead to cripple their escape. The source must have maintained a very talented control.

Finally catching its foot on one side of the big tent, the mammock came thundering down. D'artello closed in, slicing open the battle by killing the first Phantom. After that, the rest of the Phantoms were drawn to their attacker. As he fought, the mammock found its way back to an aggressive stance. It swung its mighty tusks and trunk to bat away its assailants and would have crowned D'artello as well if he hadn't ducked. The Phantoms were sent careening through the air, and he managed to tag one of them on its way by.

The mammock's feet began to tumble over one another as it built momentum, charging D'artello. Sali watched as he was at risk of being trampled by a walking house. In one fluent motion, he jumped, missing the tusks and slipping his feet in between the front legs. It ran clear over, leaving him completely unscathed. A huge support pillar for the church tent put the brakes on its stampeding advance. It was there that the mammock made its stand against the blinding cloth.

It rubbed its face against the pillar, trying to gore the material. The Phantoms got up and flew back at D'artello. He drew his father's sword and began his twin slicing techniques to vanquish his foes. Sali was tired of watching; she got up and ran over to the flailing mammock, boldly placing her hands on its side. Jumping at first, the creature almost sent her for the ride of her life. "Shhh ... shhhh," she whispered. Once it heard her voice, it began to calm down. She could even see the slowing breaths in its bulky chest. It gave one last push toward the pillar and then finally submitted quietly. Trying not to make sudden moves, she began to untangle the leathery material. She gave a hard cough, letting a dry, cold bark escape her winded lungs. Endurance was never her strong suit, but now was not the time to be weak. D'artello was being overwhelmed by Phantoms while she could do nothing but watch and wonder what it must be like to be strong as he was.

She knew of nothing else that could kill the Phantoms, just that sword held in his lonely grasp. *What pressure, he must feel, to be the sole savior. With no mentor, or allies by his side, he aimed to save the world. All alone, so brave and selfless, I do not envy him,* she thought. It stood to reason that the stronger a man was, the more responsibility bestowed upon him. Suddenly she was grateful to be the normal human untying the mammock and not the daredevil fighting the monsters.

D'artello back-flipped to escape a sword coming in at his midsection and to open a gap before he got surrounded. The Phantoms' unusual behavior was baffling. Formerly, they were a foe dealt with easily, and he could turn them away by the tens. Now, the presence of the source made them so much more aware of their only threat.

The Phantoms floated in cautiously, countering his circling steps. They hissed as if to curse at him, but no such insults came. His mobility was down in this foot-high snow, but they floated gently on their airy ground, a clear advantage even without their newfound intellect. After a few seconds, they still stood on their side. Six of them in direct vicinity now, about three too many.

"D'artello! Jump on!" Sali cried. The mammock gave another of its blasting cries as it barreled through the fray. D'artello jumped up and landed skillfully, just one foot on each tusk. On his way by, he sliced two more of the Phantoms as the other four were pushed to the wayside by the hulking behemoth. Once past them, he pushed himself up and in front of Sali, assuming their pre-scuffle positions. They rode off into the white wilderness, leaving the encampment and the last organized army in the world behind.

Chapter 16

Having never been this far north proved to be a weakness for Gina, Gerrik, Bensel, and Elan. The altitude did not help matters either. The higoat wool was just not cutting it; the wind passed through it as if it weren't even there. Gina huddled up to Elan as best she could to keep warm, and he was shivering so much that he couldn't extend his arms to grab the reins of his slepne. He had to trust Thunder to do the right thing. It was not a particularly dangerous act, as Thunder was as loyal as the sword on Elan's waist.

The ters underneath Gerrik and Bensel were beginning to hack and wheeze, and their loyalty was in question. Lizards were always harder to domesticate, and if they really wanted to turn tail to head back home, they would and there would be little the two riders could say about it.

They decided to land. Gerrik touched down, but Bensel's ter collapsed just as it hit the ground, throwing the old, cold king into the snow. They watched the animal twitch and knew it would not survive. Gerrik gave the other one a tap on the rear to send it on its way, hoping the same fate would not befall it. Elan hovered gently for a moment and then let his animal touch the ground.

"We'll have to continue on foot," Gerrik said, determined as ever to follow his son.

"Dammit," Bensel said. "We're going to die out here."

"No!" Gerrik simply said. There was really no other response. He had no plan or comforting thought to give.

"There's no one up here to help us. You saw that encampment; the Phantoms have obviously been here, which means there are no people here," Bensel argued.

For the first time in his life, Gerrik knew helplessness. He did not fear death. In fact, given the circumstances, it looked like a viable option.

"I could look for another settlement," Elan said, shivering. "Thunder is doing fine." he looked down at the dead ter. "My king, with your permission…" he began to say, but he soon realized by the lack of hope in their eyes that his orders could only be given by one man at this point. He jumped down, thumping into the snow, and raised his hand to help Gina off. She stumbled weakly as her muscles were beginning to give way to the numbing chill. She did not have the bulk that the men did. Elan mounted the slepne and Gina looked up at him with sullen eyes. The slepne gave a nasal sputter and a hard beat of its blanket-like wings as it jetted back into the sky.

Below, they all felt the same fear—that Elan would not return for them. An eternity went by and what little Gina could see was beginning to blur. Her lips were already blue by the time she fell to her knees and passed out.

* * *

On a hard floor, she awoke softly. Awake, but not yet ready to open her eyes, she let her fingertips do the glancing. What was this substance? Wood? Stone? Whatever material, it was sure as hell cold. There was no more wind or precipitation, so she figured she must be inside. Maybe Elan found another settlement. She pushed herself up to look down at her reflection, as if she were lying on a mirror. It certainly felt that way, but her hand slipped and she barely caught herself. Her shoulder gave a tight pull, emitting a negligible amount of pain. Pivoting up on one shoulder, she examined the moisture between her fingertips. *Water*, she realized. It was ice. The floor was made of ice, as were the walls and ceiling.

On those walls were candelabras made of ice and decorative carvings. Embedded in each wall were statues of Phantoms with their blades in a saluting stance that made them look almost civilized. The Frozen Steels were horizontal and centered over their would-be faces, so that each eye could see beyond its respective side of the blade. They scared her before she realized they were just sculptures. This whole location had notable architectural beauty, as the empty world did in its own way, mono-colored and very intricate. She tried to stand but slipped onto her behind, and so sat there taking it all in.

The room was a grand hall, like that of Genzak's palace, except everything was carved from ice. Banners on the walls, mounted weapons, the knights (Phantoms), and even on the far end were two thrones, one for a king and one for a queen. She stood up again, this time managing to sustain her balance. Because the wind was off of her back, it was much warmer, even in a room made of ice. Her first instinct was to see where exactly she was, so she shuffled toward a window.

Where is everyone? she thought. "Sir Gerrik!" she shouted. Her voice carried on endlessly, as if there was nothing to bar its path, and certainly no ears to intercept it. Finally reaching the window, she wiped away the frost on the sheet of ice that made up its pane. Staring over a frozen courtyard, she could not see any signs of life. There were ice carvings littered about in a symmetrical fashion; some of them looked like scraggly trees, and others like bald shrubs. It was similar to the hedge maze in Bensel's castle, except it was made of ice. Beyond it were crenellated walls. She gasped as a familiar, unsavory voice rang in her ears to accompany the realization of where she was. The timing was poetic really, as if this person gave her the time to figure out her location.

"Beautiful, isn't it?"

She spun around so fast that she slipped and fell to her backside again. Standing before her was the winged man. He had no cloak to hide his face this time. With hair and eyes colored like the snow outside, he was quite the physical resemblance of D'artello. His hair, however, was longer and hung lower than D'artello's, and his narrower face suggested that he was older too. His beauty was matched only by her hatred for him. The onyx wings shown in the reflective light of the ice palace and swept the ground gently with their primary feathers. He wore a long, black garb that reached to his knees and was unbuttoned to reveal his lean, muscular chest and stomach. Wrapped around his legs was silver armor, with black slacks underneath them, and heavy boots to complete the ensemble.

"Don't be frightened," he said calmly. "I'm only here to deliver a message, or an invitation."

"Frightened!" she exclaimed, rising to her feet, pulling her sword to a ready position. She had waited long enough for this moment, and the initial and irrational anger had not worn off. Without another word, she swung her sword. It sliced straight into his arm and got hung up on a tough ligament with a chewing sound that made her cringe. He stood there and watched on, not even flinching. Gina let go of the handle and stepped backward until she was against the wall.

"Ngh," he grunted. "Are your childish desires satisfied?"

"Childish? You killed my parents!"

"And you tried to kill me just now," he responded.

"Yes, and you still stand. Some sort of power that the Phantoms give you? Coward."

"Not in the least. This is your dream, and whatever happens is your own doing. You could have killed me, but you didn't," he explained, letting sludge-like blood drip from his wound to the floor.

"You look like D'artello," she said, her voice lowering to a whisper.

The Adventures of D'artello

"That is why your notion is childish."

"Shut it! Shut up!" she screamed, holding her ears.

Approaching her, the winged man grabbed her wrists and pulled her hands away so she could hear. Even with the sword digging into his shoulder, he was very strong. "You are childish because you want to get revenge on me, and kill me," he said, his lips right up against her ear. "But you can't do it, can you? D'artello doesn't want you to, and you know he's right, don't you?"

She bit her lip but gave no answer. His audacity was obscene. There was no bolder a man alive than this one who could slay a soldier's parents and then stare her right in the face like nothing was wrong. She had killed few men yet and was trained and taught to think that this was how war was fought, but she could never imagine facing the aftermath.

"You know, there have been many like you. I've killed quite a few parents I guess, and they all say the same thing and have the same look in their eye, yet they all come from different backgrounds. Even someone like you who can hate her parents still musters the very same response."

"I didn't hate them! They wanted something different for me," she said.

"Ah … okay, I understand now," he patronized. "Do you have any idea how painful it must have been for them the day you ran away from home? The kind of pain that a father feels upon losing his child? Sure sounds like you hate them to have put them through that for your own selfish needs."

Crying now, she did not know what else to say except, "It's more complicated than that." A chill ran down her back, making her shiver.

"I know exactly how you feel. My father wanted me to be something I simply was not. Just be happy you left of your own accord."

She turned and looked back out the window. She was able to make a run for it but did not want to. Instead she wanted to make him break down, to use her words if not her sword to cause him pain. "And was that a decent human being?" she asked.

"A human being," he responded, "clearly I am not." He gestured to his wings.

"You're a monster," she said through her sobs.

"Indeed I am, but not by self-proclamation. Monster was not my name, but that often times seemed to be what people called me for the last twenty years. You start to become it after a while."

There it was, her opening. "They called me housewife, and yet I became a soldier." She watched him in the reflection of the window, her back still turned to him, but his complexion did not change. Yet his silence was gratifying enough.

He raised his hands out to shoulder level and began to clap slowly,

"Bravo," he said. "So you've bested me in life. To a normal man, that might hurt, but I am not human."

"And what makes you so different?"

"Humans are loving and caring. I'm sure I don't need to tell you that I lack these traits," he admitted. "But, did you know that humans are selfish? The fact that you can live in a world full of intelligent beings to associate with and still feel lonely is the real sickness, the real monster. I have the physical makeup of a man, barring my beautiful wings of course, but … tell me … what makes a man? Is it his appearance? No, it is his mind, the way he thinks. Humans all wish to protect one another without knowing full well why. Humans abide by false prophecies, follow corrupt leaders, and slaughter one another for the very same sickening reasons. Religion, skin color, property, wives, these are all petty reasons that can make a man go crazy and take the lives of his kin. No one sees the big picture. Do you see now I am different? I am an idealist, or a monster as you humans would call me. Observe the Phantoms. Each one is the same creature, right down to the fiendish personality, but Phantoms don't fight or oppose, and they most certainly don't have wars among themselves.

"You see, very few men set out just to hurt. They in fact set out to satisfy a need, like revenge," he said, motioning toward her. "I … am not a man, but a monster, because I set out only to hurt. I will never be satisfied, as I have found eliminating the people who specifically called me a monster to be exhilarating. I find I just want more and more, and that I enjoy the rare, finer emotions in this world. Vengeance, misery, suicidal intent, panic, and madness are the purest, most tasteful flavors of the human psyche. They are uncontrollable, fully capable of consuming a person's soul, turning them into a monster. I have a little of all of them eating away at me, and I satisfy it by watching people become monsters so that I don't look so bad. It is from these feelings that I became a tool, a champion for a mad Peacemaker to rid the universe of humans. I have no desire to be anything more or less."

"What are you talking about?" Gina said, turning to face him.

"You will know soon enough, as you are becoming one, a monster like me. I can tell just by how you looked out the window to observe the empty beauty of the courtyard. You know that there is something exquisite about a world without people, something a little less complicated, something a little simpler and more peaceful." He clasped the sword, pulling it from his shoulder and gave a shout. The giant laceration began to seal itself up, as if it had never happened. "Now that's better. It seems you don't even want to hurt me anymore." He handed the sword back to her. "You poor girl," he whispered, stroking her hair. "I know the confusion you're going through, and I want you to know that when you fall, I will be here to catch you, because D'artello will not," he said, drawing his blade. "I'm afraid your friends are warming you up, and you are going to wake up now, but I'll see you soon."

* * *

Gina awoke to the wind blowing in her face and the echoing of the winged man's voice in her mind. She lay on her belly on top of a brown fuzzy beast that carried her on a long march through the frozen wasteland. Apparently Elan had found help. A thick blanket spread across her back and kept her warm. She could feel the contrast between her freezing face and her toasty body. Gerrik was more near the front, conversing with a large man, spearheading the advance. She had to wake up a bit more, so her ears would allow her to listen in on their words.

"From the south eh? So more of you are coming up he-a? Is it safe down the-a?" asked Zack. Gerrik trotted beside him as the others mingled in with the rest of the soldiers. Gina lay still, a little groggy from her nap, listening to the conversation.

"More of us?" he asked.

"Yes you, from down the-a," he said. "Just a few hours ago, a boy from the same place came to our encampment, ova that way the-a, but he ran off when we were attacked by the monsters." There was that word again.

A spark of hope entered Gerrik's heart. That must have been D'artello. If not, then who else?

"Them things are nasty. I survived them three times now, but they turn all o' my friends into monsters too."

"So where are you headed now?" Gerrik said, hugging the thick coat he was given to his chest.

"Up to the ice palace ova the-a," he said, pointed into the distance.

"The ice palace?" Gerrik said. "I've never heard of a place like that."

"Don't imagine many have," he responded. "It hasn't been there for long, it just appeared one day. Since then, monsters been driving people up he-a like cattle."

This was troubling indeed, what could this ice palace mean? Why was D'artello going there? Gina coughed up some words from a few feet behind. Gerrik looked back at her stirring from under the blanket, trying to throw it away from her mouth so that she could speak.

"Did you say an ice palace?" she asked, sitting upright now and holding onto the blanket tightly. His eyes narrowed, it almost made her too frightened to speak.

"D'artello said something about an ice palace." She said. Gerrik stopped and lost a few paces to the rest of the army in order to let the mammock carrying get closer to him.

"Quick, what did he say? Out with it, soldier!" Gerrik demanded.

"He said that he was challenged in his dreams, that he would have to go to the ice palace in the north to fight."

"I don't understand. Challenged by who?" Gerrik said.

"I don't know. All he told me was that the man in his dreams looked kind of like him and that he had big black raven wings on his back. We think he was there the night Fort Carrie was attacked and that he was also responsible for burning Belren to the ground," she explained.

"Wings? Black wings?"

"Y-yes."

His expression was addled and beside himself, like a ghost just kissed him on the cheek. He spaced out, his vision diving into the snow. . .

"Gerrik, what's wrong?" Bensel asked, halting his march in front of him.

"My … my son," Gerrik said, covering his mouth, his eyes welling up with tears.

"Of course," Bensel said, looking at him oddly. He kept walking.

Bensel missed the point, if even by this time he wanted to hear it. Gerrik could not express his anguish in any more than those two words. He began to daydream of a boy, a different boy, a beautiful baby boy and a gorgeous, blonde, laughing wife. Those lush tropical fields on the eastern continent would entice and tickle the foreign family as they frolicked in the dusking evening of many a mild night. It felt like a warm vortex encircled and swallowed his heart, the very same feeling when leaping over a cliff and realizing that everything you know and have experienced will be smashed at the bottom, wiped from existence. This was a loving feeling for two of the most important people in his life who were gone, and had been gone since D'artello's conception.

"Dad why, do I have to?" he remembered the boy asking. Though his parents loved him dearly, his differences, his ebon-feathered wings, were something that others did not understand. During his birth, the medic began to scream, "Demon! Demon!" and threatened to tell everyone about it if he and his wife did not get rid of their child. That man, unfortunately, had to take a mysterious fall, resulting in death shortly after. A murderer and father to a "demon," he forced his son to wear big and often restrictive clothes to go to school, to play with friends, and even to accompany his own mother to the marketplace. No one could know.

"Yes, son, not everyone loves you the way we do. They only see the outside," he would explain. Little did he know, Gerrik's words were building a rage like the world had never known. At the time, he felt that sheltering the boy and keeping him home all the time would have caused more harm.

Through the years, his boy became a regular and beloved citizen of the small village. At just the tender age of eight, everyone loved him and he made his parents very proud. Gerrik felt they could look past the physical differences of his boy. And so it was time. He went out in a shirt fashioned by his mother to have holes for the wings. The simple people of the village stared, and some of them poked and pulled just to believe their eyes. Things began to look bleak when other boys picked on him. Not knowing where else to turn, the scared child ran to the local church where he felt safest. That day was full of misfortune. Gerrik never once felt that it was his own son's fault, but the church caught fire that day and burned to the ground. When his son rose from the ashes, the people beat him within an inch of his life, but his wings could still carry him off, and carry him they did. A poor, lonely boy never came back to his parents.

Gerrik and his wife looked long and hard for many an evening, and their land of peace and rapture had turned into bitter hills of bloody violence. Every day, they received warnings to leave their home, and one day, men attacked his wife, leaving a scar across her forehead to remind her that the demon seed grew inside her. The warrior in Gerrik was not so calm in those days. He broke every bone in many bodies before finally leaving that continent. He would never forget the day that the gray-bearded easterner asked him to leave, saying he would be killed if he did not. That was too much to ask; he would have rather died punishing them for the abuse of his wife and son. His battle cry as he charged into a dozen men was, "Arbello!"

Until now, Gerrik had assumed his son dead, as the conditions and wildlife surrounding their village were far too harsh for a boy his age. When they got back to Vaukry, they had a funeral to lay him to rest in their minds as well.

By the time his memories were retold, emptiness befell him. The beautiful blonde wife that he'd loved with all of his heart was taken away shortly after, during D'artello's birth. These days he couldn't even bring himself to speak her name. A part of his past that he'd worked so hard to push away was still alive, needing him badly. Finally he could make amends. It would be like new, he and his two boys living happily ever after.

Coming to, he ran all the way back up to Zack. Bensel noticed him running and jogged to catch up with him as well. "Gerrik, wait! Where are you going?" he shouted after him.

Upon hearing the name, Zack stopped his mammock and the line behind him turned, staring back at the aging southerner.

"Gerrik" was a name Zack had heard before. He wanted to get a good squint at him. This made it all the quicker for Gerrik to catch up to the shoulder of the hulking beast. "Gerrik? *The* Sir Gerrik?" Zack asked. The soldiers behind him were thrown into frenzy. They came from places all around the world, all of which had their own renditions of Gerrik's exploits that men told to the soldiers beside them.

"Yes, Sir Gerrik of Vaukry," he stated. The crowd went silent, and all eyes were on him. "My son was the boy who visited your encampment, and I know he's gone to the ice palace. He is special, and has the power to vanquish the monsters, but I fear he is in more trouble than he can handle. Gentlemen, I love my son and I am going to save him, for I too can vanquish the beasts."

Bensel, Elan, and Gina looked up at him, shocked by his sudden dishonesty. He just told a boldfaced lie to the last organized army in the world. They listened to the words that followed.

"Despite this, I cannot do it alone—save my boy *and* the world. I need your help!" he shouted over the precipitation.

Murmurs began as the information was passed down the line to the folks in back that could not hear him.

"Men!" he shouted simply.

They began to cheer and whistle.

"Our solemn hour is passed. The hour of reckoning is now. We have watched our families, our friends, our villages, towns, cities, and kingdoms fall, and yet here we are, fighting on equal ground with such a formidable foe. Whooa!" he blasted.

"Whooa!" they repeated.

"Look around you, at everyone, your brothers and sisters. Of different kingdoms, different religions, different skin colors, but none of that matters now. You are one, the last army and our final hope for our survival. Whooa!"

"Whooa!" they cheered, louder this time, thrusting their fists into the air.

"You are here now because you are the best, the strongest, the quickest, and the smartest, truly a superior breed of man. For that, pat yourselves on the back, because salvation was not given to you ... You took it! Whooa!" He thrust his fist into the air.

"Whooa!" they shouted.

"But you need the help of my son and me to vanquish this plague forever. I beg you, here and now, let me, Sir Gerrik of Vaukry, lead you to victory in your final hour!" he shouted over them.

This time the soldiers went berserk, howling and barking as only men of war could. It had been some of their lifelong dreams to serve under the great war hero's command since they were children.

The only obstacles to his plan were the sealed lips of Bensel, Gina, and Elan, and of course, Zack's leadership. Zack dismounted his mammock then stood face to face with Gerrik. Zack's complexion was that of disbelief. Gina,

Bensel, and Elan looked on, wondering if he was to be called out before the men he'd just riled up.

A big part them wanted Zack to pick up on it, to call Gerrik's bluff. They were disgusted at this audacious move. They all wanted to save D'artello, but there was a point when they had to ask, "At what cost?" If there were no humans to protect, then D'artello's fight would be in vain. Gerrik should have been telling these people to stay the hell away from the ice palace if they wanted to live, not encouraging them to come along to their doom.

Zack gave him a long stare that made even Gerrik feel a sense of intimidation, given the recent tactic he had chosen. Suddenly he clasped Gerrik's hand and held it to the sky, taking a side-by-side position with him. "It has been an honor serving you as your lead-a, and congratulations on making it this far. To be truthful, I have questioned my own skills as your lead-a given the gravity of our situation. But as lead-a, I have to know when a betta man is up for the job, and my confidence lies with Gerrik he-a, the greatest warri-a our world has ever known. It is under his leadership that we will see victory."

And just like that, everything Zack had fought for and accomplished had been passed to a liar in mere seconds. The warriors applauded their former leader as he passed over his position.

Gerrik turned to him, wasting no time at all. "Now, how far ahead of the Phantoms are we?" he asked.

"I imagine 'bout a couple-a hours," Zack replied. "We fled the encampment. Our men were too overwhelmed, and I figured if we wanted any shot at survival, this was the only thing we could do."

"Good, so this is our plan," he said. Bensel, Zack, and Elan huddled together. With that, Gerrik became leader, and the troops were none the wiser to his lie.

During their conversation, something strange began to take place. There started a ringing in Gerrik's ear. It was low at first but asserted itself to the front of his focus, drowning out the words of his allies. He cringed and forced his eyes shut, trying to step away from it as he would a sun too bright for his eyes. When he opened them, his company was stagnant. Bensel, Zack, and the rest of the soldiers seemed to be frozen in time.

"Bensel! Elan!" he called. He turned his gaze to Gina. "Gina!" No response, not even a second look. Her eyes were affixed on where he was just standing.

"It will do you no good, Gerrik," he heard a familiar voice call. Spinning, he was now face to face with Harmony.

Dropping back into a fighting stance, he said, "You should have just left my family out of this! Damn you!"

"My dear Gerrik, no matter how angry you are, there is nothing that you can do to hurt me. You *must* listen to my words."

"I would rather break my fist against you," he said, throwing the hardest punch he could muster. Any man, no matter how big, would have been thrown to the ground by this attack, possibly even killed. Harmony though, merely blocked his attack with a lone finger. It stopped as it would against a brick wall.

Holding his fist there and pushing with all of his might was useless. The Peacemaker just stood like a mother waiting out her child's temper tantrum, strong and patient, staring him in the face.

"You are no Peacemaker," he said through clenched teeth. "You are nothing more than a witch who plagues me."

"Yes, Gerrik, wound me with your words. Enjoy it because my actions are the ultimate wounds on your soul. You are out-classed, my dear warrior, both physically and mentally. So yes, speak ill. You, in the end, are the one who will suffer."

He threw another fist, this time even harder than he ever thought he could. It incurred the same result, except this time small sparkling lightning danced around the point of impact. "Impressive," she said, examining her hand. "You actually tickled my finger a little," she taunted. Gerrik finally began to cave to the goddess's request, realizing that physical violence was futile, no matter how called for it was.

"What!" he shouted. "What the hell do you want? What *more* could you take from me? You already have my wife, my two sons! What else could you take from me? My life would be a blessing."

Harmony paused for a second, staring blankly at him as if considering the offer for his life. "Your son, Gerrik—"

"Go to hell!" he interrupted.

She ignored the disturbance and went on. "Your son, as I am sure you are aware, is still alive. Arbello."

"Don't say his name! You don't get to say his name! You did this to him!"

"Like your other son, D'artello, he is working to a Peacemaker's will. My brother Unity. Unity, my beloved brother, the only unconditional love in my eternal life, is the driving force for the plague of madness, the Phantoms."

"So you're all alike? Using mortals to fight a war that should be endured by the gods?"

"So quick to jump to petty conclusions, a mortal like you could not understand the workings of the Peacemakers. You only know what your religious dogma tells you, never knowing the truth and countless wars waged by us. Do you forget that we are all named after a notion to create peace, and you do not suppose we differ enough to quarrel occasionally? This time is different, my dear Gerrik."

No matter how much he hated her, he felt compelled to listen. He wished to know why his two sons must be pitted against each other, even if she was the only reliable source of answers. At long last, he straightened himself out and crossed his arms, finally ready to hear her out.

"Tell me, Gerrik, you remember the Molten Steel? The useless ethereal trinket, it could not even cut a man's flesh. The last sword you ever laid a hand on. I am sure that you now see its use. It is the only weapon that can kill the Phantoms, despite our lies to these hopeless men."

Bitch, he thought, as he knew she could read his mind. As if he did not feel bad enough that he was forced into a corner like that.

"That blade was created by Wisdom, but not even he is sure how it was forged, his memory an unfortunate sacrifice. I am certain no one else can wield it, not even I," she admitted. "Phantoms exist on a higher plane than even we immortal Peacemakers. I cannot kill them, just as you cannot kill me now. As you can see, the battle is well out of my hands."

"Why D'artello?"

"I do not know, Gerrik. Why any mortal? The prophecy states the blade will have a mortal wielder. As does the blade your other son wields."

"What prophecy? I have never heard such a tale," Gerrik said.

"One that men were not meant to hear, written long before the first Peacemaker. Not on paper however, or a scroll, or even inscribed on stone. It is chiseled into the minds of Peacemakers, like second nature. When we are born again as immortals, we are born with this story in our minds. We know it all by heart, for it is the salvation of the universe and is known only as the prophecy. We know that we are powerless to stop it and that light and darkness must clash to determine the outcome."

"What are you saying? Are you saying that Arbello has become evil?" Gerrik said.

"It is all perspective, my dear Gerrik. D'artello fights to maintain humanity, to maintain this chaotic universe dominated by man. The world where people die, children become motherless, and where happiness is ripped apart. Happiness, and love, as you humans view it, entails these details. His quest will ensure my dominant control of all humans, and I will lead them to true peace. Arbello fights to change it, to make all humans agree, their wills aside. They will all be the same, united as Phantoms. No free will, but no more fighting or war once the purge is complete. This is the beautiful uncertainty of it all: we *Peacemakers* are created to do just *that*. Who is wrong? Even though the prophecy says that good will prevail, we do not know who represents good. Tell me, Gerrik, which do you choose?"

He thought for a minute, scratching his scruffy face, closing his eyes, exploring his mind to find the answer. "They both sound like evil to me," he responded.

"Mortal! The end of your world is at hand, and all that you know will be lost forever," she responded with a ringing voice that he could hear with every sensation of his body.

"You are wrong," he said calmly.

"What?"

"What I know right now are my sons and that they will die if I don't do something as a father. I must stop them, stop you and your brother," he said, turning his back to her. "Sounds like the cards are in my hands right about now."

"If you try to stop this, you will perish," she warned, clenching a fist.

"Not by your hand. If you kill me, how will you get D'artello to comply with your orders?"

The normally calm goddess was now in a fit of rage. "You have been warned, Gerrik! If you interfere directly, you will die," she threatened.

"I have nothing to live for but my sons. Many better men have attempted to kill me. You're welcome try your best as well!" he said with valor in his tone.

Clearly at her wit's end with him, she waved her hand, and the usual heavenly white glow was more like a lightning strike, flashing and blinding Gerrik, returning him to his conscious state.

"Gerrik … Gerrik! Hey, aw c'mon, don't die on me now," he heard a familiar voice call. Feeling a tight pressure on his chest, he coughed for a moment before forcing his eyes open. He awoke to find himself in an unfamiliar room. The melanin walls glowed with a warm fire, and brown wooden supports lined the mammock-skinned interior. Elan was staring down on him as he lay on a warm, fuzzy cot. The coats of his friends slid off of him. They had all taken them off to cover him, trying to warm their beloved companion. He looked over at Gina as her teeth chattered.

"What happened?" he asked.

Elan cleared his throat like an unofficial spokesperson: "You passed out, sir," he explained.

"For how long?" Gerrik asked quickly.

"Only an hour," Gina chimed in, picking up her coat, as she could bear the cold no more.

"Thought you were dying on us, old man," Bensel said, slapping him hard on the back. This sense of relief faded quickly. They all had not forgotten his promises of power to vanquish the Phantoms. It was confrontation time.

Zack peeped in. "Ah, y'okay ova the-a?" he asked cheerfully as he waltzed into the tent. He handed him a hot bowl of soup that smelled like raunchy higoat sweat. "Here, drink this. It'll thicken your blood up a little."

Just one whiff was enough to put the meal aside for the time being. Gina, who happened to be behind the spot he put it down, had to turn away from its waft. "Yeah, I don't know what happened. Guess I was colder than I thought," he lied.

"I just want you to know that the men are more riled up than I've ev-a seen them. They feel that they can win this. Guess I just wanted to be the first to say: no matter what happens, I am proud to fight under the command of such a great man," Zack said. "Your battle plan is accepted among the troops, and we feel that it is genius strategy. We are all behind you." He looked around, beginning to feel the unease of interrupting a moment. "Well, just wanted you to know. I'll leave you to your comrades. I'll be out the-a when you're ready." Zack made his exit.

"Battle plan?" Gerrik asked.

"Yes, I devised a strategy, for which I accredited you because they wouldn't listen unless they were certain it was your idea," Bensel explained. However, this was not to be the topic of discussion.

"What are you doing, Gerrik? You know we can't win," Bensel said. "You're just going to get them all killed."

"Listen, Bensel ... all of you," Gerrik began. "My son is still alive, and I will do anything to save him, even if that means these soldiers will be a distraction."

"Sir Gerrik!" Elan said.

"These men know what they are getting themselves into!" he yelled.

"Gerrik!" Gina called.

"No! Stop! You all have no idea what I've been through. There is more than just D'artello on the line here. I have another son!" he exclaimed.

"What!"

"Yes, the winged man, his name is Arbello and he is my son, as true as D'artello is," he confessed.

"Are you sure?" Gina asked.

"What the hell, man?" Bensel said. "I've known you since we played pranks on our parents! We shared sweat and blood! How could you keep something like this from me?"

"You don't understand, Ben. I thought he was dead," he replied curtly. "I know you aren't going to believe me, but when I passed out just now, Harmony visited me and told me. I had already figured it out though, when Gina mentioned a black-winged man."

"Unbelievable! What a load of crap," Bensel said. "Don't start this again. He always talked like this when we were at war."

"I believe you," Gina said suddenly. "I have seen her myself, speaking to D'artello. She mentioned taking his soul away to protect him."

"You too? What the hell? This is ridiculous blasphemy!" Bensel shouted. "Blasphemy! Blasphemy! Blasphemy!" He was a regular at church and always did get slightly agitated whenever people spoke of Harmony in nontraditional means, but this was very out of character even for him.

Elan stayed silent, not wanting to get in the middle of this.

"Fine, Ben, if you don't want to believe me, then don't. But I know what I know, and you can't even believe I had another son. Look around you, damn old fool! What the hell is a Phantom? You ever heard of that miserable creature? Did church ever teach you that? You don't even know what Harmony really looks like, and you have no qualms about dedicating so much of your energy toward that stupid witch-worshipping cult!"

Bensel was too outraged for words. He opened his mouth to speak but was afraid of saying something he would regret. The old man just crossed his arms.

"Now," Gerrik began, "I know I lied, but I have to protect my sons, especially Arbello. That boy never had the chance. People nearly killed him when he was a child, just because he had wings."

"You're right, and now they'll kill him for what? How does felling an entire world of nations sound to you?" Bensel said.

Gerrik stared at the floor, pondering the statement.

"Gerrik, look at me," Gina said. He stared straight into her beautiful blue eyes, filled with idolization for him. "You are my hero. Since I was a child, my mother told me of your exploits, and I have every intention of telling my children that I happily fought alongside you, but I cannot watch you sacrifice good men's lives for this purpose."

"And you think that you can stand in my way?" he asked, raising his brow to meet hers. "Listen Gina, I don't want to see you get hurt. You just let me do what I must to save my boys, and that's an order," he threatened.

"I'm sorry, Gerrik, but I can't just let you get away with that," she said, drawing her quivering sword. The only thing more unbelievable than meeting her hero was realizing that she may have to fight him to the death. "I've got to be strong, because life is worth living. D'artello reminded me of that, and I intend to defend that opportunity for these men as well."

Gerrik knew he was wrong, but admitting it would mean condemning his son to the death he probably deserved. Even though his plan was to use the soldiers as a distraction, there were very few options anyway, given the circumstances. That could have been the result whether he wanted it to be or not. He just had to play along. All he had to do was explain it in a way that the others would understand. That part was easy. The real challenge would be rescuing his two boys.

Chapter 17

D'ARTELLO gave a blasting war cry as the last Phantom on the field charged him. This was but the last of the ear-piercing clashes that had begun hours ago. Holding back the Frozen Steel with his sword, he pounded his fist into the midsection of the ghostly being repeatedly. Even in his soulless state, rage bled through. The creature fell back long enough so that he could slice through with the Molten Steel that shown brighter than the snow around it.

Seeing the last opponent go down, Sali made the mammock hustle a few yards over to him. "I don't think he's going any further, D'artello. You should have seen him trying to get over here," she explained.

He held out a hand to help her dismount, and the mammock stared them down for a moment. Then it turned off to find the remnants of the herd.

Sali looked down at the sword glowing in his hands. Just the thought of their enemies being so close but completely undetectable was rattling. There was no tactician within her, but even she was uncomfortable being out in the open.

"Run," he whispered, taking off through the snow. He did not need to tell her twice. D'artello had always been the quickest kid in the village, but not today; keeping up with him on pure adrenaline alone was no difficult task. The ice palace grew larger and larger as they approached, encompassing their entire vision eventually. A structure of this height was impressive for stone, let alone such frail a substance as ice.

They halted within the outer cloister to examine the sight it truly was. Despite its frail composition, the structure never once gave off a sign of weakness. Its walls looked easily comparable in strength to those built from stone in other parts of the world. The archway they passed under was thicker than both of their bodies next to each other. The ice itself was free of cracks or other blemishes and was certainly well maintained. The courtyard had a garden of white powder and two translucent statues standing adjacent to the door, one of King Garo and the other of Peacemaker Unity. If there were any further doubt this was the right place, there were depictions of a winged silhouette carved into the arch above the entrance.

Most castles in the world were built with an outer wall leading into an outer cloister, then an inner wall that was thick enough to house royals and nobles, leading into an inner cloister and courtyard, then a central tower, all encompassed by the four short towers on the inward wall and the four large towers on the outer wall. This was no such castle. Most of them were built like fortresses to repel attacking forces, but this one was built to invite. Thus it was relatively easy to breach with no moat or inner wall, but it looked as if it could house only one occupant in its massive innards. It had a pyramidal base, massive and square at the bottom and tapering upward. It only had three towers, one each to the right and left, and then one giant spire in the middle that reached upward indefinitely. Its transparency against the dawning sky made it impossible to see the top. The two side towers were not straight. Instead, they leaned outward. If one stood as D'artello and Sali did now, staring at the tower, they helped form a "W" shape. They were also fashioned to look like massive wings with intricate feathers carved into their outer edges. A triad of crenellated-walled walkways, presumably the platform for D'artello's battle against the winged man, connected the perches of each tower.

"By Harmony," Sali said.

Even D'artello had to pause to admire the natural beauty of it all. The air became somehow heavier, weighted down with an evil presence.

"It isn't beautiful?" came a voice.

They turned to recognize a scrawny, middle-aged man, covered in a thick, rich purple robe. It was King Garo in all of his madness. He gave a toss of his cape, revealing the golden armor underneath it. The shoulder armor was ridden with fearsome steel spikes. A lion, the official symbol of Vaukry's inalienable courage, was hammered into the royal cuirass. Just as the robe fell, the wind kicked up and lifted it backward once again. A wide grin spread under his salt and pepper stubble that was as bright as the snow around him. D'artello remembered him being an onyx-haired king, but the darkness gripping him had aged his appearance. His eyes were settled on blood red, the way Joseph's had been, and his hair and skin had paled out to a deathly wither.

"Die you will here, bow unless to you your king." He spoke gibberish. A dark, drunken power had gripped the unstable old fool, and no shred of him was left human.

Shadows began to litter the ground, blocking out the sun, smothering the snow in ghastly shade. Sali and D'artello turned their attention to the falling, white-cloaked sky. Phantoms had always hovered, but these ones were flying, perhaps another benefit to being attached to their source for this long. Floating gently down to ground level, they advertised their sheer numbers. It had to be in the thousands, perhaps even more, all of them hissing and moaning but not attacking.

"Will now you bow," he muttered. It was strange that the Phantoms stood on their own side like dogs on a leash, but their focus was the same, set on the threatening blade in D'artello's grasp. Sali tugged at D'artello's arm to try and lead him inside, but he stood his ground and took a fighting stance, drawing the second sword from his waist.

"D'artello, c'mon, we can't fight. There are too many," she said.

"Heed you not will?" Garo asked. "Die then you miserable will worm!" he said, holding out a vertical palm. A black stream shot forth like a fountain of luminescent oil. D'artello did a quick vertical spin to get his momentum up and then slammed his sword head-on into the oncoming stream, splitting the ebon river, returning it to the heavens in mist form. The fork just barely missed Sali, who hid behind him. Garo closed his hand to end the stream, looking on eagerly to see his mutilated foe. No such luck. D'artello gave his Molten Steel a cocky twirl and returned to his initial position.

"You not did die?" Garo asked, cocking his head to the side farther than any being with a spine could. His movements in that regard resembled an owl's, as if his neck were just as flexible and agreeable.

"Get back," D'artello said to Sali, taking steps backward until he was inside the doorway to the ice palace. The Phantoms could only fit in single file and still have room to attack, but D'artello knew that they would try to force their way in three by three at least. The inside of the castle was shady. It was not as bright as the outside but still lit by seemingly nothing at all. The highly magnifying and reflective surfaces of the ice allowed for a single ray of sunlight to illuminate the entire structure to some degree. It was not the most effective lighting, but at least they were not left in complete darkness.

The Phantoms came in as predicted at first, three by three, but once a few waves were cut down with little effort, they began to grow more sensible. Even single file, they were no match for D'artello individually. They heard a roar from outside, and then another black beam ravaged through. D'artello didn't have a lot of time to react. He barely blocked it, slicing it down the middle. Apparently the occupant of this castle only wanted Garo to enter, not his army. A different roar bellowed, this one unfamiliar; it definitely was not Garo or a Phantom. This one sounded like a million hawks clawing one another's eyes out, a shrill cry that filled their ears.

"The secret weapon!" Sali shouted.

The Phantoms stopped pouring in and gazed up at the sky, very much the same way their leader did. "Hell the what that is?"

D'artello looked outside upon hearing another potential foe. He saw a stream of red fiery comets blocking out the sun, just as the Phantoms before them had. He had always heard the myths of black powder. It was a more popular weapon on the far east of the eastern continent, but they weren't even sure it existed. The blazing arrows poured down by the hundreds, sticking in Phantoms and the ground, but they were still burning.

"Get back!" Sali shouted as she yanked him away from the doorway to shield them around its corner. A loud clap of earth-shaking thunder accompanied by a devastating crimson lightning flash ripped through the Phantom troops, scattering their whole bodies. It was like smashing an anthill with a war hammer. Even king Garo was caught in the blast. When all was clear and black smoke emanated into the palace, Sali and D'artello peeked out from beside the entrance. They saw piles of Phantom bodies against the inner ice walls.

"See! Look! That's what I was trying to tell you! Zack did have a plan, see?" Sali gloated. Her happy expression faded when the smoke cleared.

Garo still stood where he had before this epic testament of human power. His purple cloak was tattered and charred, and one of his arms had been scattered elsewhere. "You damn!" he shouted. "Work did not this, will they soon regenerate!" he threatened.

D'artello knew he was right. Even now a stirring came from the bodies; this fight was just beginning. Yet another surprise came to their aid. A howling of a thousand warriors could be heard from the outer cloister. Sali placed a hand over her eyes to block the sun. "It's them, D'artello! The army from the encampment! Zack's come to save us!" she shouted, again sounding hopeful.

King Garo was not going to give them time to watch the battle, however. Despite his confident and quirky mannerisms, he had launched himself into a full sprint, hollering at the top of his lungs. D'artello and Sali fled into the entrance hall. The room was broad, square, and dual-level. The floor was an immaculate sheet ice that reflected them. Above hung a chandelier, safely assumed to be ice as well, its thousands of sword-like spikes pointed down toward the ice floor in a wide, conical shape. Just a few yards away were two sets of stairs, one to the right, and one to the left, both leading to a loft entranceway to the second level.

Just one step sent a spider-webbing crack all the way to the walls and the thicker shelled stairs. The cries of King Garo were close, growing much closer by the second. There was no time to argue with this scared girl. "Go and run into the next room," D'artello instructed. Tripping her and using his arms to caress her fall, he sat her down and then gave her a hard shove.

"What are you doing!" she yelled, helplessly sliding toward the stairs.

He watched Sali grab one of the raven-shaped banisters and begin her ascent. She stopped at the top, on the balcony, to take a last look at D'artello from behind the hand railing. Deathly cold waters were beginning to trickle up through the cracks they had made. "Be careful!" she shouted.

"Bastard!" he heard from behind. That call alone was enough to send Sali running for the high ground. King Garo rounded the corner, firing his eerie black beam once again. This one D'artello did not block. He instead took a few more running steps and then jumped into a slide tackle toward the stairs. The floor was in rough shape at this point. It was like a moving mosaic of their reflections. D'artello grabbed the raven banister, for if he slipped, a hypothermic grave surely awaited. Garo hurled one last bolt at him, but it was sliced with relative ease.

That raven banister proved a formidable foe for King Garo as D'artello gave it a quick slice of his father's sword, then another to take the head off, probably to reduce its weight for the punt of his boot. The awkward body spun through the air and crashed heavily through the ice at Garo's feet. The angry source fell through into the frigid depths below, leaving a long trail of bubbles in his wake. It was dark, so its depth as a result was hard to gauge.

D'artello was not going to wait around to try though. His boots clicked up the stairs toward the entrance of the next room, where he would recover Sali. A big, black tendril shot up from the water just as he'd reached the top of the steps. It crashed through the midsection of the loft, sending bulky chunks into the water below. King Garo was trying to take D'artello's escape away, but there still remained a narrow strip leading through the doorway. D'artello folded himself around it, into the next room.

A trophy room of sorts, it was a rectangular chamber with one entrance and one exit to the far end of it. Sali stood just inside, examining the statues that lined the walls like stuffed game. Alphas, mammocks, ters, higoats, and many people stood in scared poses, frozen into their stone forms. The winged man enjoyed turning anything he was able to into a statue. Sali must have been looking for Adriel's body, but when D'artello did not see it, he could lay to rest the thought of that man being a pure soul. "Keep going, Sali," he said, holding up his sword again. King Garo was still coming.

Just as Sali had escaped into the next room, King Garo came stomping in. The one-armed king was now pale as a sheet, and his lips were a deep bluish purple. Frozen droplets clung to his gray hair, scruffy face, and eyelashes. He let out an angry howl that ripped jagged chunks of frozen shrapnel from the floor toward D'artello. The youth responded quickly by collapsing his stance, letting the majority of them crash into the wall and the rest careen into the next room.

A quick dash and Garo was able to close the gap at the midpoint of the room. D'artello came back with a potentially beheading slash, but King Garo fell backward flat onto his back. Then D'artello went for a downward stab through the heart, to end it all, but an unseen force sent the king sliding swiftly back to the far end of the room, laughing hysterically. His body like a plank and his feet like a fulcrum, he rose. "Swords so it is you play want to," he uttered as he reached his only arm over to grab his side-mounted blade. A short black tendril shot from his severed arm and hardened into an edge, creating a dark, sharp blade extending directly from his elbow.

D'artello held his position, as King Garo would have to cross the gash he made in the floor and D'artello would have the advantage on the high ground. The first clash sounded, and then D'artello managed to get a cheap stab in the shoulder with his father's sword. He was quick enough do draw back and parry off Garo's second blade as well. Suddenly, the dark sword changed shape, becoming a tight hook around the Molten Steel. The precious weapon was yanked from its owner's hands, jerking D'artello forward a little. If not for his quickness in blocking with his other hand, he would have lost his head.

Garo had stepped up the pace a bit, not wanting D'artello to call back the Molten Steel. Thus he forced him back toward a wall next to an alpha statue. Garo sliced at him wildly, and D'artello dodged attentively, but his swords were gradually carving out the wall. It became less and less stable as more and more gashes were sliced into it. King Garo would not let up, and neither would D'artello. Soon they had dug so far into the wall that the boulder-like overhang could give way any second and crush them both. Taking advantage of this, D'artello slammed his sword into its underbelly, sending a vibrating message to the exhausting ceiling to just let it all go. He dove and skipped off the back wall to escape Garo, but Garo did not see or escape the tumbling boulder. Any mortal man would be dead three times over, but not this one. He growled and threatened revenge in his jumbled fashion. D'artello called back the Molten Steel and then left Garo pinned as he ascended the stairs in the next room.

There it was, the grand hall, the throne room with—oddly enough—two thrones. Carvings of Phantoms lined the walls, and an encircling catwalk hovered above, leading to four exits, the front-most toward the stairwell to the top of the central tower. Sali already waited at the top near that exit. There were three epic windows on each side, leaning over him and the enclosing room. He could tell they were near the top of the pyramidal base of the palace now. The windows were elongated to about the height of the Church of Harmony in Fort Carrie, allowing in much light.

"C'mon, D'artello! Run!" Sali shouted after him just before entering the stairs herself.

"Me that give weapon!" he heard the king call. D'artello looked down for a moment at him. He'd just entered, so there was no chance of him catching up. He made it all the way, uninterrupted, onto the catwalk. With a crash came the all too familiar screeching of legions of Phantoms. It seemed they were finishing the remnants of the human army, and six of them poured in to get their shot at the wielder of the Molten Steel. D'artello had not yet made it to the doorway, and they flew straight for him.

With their newfound ability to block, they occupied him long enough for Garo to catch up. Each time D'artello would block and close in for the kill, he had to block step back to avoid being sliced. Six swords were just too many. The Phantoms weren't stupid either; some were going high and others low. No swordsman alive could keep up with this kind of pressure.

"You are there!" Garo shouted. Upon observing the fight above, he began to chuckle, and then with a sharp grunt, he smashed a tendril through D'artello's escape route. Another grunt allowed him to smash the balcony running along the other direction. D'artello was now isolated on a lone, standing platform with six Phantoms.

D'artello had other plans. Knowing that he had to separate them, he ran into a flying leap across the gap, landing in with his shoulder, barreling into a forward roll. Angry that his prey might escape, Garo raised his hand to bring another tendril down right on top of him. It was a close call, but just before impact, the point of a sword poked through, between the eyes of Garo's lion chest plate, and then a kick sent him smashing face-first into the ground.

"D'artello!" Gina called after him.

She ran ahead toward the stairs to help him with the Phantoms, but Garo got back up instantly, snarling with rage. "Bitch you little," he cursed. Just before he could attack, Gerrik leapt over his head and grabbed hold of what remained of his left arm, sending Garo staggering. From there, Bensel was supposed to smash him to the ground, but instead caught the old source and stood him upright.

"What are you doing?" Gerrik shouted.

"We're sorry, Sir Gerrik," Elan said, coming in toward Gerrik, holding his great blade in a ready position. "The winged man told us he can bring Sandra back; we just have to stop you," he explained.

"Ben, is this true?" Gerrik asked, not lowering his guard.

"It's nothing personal, Gerrik. Please forgive me. I know you'd do the same for your son," he said.

"Have aid I? Aid then who will you?" the crazy king went off. Gerrik dodged the first tendril blast, allowing it to collide with Elan, smashing him into the wall next to the entrance of the room.

Gina had made it. She leapt over the gap and slammed her shield into the first Phantom she encountered. It stumbled into D'artello's whirling blades. One down and a divided effort made them a little easier to manage. Three more joined the fight from the same broken window. They positioned themselves to surround the couple, but D'artello took a bounding back step as Gina darted into the fray. He gave the back of his fists as footing for a step jump, boosting Gina high into the air. She came down stunning one very unlucky foe that was quickly tagged by D'artello.

The pair fought back-to-back now. She ducked as he slashed overhead, following through to the foes back on his side. She sprang up with her shield, knocking another one back and then covering with her sword, stunning the second one. D'artello held his blades in defensively, using his feet to slam them away quickly. Gina back-flipped, holding her sword above her head to devastate the Phantoms that broke her fall as D'artello slid underneath her to serve up a rising slash to the stunned foe. They then locked arms and swung low, like a bladed pinwheel. One circle later, Gina's blade sliced through to stun or move the Frozen Steels out of the way to pave way for the Molten Steel. Three more Phantoms went down. They swapped weapons by tossing Gina's shield and D'artello's second sword up above their heads, catching the instruments with agile ease. Then she jumped on his back, gripping him tight around the neck just before he charged forward with the shield, leaving all of the Phantoms behind them.

Coming to a sliding stop, he pivoted his body and Gina jumped, landing on the shield. He gave a roar as he whipped the shield, sending it, and Gina standing erect atop it, whirling through the air, back into the crowd. As she held the two swords out, stunning each Phantom she passed, D'artello followed her, making quick work of the remaining creatures.

Gina spun to a dizzy stop. She stumbled and almost fell over, but a passing D'artello scooped her up to kiss her deeply. Even without his soul, he still felt for her. It seemed that his feelings were returning to him piece by piece. Love for her was one of the first to come shining through.

"Run! Stop Arbello!" Gerrik shouted, dodging Bensel's sword and then another tendril.

D'artello had no qualms about running ahead, but Gina looked down at Gerrik fighting Bensel, Elan, and King Garo. She was afraid that this would be the end of her hero.

"Go, Gina!" Gerrik shouted between breaths. "Help D'artello!"

At long last, the pair made it to the triad rooftop of the ice palace.

"Help! D'artello, help!" Sali screamed at the top of her lungs. There he was, the man in their dreams, the ebon-winged man with his silver hair fluttering in the wind, his devious cream-on-white eyes locked on Gina and D'artello. He wore a toothy grin; clearly he found this sort of thing exhilarating. He bore a coat that reached his ankles, but he wore it open, exposing his lean and powerful core muscles to show that he was not afraid of his opponent's blade. He was standing right on the edge of the roof, not really a risk for him, but Sali was more scared than she'd ever been in her life. He held her over the drop by the scruff of her jacket.

"Let her go, coward!" Gina shouted. "You're strong enough, aren't you? You don't need a hostage!"

His wings gave a hard flap, and Sali yelped at the sudden jump in elevation. "How pretty you are," he said, stroking her hair. "Shhh … shhhh" he repeated, trying to quell her sobs. "I won't drop you, I promise," he said ever so tenderly.

Sali did not believe this psychopath for a second, so she kept screaming and trying to push away from him in hopes D'artello might catch her.

"Oh shut up!" the winged man yelled at her. "I would turn you into a Phantom, but a weakling like you will probably turn into a statue anyway." He grabbed her by the throat and held her over high above the roof of the castle.

"No!" Gina shouted. "D'artello, do something!"

He was already on it. He hurled the Molten Steel through the air. Arbello evaded it at the last second, but it managed to shave a few feathers off.

D'artello called it back, but Arbello was ready for that too. Sali dangled helplessly as her wind pipe was being crushed by Arbello's fierce grip. She kicked her feet while holding on for dear life but was being thrown around like a ragdoll every time Arbello made a swift evasive maneuver.

"Hurry!" he taunted. "She's turning a little pale, and do be careful, I *am* only holding her by the neck."

"Put her down! She has nothing to do with this!" Gina shouted.

"Oh but she does. She's human, and I can't stand a single one of them. The feeling is mutual though. Just watch." He pulled Sali in tight, hugging her, letting her hold onto his back until she felt as safe as could be in death's arms. "I've got you. You're okay. See?" he said, spreading an arm so that she could look down. Seeing the elevation was no comfort to her. He pulled her face into his shoulder, stroking her hair gently until her sobs slowed.

Pulling away again, his gaze pierced right through her eyes, straight into the lobe that intercepts fear. She instantly began to cry out again. "D'artello! Help! He—" She was cut off by his leather-gloved hand over her mouth.

"Now," he began, her eyes staring straight into his. "If you will just calm down, I'll let your mouth go, okay?"

Considering it for a moment through endless tears, she nodded her head, but Arbello let his glove soak up the moisture a little more before removing his hand. Then he licked the salty fluid from his glove. "Ah ... tears. Some fools thirst for blood, and I ask, why? Blood is so easy to get. I could just gut you right now, raining your innards all over your friends. That wouldn't hurt you though. It would all be over so quickly, what would it matter? Let me tell you this though, the surefire way to know that you've hurt your enemy, for your after-life reference I suppose, is when your enemy cries. When tears start to pour from their face, you know they are in that delicious moment of knowing a pain worse than death, they can't even die with dignity. Blood? Who needs blood? It's messy and merely a side effect of a slain enemy, needless. And who wants to be covered in the person they hate? But tears ... heh heh ... tears," he said, wiping them from underneath her eyes and taking another taste, "... are so fulfilling."

"Arbello! Put her down!" D'artello shouted. "Come and face me like a man!"

"Hmm ... my name. That must mean Father is here too. That must be why Garo is so late for our little play date. Just keep quiet. I'll deal with you two very soon. Man, can't I get a moment's peace?" he complained to Sali. "Now where were we? Oh yes. Let's see, fear, tears, ah yes ... Now all of what you just heard aside, tell me what you think of me. Give me your first impression," he said, spreading his wings out so that they floated down gently. "And ... I hate liars, so lying to me is risking your life at this point. In short, don't do it!"

"Please, please just let me go," she begged, not sure what he wanted from her.

"Ah, that's not answering my question, silly girl," he responded playfully. "I asked what you thought of me," he repeated. By this time, their slow descent had brought them to roof level but standing on the edge of another tower. It was still too risky to make a move.

"Get your hands off of her, you damn *monster*!" Gina yelled.

"Please let m—"

"Shh," Arbello silenced her again and gave Gina a glare. "What was it you said just now? You want to repeat that for me?"

"You miserable, Harmony-forsaken monster, put her down!" Gina yelled.

He turned back to Sali. "Oh, it will rain many tears today," he said, shaking his head. He wrapped his palm around her jaw and the other around her head. With a sharp twist and a sickening crack, he snapped her neck, spinning the head around so that the shocked eyes were able to stare right at D'artello and Gina. Then he discarded the limp body off the side of the castle, onto the battle below. He shifted his stance, pulling his Frozen Steel from its sheath on his waist.

Giving a hard flap of his wings, he shot from one tower to theirs faster than Gina could react and pull a sword up to block. Luckily, D'artello was standing next to her and was able to catch the attack. When the Molten Steel and Frozen Steel collided, it sent a rigid shockwave that blew Gina helplessly backward toward the parapet wall of the perch. D'artello slugged his opponent in the side of the face and then kicked him in the stomach to boost him into a spin, giving a backward, airborne thrust of his other leg, sending Arbello flying away. He broke his flight by opening his chute-like wings, slowing his velocity.

"So you really are my brother. You do have some fight in you after all," Arbello taunted.

Brother? D'artello, soulless, let the question quickly slip away.

They slammed swords again, once high then low, sending two more shockwaves that left gashes in the surface of the roof, spewing shaved ice over the edge. "Tell me, did you find out what you were fighting for?"

Even if D'artello were whole enough to answer the question, he likely wouldn't have, simply out of spite. All that mattered to him right now was that he fight. The reason mattered little, as he had plenty of them to choose from. For Tanya, for his friends, for his father, for Sali, and for all of the weaker souls who need protection from madmen.

"Fine then, you can't answer. I get it. Well tell me this then. What kind of savior are you supposed to be without a soul?" Arbello said. Yet another prodding question that D'artello probably could not even answer if he did have a soul. Harmony said it would protect him, and it did, maybe from Phantoms, but also from his own emotional weaknesses. In this form, he could not hesitate or cower, he could only fight, and fight on he would.

Arbello gave a kick that slid D'artello away on the slippery surface, then boosted into the air to come down on him. By using his lower back as a shock absorber, D'artello arched it and raised the Molten Steel. The delayed impact cushioned Arbello's attack but sent a mighty shockwave that collided with the neighboring tower, one of the wings of the palace. It began to crumble and toss a colossal chunk of ice down on the waging battle, crushing many more people. The Phantoms would recover, but indirectly, D'artello was responsible for more lives. His frustration showed through.

D'artello kicked out his feet and then thrust them both into Arbello's bare chest, sending him up into the air. He recovered by dive-bombing D'artello with a mighty swing, but D'artello dodged it completely. The Frozen Steel was driven into the ice, freeing up some big pieces. With D'artello to his left coming in with a vertical swing, Arbello countered with a rising diagonal. The swords slammed again, giving off a cry that even the Peacemakers could hear. This shockwave lifted even some of the clouds.

"Don't you see? These Phantoms do not quarrel. Don't you see? It is real peace, brother. Unity's ideal is proven," Arbello said.

"That's not your ideal," D'artello responded.

"You're right, but I am the champion to carry it out. My ideal is to wipe out all humanity in the universe. Unity's ideal is merely a side effect."

"The universe?" D'artello asked as they traded blows once more.

"Ah … your Peacemaker hasn't told you about the other worlds? There are five more of them, all with people like us, humans, and when I am done here, I will move on to the next planet until my revenge is completely exacted."

The next planet? What the hell was this maniac spouting off about now? D'artello thought. It did not matter, because Arbello would be ended here and now. Though D'artello did recall the story about the light and dark half-minds, he could not apply that knowledge while he was soulless. "Revenge, it's such an easy concept to embrace." D'artello responded. "Humanity's survival depends entirely on the Peacemakers, not you or me, and if you hope to disrupt this balance, I will stop you."

"You poor mislead boy, when I am done here, you will know what it means to fight for revenge. Then perhaps you and I will join forces, damning humanity to the prison it deserves … together."

D'artello rushed him quickly, uncertain of what he meant by *together*, trying to pin him against the railing, but Arbello flapped his wings hard, landing behind D'artello with his icy sword touching the back of his neck.

"Don't you see? You have no emotion, no backing for your ideal. You are not even human yourself, so why defend them?" Arbello argued, leaving a bloody slit in his brother's skin.

D'artello spun, smashing his opponent's sword out of the way. The clashing of the two blades sounded like it would rip reality apart. D'artello swept his leg, trying to take him off balance, but a simple flutter of the ebon wings avoided that. Arbello swung his boot toward the head of his brother from an airborne stance, but D'artello leaned back, avoiding the attack. He came back with a shimmering, rising slice, causing Arbello to back off a little. Moving back in, the swords embraced again, driven by supreme perseverance versus raw passion. D'artello stepped toward the side to divert the force, sending Arbello's weight forward and destabilizing him, all the while throwing a fist toward his face. His blow was stopped dead by Arbello's palm.

D'artello went for the kill. His opponent's back was to him and the timing was perfect. He thrust downward to pierce the spine, but the wings of his adversary proved too good an asset. One of them flapped, whipping D'artello's hands with a thin bone near its top, shocking his hands and sending the Molten Steel spinning away across the ice. Then Arbello came in for a swing of his own, but D'artello's boot caught his hands there and sent the Frozen Steel spiraling in the opposite direction. Now the brothers fought tooth and nail. They grabbed hold of each other, taking their cheap shots where they could, including socking in the face, upper-cutting the ribs, and knees to the hips. They rolled into the air as Arbello struggled to distance himself.

D'artello took a fist to the gut, causing him to release his grip for only a moment, long enough for his brother to send a foot streaming upside his face. Then D'artello plummeted onto the ice below. Arbello landed and walked toward his sword, leaving his brother on the ground. "You see? There is no way you can win," he taunted, kneeling to retrieve his weapon.

He was about to continue his prideful lecture but was caught off guard by a cut down his back, coming from D'artello's Molten Steel. Yelling in pain, he turned to block the second strike, sending another powerful shockwave away from the clashing of the legendary weapons. The ice continued to crack to the point of collapse. With new fury now, D'artello swung the Molten Steel, trying to create an opening. Arbello's injury made him struggle a bit more to block the rapid attacks. This went on until a fist struck the side of his face, then a kick to the side, knocking Arbello completely off his aerial footing and to the ground. D'artello leapt after him, meaning to kill him this time, but a wing took him out of the sky.

"You are really starting to annoy me," Arbello sneered.

"Not having as much fun as you thought you would?" D'artello asked as the two fighters climbed to their feet.

The pair flew back at each other again. This time Arbello went from fast to impossible to follow. He managed to get a hold of D'artello's arm, and when he did, he folded his brother over his shoulder, slamming him to the ground. Then he swung downward, meaning to execute D'artello, but his brother was too swift. One hasty backflip and D'artello was back on his feet at a good distance from his maniacal opponent.

Arbello came at him again. As D'artello raised his sword to block his opponent, he weaved around him this time. Before he could turn around to face Arbello, a kick drove him face-first into the ground, causing him to slide until he hit the frozen railing.

He turned around in time to see his brother approaching him. Arbello lifted him up by the scruff of his collar and held him out over the edge of the roof, threatening to drop him.

"Is this the best you could do? It wouldn't even satisfy me to end your life this way. I want you to watch your world end, to die by the Phantoms as so many lesser men have," he said, dropping him back into the confines of the rooftop.

Gina watched helplessly from a distance. There was no way she could stop someone that powerful. D'artello sat with his back to the icy parapet wall, writhing in pain at his injuries.

"Let me tell you why you could never have beaten me. My thirst for revenge drives me. My *passion* has become to destroy the human race. I have passion, while you are a string-less puppet. You could never beat me. And once King Garo makes it to the top of this castle, it will be complete. There will be no saving this world or the people on it. Good riddance!"

"Arbello!" came a voice from behind. The winged warlord pivoted to the left, opening D'artello's view to his father standing in the stairway. "My son! Arbello!" he called. He had miraculously made it through Bensel, Elan, and the tainted king, only to face his sons in battle.

D'artello gawked at the words coming from Gerrik. So it was true, Arbello really was his brother.

"Dad, so glad you make it," Arbello responded.

"Yes, my son," he said, examining D'artello and the battle scar across Arbello's back as well. "Please, you don't have to fight anymore."

Arbello began to laugh. "Heh, do you really think *all* can be undone just like that? Do you think that I can forget what humans did to me?"

"Humans?" Gerrik asked. "You are human, Arbello."

Gina ran to D'artello's side.

Giving Gina only a passing glance, Arbello said, "No ... I'm not. I am an avatar, an avatar of punishment, justice, to rid the universe of their cruel rule. Clearly, you know as well as I that I am not accepted as human. Look at me, Father! Look at these wings! Look at this sword and what I have done with it. You people call me a monster for this, and Unity calls me an avatar. I am no human. I am not so weak as to rely on my feelings to find justification. Instead I've moved on. I simply see something wrong, and I wish to correct it."

"What are you saying?" Gerrik asked, heartbroken. It was not his way to give up, and even if he wanted to break down now, how could he? What could he do? Could he really bring himself to fight and slay his own flesh and blood? He remembered again the poor child being covered up, restrained, wondering why, too young to understand. This was not that boy. That very boy had grown into a very angry man. He had to be stopped.

"Gerrik!" Gina yelled, tossing him his old sword. As the blade pin-wheeled through the air, Gerrik watched it and relived the birth of his first child. The eight years they'd spent together, and for what? For this day to come, when he was given no other option? To save the world that took his boy from him? To do the bidding of the goddess that took his wife? What strength did he have to rely on? No strength. Nothing but the sword spiraling through the air toward him, just like the old days.

Catching it by the hilt, Gerrik felt the familiar blood soak his hands and the heartless euphoria that came along with it.

"So, what now, Dad? Are you going to fight me as well?" Arbello asked, watching his father gaze deeply into the sword. "Then prepare yourself," he said taking an offensive stance. "It's all or nothing. Either way, I will come to rest with my hatred."

"It doesn't have to be this way!" Gerrik shouted, taking his eyes off the magnetic pull of the blade. Suddenly he was unaware that he was even holding it.

"You fool!" Arbello shouted. "There *is* no turning back now. These hands …" He stared down at his palm. "I have done more than just get blamed for a church fire this time. They thought I was a demon then. Well how about now!" he yelled at the top of his lungs for the world to hear. "Do you fancy this a fairy tale? I have felled armies, felled nations. I have felled a planet of what you would call innocent people. I am already in hell's doorway, and now I will either pass through or stay and continue to deride death."

Gerrik was speechless. He glanced over at Gina, who was tending to D'artello. She looked back and then stumbled away with fear. Gerrik's eyes were as cold and frightening as D'artello's. Gazing upon her as a barbarian would, sick with rage and animalistic instinct. Just that sword in his hands was enough to send him back, delving deep into his inhumane nature. When it came down to it, the great Gerrik, the best warrior in the world, was a killer. For a time, he was able to take the tool from his own hands, but now, like an addict, he returned to the one ecstasy that once cradled him dearly.

A shocking cry came from the stairs that led to the roof. It was King Garo.

D'artello called his Molten Steel to his hands and then pulled himself to his feet.

"Wait! You can't!" Gina gasped, trying to hold him down. Even in this weakened state, without the hindrance of pain, he was much too strong for her. Soon he was standing with the weapon at his side, readying himself to take on the much-tainted king.

They heard Gerrik cry out as he charged Arbello. Following it was a series of speedy clashes, far faster than those of the brotherly feud that had previously taken place. They circled each other while their swords slid and brushed off of each other. Arbello kicked him in the stomach, causing him to take a few steps back.

"You're holding back, so this will be easier than I thought then?" Arbello taunted, cracking a cocky grin. "Do you think you can kill your own son?"

Just then, D'artello pounced at him with a daedal flurry of swings. He did not want to make it easy for Arbello to make a move against him again.

Gerrik watched as D'artello went high then low and then high again. He was definitely trying to kill his brother this time. He thought about Arbello's words. Could he really take the life of his son? Then about his own question—could he really let his boys take each other's lives?

He would not have time to think it over. King Garo had already made his advance to the roof, now howling for some attention. "Gerrik!" he yelled. Garo outstretched his severed arm and did the very same blade trick he had used on D'artello. "Now," he said with a maddened grin just before murmuring gibberish about him and his sons bowing to their king.

Gerrik and Gina charged at the poor soul to protect D'artello's rear, cutting wildly at the laughing man. Together they were able to hold him and his toying antics back.

D'artello found an opening and was able to land a crippling kick to the outside of Arbello's knee, to which he fell quickly after. Still though, the fiend was able to keep up with his speed. One of the black wings swept D'artello off of his feet, knocking him to the ground and sending him sliding across the ice. Arbello then flew at King Garo. He seemed to be fighting to engage him as well, but competing for the killing blow. He grabbed Gina by the collar and threw her effortlessly through the air, toward the edge of the roof. She closed her eyes as she awaited the free fall to her death.

At the last second, D'artello tackled her out of the air, holding her tight to brace the impact as they landed hard. They both would have stood up at the same time, but his hand against her chest forced her back down as if to say, "This fight is not safe for you." This both irritated and eased her at the same time.

"D'artello!" Gerrik yelled as he danced in the three-way melee. "Kill Garo!"

Arbello then managed to boot Gerrik away too. He grabbed hold of Garo, arresting his arms behind his back. Then something that no one saw coming came out of his mouth. "Go ahead, do it! Stab this power-drunk fool! If you do, all of the Phantoms will disappear forever."

D'artello looked at him oddly for a moment. Was he handing him victory? What was his plan?

"D'artello, it has to be a trap!" Gina yelled.

"Take the shot, D'artello!" Gerrik yelled, still believing that there was a chance to salvage his broken son.

"Do it, dammit! Just do it! Why do you hesitate now, you miserable, soulless creature? Why don't you swing!" Arbello yelled.

Part of D'artello wanted to do it. He approached the struggling king, who was murmuring cursed broken sentences at his current misfortune.

"We've got all day!" Arbello said. "He can't resist me while being this close to my sword," he explained. "What's the matter? Confused? Well it seems you still have some feelings, so let me see you cry too. No matter what happens now, you can chalk one up for Unity, because this world has already been conquered."

"What do you mean!" Gina said. "The end of the world? No! Not yet!"

"Stop this, Arbello!" Gerrik shouted.

"How did you ever make it as a warrior, Father? I can't stop it because it's already done. War is no place for love. The capital was desecrated months ago. I started exacting my revenge about three years before Harmony even visited this fool you call my brother. Fort Carrie? Belren? Hell, even the capital that far back was in the final stages of my plan. Didn't you notice the composite army patrolling the north, calling themselves the last organized force on the planet? Did you ever think they weren't lying? There were men from every continent in that army because they were running from the Phantoms and sources. You know, when the alphas migrated south, I was actually afraid that you might make it here too soon. Pity me for thinking you were that smart. But now? It's too late to stop me. I know no cure for becoming a Phantom, but if you cut the source, they will all be gone forever, and my revenge will be complete. So please, go ahead and cut him now."

A bright light came to the rescue, enveloping the top of the ice castle. It blinded all of its patrons for what seemed like an eternity within five seconds. When it cleared, a powerful looking man stood behind Arbello. The man was broad with red hair tied neatly back, and a chiseled, hairless face. He wore thin leather armor, carrying with him a targe and gladius. Peacemaker Unity, cause of the entire Phantom outbreak, now stood before them.

Where Harmony spoke soft and seductively, his voice was bold and intimidating. "Arbello, what are you doing?" he thundered.

"Silence! Worthless immortal," he spat back. Unity showed his discontent by lowering his brow. "I am changing the rules of your game, and there's nothing you can do about it, for I am the only champion who can wield this blade, and you know it," he hissed. Turning to D'artello, he commanded, "Now do your Peacemaker's bidding! Slice him and end this!"

All Unity could do, despite all of his power, was try to reason with him, but everyone else had tried that. Arbello was right. Cutting King Garo would disperse the Phantoms, killing everyone who became one of them undoubtedly.

If D'artello did not slice the man, there was no reversing the effects of becoming a Phantom. Everyone was powerless now, both man and gods.

Either way, D'artello could not give him the satisfaction of being the one to do it; Arbello wanted it too much. D'artello threw the Molten Steel to the ground, letting it slide almost over the edge of the tower.

Arbello watched with extreme disdain. "You pathetic! Weak! Insolent waste of life!" He could control his anger no longer. He thrust his foot into Garo's back, smashing him to the ground then shooting straight at D'artello. His charge was interrupted by another white flash, a more familiar entrance. Now Harmony stood in front of her champion, blocking Arbello.

"Stop this," she declared with obvious frustration.

"You dare interfere with the champions?" Unity said. "You know the rules. That gives me a free move as well." How awful, they were arguing over these lives as if they were some part of a childish board game.

"Then this planet is yours, brother," she offered.

"What? Bitch!" Gerrik yelled. Unity shot him a look shortly after, but Gerrik was not scared. He locked gazes with the immortal as if he were his next victim.

"No," Unity said. "This is no gift. My champion has already won the day here, as he has made very clear. Now, Arbello, claim your victory," he commanded.

Arbello followed the orders with the heart of a defiant child. It was not his way, and not how he wanted to win it. In his mind, he had lost.

That fact aside, he took one last grinning glance at D'artello, knowing that Harmony would make him follow to the next planet. "There's always next time. This isn't over," he threatened as he took a fighting stance in front of Garo. They all watched as Garo took the last swing he would ever take, and with ease, Arbello dodged it and landed his slash, cutting open the source and freeing the Phantoms from their ethereal shackles. They were now bound to this world.

Garo collapsed to his knees and began to transform into one of them himself. "No!" D'artello screamed.

"My son! What have you done?" Gerrik shouted. Charging Unity, he said, "I won't let you take my son from me again!" Unity batted him to the ground like an insect.

A red, opaque bubble wrapped itself around D'artello. Harmony's magic was beginning to carry him off toward the sky. "No!" he shouted. Gina ran to him, trying to force her hand through the bubble, but was pushed away from it when she saw the Molten Steel flying toward her exact spot.

"Where are you taking him!" she shouted at Harmony.

"Mortal wench, you need not know. It is far beyond your comprehension," she said, her expression unchanging.

Getting higher and higher, D'artello's emotions were overriding Harmony's efforts to suppress his soul. "Stop it! Stop it!" he yelled, pounding on the red barrier. It was gelatinous and folded around each fist he threw into it. There was nothing he could do except watch his ascent.

The two Peacemakers disappeared, leaving only Gina, Gerrik, and Arbello on the roof. Gina and Gerrik stared up at him, but Arbello was approaching from behind. His father had fallen to his knees in hopelessness, but Gina, seeing D'artello's peril, tried to comfort him still.

"Everything will be all right, D'artello! Everything's going to be okay! I love you, D'artello!" she yelled to the heavens.

It was the last thing he heard or saw before Arbello made his charge beside thousands of Phantoms covering the roof like a swarm of rats over a corpse. D'artello never cried harder in his life. He would never see his family, friends, Gina, or his home world ever again. "Gina!" he shouted. "No! Dammit no! Let me back down there! Listen to me, damn you!" he shouted at Harmony. "Arbello! You'll suffer for what you've done! Do you hear me? That I promise you!"

The stars became neighbors as his home grew smaller and smaller until he could look upon his entire planet. Leaving the calamitous battlefield behind, he trailed off into silent space. The lone traveler drifted on toward his next destination with nothing but the books in his pouch, and the sorrow, vengeance, and hatred in his soul.

Epilogue

GERRIK looked up as his boy was carried off but barely had enough time to pay him even a visual good-bye. Somewhere inside, this broken old warrior found the will to fight on. The Phantoms charged the roof and rampaged toward him, swinging their blades, ready to gnash him to mincemeat. He grabbed the first appendage he could get his hands on and broke it, as if a Phantom's arm could break.

Somehow he avoided all lethal strikes. Unfortunately for him though, all he needed were his rapidly accruing scratches. Gina screamed over the grunts and roars. He did not have, and would not be given the time to work his way through the crowd to her. The poor girl was probably being ripped apart.

Arbello shot up over the crowd and then dove down at him, slashing across his chest and then kicking him, launching the old man off the side of the tower. Gerrik plummeted down far enough to come to the realization he was falling. This was going to hurt. An entire lifetime as the greatest warrior man had ever known, undone by his own offspring. In this, he found logic; no matter how much he had tried to raise his boys right, his own violent and monstrous tendencies had passed on to them, and there was no saving them now.

With no will to live, as if he'd had a choice, he accepted his fate and braced for impact. What would his sentence before the Peacemakers be? He had killed so many men and had only one person to blame, Harmony. And with that final thought, his body touched down, crushed under the velocity of the fall.

From above, Gina did not have the time to look down but was aware of

Gerrik's fall. She hid behind her shield as long as she could before a hand finally pulled it aside.

"Help! Somebody, please! Help!"

A voice, Gerrik thought lying in his snowy grave. *No one can help you now,* he thought as he listened to a woman scream. *Can I help her? No, I am dead. I can help no one, not that it is much different than life.*

"Help!" she shouted through hysterical tears.

What is she doing here? Did she come with the army? Can I help her? Is this perhaps the first test of the afterlife? Can I move? A hideous laughter cackled through the chasms of his mind, getting louder and louder until he was sure his skull would explode. His hands flew to his ears. When finally he began to kick his legs uncontrollably, the laughter died down. He sat up in the snow, taking a deep breath, clinging to life.

He looked up at the ice palace from its base, then at his hands. A glinting in his eye revealed Gina's sword. He grabbed it and began to mirror himself in it, starting with his face and down his chest and back. No damage, no wounds he didn't know were already there; everything in his body seemed to be functioning normally. He could move his legs and feet with little problem. No doubt about it, he survived the fall. *Alive? But how?* His stomach sank suddenly, having an epiphany as he ran his hand across the wound on his chest. He had been cut. He was becoming one of them, a Phantom.

"You there, please help me! My husband!" a woman's voice called.

Gerrik sat a moment and stared at the sword in his hand, then stood up ominously, his eyes never leaving it.

"Hello?" she asked, looking at the sword in his hand.

By Harmony, he wanted nothing more than to dive on her and cut into her, to slice her apart as if she were his worst enemy. He hated her. *Why do I feel this way?* he thought. *I want to kill her. I can kill her ... No! I won't. She's done nothing to deserve this,* he fought. He came out of his trance, throwing the sword into the snow beside him.

"Oh thank Harmony," he heard her say as she romped through the snow, soaked and freezing. "My husband, they took him," she called out to Gerrik.

"C'mon!" he said, taking her by the hand. "I'm sorry, he's gone! There's nothing we can do, but you can still get away!" he yelled.

"Wait! You don't know that!" she cried.

Gerrik wasn't going to leave her though. "You have to trust me if your life is important to you. What's your name?"

"Marilynne! Please, we have to go back for my husband!" she persisted. "Do you know what it's like? He's all I have!"

Gerrik stared into her icy blue eyes. "I lost all I have on top of that roof.

They are gone, and I'm not okay with it, but there is nothing we can do if we are killed as well. I choose to live. How about you?" he said, releasing her hand and beginning to walk off.

    She stood for a moment, biting her lip and letting the tears pool up in her eyes, thinking about the loss of her husband. But as she watched Gerrik walk away, something inside compelled her to follow him away from this horrible place and toward a world that had officially ended.